CURVE OF THE EARTH

—.—

A NOVEL OF LAZARUS

CRAIG A. BROCKMAN

Printed in the United States of America

First Printing 2022

ISBN 979-8-218-00637-2

Curve of the Earth Publishing

craigabrockman.com

Contact: craig@craigabrockman.com

Tecumseh, Michigan

to my Beautiful Friend

CONTENTS

Stephen to Lazarus

But was I the first martyr, who
Gave up no more than life, while you,
Already free among the dead,
Your rags stripped off, your fetters shed,
Surrendered what all other men
Irrevocably keep, and when
Your battered ship at anchor lay
Seemingly safe in the dark bay
No ripple stirs, obediently
Put out a second time to sea
Well knowing that your death (in vain
Died once) must all be died again?

— C.S. Lewis

I. Introduction

Dear Sister Athracht

Sweet mortality, I pursue its venomous sting. Those fierce Immortals, of which I have written, have yet to extract this Methuselah life from my grasp, but my interminable years do not confer upon me significance or exceptionality. Whether an ill-fated child or a feeble codger, each person lives their entire life span and has fulfilled the life intended for them. At the time we spoke I was confused, but now I understand that wise secret of Solomon you blessed me with as we parted: "All the days of this meaningless life that God has given you under the sun—all your meaningless days." It is this meaninglessness that we ponder.

It has taken me all this time to learn how meaning is cradled within meaninglessness, how mortality and immortality are two sides to the same coin, and how I carry in my heart both the quiet contemplation of my sister Mary and the restless conscientiousness of Martha. With your guidance, these parchments reveal what I have discovered. There are so many scattered fragments and scraps of writing that I weave in where I can.

God's love is the currency of the universe, the secret economy, and you have shared it generously. You and I stood together along that last coast of the world with emerald valleys at our backs, rocky cliffs at our feet, pondering what lies beyond. Not only what lies beyond those endless seas to the west that few dare traverse, but also pondering what lies beyond endless seas of our eternity. Each of your rare and precious letters has been treasured, building upon and growing that first treasure you deposited into my soul at our brief meeting long ago. Through that encounter and through all our long years of correspondence, I feel as though we have been dear friends and will remain fellow sojourners forever. Your sharp insight cut to my heart, helping me to comprehend this vain existence.

Like a child clutching the last filthy threads of her favorite ragged blanket, I will hope a remnant of the fabric of my life may be preserved. You reminded me of how an imperfect glass nevertheless transmits light. Though I may be only a candle flame, I am yet a fire.

It is my great passion to return to your distant island of Hibernia, but if I do not, then I trust your wisdom to care for these journals. You may arrange and hone them under your wise and gracious hand as you see fit. You need not be kind so much as honest of my imperfections. Soon fades the tapestry woven without black.

I need not tell you that you must take every precaution not to allow one of these parchments ever to fall into the hands of your brother, if he lives, or of his acolytes.

Sincerely,

Lázaro a Bethania

So I begin.

I am less enamored of change than constancy. I am enthralled by those things that have not changed for me: wheat fields, my fingers skimming awn soft as kitten whiskers, a rosy-cheeked toddler gleefully exhausted from her first tottering dash, and a certain quiet burble of a creek that folds and crests to create the exact murmur of depth and sweetness. Those things have never changed. Nor have I seen change in the boundless pride of humankind, the thrumming terror of battle, or the wan sadness of a mother holding her dead child.

I am not a scholar, historian, or theologian.

Not a theologian because I am chief among skeptics. The pendulum of my life swings between the bliss of eternity and the bleak finality of life, and I cannot seem to brace against it. My theology is the simplest theology of all men: I believe what I see. If I cannot see it, I will not believe it. When I do not see God, I do not believe.

If I am a blind skeptic it is merely because my eyes are closed. I open my eyes to behold a magenta sky—Why magenta? Why birdsong or melody? Beauty is cast randomly abroad in abundance, and for what purpose other than the hand of a loving Creator? A rock badger ponders me with its curious face, shakes its head, and ducks into a crevice. I laugh. The world lives in beauty and humor. Why? To what purpose? It is far more difficult to reject the existence of loving elohim than to accept their existence.

Like the curve of the earth: We stand upon an orb too vast to behold. Its curve can be seen only by a shadow cast in eclipse or by the parallel curve of the sky and the fading shoreline. Because we stand upon its great surface we are hidden from viewing Earth itself. So, it is from where we stand within our infinite Creator. We are surrounded by him, and we may be too close to perceive his face until, like the curve of the earth, it is reflected in the face of another or across the span of our lifetimes.

In my musings are gaps through which a Roman fleet could sail and things I have forgotten or ignored in my dim perception. Wracked by why I, of all men, should have been handed this long life, I dwell upon my unworthiness.

If I must chronicle, I fear my earliest years were lost to that swirl of hazy memory. I will stitch it in as it comes to me, but sadly, there is extraordinarily little I can recall.

Though I yet hold on to one dear early memory.

It was raining. Children feared the rain in arid Judea because often a cloudburst would lead to a flash flood that swept a child tumbling and screaming down a swollen wadi. At the time, I was little more than a toddler. I remember running through the rain, trying to hurry home with my sisters... Now I remember how old Mary was because I distinctly remember the gap from her missing front teeth. I see it all: I must have fallen in a puddle, my soaked tunic, the girls in their dresses with veils clinging to their long, wet hair, Mary's gap-tooth smile and red cheeks as she giggled at me uncontrollably while Martha, always the older sister, a few steps ahead of us, was scolding and scolding like an angry crow. Mary strained at my arm while looking at me with her beautiful dark eyes and breathless laughter until she was nearly pulled into the shallow puddle with me. I wanted to pull her in with me so we could swim together. But that is all I remember. I do not remember arriving at our home, drying off, or what mother would have said. She was never as stern as Martha, though I would never want to disparage Martha. She was a person of honesty, integrity, and spirit, and she grew to be the most reliable sister you could have. I will tell more about my sisters as the years unfold: about Mary, the quiet woman of contemplation, never harried or harassed, led by what was revealed in her narrow gaze, and about Martha, the tireless pursuer, always attempting to enhance and amend the contents of this simple chalice we have all been served. In my soul, the hearts of my sisters wrestle: Mary's accepting serenity and Martha's faithful duty.

As I review these pages I realize that I want to be remembered for nothing. If I could erase my name and my singular status from these documents, I would do so in an instant. All legacy is vanity. All hope of reputation is a mist. My reputation and legacy have changed and will change a thousand times, and none of it will be true to my existence because no one, myself included, can fathom what this existence means. Not now and maybe never. I chronicle because, from some force, I am compelled. I can discern no other reason.

A loom stands before us, but we see only the warp in a blur of infinite threads made of infinite fibers and colors that one day weave into a tapestry of profound complexity seen by the great I Am. Never ask for meaning. We would not know it if we saw it.

This is my life; these are my chapters, and I remember them as I have lived them.

II. KNOWING YESHU

I HAVE KNOWN GOD; I have walked with this man.

Reaching back in time to extract those precious years with Yeshu elicits more pain than solace. I am both chief witness and prosecutor for my own conviction. After walking beside him and seeing his face how could my soul have been decimated by years of doubt and debauchery?

I am not a historian. There is scant history here and it may be unreliable. We live history not as a broad panorama but day by day, minute by minute: it is never historical as we live it. To this disheveled history we add our shoddy memory in bits and scraps whether it is remembering this morning's breakfast or a previous century's great war. I do not recall the countless meals my mother lovingly prepared, but they all contributed to my growth. Likewise, the person I became arose from a granary of countless memories, most of which have been eaten by locusts and lost to eternity.

What was it like to know him?

I forever thought that I could love all of creation because of what I saw in it of Yeshu. Returning from death, my life was restored and filled with wonder: water was turned to wine, crowds were fed from a basket of fish, the blind were given sight, and people were raised from the dead. Everything was swirling mystery; changing as I listened to him and watched him transform the world by his touch.

I have yet to reveal all that went wrenchingly wrong with my life, but first, I must recall to myself that brief time when everything seemed exactly right.

Judea and our cities had seen no shortage of pretenders and messiahs, yet Yeshu was none of these. He had no similarity to those false prophets. He was not *another* anything. He was someone wholly new and different.

I ponder those face-to-face days with him. He was always Yeshu to us, then Rabbi. He became Yeshua to the authorities in Judea and later in the early Church after his death and return. To us he was common. Not common in personality or insight, but common in his presence and appearance.

Our father was the first in our family to meet him and welcome him into our home. He had left his mother's home in Nazareth and lived nearby and was known at the synagogue and in the city but had not been baptized by John. It was not unusual to see him in Bethany. He had grown into Joseph's trade and was a skilled carpenter—merely a carpenter. Could there be a trade more appropriate for one with a Creator's mind than to be a builder?

When our father met him, Yeshu had been framing a shop that connected to a merchant's home in Bethany. My father was the mason. They struck up a friendship, and Father invited him to our home. I suspected Father imagined him as a worthy prospect for my sister Mary, who was not betrothed at that time. Father always had an eye in search of a tradesman with a good heart who would take care of his little Mary. However, it was obvious to everyone that this man was more than a handy marriage prospect.

In our home, reclining at table with our family, Yeshu studied us. Smiling, the corner of his mouth pulled into his mustache, he was attentive, almost unsettling. But as soon as he sensed awkwardness, he smiled broadly or made an aside to dispel tension.

Yeshu asked if we knew of the one called the Baptizer. Our surprise was obvious when he told us that John was his cousin. Everyone knew John: his Nazarite hair long and gnarled, his clothes of ragged skins, and his crazy rantings about the soon appearance of the one who might be the Messiah. We said nothing when Yeshu revealed this, but our surprised reaction made him laugh. The neat, well-spoken carpenter bore little resemblance to the crazy, locust-eating prophet.

"You have nothing to fear." He chuckled, holding up a hand. "I promise that you will not have to serve locusts if we are ever to grace your lovely home." By the look on Martha's face, she was not convinced.

From that first visit, my sisters were captivated by him. None of the pompous rabbis would allow women to join them at table, to debate, or to sit within earshot when men were talking. But he joined them in lively discussion. They formed a bond with him, and he often sought them out.

In later years when Yeshu was in our home he was rarely alone, yet no one—man, woman, or child—felt ignored in his presence. He never taunted or coerced, and never disparaged someone who offered an insight that was less than inspiring.

What else can be said that has not already been recorded a thousand times? He loved, pondered and dissected everything he saw, and his energy and inquisitiveness were contagious. To be near him was to be drawn in and included. He was irresistible.

I recall a day after he had called me back from death. He was with us again in our home. As always, distracted Martha bustled about with preparations while devoted Mary reclined nearby. In addition to our family, there were members of his family, and many followers scattered in our small courtyard and spilling onto the street. We were fortunate to have four rooms in our home. In the houses adjoining our courtyard were relatives and one elderly couple who were old family friends and tolerant neighbors.

Amid the bustle, Yeshu was telling me that soon I would be forced to leave. I thought I misunderstood him. I could not bear to think of leaving my family or of leaving him. I waved my hand toward the noisy crowd and cupped my ear. "Rabbi, I have just returned from death, and now you are telling me to leave?"

He frowned studiously at his interlaced fingers, then tilting his head quickly toward the doorway to the courtyard, he led outside into the brilliant day. We sat against a wall in the shade, his hand shielding his eyes, while he smiled at the children at play with clay horses and ragged dolls.

"I cannot leave," I continued. "My sisters! What about them? I fear more for their safety than for mine."

"They will be safe," he said. "But you are not safe if you stay here."

"How will they understand if I leave them at a time like this with the fear and confusion worse every day?"

He shook his head and smiled. "Do not fear. They will be safe."

With his compelling sincerity and that distant thunder of his unhesitating authority, he was not to be resisted.

"Seek me and I will show you everything. I will care for everything that you care about." He grasped my knee. "You know that!"

On the verge of tears, I knew I did not want to leave my sisters—or him. The courtyard and the banter fell away while I drank in his presence in the time that remained.

The issue had been settled as far as he was concerned; there was no more to be said. Soon he was distracted, raising his arm and rolling back his sleeve. An ant was stumbling through the hairs of his forearm. He brought his arm close to examine the insect's twisting path. With the merest touch of the tip of his little finger, he parted the hairs, then gently tapped it. The creature paused, hastily cleaning its antennae to consider the sensations. Yeshu smiled, touched it again, set his finger in its path, and watched it crawl over his nail and along his finger. He slowly lowered it to the ground. At that moment, the gulf between uncomprehending creature and all-knowing Creator could not have been greater. As it was for the ant, it would be for me, always.

He was too familiar and finite to be Creator. But in beauty, love, and humor, everywhere his face I see. And children of the Creator, we resemble him.

Yet his strength was fearsome and unpredictable. The powerful Sanhedrin feared him and could not defeat him, either by argument or by death. Though entirely accessible when near, he also possessed a stark and restless character. He would withdraw within himself and wander away alone for days, not to be followed.

Always more enthralling than his power was his ordinary humanity. The same as any of us in that circle of believers he ate, slept, washed, and relieved himself. But it was in those moments of sincerity and severity, of frailty and magnificence, that the entirety of Yahweh seemed nearest. Here was Yahweh: more like a man than mankind itself.

One who has seen him will never stop seeing him or his character in everything: his creation, his love, beauty, integrity, and his humor.

His humor! When he threw back his head, his laughter would tremble like a gong and peel like chimes: a waterfall of joy pouring over us. While he relished our silly foibles and tolerated our struggling insights, we felt cherished as children. I will not admit that the Son of Yahweh was a prankster. Blasphemous. But his quick wit and eye for hilarious opportunity kept us on our guard.

His teachings could be complex, yet utterly simple. It is unfortunate that so little of it survives. He did not admonish Jews to abandon our faith, but we drank in his teaching because the words he spoke completed the faith we had cherished throughout generations. He did not destroy it. That reality, more than anything, first persuaded us. Our ancient faith grew clearer and was not contradicted by what he taught. In time, as the old faith was eclipsed for us, his lasting words served to clarify and expand what our faith had meant to us. However, the power of the greedy Pharisees had been challenged. Their lives and wealth depended upon blind loyalty.

Should I seal my fate so early in these journals by confessing how thoroughly I eventually grew apart from him? As my own prosecutor, what else can I say about him to make the case against myself?

How he loved children: muddy-faced, shat-pants, and sticky-handed. It never mattered. He would never avoid them or push them away. He sought out those rebellious and forgotten orphans that we found on the city's edges. His disciples would try to brush them aside, but not Yeshu. They warmed to him because he knew their pain and their simple desire for mere scraps of peace and happiness. They were no different than all of us: He understood our sad hearts.

Yeshu wept with us and for us. Some claim that he wept from grief when he arrived to meet my sisters after I died. Not grief—it could never have been grief. Grief arises from our sad longing and ignorance. He wept in empathy. When he saw my sisters crying, he cried for what he saw of all of humanity, for all our sadness at our finite and broken lives. He wept because he saw the pain we all suffer, and he pitied us for the pain we endure and that we have caused ourselves. He saw us as the foolish, lost, errant children we are, and because, in that moment, he could not embrace us all, he wept for us all.

That was to know him.

I have tried to share fragments of my memories of him. Though it seems I have occasionally felt his presence and I have seen his face in the grace of others, I miss him dearly and cannot wait until we are together.

I did not witness the execution. My sisters insisted I stay in hiding, knowing I was evidence of his power, and the Pharisees could never let me live.

But killing our dear friend was an indescribable injustice. I have gained a long perspective and understand its relevance. But the pain, shock, and injustice have never abated. I often consider: What if I did not have a Savior, and the one way to gain eternity with Yahweh was to endure torture and die that heinous death; could I do it?

III. Knowing Death

A searing ligature tightened around my eyes, all daggers and retching: vomiting twisted knives deeper into my brain. My head felt skewered, spinning on a hot spear thrust from the base of my skull to my forehead. My screams stuttered with wracking chills.

My sisters were in a frenzy, Martha bustling with mother's poultices. "Where is he? Where is Yeshu?" And Mary's worried, tender nearness as she stroked my hand, trying to quiet my thrashing. Night flashed to daylight, then night again. People would come and go while existence slowly coiled to a heap on the floor. I was not fearful of death. I would have gladly traded life for release.

Why had they lowered me into thick, black grease when I was already beyond exhausted? In my confusion, I pondered what a strange remedy this was. I could not open an eye or lift one finger. In this slowly turning vortex of tar, I may have dwelt for days or months, spinning inexorably toward the center.

There was finally that moment when I joyously realized that pain had left me. But then inexplicably they lashed my feet to a windmill blade: my arms flailed as I spun. I broke free and was flung far and away, twisting and falling, accelerating insanely.

After hours or days, my descent slowed until it felt as though I was being lowered into an infinite depth of carded wool. There I floated, slowly settling again on my bed like a leaf, waiting fearfully for that horrible pain to slither near again.

But there was no pain. While I lay there, everything began to fall away, tile by tile like a crumbling mosaic. At that moment, I was made aware that my body had never been possessed of a spirit, but that my spirit had always been possessed of a body. My body had been played like an instrument by my spirit. Disrobing myself of flesh, I laid it aside and passed through gossamer.

Only that which had been substantial remained.

When I was a boy, I remember walking in a graveyard on a beautiful spring day. Beneath the ground, sequestered in tombs lay a world of death, melting into black ichor and decay while above, separated by the thinnest veneer, was a bounty of sound, color, freshness, and life. I had then imagined the fragility of life and the wavering wall, thin as a knife's edge, that we walk upon between life and death: our world of light and life a mere skin covering the vast darkness below.

Now I saw it.

But I had not *gone* anywhere. I was not taken. My room, the bustle of the house, and the world I had known simply fell away. And *There* I had come to be. Wherever *There* was—or is. I learned that while I was *There*, the world slid past several days, but I was not *There* for days or minutes or millennia. Time does not fit into that place: no passage of time, no concept of a sequence of events. We are present and will always be.

Everything I describe about this place will sound ridiculous. When we went to Jerusalem, my sisters and I would be enthralled on those rare occasions when we were able to watch puppet shows at the market. Or we were breathless when we watched the Roman actors mime sweeping scenes of tragedy and comedy. Most parents shielded the eyes of their Jewish children, but I believe our father was as smitten as we were. When the puppeteer was done or the play was over, we turned and left with the crowd. The characters portrayed by the puppets or actors no longer existed except in our memory; the story was finished. Certainly, the puppets do not care that the show is over. The characters do not care that you have left the amphitheater. Like death, they no longer exist. The story is not altered by the audience's departure. It is finished. So, it seemed to me when leaving behind the life I had lived. The panoply of my life and all the characters I had known on that stage of existence where I, my family, and sisters had played was finished, and I had extracted myself with scarcely a thought.

Heaven does not capture the sense of where I found myself. I was in a place that forever surrounds us, is always nearby. All this material world merely obscures our vision for a time. I was not in a place of primeval forests with snowcapped mountains set above lakes rimmed with Romanesque mansions. I suppose there may have been all of that too, but the unseen that exists inside and outside our universe is far more wondrous and mysterious than what we can behold with mortal vision.

My first overwhelming and immediate impression was holiness. "Holy. Holy. Holy." I do not think I heard the words but felt them. There was a sense of pure love, but holiness eclipsed even that. Holy was deep, cool, and clear like a vast ocean. I lay back, sunken deep into the holiness; the utter, all-encompassing purity without a speck of anything else. I swam in unbroken holiness.

I realized I was not simply in holiness, but I was also in the presence of Holiness. Perfection. The tiniest grain of imperfection, transgression, or defect would dilute this universe, decay flawlessness, and never be tolerated. This endless sea of holiness would have evaporated in an instant.

My next impression was unutterable awe. Not wonderment for the indecipherable intricacy. Not astonishment for the depths of the infinite. But awe. Awe for the utter and complete simplicity of it all. Bathed in simplicity, the universe is obscured solely by the distracting complexity of our physicality.

I cannot understand a way to say more. It was the Place Behind It All. That sounds trite. Because in truth it is the Place Before All.

From this new vantage, I saw more. I saw in a flash the universe. This may be where words entirely fail as it all becomes too fantastic, but I must try to sketch what I saw.

I beheld a form like a cube.

I understand how the prophets have struggled to convey with human words the realm of the infinite. Their descriptions of wheels within wheels and fantastical creatures are all clumsy attempts like mine.

Simplicity.

Imagine floating within a cube that is lined with polished silver mirrors so that the ceiling reflects the floor, and the floor reflects the ceiling while one wall reflects the other into infinity. As you move toward one plane, you can see reflections of the other planes. It all connects. Now add mirrors in the corners of the cube, and suddenly, there are many more reflections. Add a hundred, a thousand, an infinite number of mirrors and the cube has become infinite reflections and connections.

At once, take this whole infinite cube and turn it inside out. You have a jewel with infinite facets reflecting other jewels of infinite facets. I saw a universe that exists as a cohesive whole, so that in an abstract way, a leaf falling on earth may connect to a whirl of dust on a distant star. I saw this. One massive, connected world. Yahweh's mind sees all this, and it is forever in the *present* to him. All is now—forever.

It could have been minutes, years, or centuries until these threads of the universe wove into tapestry. This tapestry resolved into a scene.

There were others, other people being woven into the fabric. And I believe other entities were there, too. It became—or is—a merger of places and persons. I am not wise to explain how the presence of persons and entities was also the presence of places, but each person and each entity seemed to bring its own place or realm of existence with it.

When my vision fully resolved, the scene was emptied of all entities. I beheld a moment of infinite solitude. Not loneliness, but sweet aloneness.

Before me was a glimmering lake surrounded by emerald grass that swept into hills lined with great oaks and tall pointed cedars. The trees loomed like thunderheads, rising golden, fading to lavender and blue as they receded into distant haze. There was no sun, yet radiance spilled from everywhere; it cascaded from above with colors and in a form never seen. The living light cast upon the land from a vision of three interminable prisms, each refracting light and color, one to another in an infinite array. Flutings and whistles from hidden creatures were carried on a fresh breeze, spicy with the humid aroma of pine and grasses.

From distant mountains came chants, choruses that were speaking and singing refrains so complex and compelling that no human ear could tolerate the music or the message. While distracted in speechless amazement, I had not seen that a person had stepped from cover of the forest and was striding toward me across the grassy slope. A woman approached wearing a splendid silk gown, which moved with her like water. Her face was child-like glee. On each side of her stepped two children with long, black hair and dark, almond-shaped eyes that watched silently. The children were arrayed in purple gowns trimmed in gold, made of a material that flowed with their hair. At their sides they carried small, glimmering swords seething with runes beyond earthly interpretation. Both the children and their swords were menacing beyond their size.

Her two Watchers stepped back as she kissed my cheek and embraced. Her beauty was not defined by femininity, as in our world. She did not wear femininity; she possessed it.

She greeted me in a voice lovingly warm and familiar while I remained wary, though intensely curious. As unfamiliarity slowly lifted from her features, I was astonished beyond words. In a mist of remembrance, like the face of a surfacing swimmer, I recognized her: my grandmother, Martha, now a young woman again as I had never seen her. Her hug was homey, sweet, and natural.

Without hesitating, she spoke earnestly the pageant of my family, our history, our story, and our legacy. Regrettably, I recall little of what she said. But in this story, she spoke of my parents, my beloved sisters, and me. Echoes of our existence rang through millennia past and forward into millennia to come. She spoke of the land where we stood, and of sweet Yeshu who was all and in all. But it was like dreams in which something profound has been learned, or you have written or discovered something so vital and remarkable, but it is all swept away when you awaken.

After hours or years, she led me near the forest. She held out her hand to motion me to go ahead of her. I walked into a darkening woodland laden with dew and moss, over roots that tangled like arms of giants, through clearings as large as stadiums. Overhead were broad leaves and soft needles that shimmered on swaying branches. Down aisles of trees stole thin blue and green light. The massive, twisted trunks and the fragrant forest floor, twining with vines amid ferns and flowers, seemed to stretch on forever into gray, shifting haze. Our journey was long. I think we continued to speak. I had so many questions, but I doubt there were answers that could be understood in this life. Gradually, the forest became deeper, the trunks nearer, and the limbs closer to the ground.

My grandmother had grown silent. I continued to contemplate this world and our encounter until I tilted to walk under a limb, and when I turned, she and her young companions were gone. I knew I would soon be lost, but I was not frightened, I was warily curious.

I sensed I was not alone in this wood. I wondered whether the child-like Watchers might have continued to follow, remaining hidden among the trunks and hillocks, along with other entities of this world. Indescribable creatures flitted among the pillars of trunks or disappeared before revealing themselves. Compelled, not forced, I pressed on to find a path or way out of the darkening tangle.

Under limbs streaming dark vines, I stepped high through deepening moss. I was about to turn back, because ahead was becoming too dark, and too narrow for me to enter. Behind was the infinite; ahead was the narrowing finite. That is when I sensed I was back in the dank, reeking tomb. Like a veil falling over me, decrepit and despicable, I found myself once again clothed in the burdensome weight of old flesh, with the odor of withering rot encasing me. Although my arms were bent at the elbows, restrained by grave clothes, I felt myself stepping out of the old flesh while pulling on new.

Laid upon me as a heavy robe, I felt the moist, elastic weight of my flesh like an animal hide. As if wrapped in the fresh skins of a wolf or lion, the bloody animal scent enclosed me and shaped to my form. Fiber by fiber, I felt my animal body once again woven and laid over my bones. Cord by cord, the muscles and sinews were sown in while organs inside were restored and replenished until, crackling with brute vitality, my new flesh seethed with primal vigor. I was not becoming an animal—far from it. I was more human than I had ever been. I had been remade.

I walked in darkness. Nothing other than the sound of my breath and my scraping feet rustled against the clammy stones until a swirling cold embraced my ankles. Cold fingers scratched at my feet while clattering bones and dragging flesh hissed in the crypt. Angry and betrayed, the wraiths at death's door pursued me. I was not to be allowed to cross over. More frantic to escape, I hurried.

Nearly at the mouth of the grave, something was pursuing me and did not release its grip. Though I did not turn, I felt others following unseen, determined to harass me.

I was distracted from those entities and all that lay behind as I began to see the crisp highlights of glittering landscape, the edge of each leaf, insects scuttling from the grave and birds far away in the clouds.

I did not recognize Yeshu with his hands resting on the shoulders of two little girls. For a moment, in wavering shadows, I saw gap-toothed Mary and stern Martha. The stasis of time vacillated and shuddered, then began grinding forward again. The images shifted until I saw the women I knew, my sisters with arms outstretched for me. Wailing with joy, they hugged me, and I melted into their embrace.

Though it was midday, all seemed cast in an evening of earthly dimness. And beyond this veil, I sensed the nearness of rustling creatures that had either followed me from that world beyond the grave or had simply existed here unseen all along: indescribable entities, dodging and weaving, just beyond the realm of sight, scurrying among the small crowd or diving into undergrowth, leaping from rocks and escaping before their forms were seen. It was dizzying and unsettling.

Soon, my boiling sensibilities lowered to a simmer, shrouded so I could see again. But throughout that day, as my reeking grave clothes were removed, as I was washed and restored, I was silent, listening to whispers of those entities that remained while my existence was being remade.

IV. He Lives

I had been one of the few brought back to life in those days. But we merely left ajar the door between this life and the next. He smashed it down. Beyond repair, he splintered the planks and ripped the door off its hinges. Destroying death, he throttled its neck and severed its head.

I am reminded of standing at the docks watching peasants and farmers stream onto ships clutching a lamb, swinging a cage of doves or hefting bundles to market. Others stream off the ships looking much the same as those who are boarding. You cannot tell the departing from the arriving. Those who are leaving may as well turn around and walk back on shore. Then suddenly, one princely couple will strut down the ramp in fine clothing from exotic lands, carrying gifts and treasures. They are returning from somewhere *other*, and they have returned different than when they left.

That is what it was like when Yeshu returned. He returned as different from when he had left. He had been somewhere *other*.

The stories of his horrific death were told to me secondhand because I fled before he was apprehended. Grizzly details of torture and execution filtered to me, while hiding in a shepherd's hut near Anathoth, enduring dizzying days of remorse.

Yeshu's aunt Mary and Zebedee's wife, Salome, had found the empty tomb.

No one could have been more reliable. The sister of Joseph and the mother of Zebedee's sons were among the group of women tasked with caring for the body. And it would have been a daunting task. Because of the Sabbath, his remains had lain in the grave unattended. Rules required proper washing of the body and removal of the shroud that would have been crusted to the body with blood and flesh from the horrific scourging and crucifixion. His matted hair and beard would be cleaned and straightened, and wounds would be packed or approximated as neatly as possible. The women would require jars of water and yards of linen in addition to perfume and spices.

They did not want to raise suspicion. Carrying a few items that would be left at the grave until they returned with more supplies, his aunt Mary and Salome went alone with the intent of scouting the tomb to learn how it was guarded, and how the stone could be rolled away. There would be no help from Roman guards who would be watching their every move. The Pharisees were tense and the Roman guard wary.

But two women on a mission to conceal death's decay returned with the message that death had been vanquished.

I fled, taking refuge in Anathoth. I was holed up in one of several huts built by my father for Amos, a wealthy landowner and supporter of The Way, as Yeshu's people became known. As children, my sisters and I had traveled with Father to carry stone and mix mortar. But we spent more time playing in the fields chasing the lambs while he worked.

I hid throughout the times of turmoil, stealing back to Bethany only twice.

The hut was adequate. I learned to shepherd with Amos's son Thaddeus, an odd young man, barely more than a child. Amos and his wife, Rebecca, were kind and generous to their children as they were with everyone else, but I could not help thinking that Thaddeus had been set on the path of becoming a shepherd because of his awkwardness. He would sit distractedly gazing over the valley picking incessantly at ugly sores on his arm that he claimed were sheep pox. I am sure these were not sheep pox, but merely the result of his anxious habit of scratching himself. Despite his faults, having learned the trade from his father's esteemed shepherd, he had been given stewardship of his father's flocks. The role suited the lad, and he had grown into it with honor.

The days in hiding crawled by for me. But Rebecca kept an ear toward what was happening in the city. It seemed the entire movement had ended bitterly. Hope was dying.

It was such a vivid, painful time. I remember everything about that little hut. Lost in reverie, I tried to keep myself from sinking into the darkness which had been my companion too often before I met Yeshu.

And the strange sense that something had followed me from the tomb still haunted me. I would see things out of the corner of my eye or hear whispers in that strange tongue from that dimension just beyond the veil.

I would lay in the hut pondering the tragic events that surrounded us while I traced every mortar line, thinking of my father's hands. I followed the lay of the stones and the way the poles and thatch formed the roof. Though turmoil surrounded me, I felt sheltered and embraced by my father in that stone nest. I saw his artistry.

The stones were fit by shape and color; the small window had been planned from the foundation so that just the right stones would fit squarely to the opening. Near the roof, the edges of the walls were carefully offset outward to allow spaces for the rafter poles and to prevent rain from entering the hut. Narrow gaps under the eve kept the air moving so that in the heat of summer, the stone shelter would be cool in comparison to scorching hillsides. Though it was no more than a shepherd's hut, my father built it with the same care he would have applied to a senator's loggia.

These walls also sheltered my faith during this impossible time. I thought often of the Creator while the face of Yeshu was never far away from memory. I longed for form and design to my life, but there seemed to be none. However, in this hut I saw a ray of the hopefulness I thought had been lost. With these stones and sticks, my father was simply rearranging materials supplied by the Creator. We create nothing; we rebuild, and all that we rebuild is merely an imitation of the Creator. I pondered how we are his creatures, glorifying him with his creations.

My father's trade provided a comfortable living and created opportunities for us. His skill as a mason was sought not only by local merchants or haughty Pharisees of Judea, but he caught the eye of several centurions and Roman citizens.

Through this door of opportunity entered Demetrius, the grammaticus, who I owe an eternal debt for any scholarly proficiencies I preserve.

Demetrius was a teacher attached to one of the imperial estates. Father had arranged to expand and enhance Demetrius's dwelling while working on the courtyard of the teacher's wealthy patron. In exchange, Demetrius agreed to a year of lessons for my sisters and me. But after the year had passed, Demetrius stayed on, eager to continue teaching languages and other subjects. I always suspected that it had less to do with me than with my brilliant sisters.

Demetrius displayed none of the typical peevish abuse common to Greek pedagogues. He was joyous, engaging, and enthusiastic. My gifted sisters caught the attention of his keen insight while he pleasantly tolerated me.

Along with Demetrius came another enormous benefit. This benefit was of greater value for me than for my sisters. I would have never learned the languages that served me throughout my life had it not been for that small incentive arriving at just the right time: the beautiful girl, Zenarion.

Demetrius would not have been allowed to entertain his Jewish students at the estate of his wealthy Roman patron; therefore, in the interest of expanding the cultural perceptions of the patron's daughter, he brought Zenarion to us. My lessons were never the same.

She was Mary's age, a couple of years older than me, but I was at that age when I was laying aside childish things and noticing *other* things. And if I were looking about for something to notice, Zenarion could not be ignored.

And she knew it.

On one occasion, she arrived in a long cloak that closed with a hasp about the neck and a sash wrapped around her waist. I did not notice her until a magical scent of cinnamon and cypress wafted across the low table where we worked. To this day, those fragrances recall one Roman girl.

She had chosen the seat near my corner of the table and pretended to ignore me as usual. Her flowing black hair was pulled through cuffs of silver. I quickly looked away when she caught my gaping stare. Without looking at me, she smiled coyly and began slowly to untie the sash, unbuckle the hasp, and slip out of her cloak. She wore a short, filmy tunic that left little to my highly active imagination.

My mouth went dry until I heard Demetrius say, "Lazarus, repeat the phrase in Greek."

I spun my head toward the teacher, blushing and stammering while Zenarion covered her mouth and giggled. My sisters looked up confused.

"Zenarion, cover yourself! Then wait for me at the gate." Demetrius glared, his silver hair flaring around his balding head. Hastily he brought the lesson to a close. Any other teacher would have soundly beat me, but not Demetrius. The girl pouted while she pulled on her cloak and left the table. After our teacher hustled his charge back to his patron, I feared I would never see her again.

But she returned the following week, though I was less delighted with her modest attire. Zenarion was not merely fetching; she was also a brilliant scholar. As our lessons unfolded, I knew that although my love would remain unrequited, I hoped at least to dazzle her with my brilliance. I am certain I never accomplished that, but week upon week, I studied harder and became more proficient in Greek and Latin in hopes of impressing this goddess. She grew bored with her seduction and devoted her full attention to her teacher and my sisters. I now know I can attribute my facility with languages as much to Zenarion as to Demetrius. Yahweh uses the tools at hand.

In the dreadful days after the execution, we seemed lost in despondency, until that day I recall as if it were yesterday.

In the hills tending sheep, one of Amos's daughters would bring food. I recall the crumbly bread of cracked grains, along with a skin of dried meat or lentil stew. I was leaning against the hut, fitfully dozing, while Thaddeus sat nearby, annoyingly picking at his arm. As he would often do, he threw a sheep's turd in my direction to awaken me. Maybe his arm would not have been oozing with sores if he had not played with sheep's dung all the time. He pointed in the direction of their house.

Bleating and bounding, the herd was parting in a widening wake. I thought it was Thaddeus's sister, Sharon, running with the full abandon of a young girl. But skipping from the sheep herd and careening along the narrow path that led up the hill toward us was Rebecca, the stately wife of the wealthy landowner. Thaddeus and I stood, my knees wobbly with fear that another terrible thing had happened: My sisters had been apprehended—or worse—I thought.

A hundred yards away, she yelled, "He's alive!"

Thaddeus and I looked at each other, her laughter echoing across the valley. "He lives! Yeshu is alive! They have seen him!"

She bounded the last steps to the hut, flushed and breathless, giddy as a child. "They have seen him! Mary, Joanna, and Salome, and now the men, too."

Finding the chief shepherd nearby, we left the herd with him while we rushed with Rebecca back to the farmstead.

By late afternoon, we were gathered in the large home of Amos and Rebecca, while other followers from the city continued to arrive.

A cheerful afternoon stretched to setting sun when a spontaneous feast was assembled that spilled out the door and into the courtyard. We were reclining after the meal, talking excitedly among ourselves, eager to hear all the news streaming in and being shared. Skepticism lingered, but there was a simmering thrill.

Then the extraordinary happened. We all felt it, as if the entire house acquired a droning heaviness lowering us into a quiet glade. Our conversation became muffled and slow until there was only the lingering laughter of the children in the courtyard. All conversation and laughter trailed away while we sat curious and bewildered.

"My Lord?" The haunting silence was broken by Rebecca's whisper.

This was soon followed by murmurs from others.

One of the men said, "Yeshu!" As if emerging out of the surreal, viscous pool, Amos and the other men peered in from the other rooms, and the children found their way in from the courtyard.

He was here! As though he had been among us all along, and we had not noticed.

It should have seemed more mystical or fantastic than it was. Most of us stared, trying to comprehend, while others were inspired to outright laughter. It was astonishing, while somehow amusing. Exactly like something he would do. More than anything he could have said, the manner of his appearing was proof that it was him.

It was joyous—ecstasy—having him among us again. Except for the wounds on his wrists and between the straps of his sandals, it felt as though he had never left. I try to clutch this memory as a reminder, but it often escapes my grasp. When I am separate from him, I am easily distracted from him by the world, but when I am in his presence, I am wholly distracted from the world by Yeshu. He fills my vision.

A little girl, all tousled hair and white teeth, giggled, a hand over her mouth as she offered him olives and fruit. He carefully selected a fig, wrinkled his nose, and casually popped it in his mouth, raising a brow and grinning at her. She skittered away in laughter.

We should have fallen at his feet, but we were stunned. He ignored our shock and engaged the bewildered flock in conversation. That was his nature. I remember gazing at his beautiful face and thinking how, mere days ago, this countenance was covered in blood and wounds. Some in the room had seen this. Now they saw the same man, new body. He said little that we had not already heard, and we would have been too overwhelmed to remember much, but now we understood what we should have seen and known all along.

Eventually, he found his way where I reclined. I probably spoke nervous drivel, but I remember what he said as he leaned in. "Lazarus, be mindful that the thread of your life will not be like these others." He motioned around the room. "You will not die again soon. Though your body is not like mine, it is also a new creation. I am new. Nothing has gone before. I possess neither a body of clay that has been remade like yours, nor is it a spiritual form like the angels. It is something new made for a new age that waits at the door. But your resurrected body is like those before the time of Noah, you may not die again soon."

"What do you mean, Lord? How am I to live?" I asked.

"I have told you what you need to know, and I do not need to say more. You must live your life. I command it." He smiled. "Lazarus, you are the one who asks no questions, then you ask too many questions." He laid his hand on my shoulder. "But you never ask the right question."

"What is the right question? What am I to *do*?" I asked.

"Ah, more questions!" He laughed. Then he stared into me, my heart pausing. "I promise you will live long enough to know the right questions."

This left me only quiet and bewildered.

"I do not mean to make you more confused, dear friend. You can be so much like your beloved sister, Martha! You do not need all the answers, and you do not have to *do* anything. Remember two things. Now, listen to this." He held up his index finger. "If you will do *alpha*," he raised the second finger, "then I will do *beta*." Then he crossed the two fingers. "If you hand to me whatever trouble, burden, or worry you have, I will take care of it. If you give me your life, I will take care of it. It is that simple. And it will be that simple forever." He patted my shoulder again and stood.

His visit was far too short and ended as mysteriously as it began. He went out to the courtyard with the children. Several stood to follow him, but he lifted his hand and we stayed. In the courtyard, we heard him speak to the children, low and gentle, the children twittering. Stillness for a moment, then his pure, resonant voice, drifted through the house, singing the verses of the lullaby from Psalms that all our mothers sang to us:

"Little lambs be still, be still and know,

Be still and know your shepherd is near.

Be still and know, be still and know,

Be still and know I am with you."

As we listened we looked at one another, smiled; some sniffled and wiped an eye. Then it was silent again. After a while, the children wandered in. We expected him to follow, but they said he had simply left. He could not have left the courtyard without going through the house.

He was gone before we could say farewell.

Despite all I had seen and lived, how could I allow myself to inflict pain upon innocents and turn my back on all I had held sacred?

V. Miriam

It was not long ago, while my thoughts floated in that clairvoyant space between sleep and wakefulness, that I saw Miriam as in a vision. Her fresh, girlish face looked up at me with wonder; confident smile, lower lip slightly protruding, cast in a flush of warm light—fire light or the last rays of setting sun—illuminating the green flecks in her irises and red strands in her black hair. Her gaze riveted me; my betrothed had been just a girl.

I had vowed to become the cutting edge of the Spirit in my beloved's life. And she was my beloved. I had poured my life into her and she into me. After all this time, I cannot dispel the guilt I feel whenever I consider what I did to her.

We escaped to Cyprus after Yeshu was executed and resurrected. If we stayed in Judea we would always be in fear of capture and execution. After the brutal stoning of Stephanos, we knew to stay clear of the Temple and the forces in Jerusalem aligned against us—including Saul.

Miriam's father scraped together a small purse, so we could leave and start a life on a strip of land at the edge of a small village.

With the disciples in disarray, we were grateful that Barnabas had reached out to us and made an agreement with his uncle Zechariah. The old man was ready to yield his humble house and land if we would manage his farm for him. After generously offering us his simple home, I helped Uncle Zechariah restore a hut where he would live on a corner of the property.

Miriam was a capable young woman, but she was overwhelmed by our circumstances. The farm provided a home, but it was still too small to provide for a family. I thought I could supply our needs by using those skills my father had taught me. Young as I was, we were thrown into a challenging situation far from our families with no idea how to build a homestead. I am ashamed to say that despite my skills, I had been a sheltered younger brother, spoiled by my sisters.

We were on Cyprus a short time when Barnabas returned with a small band of followers. They wanted me to leave with them and return to Judea to be an exhibit for the miracles of Yeshu. I was too naïve to turn them down. We had no children, the farm was small, and with the help of Uncle Zechariah, Miriam would not be alone. She wanted to accompany me to see her family, but I thought I would play the stern and foolish husband. I convinced her she was to be a dutiful wife—to stay and take care of our home.

It was a ridiculous and perilous adventure. Throughout Judea, the political climate was unsettled for followers of The Way and our leadership was disordered. I was away two months, leaving Miriam and the old man to take care of the tiny farm. When I returned, she was despondent. She seemed to come around eventually, but it pained me when I saw the damage I had inflicted on this girl.

And she was a girl. We had not consummated our marriage before I left, and I was determined to be gracious by honoring her. A girl may be ready at the time of marriage, but often she was not. A woman's life could be brutish, and it was not unknown for a callous older man to ravage his younger wife. But this was uncommon, especially within The Way. I had known her throughout her life, and I humbly respected her, and I wanted her to respect me. All things happen in Yahweh's time.

After I returned to Cyprus, our life was quiet. She asked me little about my journey, and I told her less. I imagine this girl was at least playing at being the dutiful wife. I farmed our patch of land and worked in the village using my few abilities. A subtle love entwined our humble lives as we grew together. I believe she quietly forgave me for my absence, though I woefully regretted it. I never wanted to leave my betrothed again. She was becoming my love. In fact, I became dizzy in love with her as finally, in joy, our desire consumed us, and warm Cyprian nights were filled with our passion.

Mary, then Martha arrived to help Miriam set up a home when our first child was due. But Miriam's small frame was barely capable of childbirth, and we were heartbroken, devastated when despite my sister's expert care, the child died at birth. I nearly lost not only my first child, but also my precious wife: another thread that knit us closer.

Mary had to return home soon after that tragic birth, but Martha stayed to care for my Miriam like a beloved mother. Martha's bustling and busyness distracted us from our grief of losing our first child. My sister reshaped our humble quarters into, what was for us, a lavish home. While she hung simple tapestry and curtains, she pressed me into remodeling rough shelves into simple cabinets, framing and hanging new doors, expanding our meager courtyard, and rebuilding a sad little stable to create a corner for drying herbs and to store our granary jars. Under Martha's direction, I built racks to dry fish and meat. I do not know where she acquired a sack of blue dye, but she stirred this into a slurry of plaster to cover our house inside and out. When she was done turning our home blue, she found a porous, glittering stone that she crushed into powder, mixed with oils and pigment. Inside the house she painted a thin, golden line all around our walls. She continued that lovely ribbon out the door, circling our entire house, inside and out, with an unbroken line. Miriam was cheered by this simple adornment, and lovingly referred to our home as our private patrician mansion. However, I am certain there were no Romans of any class who were happy as us. We felt the embrace of that unbroken golden thread surrounding our home and our lives.

We worried when Miriam became pregnant again. Our second child was ready to arrive a year after we lost our first, but now it was just Miriam and me, while Uncle Zechariah waited nervously outside. My sisters could not be there. They had families of their own to attend to. But Martha had given me careful instruction, and I felt a shred of confidence from having witnessed the rhythm and intensity of birth when I had assisted the shepherds.

This child slid into our world boldly, thrusting his tiny fists and letting loose with a single long scream that sounded more like a victory cry than birth. He was wonderful. I recall Miriam with her sweaty hair and flushed face weeping for joy, laughing at her precious child. We embraced as one—until little Lazarus kicked me away, rooting for the breast.

It was good fortune that we named him Lazarus. The expedience of naming sons after myself became apparent with time.

Through my sisters and others, we were able to keep in touch with the Believers in and around Jerusalem. Barnabas returned, this time with Paul and John Mark. By then, Miriam and I had grown to five: Lazarus along with the two girls we named Mary and Martha, of course. On Cyprus, we had a circle of Believers who received the Disciples warmly. But at every turn, it was becoming more difficult for The Way. The ecclesia on Cyprus tried to avoid trouble by keeping to ourselves and staying out of the way of Roman and Jewish authorities.

But an enemy just as dangerous was at our doorstep. We were becoming increasingly aware of Elymas the sorcerer, who was a growing scourge to Believers. After Saul converted and became known to us as Paul, he was a fearless leader and pushed the boundaries of The Way. While on Cyprus, he confronted the fraud Elymas with impunity. But the diviner had an arrangement with the Proconsul Sergius Paulus—until the proconsul himself later converted. Before the proconsul's conversion, the political arrangement with Elymas would have destroyed us if Paul had not bravely interceded.

Elymas had been antagonizing the believers on our end of the island near Patmos, but his wicked eyes and ears seemed to be everywhere. Everyone knew that sorcerers were often the equivalent of swindlers, a laughingstock, but Elymas did not earn derision; he earned fear. A cunning merchant of sorcery, he had enthralled authorities with his knowledge of astrology and the dark arts. His ragged, stinking minions would follow him to the cliffs to listen to the bleak auguries he beheld in the flight patterns of sea birds, or they followed him deep in the night, clustered around a weak flame, while through gory haruspicy, he twisted his bony finger through stinking entrails to teach them horrid revelations of his ominous craft.

When Barnabas returned with the two Disciples, Paul wanted me to accompany them on a journey north across the sea. I did not want to leave again, but Paul was relentless. I felt Yahweh had put this woman, my family, and this land in my care, and I did not want to leave again to be the Disciples' show horse.

I am certain another factor was simply my pride. I was aware I had gained a following among Believers who knew my past and knew why the Disciples had come to recruit me. I enjoyed a small following of my own. Though it might result in no more than a nod at the marketplace or a visit from a town official, I secretly relished the occasional gifts: the prize sheep, the broader plot of land, and the fine linens for Miriam.

The Disciples stayed on for a season. Paul was a creature of the city, the temple, and that shoulder-to-shoulder bustle that was Jerusalem. However, honing what had been a mere diversion using leather and cloth, he had developed an impressive trade by applying his curiosity and hungry intellect. These skills also provided a means for him to connect with other craftsmen and farmers. We worked together as he mended harnesses and implements, spread fabric shelters, and worked on ingenious hasps and fasteners. He talked incessantly. Though I loved him, I worried for him and for the attention he might bring to us from Elymas and the Roman authorities. He openly ascribed titles to Yeshu such as Lord, Savior, and Son of God. I feared the Romans would arrest us for blasphemy against their imperial cult, which ascribed similar titles to Caesar. Fortunately, our Roman occupiers considered us as merely another Jewish sect and continued to ignore us.

Elymas was obsessed with Paul, but he feared him and would never approach us directly. But I feared the sorcerer. Because of Paul's presence in our home and because of my notoriety, he had his eye on me, too.

Though confronted, Elymas and his followers remained fascinated by Paul, believing there was no higher form of the dark arts than dreams. They had heard the stories of Paul's conversion and of his profound revelations, which the sorcerer believed arose from the dream world. This evil cult had suspicions that Paul might emerge as a rival sorcerer. However, Paul never sought notoriety, never sought his dreams or promoted any of the mysteries that surrounded him. Though outspoken, he never preened like the garrulous rhetoricians and sophists. Though he was not eloquent of speech like them, his education within the leading schools of thought, his intelligence, and argumentative skill far exceeded their own. He put the sorcerers and educated classes to shame by supporting himself as a common man, by being open and generous with his talents, and by never pilfering from his acolytes or from the ignorant.

Paul tried to persuade me to share his deep desire to push the geographic boundaries of the knowledge of Yeshu. He wanted to go places where no one, Jew or Gentile, had heard of the Gospel. Eventually, I relented when Paul assured me the Disciples would provide help for Miriam and the small enclave of followers that had developed around our home. I agreed to travel as far as Perga and Attalia on the coast, no farther, and return in a couple of weeks. Paul was sensitive and supportive of my commitment to Miriam and provided what he could to secure her wellbeing.

She was stoic when I left that morning. We held each other, and I kissed the children. Then as I was leaving, I traced with a finger the thin gold ribbon that surrounded our home.

I left.

VI. Flight

Paul and Barnabas expanded their campaign to Antioch and beyond after we set sail. I am certain they would not have hidden their plans from us, only to spring them on us later. That was never their way. They were transparently honest men to their core. I believe that once they set sail, they became exhilarated by the adventure and with assurance that they were being led by the Spirit to go further. I could not argue with how they were being led, but John Mark and I did not agree with them. It would have been cruel and faithless of me to put Miriam through months of separation again.

John Mark and I returned to Cyprus. Paul was angry. He later patched things up with John Mark, but I never again saw Paul, my cherished friend.

I honestly cannot fault Paul and Barnabas. Like me, they were fully human. Like all the Disciples, they were people who at their core were incapable of serving Yeshu, yet they lived within a fortress of faith. I was weaker. I had determined my life would be confined to my commitment to my wife, my children, and my existence on Cyprus. The Disciples had broader visions.

To me, the work of the Disciples and the work of our small ecclesia should have been simple. When in the city on market day, the authorities might be called upon to block the streets or direct the carts and crowds so that all the traffic would move in one direction on one street and return in the opposite direction on another street. A guard would stand at the intersection and direct crowds. My job and the task of the Church was to be as simple as the guard at the market: Stand on a one-way street directing my family and anyone who was interested, in one direction, toward Yeshu. If someone were headed in the wrong direction, I would clearly point the other way. It was that simple. Paul and Barnabas felt it was their task to create new streets with more thoroughfares leading to the Savior. They were not wrong.

I do not disparage Paul. He was not the dire, harsh person many believed him to be. Though I said he was adamant, and he was, he was never severe. I think of him as gentle, brilliant, tireless, insightful, and the nearest to the personality of Yeshu of any of the disciples. He was persuasive and passionate but never overbearing. He possessed the true character of the Christ, which was why he was so readily accepted by the Disciples and why he was given the position and authority he was granted.

In later months, Barnabas returned one more time to ask me to develop a leadership position for The Way on Cyprus, but I refused. I was not a leader like them. Many years later, my son served honorably as bishop, but I had no interest whatsoever. Paul, Barnabas, and Peter were competent leaders and had gifts of administration and development that few people possessed. Their gifts were instrumental to the survival and expansion of the early Church. In mere generations after the Disciples, the greedy domination of less competent men would yield to staid ritual and barren religion. I have rarely seen anything more.

My first love: It torments me when I think back to how my time with Miriam ended. On Cyprus the love between us grew with passion. We had become one. We had grown up in the same community; she knew who I was, and we were both familiar with Yeshu and those around Him. More importantly, she loved my sisters like I did.

At more than five decades, I should have been an old man. Though aging, Miriam was lithe and lovely. She carried her small frame like a young woman. Sadly, the inevitability of age, childbirth, and the rigors of farm life overtook her. Graceful aging caused her to gray and wrinkle until an old woman replaced my girlish Miriam. We lived well, but hard work had taken a toll on this mother, grandmother, and farmer's wife. She would totter after a long day of harvest, shearing sheep, or chasing grandchildren. I was becoming selfish and vain, dreading her aging. I looked like a man in my prime; my son and I were often mistaken for one another. I could no longer be seen in the market or in our fellowship without someone commenting.

There were those in our circle of Believers who understood that this abnormality was due to my remarkable history. I was learning what Yeshu had meant all those years ago when he spoke to me at Amos's home and told me that my body was unlike others. I was realizing—and fearing. But it was mostly beyond my comprehension, and I spent many sleepless nights pondering what this would mean for Miriam and me.

We had three surviving children who helped with the work. We had endured the misery of losing our firstborn, but then we lived through the horror of seeing two more of our children die. Like all parents, we waited for illness and disease to take their bitter share, hoping they would leave us at least a portion. Disease and death are the mirthless playmates of childhood. We had one child who died of a sickness in her chest at less than two years. Then there was the tragedy of our Thomas, who was seven when he fell from a tree and injured his stomach. He died a long and excruciating death days later.

We never recovered from Thomas's death. Miriam never spoke it to me; she did not have to. I was thinking the same thing: If Yeshu could raise me from the dead, and if others had been raised from the dead, then why could Yeshu not spare this innocent child from a horrific death?

I fear Thomas's death was the first bite of an axe that would bring down my tree of faith. Maybe I was incapable of seeing more dead children. I would rationalize that was part of the motivation for what I ultimately did.

Miriam seemed to understand our fate better than me. She knew the truth as we grew apart and seemed to be waiting—waiting for something to occur that I had not accepted, yet. She would no longer allow me to watch her dress or to share intimacy. It was devastating for a couple who had grown together over many years, through many trials, to begin to cleave and grow apart. Our souls were entwined, but the strands of our life were unravelling.

The fellowship of believers was also unravelling in disturbing ways. The poison of pride was creeping into the ecclesia causing internal conflict and squabbles. Those who visited from Judea shared how the love and caring maintained by Paul and the Disciples were dissolving into petty strife. Social and political concerns invaded communities of faith across the region and the bonds of peace were broken despite the grace of Yahweh. Our fellow Believers on Cyprus were being similarly afflicted. I grew weary of the bickering and pride, and I slowly separated myself from them. There was no point enduring this foolish strife. At the same time, deadly persecutions were increasing. We were being torn asunder by conflict from within and fears from without.

I was vain and foolish. I could not watch my Miriam growing old, and I could not stand to see the life we shared wither and gray. In my narrow view, I could not see a way for our life to continue. In truth, I was not interested in or capable of finding a way.

I feared my youthful appearance would cause me to become a mere spectacle, an attraction on Cyprus. As Believers, we are never to allow any quarter for fear. Insidious fear will always manipulate us into irresponsibility and betrayal. I feared losing Miriam, I feared for my life and for hers, I feared the strange life that had befallen me, and I feared not knowing our future. And as the fellowship of believers disintegrated, I feared the loss of my faith.

Early one brightening spring morning I stepped out the door. My grandson Laban, nearly a year old, had been laying near his mother, her tunic over her breast and the child clawing at the covering. Bleary-eyed, he looked up at me in the dim room, hopeful I could help him secure his breakfast. His long, curly hair billowed like a tiny thunderhead at his mother's side. He changed his tack and reached for me. I called him Leben, because he often smelled like buttermilk, and he had wet his leather wrap, which added nuance to his odor that morning.

I held him close, as though I were embracing my entire family while his pudgy fingers clutched toward the doorway. He loved to venture out in the morning, to find the animals and throw scraps.

I carried him out the door to take in the valley and fields, hear the lambs calling, and see the haze on the hills. He popped a finger out of his mouth and pointed. I had to name whatever he pointed at. Then he would return his finger to his mouth until he saw the lamb, or the hen, or a hawk soaring to reach the rays of rising sun.

Looking around, thinking of the Psalmist's words, I allowed myself a prideful boast: "From the womb of the dawn to you belongs the dew of your youth."

Soon, the morning chatter of family and the smell of breakfast followed us out the door. I had not seen Miriam as she stepped into the morning and I did not know she was beside us until she slid her arm in mine and leaned her head on my shoulder. Laban patted her head. The corner of her mouth worried into her cheek; she was about to speak, but her head shook once quickly and she fluttered her hand, trying to brush away regret. She knew. If it were not this morning, it would soon be another. In a sense, we had already separated. But we embraced in a way we had not in years. I kissed her head and felt a warm tear on my arm. With resignation, she took Laban and walked with measured steps to our home, her fingers tracing the faded golden ribbon that still encircled our house.

I spoke an insincere excuse to her back. Without turning, she briefly waved backhanded. I said I was meeting our neighbor, Judas, and we were going into Salamis to pick up a young ram and other supplies for him. We would need to take his cart, so there would not be room for my eager son Lazarus to join us. It was all empty chatter and excuses. As I walked backward the last few paces, I watched Laban, wide-eyed, opening and closing his stubby fingers, reaching for me over his grandmother's shoulder.

None of them saw my tears, but my mind was bent on doing the most foolish thing I would ever do. I had a vague plan. I was not brilliant to conceive a broad scheme or to understand the consequences.

I walked away; that is what I do.

Along the road, I turned toward home. Miriam had stepped into the doorway again. I waved. She stared unmoving, resigned.

Could I do this? Foolishly, I told myself it was my duty to protect my family from rumors and suspicion. If I stayed, I would attract more attention to myself and risk harassment from the sorcerer Elymas, who yet slithered on Cyprus. That was partially true. But I was lying to myself. The truth was I could not bear to watch my Miriam grow old and die and I had become weary of the attention of curious whisperers. I was not able to reach inside myself and marshal the courage to stay. I knew it was wrong. By the heavens, I knew it was wrong. Throughout my long, tortured life, I have known it was wrong.

It will forever haunt me.

In Salamis, I helped Judas load his feisty ram and his supplies. Then I told him I would stroll along the docks while he bargained for more grain and reconnected with merchants that he knew. The city was large, and the docks were hectic with Roman ships and other foreign vessels. It was easy to disappear into the tumult.

I ducked into an alley to find a way around the crowds and circle back to the docks. Suddenly it was like the world stopped, the bustle of crowd noise fell away, and I was stunned into fright. Like seeing something completely out of place: a scorpion in your cup or a wolf in the barn. The first time I saw the two of them was surreal and horrifying and is burned in my memory. It would not be the last time I would be tormented by their dreadful countenances and by their sudden appearance. Across oceans, continents, and down through time I foolishly thought I could elude their pursuit.

They hovered at the end of the alley blocking my escape. I was riveted by the sizzling dread of their presence. Taller than men, their long black hair and fine features were as men from the East, however ancient and severe, ghastly, yet like raptors or serpents, intriguingly beautiful. Creatures, not men, robed in brocaded garments of deep purple and green, trimmed golden, carrying fierce polished swords, engraved with roiling runes and images. They knew who I was, and I was certain they wanted to kill me.

I surmised they had been sent by Elymas the sorcerer. The sorcerer had frighteningly defied mortality and had become increasingly powerful. Now his followers had once again infiltrated the government on Cyprus. Miscreants from across the sea in Perga and Attalia had arrived in his thrall.

During a brutal exchange with Paul, Elymas had been blinded in the proconsul's court. His tribe became increasingly dangerous and often would boldly disrupt activities of The Way. As Believers, we never took their powers seriously because we knew that the powers of evil were minuscule compared to the power of the living Yahweh. After several years, probably because Elymas's cult had lost the proconsul's protection and attention, they resorted to a degree of witchcraft that was terrifying to many on Cyprus, including many believers. Rumors spread of bizarre rituals with animal sacrifice, and many feared child sacrifice. Eventually, the proconsul intervened.

Now there were rumors of something more bizarre. Reports claimed that people on the island were seeing beings described as Immortals, strange apparitions from the East thought to be ancients. The cult of Elymas claimed that these beings were old ones, bidden to Cyprus to teach ancient crafts and the attainment of immortality. We had been convinced it was merely a strategy to counter the Disciples' teachings.

I was no longer skeptical.

When I saw these beings in the alley, I knew what they wanted of me. Panicked and confused, I slipped between the rotting shacks that lined the pier and through a door. I dashed up the first gangplank I could find.

On deck, a couple of sailors were milling around, scarcely noticing me until I approached. Before I could speak, they pointed toward a young, shirtless man among the cargo, shuffling jars and crates while he scratched figures on a tablet cradled in his arm.

As I approached, he looked up. He was younger than I had assumed. A youth, he could not have been as old as my son. "Passengers pay upfront," he said as he waved me aside, then paused and grinned, "but we can bargain if you are willing to push cargo or pull rope."

Frightened, I could only stammer. Though I had decided to leave Cyprus, I was not certain when I would leave, and I was not entirely prepared to start a voyage. I was afraid to glance back to shore, fearing I might catch the Immortals' eyes again.

He knit his brow, looking along the docks, something catching his eye. He shook his head once quickly as though dispelling a bad dream. I imagined he must have briefly glimpsed the reason for my panic. Sailors were accustomed to seeing strange anomalies along the docks of the world. He looked back to me, sensing my fear. "I'm Markos." He extended a hand in greeting. "Captain of this grand vessel," he said proudly, an ironic smile crossing his fresh face. A Greek sailor, he had a short, black beard, and indulged himself with a silk neck sash and large earring.

Along these docks, it was more common to meet grizzled skippers and gnarled sailors who reeked of fish than handsome young men professing to be captains. Wary, I gazed around the ship until I caught the eye of one of the old sailors who winked and nodded assurance. What did I have to lose? My feet were on deck; I was already running away from a life I might lose to those creatures on shore. I had to make a choice. I glanced nervously along the docks, sighed in resignation, grasped Markos's hand to seal an agreement, and paid his fee upfront.

"In for a lepton, in for a drachma," he said, his grin beaming. Though, I had never been a gambler.

The sails were unfurled, and the ship was cutting into waves before I could reconsider. We would head west toward Crete; then after a layover, if they could gather adequate cargo, we would continue farther along northern shores.

What I was doing was inexcusable, despite all my tepid rationalizations. The reality was that I was leaving Miriam, my family, my community, and my home. My foolish plan was to sneak back in a few seasons or years to find a way to live a deceptive life among my family. Foolish. I was lying to myself and worst of all to Miriam.

In Miriam, I had seen a dimpled, brown-cheeked child: budding breasts, black hair with wispy copper strands, her green-flecked eyes—all changed, seemingly in a day to the dull gray of a huddled grandmother. I had witnessed the extent of a lifetime, lifted this tiny piece from a game board, regarded its short span, and then tossed it over my shoulder. I imagined she would become withered and bedridden, cared for by our children, and possibly dying alone.

I never returned to Miriam's side. The winds were never under my command. Storms, wars, earthquakes, and all the mayhem of earth and man were thrown in my way. Those were my pathetic excuses. How do you apologize to someone you destroyed so long ago?

If this had been the single love I had ever abandoned, the single foolish course I had plotted, then maybe there would be a place for wilting excuses or vague exoneration.

But this was far from my only failure.

VII. At Sea

Men and cargo were boarded, the riggings whined, and sails unfurled. My prior experience at sea was merely ferrying to Cyprus or Perga. Despite my trepidation and confusion, the day was glorious—clear and bright, gulls soaring, and the spray kissing my face and drenching my tunic. Farther from shore, the cross seas swelled, we rolled and bucked, and then steered westward, skimming over crests and thumping into troughs. With ropes singing and cloth snapping, I stood on the bow, inhaling briny haze.

Wait until I tell Miriam and the children, I thought for a moment, then woefully forced those ghosts beneath the waves.

Standing beside me on the bow, Markos thankfully distracted me from regret. He grinned broadly while taking in the spectacle as though he were a novice like me. Warily glancing at his muscled arms and giddy youth, I sincerely hoped he was not a boyish novice.

And he was not. The crew loved Markos. All of them had worked for captains who were brutal cheats, willing to risk the lives of their crew for a few pieces of silver. The sailors were eager to tell me stories of Markos's generosity and exploits at sea. Acknowledging his youthfulness, they assured me he was deft with rudder and sail while shrewd at procuring and selling cargo: far from the clear-faced adolescent he appeared.

Markos's mother had died when he was a guppy, and since Markos was an only child, his tender father could not bear to part with him. A sailor's family is held together by his wife. If she dies or runs off with another sea hack, their children are scattered—or worse. Instead, Markos's father took him to sea. Through a harsh school of storms and treachery he emerged as a brilliant, young sea captain.

After days at sea, I sat alone at the bow, contemplating an unquiet ocean of shifting waves etched in flashes of gold and silver. I brooded while gazing across the expanse of shimmering beauty. Lonely at sea, I had arrived at a place worthy for one who had abandoned life and love. Already grief and guilt were building on the horizon like a cold, black November squall. Having loosened lines that had secured me to the anchor of my faith and to the sails that were my family, I foundered far from shore. I thought of tiny Laban—my little Leben—sweet Miriam, and the delight within my family's embrace.

"Where are you, Lord?" I said aloud. "Who are you and what will you have with me? Is there forgiveness for someone who has fallen so far?"

As though receiving the damage report after a storm, my mind dwelt on all I had left behind on Cyprus, until I was distracted by the panorama that lay before me. Stricken to silent submission, I began to examine lessons learned from Yeshu: how we were created for praise, and we are to live in awe. Dutifully excoriating myself, I tried to force myself back to my reflections on Miriam and my family. But the created wonder I was beholding spoke powerfully to me, demanding adulation while offering counsel.

Yeshu taught and the Disciples affirmed that we were created because, wherever it exists, great beauty and boundless genius cries for—demands—awe. It demands adulation meant simply to satisfy Yahweh's magnificence, not to satisfy the rogue arrogance of a vague Elohim or other omnipotent deity. The created world demands witness whether this vast sky and ocean or something simple as the curve of a shell, the curve of a growing fern, the curve of the crescent moon, or the curve of the earth. Our forced or involuntary adulation would have been meaningless—tyrannical. So, we were granted a single sacred *flaw:* choice. In leaving Cyprus, I had exercised an act of will. Yet, it is often our choices that speed our downfall and explain why we would need to be rescued by a messiah mangled and crucified: his death becoming our rescue from our bad choices.

As loving father, he offered himself in our place because there could be no communion with Yahweh without absolute purity. And imperfection cannot be merely covered over, it must be abolished. Yahweh provided the means of restoration by putting himself in our place. Through Yeshu's perfection, each speck of our imperfection can be erased whenever we ask forgiveness, and we are restored to fellowship with Yahweh.

Despite all that I knew, it was not difficult to swing back toward remorse. Through disappointment with the ecclesia on Cyprus and my betrayal of Miriam, I had allowed my relationship with Yahweh to be scuttled. I chose to sit there and dwell on myself and my pitiful incompetence. I felt empty, wholly adrift and lost.

I had abandoned Miriam solely because of a bizarre rationalization and a vastly distorted sense of what I thought was right. I had told myself I would bring shame to my family, that my warped existence would bring derision and threats if I lingered with Miriam and my family longer. I was a fool. A fool who had made a choice that secured safety not for her but for my own vanity and safety. There was no way to turn back.

In this place, I could not decipher what I had done, and I could not untangle the overwhelming jumble of feelings from confusion and guilt to grief and loss. One blended into the other. I allowed myself to deeply ponder whether this immortality granted me by Yeshu was a curse, not a gift.

"I did not ask for this long life! I do not want it," I said to the sky.

I thought of those small tokens that would be purchased before a short voyage. When the time for departure arrived, we would hand over the token, board the ship, and leave. I longed to be given a token I could hand over and depart this life.

"Let me die. What is your will in all this, Lord?" I asked. No response, I thought. When in fact, response was everywhere. How blind I was. Would I ask what is the will of the ocean as I was tossed on its back? Would I ask the will of the sky as I sat under its vast dome, tossed by wind and weather? Overhead, wispy clouds arched away to infinity while a film of distant islands wavered and disappeared on the horizon under a sliver of moon and a round, brilliant sun. Sailors knew of the curve of the earth. They did not need the ancient Greeks to teach them. They knew that they likely sat on a globe or half of an orb as perfect as the sun and moon that hung above. They had skimmed the ocean into the darkening edge of a solar eclipse or into those eerie red nights of lunar eclipse. It was all around them and under their bow day and night.

Because we stand on its broad surface, hidden is a view of the earth itself. We see the curve only as it is reflected upon something else: an eclipse or a celestial display that betrays its vastness.

Where are you, Lord? Like the ant on Yeshu's arm: The Infinite is unseen only because we walk too near.

Markos's joy with his life at sea was a stark contrast to my overbearing guilt and sorrow. Like something from the tomb, I pulled the ragged cloak of despair and melancholy around my shoulders and wrapped my soul. It was comfortable and familiar as I slipped it on, its stains and tatters surrounding me. Upon this garment was embroidered a dark portrait. Silk threads of black emotion provided perspective, certainty, and depth to my bleak life.

I had fled meaning to embrace meaninglessness. By casting myself at sea, I was desperate that this hapless venture could somehow untangle the threads and restore meaning. Foolishness.

Had all my long hours of precious learning in the presence of Yeshu and Paul amounted to nothing? Like a foolish child, I was in the throes of my helplessness and sin. From their wise counsel, I had learned we were not supposed to dwell on sin. We admit we are wrong, confess it, make restitution if needed, and then move on immediately. Forget the sin; God has.

I recalled the prophet Hosea spoke of "taking words to God." In the mind of the prophet, we seek repentance to restore communication with God. Is that what I am to do—to speak the sin and ask forgiveness? Restore communication, heal, then find my way back? I could not. I was too humiliated at my unrelenting, profound weakness. I was deeply and utterly ensnared; drowning, flailing, trying to swim free from this net.

Mesmerized by the motion of the sea, I sat devastated by my powerlessness, wallowing in my despondency, and contemplating. Maybe those devils we nurtured as youth never leave us; we merely feed them less; we become more adept at controlling them until they return with all their snarling horror. Have I been merely digging graves and burying my sin my entire life? Have I fooled myself by believing that once our sin is forgiven, it is truly gone, buried and forgotten? It did not feel forgiven or forgotten. All the while, there it lays, our lives becoming more constricted by a landscape of restless graves. For a time, it may seem forgiveness has granted us a bit more property. We build new dwellings over the old bones. But then the ghosts return. The cycle of our transgression never ends until we are defeated.

Slouched on Markos's ship, feeling pitiful in sin, I was defeated. I did not stand defiant with fists clenched at God, but skulked fearfully with knitted brow, caught in the act like a worried child. Weak, impulsive, and controlled by vice, I cannot help myself.

"Who are you, Lord? What is your will in all this, Lord?" I repeated.

"Is the sea your lord, Lazar? Like it is for me?" I had not heard Markos's approach. With sparkling laughter, he continued, "Sometimes the sea is my lord and sometimes my lady."

"No, I talk to the Creator," I said awkwardly, looking at him and then back to the sea. It would not surprise anyone; no one would be offended, whether Greek or Roman, by devotion to a deity or to a multitude of gods. Every ship was replete with small banners, figurines, and shrines depicting every god or goddess, east to west.

"Oh." Markos flipped his hand. "I believe none of it. Not a bit." He looked around to assure himself that none of his sailors heard. They would tolerate any god, but no one would abide the blasphemy of claiming to be without any gods in this god-filled world. He leaned in conspiratorially, animated, his dark shoulders, flowing hair, and brilliant eyes seeming to move with the sea. "Oh, I play along with the men and all their superstitions and ridiculous fears. Gods create more fears than they relieve." He clutched the tiny phallic trinket that hung around his neck and smiled. "I play along, but I believe none of it. I know you are Jewish, my friend, but you seem like a sensible man, so I am sure you do not want to hear my ignorant ramblings." With his arms embracing his knees he sat looking across the shifting sea. "I have been at sea long enough to know there is nothing one can do to change the whims of water or weather." He scanned upward. "If there are gods, they do not care. It is chance, merely chance. I intend to live as long as I can and grasp for all in my reach." He clutched at the sky then looked at me. "I know there are few old captains. 'I was not. I was. I am not. I care not.'" He counted four fingers. "I transcribed those words on my own father's tomb because that is how Father saw this world of chance. I have heard all those sad, believing souls say, 'Praise be' to their god. I say, 'Praise be Chance! My god is Chance." He bumped my shoulder with his. "And what is the name of your god?"

"In truth, he has no name," I replied.

"Ah...! Then how would you conjure him?" He snorted. "You must know a god's name to control him; to get him to do your bidding."

"This is not a god that you control," I said cautiously.

He nodded thoughtfully. An imageless, nameless, unmanageable god was perplexing.

As days turned to years and our friendship grew, Markos was not antagonistic toward faith, but held a vague curiosity. More learned than anyone I encountered on the seas; his questions were sincere. He read Greek and could enthusiastically discuss the ancient philosophers. That my faith had cohesive scripture captivated him. Of the hundreds of gods and goddesses that he knew of, there were only scraps of holy writ. In the years that followed, he gathered an impressive collection of Talmud and would listen as I translated. He acquired several copies of the Disciples' letters, written in Greek. I thought that he might become a convert, that he might acquire the faith I ironically struggled with.

That would tragically never happen.

Markos and I were sailors and became business partners for at least a generation. Teaching me the ways of his goddess, the sea, he was an enthusiastic priest.

He never married. I believe it was because of the pain and responsibility that marriage required; the faithfulness he had seen in his father. In the early days when I knew him, he was not one to leave the ship and whore like many of the crew. He was a lone man with secret passions.

The seas became my hiding place as I hopped from vessel to vessel, scudded behind rocky islands to escape a storm or lay over in a forgotten harbor. I lived like a man fleeing banshees—which I was: banshees real and imagined. The memory of those horrific Immortals on the docks of Cyprus was not all that haunted me. Phantoms of grief, guilt, loneliness, and regret mercilessly assailed me. I became like most sullen sailors who had forsworn life and love or fled crime and regret.

I was not always with Markos in those years, and I would learn later that he was not always at sea. With or without him, I chose the deadliest voyages involving the greatest risk. My hidden desire was to find the token that allowed me to leave this life. While hoping for mortality, I lived as one who believed himself immortal. Though eventually paying the price, I mocked injury and death.

I fled meaning and cast myself into the dark waters of meaninglessness.

Despite my unflagging quest for danger, I always found a way to avoid those voyages that might take me near the eastern seas. I avoided Cyprus and Judea, always rationalizing that time along with earthquakes, storms, and the severe persecution of The Way had scoured those lands of any trace of my life and loves long ago. Of course, I was lying to myself. That's what I do.

I was careful never to reveal myself to anyone who was familiar with Yeshu. If I encountered his followers or those who had known his disciples, I was silent, feigning ignorance or scoffing, too ashamed in my transgressions, having drifted an ocean away from what I had known and believed. And I was terrified of revealing my identity. If my existence seemed remarkable and unbelievable to me, how would it appear to another?

In the early years, Markos and I remained friends. But there seemed a line he did not want to cross, and never allowed anyone too close. He could withdraw for days or months or disappear from the seas without a trace.

When friends, we laughed at danger; he because of his youth, me because I was tempting death. While I tempted death because I wanted relief from my guilt and because I deserved retribution, Markos tempted death because he was enamored of fate and prized youth above all. His motives became shrouded and more desperate. Beyond merely tempting death, he taunted death, sneered at death, with a simmering hatred of his mortality.

Losing his grasp on youthfulness, Markos launched into headlong pursuit of living. This man, who had disdained prostitutes and carousing, became consumed by loathsome debauchery. Though my risen body was not given to much depravity, I confess I followed him into some of these dens of desperation. I regret my share of the shame. But his spiral through younger women and stronger intoxicants was an unabated race toward decrepitude. He hated me because that same mantle of decrepitude was not enshrouding me. Squinting eyes cornered at me, his lips would purse in veiled rage, then he would wonder loudly why I was not aging like him. He would challenge me to foolish contests or try to force me to tell others my age. It was ridiculous, infantile. While he taunted me, he would often have a small entourage of disheveled, childlike harlots who would try to focus on me, unable to acclimate to the motion of the seas as they swayed drunkenly at his side.

Our friendship withered until he regressed into one of those bitter, old sea captains. He cursed and spat, raging at me for the smallest miscalculation, real or imagined. Twice he left me on a pier, until I could catch up with our ship weeks or months later. Begrudgingly, he would allow me back aboard simply because he needed my experience—and the gold I had earned to fund his expeditions. There became fewer sailors willing to sign on with him. Whenever we were separated, I would return to see a man older and more desperate. My youthful appearance made him seethe, but he would shake his head, turn away silently, and sign me on again.

He had motives that went beyond hiring crew. He had another reason, eerie and dangerous, why he wanted me to return each time: He was desperate to learn the secret of my immortality.

Markos's anguish was more evident after we had lain over in his home port of Syracuse. He had secured cargo intended for Barcilonum, but he planned a stop in Sardinia, supposedly to load bales of leather from one of the native merchants who lived in the island's interior. But we knew that Markos kept another girl in one of the shacks near the docks of Sardinia, and that she would soon be exchanged with his current onboard mistress, Elnora.

Not long after we left Syracuse, a wind that had blasted like a furnace finally abated, leaving us to row for a couple of hours until Markos called a halt, allowing the men to rest. In brutal heat, sweat poured from our backs. The sails hung limp above a sea flat and hot as slate. To reach Sardinia was normally a voyage of two days—one with a strong easterly, but we crept, rowing until we were no longer able, resting and splashing ourselves in tepid seawater, then rowing again. The morning of the second day, Markos sat on the bow watching the horizon for any sign of a cloud front or breeze. Elnora snored in his cabin.

His face was fixed in a scowl, deeply lined and jowled, eyes rimmed red.

I stepped beside him and shared his gaze over smooth waters. He was unusually sullen and placid like the seas; I could smell the drink on his breath. I did not speak.

After long silence, he said, "Long ago, I picked you up on Cyprus; you were fleeing someone."

I did not answer.

"On Cyprus was the cult of Elymas. I know this; you do not have to feign ignorance anymore," he said, looking near his feet, then around the deck, expecting a bottle. He wiped his lips with the back of his hand. "It was said that this sorcerer Elymas knew the secret to eternal life, and that his followers would never grow old and die."

"I heard of such things, but there were many rumors spoken to scare the children," I quickly said, trying to head him off.

"You knew nothing of such things?" He looked at me sideways, brows drawn together curiously.

"No, Elymas was evil. I was of The Way. He hated us. I have told you all this before."

"This is merely another of your convenient stories, Lazar," he said.

"What do you mean?" I asked.

He huffed. "You know nothing of the ageless? Of the Immortals?" He became restive. "Is that not who you were running from that day?" He looked me up and down. "Do not take me for a fool. Do not lie to me. All these years I have been exploring, trying to find the answers that every man wants to know. The answer that *you* know."

We had talked but one time, and very briefly about that day I ran onto his ship. He knew I had been chased, but I always believed he had seen more, and possibly knew more of those creatures than he had been willing to tell me. More than once, he had plied me about the rumors of immortality that swarmed around the work of Elymas. I tried to avoid the subject, knowing of Markos's jealous need. "I have told you; I did not know who they were or what I saw. They were terrible, and I had never seen anything like them before."

"Look at you, Lazar. After all these years, you must know why—you *have* to know why—I would be curious about the cult of the Immortals."

"I do not know what you are talking about," I lied.

"Could it be a mere coincidence, some quirk of the gods, that you do not grow old and gray?" I could not dissuade him. He had never pushed for details, and I did not know how to respond. He pressed on, terse and calculating. "Word has it that Elymas fled Cyprus and went north, beyond Byzantium, maybe as far as Odessa or farther. I intend to find him. I want what you have, what this sorcerer gave you. You need to tell me and tell me now."

"I do not know what you mean. I assure you that evil wizard had nothing to give. If that blind charlatan lives—which is ridiculous—then you must do everything to stay away from him. Like all sorcerers, he is a fraud." My mind was reeling. I had obviously avoided talking to him about those whom Yeshu had raised from the dead, but I always assumed that somewhere in Markos's travels or in the documents he had acquired, he would have heard or read of those miracles. But much of the Greek and Roman world had walled themselves off from these Jewish *myths* and paid no attention. Markos was a man of the world, and his curiosity and knowledge should have prevented him from following fables. Unfortunately, much of my faith had fallen away, so I had difficulty maintaining a defense, and I was no longer an example to him. And those rare times when I tried to discuss supernatural things, he would scoff, no longer wanting anything to do with it.

"Markos, I accept my youthful appearance. I admit that." I proceeded slowly. I had to try something to distract him from his vain pursuit. "It is a gift that I do not deserve that was given by one whom I cannot describe," I said cautiously. "It was not Elymas; it was the Messiah of the Jews, this Yeshu whom I have told you of." This was more than I had told anyone, but I feared what he would do in desperation if he sensed I was hiding the truth from him.

Stroking his chin, swiping a fly, he continued to gaze over the flat seas of lazy doldrum that spread to the horizon. We were a speck sitting on an infinite mirror that spread beneath our bow, yet this sailor, fraught with his vanity, could not bear to look down into the water at his aging reflection. He slowly shook his head, clenching his jaw, wrestling inside.

"I do not believe you," he said. "The Jews are all Zealots. The day you boarded my ship, you were frightened nearly to death. I know what you saw. Do you think I did not see them, you idiot? You see frightening Immortal creatures, you come aboard my ship, and you never grow old.

Maybe you were simply a victim—a toy—of theirs, but I will find Elymas, and as the gods are my witnesses, I will find those immortal ones!" He made fists, his voice rising above the calm. "I cannot survive like this. I will not grow old! I will defy this body." He thumped his chest. "I will not succumb to death! If there is any way out of this, I will find it!"

I hesitated, his rage simmering. A shark fin surfaced, momentarily wavered, then sunk into depths. I had traveled with Markos for a generation—more than a generation. Why should I lie to him? Why had I been lying to him? I breathed in, then exhaled a whisper. "I am Lazarus of Bethany."

There was a long pause. He scratched his arm rapidly, he explored his lips with a clumsy tongue, then spit. "I know who you are, you son-of-a-whore! At least I know who you think you are. It changes nothing."

He stood, whisked his robe over his shoulder, and fled to his cabin where I soon heard Elnora whimper from Markos's brutal assault.

Because of his fear and loathing of me, I have always believed what happened next was by Markos's design.

VIII. Marooned

The winds recovered, blowing us to Sardinia in a single night. Intent upon taking advantage of steady winds, we did not stay long, but launched again from Sardinia, heading west, and had an uneventful landing in Barcilonum.

He left his battered Elnora in Barcilonum and we embarked on the long voyage destined for Egypt. I heard Markos telling one of his men that, after we unloaded in Alexandria, he had a commission to deliver cargo that was headed far north into the Black Sea. I knew his plan would be to follow his myth of Elymas and immortality all the way to the northern reaches of Odessa and beyond if he had to. The cargo he would carry to the Black Sea would be nothing more than the poison of hopeless desperation for youth. I knew he would not permit me to be part of the crew when he decided to take that voyage.

He betrayed me after we left Barcilonum, and we would not speak again: Not until we would meet again in a land we dream of in nightmares, at a far distant time, across those seas that are heard of only in song.

By the second day out it was clear the seasonal doldrum had left us for good. A strong westerly was at our back. We were plowing underway when the main sail slumped and began snapping loudly in the gale. It seemed strange, because knowing the gales we might be facing, Markos had been up there himself to check the rigging that morning. He was the best sailor on any vessel I had sailed, so it was not unusual for him to scurry up the mast, if for no other reason than to prove his virility to younger sailors.

As the sail sagged and whipped like a house servant shaking rugs, the wind grew, and the seas swelled. Markos nodded to me, and as was my habit, I eagerly volunteered to take the risk and shimmy up the mast to repair the sail.

The seas were increasingly uneven, and the repair would be challenging. With rope and a roll of sail cloth in hand, I was about to secure the main. I saw the men below looking up with worried smiles, accustomed to my risky behavior. It was not unusual for them to cast lots on the outcome of my misadventures.

I heard a call seconds before impact, the sailor at the bow crying, "Whale!"

I looked over my shoulder to see the black monstrosity, waves cresting its back, plowing directly starboard. I had been aboard ships that collided with whales. While the impact could be jolting, the creature would slide under the ship, the vessel would rock and veer, and damage would be minimal if any. But I was hanging onto a swaying mast with a thin line around my wrist. Just before impact, I reached to hitch the line again around my wrist and secure myself to the mast when I saw something more frightening than the sleek, plunging whale: The larger downhaul line had been severed and the narrow trim line to which I was secured was cleanly sliced with only a few strands remaining. It was too late to scurry down or reach for another lash. The impact was tremendous. The mast bent far toward starboard, leaving me hanging over the broad back of the monster with one arm slung around a rough crossbeam. The mast corrected sharply to port side like a catapult flinging me outward. I was yanked from the crossbeam, and the line around my wrist snapped cleanly. In that instant, scrabbling while trying to grab at the mast again, I chanced a last desperate glance down to the deck to see Markos, eyes wide, his rueful smile folded into his gray beard as if he had swallowed a live squid and could not decide if it were delicious or deadly: how to digest his good fortune. That was my last vision of Markos or of the ship.

I am not certain where I awoke. It does not seem possible that I could have drifted that far, but over the years, I have come to believe I had drifted to Anafi, though other mariners assured me it could not have been that tiny island. However, when I left many years later, I discovered I had been somewhere off Kalliste, near Greece.

When I told this tale to mariners, they would not believe me. It would not be possible to drift that far, and they had never heard of a tribe like the one I described on any of those islands. To them it is all a sailor's yarn. Everyone knew there were nothing but a few bloodthirsty cannibals and pirates on the islands near Kalliste. There could be no one on the remote strands of rock and sand who was as civilized and as peaceful as those I had encountered. And no one would believe that anyone could have had the skill to heal me from injuries that were as severe as I described. But the mariners could not have considered that I would not need to be healed by anyone other than Yahweh, the gifted Physician under whose care I remained.

I can relate nothing except what I was told. After I gained ability with their language, I pieced together the story of my rescue and recovery. The natives said I was found by children playing near the sea. They were horrified to find a smashed, waterlogged corpse abandoned by the receding tide.

Adding to the children's horror at my grievous wounds, they saw terrible specters hovering nearby. By their description, they had seen the Immortals: those evil apparitions that had haunted my dreams since Cyprus. Capricious: I never when they would visit or for what reason. For years I had imagined they pursued me along bustling docks or city streets, or my eyes may trick me into seeing them aboard passing ships or even hovering at the horizon. Either the creatures had deposited me on this island and attracted the children to prove I was finally dead, or they had appeared to merely claim my corpse.

After I was found by the children, three men returned later that day to drag me from the beach and burn my pale corpse. They were shocked to find breath in that battered body. The condition of my flesh was appalling. They did not want to touch me, convinced I was a voyager from the land of the undead.

Two of them built a fire and had courage to drag me near the heat, while the other willingly ran to call for their medicine man—to protect them, not to heal me. They kept a vigil through the night. By morning, color had returned to my flesh, my breathing no longer grated on broken ribs, and my wounds seemed much less severe than they first thought:

They no longer saw bones jutting from my thigh or from my twisted arms. The eyeball that had lain on my battered face had somehow retreated into its socket.

Hoping to take credit, the medicine man proudly marched the troop back to the village, dragging my bier.

Full recovery took weeks. I eventually met the men who had stayed with me and brought me back to the village. They demonstrated my injuries by slashing with their hands and jabbing at their bodies. They grabbed my arms and poked and gestured at my legs while cupping a hand over their eye, indicating how my eye had been extracted from its socket. I had other grievous wounds they were convinced had been inflicted by sea creatures or by sword. Speculation abounded in the village about how I had arrived on their island and who I was. A faction arose that did not want to keep me in the village for fear I was one of the walking wraiths that rises from the sea at night, roaming in darkness to devour their infants.

A woman came forward who lived near the village. She was a healer whose name simply translated as Auntie. She waved off their tales and had little to do with the medicine man or his embellished stories of my rescue and recovery. She carefully laid me out, cautious that my limbs were well-aligned; then she covered my remaining wounds with herbs and dressings. Though my healing bones would have been an effective tether, the villagers insisted I be restrained. An amazing feat of healing could have been credited to her, but being confident in her standing in the community and in her abilities, I do not believe she ever acknowledged she had any role in my recovery. Rare are those who do not feel a need to take advantage of a situation when it seems obvious it would improve their status in a community.

I was awakening from a restless dream the first time I saw her. I feared I had been cast into the Greek underworld with Medusa herself as my keeper. As she ministered to me on my cot, ropes of matted black and gray hair swirled and flowed over her shoulders and down the back of a nacre-trimmed tunic. Intricate beaded letters and characters adorned the garment.

"Pshht, pshht," she tutted.

In the trim hut, hung with sage-sweet herbs and beeswax, her gentle words and quiet hands comforted me.

I learned that Auntie lived outside the village because she was foreigner. Like me, she had been marooned on the island years ago. She spoke Greek, and I was astonished to hear a few words of Aramaic sprinkled in. She would not tell me where she was from, only that she had been a slave at sea with her master's houschold on holiday aboard a lavish ship, streaming banners, until a harrowing shipwreck drowned the crew, along with her master and his family—she added with a faraway smile. We discussed our circumstances, but she shared little more about her past.

She marveled at my healing, studying my wounds like a curious physician, while noting my straightening limbs and fading scars. Auntie was interested but remained distant, possessing a certain fear of me. It would take a while before I could decipher its meaning.

While caring for me and tending my wounds, she had obviously discerned I was a Jew, circumcised on the eighth day. It was my heritage that disturbed her. She would one day let slip that her master had been a Pharisee, and I discerned she might have been more than a servant, but also his concubine.

Despite the distance she maintained, she soon ignored the tethers demanded by the villagers, allowing them to hang loose so I could move freely about the tiny room that had been built against her stone and mud hovel.

There were mysteries about her that I never uncovered. She was a woman with the wisdom to believe frightened children. With her understanding of the Jews, she often circled back to ask about the Golem, as she called them, the Immortals that had hovered over me when the children found me. With interest, she had interrogated the children as she had interrogated me: Who were these creatures? Where had they come from? When might they return for me? I tried to explain the cult of Elymas on Cyprus, but I discerned that she was fervent to find them for reasons entirely her own. She may have felt it destiny, or that they possessed a knowledge she needed to acquire. I never discovered the reasons for her curiosity.

Her wonder concerning these creatures could have never exceeded mine. Who sent them, and for what purpose? I had often thought of that scrabbling, grasping fear that had played about my ankles as I walked from the tomb, and I often pondered whether I had brought back some horror that had stood guard at the gates of death.

When or where they would appear again, I never knew.

After I revived, I was shunned by the people of the village. They could not dispel their fear that I was a demigod or demon. A mythology was developing about the Immortals and me, though it was likely that Auntie and I were the only ones who honestly believed the children's description or understood the gravity. The villagers were hungry for mystery and gradually expanded the legend to cast the creatures and me in a great struggle where giants from the spirit world were trying to kidnap or destroy their rival.

Realizing the villagers' increasing fears as the legend grew, and with Auntie's help, I moved into the hills and built a dwelling. Auntie always suspected there was something more about me, and she would occasionally make a pilgrimage to visit. This wise and kind woman became a confidant, and because I was stranded, I had nothing to lose by telling her the truth about who I was. I am not sure it made a difference, or that she believed me. Like most, she was more enthralled by mystery than veracity. I cannot blame her. Everything about my arrival and healing would have been bizarre, yet she had used her courage and compassion to care for me as I healed.

These were hermit years. Auntie grew old, people avoided my distant hill, and I was soon consigned to legend. My hut was surrounded by a small garden of herbs and fruit, the way Auntie instructed, but I lived mostly from sea birds, fish. I had stored up more than a lifetime of recollections. Alone, I was able to visit these thoughts and ponder like the wizened old man I should have been.

Marooned and captive to my tortured memories was my just penance. I was in a place that I deserved, learning to accept solitude and contemplation. For a brief time, I was able to make a tenuous peace with my life and with Yahweh. Long hours of solitary toil were invested in my small plot of land, and I hunted and fished in quiet contemplation. Healing and repair were administered to more than my broken body—but also to my broken soul.

On a ledge overlooking the green sea, with the pattern of terns stitching the reddening sky, and the graceful dance of swans across the horizon interrupted by the crescendo of a pelican's plunge, I sat contemplating my weariness with this one-sided dialogue: I talked, Yahweh listened.

I edged near him haltingly like the knobby geckos along the ledge. What if I were simply to quit talking? What if I were to stop my banter, waiting for a reply that never came? I would stop asking for assurances of restoration, or answers to my thousands of questions, or forgiveness of my myriad transgressions and dark thoughts. I would stop. Stop the eternal, one-sided conversation. And stop trying to imagine a vague, private message in response, or looking for signs on the horizon, laying a fleece, or listening for a voice in my head. What if I were finally to quit seeking a response?

Below the cliff's edge, the ocean lay silent: an ocean that abounded not only in beauty, but wealth and sustenance—and terror. But it was a place from where I had been rescued and restored. It was from the ocean I had been brought to this place where I had been cared for and fed. I had asked nothing of the ocean and done nothing to alter its course.

Yes! What if I were to stop asking—and start receiving?

What if I were to stop pleading and start watching, stop asking for forgiveness and start accepting it? What if I were finally to quit talking and start listening?

In that moment, the conversation was no longer one-sided. Too often, I had been distracted from the Creator by creation. Now here I was, no one between us, no intermediary; it was the Creator and his creation before me. It spoke to me more than all the scrolls that had been kept in the Temple. For much of my life on the seas, I had lived among the pagans and animists who worshiped creation instead of the Creator. I had always examined these beliefs with wonder: Why would you want to praise the work instead of the workman, the pottery instead of the potter, the image instead of the artist, or the creation instead of the Creator? Everywhere I traveled, nearly all of those who were not of Abraham or Yeshu had fallen into this fundamental foolishness. My error was more subtle; I had ignored the Creator's voice; I had been distracted from his voice by creation.

"I want you to be my God," I said aloud. It is the sole essential prayer from the heart of a man.

Because the inward gaze is fraught with hazards, I had tried to avoid it. We had been taught that scripture examines us; we do not need to examine ourselves. We walk upon a narrow fence between the intense inward gaze on one side and dangerous ignorance of our self and our motives on the other. We fail when distracted from Yahweh by self. Yet, when we ignore ourselves, we fall into another snare. We may be guilty of both excessive inward and outward gaze, often at the same time. I had allowed myself to be vanquished in the endless battle for the mind. The frontline battle in every soul is the battle for the mind, and I had pledged that while on this lonely island, I would reclaim victory. At least for a time, I may not reach the heights, but I would claim a foothold.

Now a choice lay before me, a choice that had been forced by my flight from Miriam and from my life, a choice between the debauchery of my desperate life with Markos or a restored life of simple grace. When all else fails, we finally make a choice, but we never see that a choice always awaits between happiness or sadness, torment or bliss, slavery or freedom. The choice is made in the mind: the realm of our real existence and the bridge to our soul.

In my musings, I knew it had not been earthquakes and devastation alone that kept me from returning to Cyprus; it was this sewer of guilt and shame. My life had become meaningless not because of my circumstances but because I had created a life I thought was outside the reach of guilt's brutal hand. This is the pinnacle of meaninglessness: To be outside the reach of the soul and to have withdrawn ourselves from the Great Force of the Universe that desires to know us and love us.

This man I had become refused to surrender and was now being held down, his face in the dust, forced to capitulate. And here, on this lost island, I surrendered. I was here alone, detached and marooned, a citizen of no earthly realm. Alone in the world, I would accept my citizenship in the eternal Kingdom and no longer claim any other citizenship on this side of the veil.

Life would no longer possess meaning because of anything I ascribed to it, but simply because the Creator who made the swan and the gecko had made me and the world in which I lived. I had reached a pinnacle.

If only we could sustain our lives on a pinnacle and not in the valley where we commonly dwell.

After years of repair, first to my body then to my soul, I had finished and was determined to leave. They could not see me, but from my high perch on the hills and cliffs I could watch the daily comings and goings of villagers and fishermen. One fisherman whom I had observed for weeks was certainly a trader. He regularly put to sea with large catches of fish and bundled cargo, returning in several days.

In my years on this island, I had built a tiny skiff of skins and boughs that I paddled, tending a few nets or exploring the shoreline. By this time, most of the islanders had forgotten about me or what I looked like, convinced I was merely a myth. When I knew I could rendezvous with the trader I had been watching, I set out with my few possessions. I navigated my wobbly boat near their dock built of sticks. They would not know me and I doubt they believed the story I made up: that I had been adrift from another island and needed to find a way back. They were wary, but I spoke enough of their language and knew enough about their village to put them at ease. I boarded the small craft with the trader and nestled into his mound of cargo.

That is how I came to Kalliste, where I approached the first sturdy vessel I saw: a Phoenician trade vessel.

Looking like a young man with sailing experience allowed me to sign on wherever I chose. I could have been a captain, but I would rather stand back, choose competent, wealthy captains, and enjoy my status as a first mate or common sailor.

I was like a cork on the seas again, and generations slid past like the waves. After falling off Markos's vessel, I had washed ashore on a lost island as mere flotsam, and again as flotsam I was adrift. And of course, the waves of time eroded my spiritual resolve again. Though much of what I learned in solitude would be stashed for later use, as a dog returns to its vomit, the pendulum swung, and I was soon floundering again.

In the ensuing years, I learned where every loose plank and failing seawall stood on every pier from the Iberian Sea, around the Ligurian, across the Tyrrhenean Sea, the Gulfs of Tacape and Syrtis to the

Egyptian Sea. There were two places I avoided: that one dark island, Cyprus, and that one port in the Syrian Sea, Judea. Though Miriam and all my family had vanished in the murky past, I avoided Cyprus and I never returned to Judea. Foolish man that I was, I had assured myself that the grinding earthquake, which had struck soon after I left, had wiped all traces of my former life from the surface of that rock. And Judea would only be a home for dashed hopes and decimated family.

After near drowning and recovery near Kalliste, I was convinced that I might never die. However, it may have been merely the brutality to my body after falling from the mast, I was beginning to see subtle changes occurring in this flesh. Whatever it was, I knew that, though I appeared young, I was no longer a mere youth. I relished the rare flecks of gray in my beard. This body had withstood toil on land and sea, had succumbed to temptation while sailing with Markos, and had been broken, battered, and washed ashore. But would it ever know death? I thought I may not be released from the curse of my risen body. The great pendulum would endlessly swing between debauchery and restoration, meaning and meaninglessness, mortality or immortality.

And whenever I thought of Miriam or Markos, I realized this body could also be a weapon, and I might never cease to cause pain or jealousy for anyone who came near.

IX. Sardinia

Another generation had fled while marooned near Kalliste, and more decades passed at sea. I arrived at Sardinia aboard a Greek vessel.

Sardinia had changed.

On most of my stops at Sardinia we would stay on board, or brave the few hovels scattered onshore. On one voyage, when Markos and I were still friends and business partners, we ventured inland to hide treasure we had earned or extorted at sea. Though Markos and I were cordial, we had been together for years, and I sensed something had infected our relationship and that our friendship may be steering toward the rocks.

The time I arrived with Markos to hide treasure, there was no suitable dock for a large vessel. We anchored offshore and launched a dinghy to circle the broad beach where the River of Thomas flows into the Golfo de Orifiano. I knew it would be a long layover on Sardinia: winds were flat, and Markos would be in the safe harbor of the arms and legs of a Sardinian mistress.

Zeus's Oysters was the tavern near the strand of beach where the sailors of Markos's ship usually gathered whenever in Sardinia. Tavern is a generous term when compared to those genteel establishments in Roman and Greek cities. Among scattered port cities, a tavern was little more than a dank meeting place where miserable food and drink were served, business was done, partnerships were forged, and scores were settled. Sailors and merchants reclined on straw mats or sat on crude benches pulled near planks scavenged from wormy wrecks.

Markos wanted me to find the village of the Sardinian natives with the hopes of one day dealing with them directly. The Nuragic were the rancorous, heavily tattooed tribal Sardinians who frequented the tavern to sell their wares, learn news of the world, or seek opportunity for hire.

With the help of a few eager tribesmen, we were able to secure a small boat and a native guide. With our guide, two Natives, and our crew of three from Markos's ship, we ventured deep into the heart of the island.

The Romans derided the Nuragic as mere barbarians. But in truth the Romans derided them because of the damage these tribes had done to Roman pride. These warriors had resisted and defeated the empire for generations. I was fascinated by tales of their battle strategies and brilliant techniques as they had fended off the advanced warcraft and military might of the Romans.

These were people who could be trusted to secure my treasure and guard my future. I would do more than establish trade for Markos, I would leave my gold and silver in the care of these tribesmen. I felt urgency to create a haven for my riches. Sardinia was one of the few islands that was relatively immune to the calamities of earth and weather; it was located centrally in the Mediterranean, and it would serve as a convenient way point. As trade partners, the Nuragic were esteemed for their honor, loyalty, and trustworthiness. By might and ability, they had retained their land for generations. I was wagering that they could preserve and protect my treasure. Sailors across the region assured me I would be purchasing a haven for my treasure among a community skilled and willing to protect it.

Ceri was our guide. His mother's people lived in one of the many small villages built among the countless nuraghes—those elegant round buildings and fortresses that spread like beehives across the mountains and rocky fields.

Our small crew launched upriver from the port on calm waters that wound between rolling hills of pasture. As the broad river narrowed, we portaged cascading rapids below cliffs covered with evergreens.

A narrow stream led deeper inland within view of hazy heights. On our small boat, amid the banter of a bawdy and boisterous crew, the excursion had made me once again long for the calm and simple life I once had as a sailor. Life with Markos was becoming torturous. His pining for youth and his bitter rants were intolerable. He had already become a devilish carouser and sloppy captain. I was certain the other crew men felt the same way about Markos that I did, but even off-ship, it would be mutiny to talk poorly about your captain.

As we plied the river, those we encountered along the shores were not threatened by our small crew. It was obvious we were not Romans. And Ceri loved to chatter. He would bark to people on land and prattle with them when they scrambled to the water's edge to hail us or make bargains. He would try to impress them by bragging about the boatload of foreigners he had been hired to guide.

The journey was five days of rowing and poling upstream. As the river narrowed, we dragged and winched our small boat around rapids and stone flats until we came to Ceri's village far inland.

Ceri held up his hand. We stopped rowing and drifted to a white beach on a flat corner of the stream. He pointed toward a twisting path that rose to a winding stone stairway through a crevice in the rock. As we scrambled out of the boat, we were famished after days of shoulder-wrenching poling and stumbling around slippery portages.

An aroma of meat and spice drifted down the winding stone path. Like Esau's stew, the scent might be worth all the treasure we carried. We had survived on dry, tasteless fish and a bag mixed with rancid grain, so the rich smell wafting down the alley was tantalizing. Ceri sensed our anticipation. Though excited to show off his travelers, he was also keen to deliver to his village gifts he had gleaned from all the things the world had brought to Sardinia.

We eagerly scaled the canted steps, deep in the cool dampness of the jagged fracture until we emerged at the last chiseled stone.

We halted.

Four men and two women, all with glinting blades on long spears, stood in our path dressed in animal skins and decorated with shells and bones. Two of the men had devilish-looking, double-curved knives thrust through sashes at their waist. On the seas, tattooed sailors are common, and an abundance of dockside women love to lift their skirts to tempt us with their hidden tattoo maps of carnal excursions. But the Nuragic were covered in serpentine blue and black interwoven runes and patterns. We were seasoned sailors, yet these tribesmen looked frightening. Though Ceri tried to assure us, we hesitated. My crewmen began to turn back, but I feared that fleeing might provoke attack. I grabbed the arm of one man while the smiling Ceri laid a hand on the chest of the other sailor and gently turned him around. The sailor hesitated, wiping his arm across his mouth, squinting.

One of the tribal men wore a mask made of a ram's skull painted in blood while, leering at us, the women were bare-breasted and equally fierce.

Then, like the moth that spreads its wings to reveal fierce raptor's eyes etched upon its wings, or the harmless toad that bloats itself into a ferocious-looking, spiked monster when attacked, the warriors transformed from spiny caterpillars into butterflies when they saw their friend and cousin Ceri. The ram's mask came off, they laid aside their spears, and their faces shone child-like joy.

Because we were with Ceri, we were quickly received with the same warmth. In moments, we sat encircling a stone firepit, while they thrust heaping wooden bowls laden with the stew that had been the source of the delicious aroma: lamb and cabbage blended with spices I had never tasted. We bolted the food and held out our bowls for more. Ceri's gifts to his people were met with shouts of approval. When we could pause between gulps of our food, Ceri translated what they said and explained more of what we were seeing in his village.

The man with the ram's mask was their chief. As my relationship with this tribe was sustained through the years, Chief Maro would become a friend and teacher. He and his wife, Matia—one of the fierce women of the bare breasts—would remain enthusiastic tutors of Nuragic values and language.

With Ceri's help, I was able to make clear what I needed, why we had arrived here, and how much I was willing to pay for their service. I would need to entrust them with my wealth for a lifetime and beyond. They were shrewd partners who asked few questions but were eager to bargain.

Maro took one of my gold pieces, turned it over, scratched at it, and bit it. I thought he was skeptical of its value. Ceri told me the man knew the value of my trove, but he was more interested in the coin's alloy, composition, and density. These artisan natives were experts in metal work.

At that first visit, I left my treasure in a hidden cave. I returned often, memorizing the river and the passages leading to the village, and developing a deep relationship with the Nuragic.

After having been marooned and then spending a long time at sea, I returned to Sardinia to reclaim a share of the wealth I had left there long ago. I did not know how I would approach the village again. Ceri and Chief Maro would be gone, and it would be unlikely anyone would remember me after all this time. I was prepared to discover my treasure squandered, and I did not know how I would find a guide to offer safe passage inland to the village. I was afraid to trust anyone. The docks of Oristano had changed.

But once again, I was soon to be less enamored of change than constancy. There it stood: that decrepit old tavern, Zeus's Oysters. It had been decayed and ready to crumble long ago when last I entered it. It had the same name scrawled on the same sign, though it had been painted over many times. However, the illustration of the god's oysters had grown larger with time. The place also had the same piss and vinegar smell to it: The men pissed on the wall outside the back door and most of the wine tasted like vinegar. I stepped through the door into the dark room. The tavern-keeper's wife looked the same—until my vision adjusted and I realized it would have to be her daughter—or granddaughter.

I said nothing as I entered the dank tavern. The patrons looked more treacherous than they had in former days. Reclining on mats or scattered at the same scarred tables, they were the typical rabble of the sea that had streamed off every stinking vessel from every port in the world for centuries: smudged tattoos, crude jewelry, and matted hair plaited with shells and bones. Some huddled over games of chance played with bones and coins while others conspired, whispering over maps scratched into the dust, looking around cautiously at the other pirates and thieves. One man, his nose scarred and broken, leaned against the wall, his cheeks puffing as he snored; he was apparently more fearsome than he appeared: No one disturbed the purse he clutched in his hand or the knife he held in the other. Two or three sat on the bare floor, hugging their knees, staring through lenses of terror and loneliness.

One man was different from the regulars. He sat quietly alone near one of two slatted windows, unconcerned by the threatening mob surrounding him. He calmly polished a bright copper figure, his muscled arms swirling with Nuragic tattoos.

I grabbed a cup of the stinking wine from the surly woman and strode over to a crude bench nearby where I leaned my back against the wall. I casually engaged the man, using a Nuragic phrase I recalled that described their metal figurines, adding their word for beautiful.

He said nothing. I thought he had not heard me, or he was ignoring me. He would know that one could not be too cautious in a place like this. I cleared my throat and began to repeat the phrase. His head of curly black hair dipped, his shoulders shook, he threw his head back, and he laughed aloud. The other patrons turned toward him, wiping their mouths and frowning. He slapped the table and tried to catch his breath. I waited, clueless.

"No," he said in perfect Latin, "my hard pestle is not cracked." He could scarcely catch his breath, his sparkling eyes and hearty laughter wholly Nuragic.

Embarrassed, I pressed the heel of my hand to my forehead and looked at the floor, stealing a glance at smirking drinkers, hungry for any bit of merriment. The stoic barmaid raised a brow and showed her scarce teeth.

Smiling, he held up the figure, pointed, and slowly corrected my garbled words. What he said sounded remotely like what I had tried to say.

I shook my head and scratched my brow, humiliated.

"It seems you are not a stranger, here. How did you learn my language, and more importantly, who taught you so poorly?" He grinned.

"Ceri taught me," I said quietly.

His smile floated away like a gull in a gale. He set down the figurine, carefully folded his polishing cloth, and spread his hands on the table. Staring at me, he took a deep breath and said evenly, "Lazar a Bethania."

I looked around the tavern nervously, though my name would mean nothing to these denizens. Scratching sopping beards, they returned to their sour wine and ale.

I looked at him and nodded quickly.

"I am Maroceri, as was my father and his father before him. We have been pledged to protect and secure the legend of Lazar's treasure until he returns. You have returned!"

He handed me the figurine. "This is yours. Made from the stores of treasure you left in our care."

I started to object. Had I merely been a fool to believe all my treasure would have been kept safe by a pack of savages while it sat in the cave where Chief Maro and I had placed it long ago? But the chief and his wife had given me their sacred word, and over all the years I had known them, I had trusted them implicitly to care for my wealth. But had their descendants smelted down all my precious metal to make their silly icons?

He held up his hand to stop my protest. "Not a single coin, not a grain of your treasure has been lost. It is our people's sacred trust."

I was doubtful, but the sincerity of his face assured me.

He looked nervously around the bar. "We leave—now!" he said.

I touched his shoulder as we stepped onto the dusty street. "One moment, Maroceri; how did you know I would be here?" It was too much to expect that this encounter at the tavern was by chance. They would not keep a vigil at Zeus's Oysters for generations, and I never believed their claim to possess magic and the ability to reckon the future. It was primitive conjuring like that of every other ancient creed, cult, and religion.

"We knew you might be arriving soon."

"How? I sent no envoy. I barely knew when I would arrive here until this very day when I stepped off the boat."

"Your pursuers were here, Lazar. We knew you were coming because your enemies were already here!"

"Who?" Dreading the answer, sweat breaking on my brow.

"They are a part of the story shared about you: The robed ones with great swords. The Nuragic people fear no one, but none of us would ever approach creatures like these. They are terrible. One of our shamans was murdered. It is rumored that they were trying to force him to confess your arrival."

How would they have known this? Their conjuring was better than I had credited them with.

My guilt was rising. I thought I had brought my wealth to these splendid people, but now I had also brought my terror.

Maroceri led the voyage upriver to the village. Throughout our passage, I kept a wary watch on every cliff for the Immortals. I could hope that when they had not found me, they had left again. But their appearing never was predictable or reasoned.

The village had changed little, and I was again greeted by a masked chieftain and his bare-chested warriors. I ate the same goat stew and drank the same musty brew that had been my reception at previous visits. The only changes I noticed were those men and women who had appropriated traces of Roman dress and ornamentation. I expected Maroceri to escort me to the caves, but tradition dictated that I be accompanied by their chieftain.

Over rocky terrain and scruffy forests, we scrambled until arriving at the cave. Out of respect, he remained at the entrance, though I still suspected he had been here numerous times to appropriate my metal for his craftsmen to rework.

Lighting a torch, I stepped from the arid mountainside deep into cool silence. In a crevice were the same leather packs. Moldy, with stiffened flaps and rotten cords, they blended seamlessly with the rock walls. Lifting the flaps on each bag, I found that all my treasure had been neatly stacked and meticulously cared for—but not in the way I had left it.

I discovered they had removed, then smelted the coins and ingots into countless figurines. Their skill had likely tripled the value of my savings. Nuragic figurines were precious on markets everywhere. Transforming them to figurines would also provide a convenient means of transporting silver and the bits of gold I possessed. I laughed in amazement to see green tarnished warriors, angry gods, and voluptuous mermaids. I unfolded one bag containing an entire set consisting of a ship long as a span with sails hammered from silver and a score of sailors. My modest cache had been turned into a vast treasure. I had become enormously rich. Their skill had paid dividends on my investment.

Using his skill, my Judean father had translated the wealth of creation into another wealth made by his hands. Similarly, the tribal craftsmen had transformed my wealth into greater wealth. I had placed my treasure into the hands of trusting craftsmen for safekeeping, and they had made something of far greater value.

But these were all lessons lost on me. While I should have learned by now to have placed my life into the care of Yahweh, allowing him to expand my fortunes, sadly, once again I was on the verge of allowing the pendulum of my life to swing far from the quiet contemplation of my marooned existence, back toward a life untethered.

X. Egypt

With wealth in my sea bags, I left Sardinia again as flotsam, careless as thistledown. After contemplative years marooned, I ought to have been enlightened to leave nearly all my wealth behind on Sardinia to curb the risk of temptation. Though I should not have been smitten by wealth, a sailor's greed had been reignited, and I was easily distracted by the sight of all those trinkets and figurines. I did not devote the following years to total debauchery, because this body was not easily given to abhorrent appetites, but my life became a blur of dissipation: I wasted my time. I roamed from port to port, settling for years in a village or dry farmstead, then returning to sea.

At least I was wise enough to avoid marriage again. I was tempted to yield; longed to give into the opiate of flesh, of passions and lusts, the yearning for the soft touch, to melt into the warm embrace of human skin. But I could not trust myself to avoid what I had done to Miriam.

Centuries swayed and listed, receding over the horizon like great, ominous vessels. Yet guilt for what I had done to Miriam and for the sins of my subsequent lifetimes was not diminished. What I had done to that girl was pitiful because it was an insult to all I should have learned from my sweet sisters and from dear Yeshu. I had come to learn that while most memories soon faded like foam on the waves, memories like those I had of Miriam remained as enduring as this remade body. So many memories: Most are accumulated and stored in the dusty volumes of mind and soul until we are handed a key beyond the veil and their meanings are explained to us by angels.

The Way was spreading from village to village, across the islands, bays, and harbors. When not distorted by pride or contrivance, the saving words of Yeshu and his disciples were spreading like a flute on the breeze. Where Believers gathered, I would often slide into a seat or recline at their table. While my prodigal heart lived abroad in the world, my soul often returned, hungering for the Bread of Life. But whenever I found myself in the presence of Believers, I was tortured again with yearning for Mary, Martha, and Miriam. Invariably, the pain and guilt would tear at my guts and obliterate the simple message I was hearing from quiet people of The Way. Though I was stubborn, the still small voice I had left on that lost island near Kalliste returned often, whispering to me.

I was repulsed by the legalities and outrageous opulence working its way into the Church. Everywhere the gentle, generous saints of The Way were being transformed into greedy, grinning Pharisees. Whenever these scoundrels sensed that I had a coin, they would slide up beside me like stinking jackals pawing for my gold.

It is as though I had been asleep on that distant island near Kalliste and had awoken to find the Faith already dead. I awoke to find a corpse where I assumed there would be a living Church. Not life, merely zeal: a religious fervor concerned with interjecting itself into the fleeting power and governance of this world, rather than striving for the eternal Kingdom. Corrupted by the vanity of goodness, they were more concerned with parading their good deeds as salve for their conceit rather than a balm for those desperate and impoverished whom they enslaved with gifts of food and trinkets.

Remarkably, I found that these craven churches had a wealth of written scripture at their disposal. Much of the writings and letters of the Disciples had been meticulously copied and preserved. It did not matter that they possessed truth. As far as these churches were concerned, these words were not worth the parchment they were written on. They were utterly unconscious of the heft and power of the writings they wielded. Instead of navigating according to discerning men and women who followed the authoritative charts left for them by the Disciples, they looked to the rich, powerful, and deviant to set course for this foundering Church.

The body of Believers was deteriorating to where they looked to the world, their society, for advice on how to live instead of to their scriptures. Whether in matters of their heretical materialism or their deviant sexuality, they looked at the cities, kingdoms, and teachers that surrounded them for compelling evidence to defend and support their lusts. At a time when there was a deepening chasm between the Church and the world of man, instead of throwing off its fetters, they were looking for ways to cast moorings to the world.

I had learned from the Disciple Paul that no matter how desperately we wish something to be true and inspired, or how thoroughly justified it seems to be, if it is not derived from a deep conviction arising out of study of scriptures it is to be rejected. As insignificant and unlearned as I was, I knew that scripture must inspire our hope and design for reformation of the world. We can never bring the world to bear on scripture; we must bring scripture to bear on the world.

My arguments were lost on these depraved sheep. But their depravity inspired in me a quest to see if there were still a place where I could simply and quietly seek the remnants of my beautiful friend Yeshu and his Disciples.

I was hearing of communities of Believers in Egypt who were given wholly to prayer, study, and separation from the world. I needed separation, peace, and solitude to see his face and hear his voice again, to seek that simple kernel of Truth.

Though I possessed this strange lease on immortality, I determined again to find a way to live my life with a clear course in mind. During the long years near Kalliste, I had found a comfort in my hermit life; the ebb and flow of seasons were like the waves under my bow. But though I had treasured the solitude, I had determined that I did not want to continue to be alone. I would need to find a place where I could live with anonymity, where I could avoid harming innocents like Miriam, and where I would not see others destroyed with jealousy for my immortality like Markos.

Through my struggle with the confusion and disdain I had for the Church, I was convinced I could find solace in a community of faith, growing together in the knowledge and life that Yeshu had given. Somewhere such a community existed.

No one could have prepared me for how wrong I would be.

Pachomius and Anthony were among the men associated with these enclaves in Egypt. I never met them, but I heard of them through elders. It could not be their fault, but the reverence granted these two men seemed immediately out of proportion. The simple disciples would not have allowed themselves this veneration. Nonetheless, I felt drawn to these isolated communities. I remained interested and vigilant, hoping I could find the serene refuge I thirsted for.

Alexandria was a sprawling port at the center of the world. It was also home to that ostentatious cult of worship foolishly thought by some to be associated with the Lamb. Pretentious temples with gilded walls proclaimed ritual to the risen Christ, yet they exceeded the most decadent edifices of Pagan debauchery and Judaic covetousness. In Alexandria, church prostitutes were as common as temple prostitutes—and more egregious. Naked, stinking mockeries of flesh preened and clawed outside basilica palaces of debauched spirituality.

Like every other city from Athens to Jerusalem, I hated Alexandria. I had tried to avoid disembarking every time I had docked there. The smell, the chest to back bustle, beggars picking at your hem while your sandals are crusted in the excrement—both animal and human—that squeezed between your toes. All cities were utterly despicable to me.

There were sailors who loved the bantering at the market, the prized bargain, the flood of wine and degeneracy, pinching a plump and toothless girl's ass, or cupping a breast and then taking her into the alley for a spin. It was all horror to me. It always had been, and will always be.

Like endless days in hell, I waited in Alexandria to discern where in the deserts the hermit communities were located and how to secure passage aboard a reliable caravan. If my years on the seas were of any value, they taught me how to know a competent captain, whether aboard ships or in a caravan. I had learned of a few caravans that would be traveling near the vicinity of the communities of Believers that I was seeking, but none were led by men I could trust.

Rumor had it that a captain named Tulio had the qualities I was looking for, and he would also be delivering supplies to several of the dispersed priories. Another week or more dragged by in the dung heap of Alexandria until he returned, and then he had to secure cargo and passengers for the monasteries, replace pack animals, and hire men.

Tulio seemed pleased to add me to his passenger list along with several others destined for the settlements. According to Tulio, there were several communities within a day's travel of each other, and I could decide enroute at which I wanted to stay. He was gregarious. Though I did not need to know all his plans, it seemed he wanted to tell me anyway. My only concern was to be blessedly far beyond the stench and noise of Alexandria.

He assured me, if all went well, it would be a journey of weeks. We would spend days aboard a flat barge up the placid Nile; then we would secure carts to carry us across the rocky desert that shimmered in a blur of constant heat. Camels would be available where we disembarked from the barge, but Tulio had never gained experience with those stupid and ornery animals, preferring the smaller, and to him, more reliable donkeys. Despite the trouble to him, it was worthwhile to secure the animals in Alexandria where the selection and price were in his favor, then bring them with us upriver before departing across the desert.

Tulio and his crew were accompanied on this trip by three destitute and disheveled men traveling as pilgrims, and two other men who were novices destined to enter the ranks of the hermits. I did not know to which of these two camps I belonged: the pilgrims or the novices. Two young girls, sisters, also accompanied us, Iris and Senti. They wore black and purple robes with the sheen and heft of lavish garments. Like those of royalty, their robes were trimmed from collar to hem with intricate interlacing, gold and yellow brocade, and tinkling silver beads. Despite the grueling journey, not a spot of dust, nor a nettle or burr marred their finery. Veiled and covered, we could not see their faces, and the sisters did not speak. But they seemed to have a special relationship with Tulio. He kept them near and protected their privacy as if they were his own. He spoke of them as one—Irisandsenti.

Thinking of my own sisters, I became very curious about these women, but Tulio deflected every question about them, intent upon allowing no one to speak with them or try to get into their graces. I did not ask more. One of the crew offered that a few communities of women separated themselves like the monastic hermit communities. I assumed this was to be their destination, and Tulio had been paid, possibly by a wealthy father, to keep them safe.

Tulio was Roman, but I assumed the young women were Egyptian. His short military hair, clean-shaven features, and meticulous appearance underscored his prior life as a centurion. He had been a transport officer moving supplies for the Empire. Seeing an opportunity for wealth amid the declining Roman armies, he had built a transport venture, employing his leadership experience and ability to manage caravans.

I had a vague idea where I wanted to go and what I was looking for, but I had not made up my mind. Along the way, I would learn what I could from Tulio and the crew about each colony and then decide where I would seek fellowship.

Disembarking at docks upriver, we traveled two days inland. We climbed the wall of a steep valley and over a rise. Below us on the plain, laid out with precision, was huddled a small grouping of stone and wattle buildings. It was not a farm or fortress, but to us passengers on the caravan, it seemed like a mirage. Gleaming in late sun, set upon a floor of red sands and scattered among scrubby cedars, the structures were adorned with short spires above white walls set with round windows. As if part of the architecture, reddish rock formations jutted amid the walls.

Enraptured by the beauty of the layout, we were told this would be the smallest of the three enclaves we were to visit. It looked inviting to me, assuming that fellow wanderers like me were dwelling there, but Tulio gave us strict instructions to stay. The sisters had never left his sight the entire journey, and he hesitated to leave them with us. He contemplated taking them with him, but he indicated to his men that he did not want the women seen by anyone from this monastery. In the end, he put them under the protection of two of his well-armed crew members. With strict instructions, he handed another short sword to a third, larger assistant. Taking one of the carts to deliver and receive cargo, he left with one of his men and one pilgrim who was seeking to join the hermits at this settlement.

Nearby, across an area of scrabbly, tended fields, was another settlement connected with the community: not much more than an encampment of sticks and leaning tents. It had none of the humble gracefulness of the larger structures. We were told this was where pilgrims stayed along with those novices who wanted to gain admission to the order. The pilgrim split away from Tulio as they neared the walls of the monastery and followed the path across the field that led to the smaller settlement. For a moment, the sisters opened their veils, but I could not see their faces; they seemed to nod to each other hopefully, then looked back toward the white walls and back at the lesser settlement. They quickly covered themselves and huddled together in the shade of the carts.

By then I had decided I would stay at the second and largest of the three monasteries, about another day's journey. Because I remained uncertain exactly what I was seeking, it might be the most likely to aid my spiritual quest. Tulio curtly discouraged me from going on to the third settlement, but I did not know why. Considering that he was more familiar with these communities, I was satisfied. Tulio and his crew knew these scattered enclaves and made this supply journey two or three times a year, depending on supplies that became available, or if requests were made from one of the communities.

Late in the afternoon, Tulio returned from the monastery with his man and the cart, which now contained goods prepared by the hermits: a few baskets of simple crafts and jars of preserved goods and oil. He immediately checked on the women, brought them water and dried fruit, then directed his men to balance out the goods in the carts to make room for the sisters to ride. If light remained, we would press on for a couple of hours, until we reached an area where Tulio said we would camp for the night.

As the sun kissed the flat horizon, our carts trundled up to where a pile of stone rubble lay scattered with curly wigs of samwa plants scattered among cedars and acacia. Dying palms with fronds at their sides like tired arms leaned over a dank pool circled by a low rock cliff. Away from the pool, we dug near the stone wall, scooped away the sand, and waited as the bowl filled with clean water—clean, not fresh. We filled our water skins, then pushed the finicky donkeys toward the meager spring. For centuries, this wayside had been visited by travelers and caravans.

The crewmen were withdrawn and silent. Tulio seemed nervous, climbing over the rocks, and rustling in the bushes as if to flush hiding thieves. At one point, he came back to the camp, unsheathed a sword from his pack, and left again with one of his men.

I looked at the crew. They shrugged. "Ghosts and thieves," two of them said nervously at once, then smiled with embarrassment showing long, crooked teeth. The older one continued, "This is not an oasis only for the living. There are few places for the caravans to rest out here, but sometimes we are not alone." He pulled his robe closer around him and looked to his mate, who nodded solemnly.

Under gaudy desert stars, tar-scented smoke from crackling knots and sticks blended in the cool, heavy air with the brackish odor of the stale pool. As we would drift into reverie, wayward zephyrs, rustling the brush and moaning in the cedars, awoke us from anxious silence as haunting descended upon the oasis.

"Lazarus of Bethany." Deep in the night, I flashed awake from a nightmare that had been a squall of blood and screams. I was not aware I had fallen asleep. Dreary awakening spiked to horror. The small oasis was no longer silent but swirling and seething, crackling with fear. From behind me, pressed against the rock, the sisters whimpered. I followed their gaze where the ember glow from the dying fire cast flickering red light on bodies twisted, ripped, and scattered. The desert air reeked with the salty stench of evisceration, blood, and death. I scuttled back against the rock, next to the sisters, withdrawing my worthless eating knife. Though the camp lay in near darkness, suddenly from behind the mound of rock a light grew like the sunrise of dread rising over a battlefield. As the light became searingly brilliant, I knew. I knew before they appeared drifting across the clearing, their robes skimming the sand.

Other than their whimpering, the first sound I had heard from the sisters came as one of them wailed, clinging to the other shaking. The other sister pointed and whispered frantically in Greek, "Dolofónoi!" her voice rising, "Murderers, murderers!"

The Immortals had found me.

XI. Monastery

In their presence, I was emptied: our breath smothered in depths in viscid terror. The spawn of Elymas had trailed me through time and stood before me more terrible than I had remembered or could have imagined.

Over the ashes of the campfire they hovered, their luminosity spreading across the grim, decimated bodies of Tulio and his men. They had been either sliced through and scattered where they slept, or they had been cut down as they stood to defend themselves. The slashes had severed and seared, mingling the stench of burnt flesh and blood.

I knew these swords were the instruments that could finally deliver to me the gift of mortality. With the sweep of their hands, I would be rendered finite. Someone was shouting. I did not realize it was me. "Take me, then, damn you! Get it over with. I do not want to live!"

Churning and changing, their countenances were inscrutable. On Cyprus, when they had chased me onto Markos's ship, I had seen their faces. They may have been men from the East, but something profoundly ancient transformed them into undefinable, blank canvases that shifted and reconfigured as I watched.

"Lazarus of Bethany, you are spared. Until our mission has been altered, we follow to behold and discern the way of The Almighty." They spoke as one, with voices like clanging gongs and screaming leviathans. I looked away, unable to bear their gaze. "Take these women to the Abbey of the Cliffs," they said.

There was a flash of blazing prism light. I do not recall if I fainted, or I was rendered unconscious.

I awoke slowly, lying on my back amid the scent of brackish water and cedar, in a glow of fuchsia light. The tops of the rock mound were bathed golden, and the dead fronds of the palm trees rattled in a warm breeze. I was pondering the strange nightmare when I turned to see the sisters still huddled against the stone next to me. In gasping fear, I rolled over, expecting to see the torn bodies of Tulio and his men, but there were merely the cold ashes where the fire had been. One of the young pledges, wrapped in a blanket, sat transfixed by the rising sun, mechanically rubbing his arm.

Entranced, he turned slowly toward me with a confused smile. In scarcely more than a whisper, he said, "The creatures took the bodies." He swept his arm across the oasis. "The demons swept them away, just swept them away."

That was the last time I heard him speak in the days that followed.

Tightly holding hands, their motions mirroring one another, Iris and Senti stepped cautiously around the fetid pond to stand at the center of the clearing. They circled the cold firepit, searching the rocks and brush, then edged back toward me. I stood and brushed off my robe. They removed their veils to reveal identical faces: Aksum Ethiopian twins, scarcely more than children. With narrow features and wide eyes, they quietly regarded me as serenely as fawns. I understood why Tulio would treasure them. However, his motivations proved despicable.

"I am Senti, and this is my sister Iris," she said, in perfect Greek.

Without hesitation, Iris continued, "We are sisters of The Way, sent to find our brother, Julian, among the hermits. We have come to beg his return."

"Our parents were slain by thieves and our brother alone can secure our family's inheritance," said Senti, nodding.

"After the matter is settled, he may return to his desert hermitage if he must," the twin added.

I did not know what to say. I knew of the Aksum kingdom. The entire realm had adopted the Faith, but I had never met Believers from the depths of the southern continent.

Having not moved from where I saw him, the pledge sat staring into the sun, ignoring us while the sisters continued.

"We were taken by Tulio. He knew of our brother, and he knew that Julian was porter and doorkeeper at the Abbey of the Cliffs," Iris said.

"We were taken under Tulio's care, as is required for virgins to travel. We soon discovered he had tricked us." Senti spat her words in anger.

"We overheard him laughing with the crew that we would never see our brother, but we would be sold to the superior at a distant monastery."

"When we attempted to confront Tulio, he warned us if we spoke to anyone or tried to escape, he would see that our brother was expelled from the monastery or murdered."

"We had no choice," Iris said.

Senti stepped closer. "That name: Lazarus of Bethany. Why would those terrible creatures call you that? This is a name from the Gospels of the Disciples."

Iris added, "Our teachers have shown us the accounts written by the Apostle John. Lazarus was raised from the dead by Christos."

"Have you been risen, traveler? Is that your name?" Senti squinted one eye and allowed a shadow of smile.

"My name is Lazar, sister. I cannot pretend to be worthy of any attention from the man—Christos."

"But no one is worthy..." Senti began until Iris rested her hand on her sister's arm. They both nodded slowly with a narrow expression that assured me they were not satisfied with the answer. They had said enough; they would wait.

I helped, but the girls, scarcely more than wisps, were more competent than me at sorting through and discarding Tulio's gear, repacking the carts, locating the donkeys, leading them back, and hitching the harnesses.

Wrapped in a blanket, the silent pledge continued to sit motionless.

While we were busy with our preparations, we were startled by a shout. I quickly took Tulio's sword, shielding the twins. Someone peered at us from where they were hidden among cedar branches.

"Who are you? Show yourself," I demanded.

"I will not harm you. I am afraid to approach." It was the other pilgrim we had assumed had fled or been killed. Unfazed by the shouts of the other pilgrim, the silent pledge had not stirred.

"Tell us your name," I said.

"Darius, the pilgrim."

"Come down. We do not fear you, and there is no longer anything to fear here." I smiled assurance at the twins, and they smiled thinly as they packed and strapped the carts. Their heads were uncovered, revealing blue black hair coiled into ropes of intricate braids, iridescent in the early sun.

Darius approached. "I only...I only just awoke, and...."

"Nothing to fear, no need to explain," I said.

He looked quickly around the camp. "The demons, I saw the flash and fled. I am so sorry. Then I fear that I was smitten or dealt unconscious. I do not know...."

"We do not know and we need not speak of it," I interrupted.

"I know the way. I have a chart," he said, eagerly reaching into his robe and unrolling a parchment. "I had it charted before I knew I would be traveling with Tulio. A priest in Alexandria sketched it for me when I sought his help. I can show you the way to the next abbey, and beyond to the third abbey if you are traveling farther."

In our eagerness to leave the encampment, we had not bothered to give serious thought how we would get to the next abbey. I imagined we would have followed the traces of prior caravans heading west, and may have found ourselves lost in the infinite fields of sand.

"The Abbey of the Cliffs is our destination. We will go no farther. The supplies will stay there until the third abbey is able to claim them, or someone ventures on," I said.

In two days, as the sun was sinking toward the horizon, we arrived at the Abbey of the Cliffs. Like a lovely Roman mosaic, it lay painted in orange light beneath red cliffs surrounded by yellow desert. The abbey's crosshatch of walls and patchwork fields were graced by a meandering stream lined with palms, cedars, and acacia. The road wound through scrub and cedars up to the doors of the priory. The cliffs loomed large as we approached the enclave. Like the smaller abbey, a rustic settlement was within sight of the abbey walls. Unlike the ramshackle settlement near the first abbey, this village, with brushed streets and small spires, seemed as orderly and clean as the abbey.

As we approached, several small barns were huddled a stone's throw from the monastery. Fences held goats, donkeys, and sheep. A rooster crowed amid its flock and led his hens scurrying and scratching among hooves and through manure.

I smiled to myself at the familiarity, imagining I might at last find a home here. I could not have guessed how unfortunate and brief our sojourn in this sanctified enclave would become.

We approached the doors and were at a distance when a dark face peered through the small, barred window. "Sisters! Senti. Iris. You are here!" the doorkeeper shouted.

They lifted their lovely robes from their feet and rushed ahead, but stopped at their brother's command. "Oh, forgive me, forgive me, my lovely sisters, but I cannot allow you to enter. Please, stand where you are." His voice was shaking. "Oh, my dear sisters, you have arrived. And you are safe? But how I fear what news you may carry."

They hung their heads, held hands, then glanced painfully back toward me for an answer. I shrugged and began to call, "Your sisters are here to...." But as I began to speak, the gate slowly opened. Julian stood rubbing his hands helplessly as a circle of men pushed in behind him, several with long sticks as though ready to defend themselves. An older man angled through the pack and stepped forward. A gray beard framed his face and lay onto his chest, blending with the disheveled hair around his shoulders. He lowered his hood. "Julian, let these sisters come forward." He called to the twins. "Sisters, please cover your heads and do not...."

Robes lifted, they were already running, but instead of falling into his arms, they stopped to face Julian. They greeted him by merely bowing and touching foreheads with their brother as he grasped their shoulders. They began desperately speaking in their tongue, but Julian, already stricken by what he was hearing, tried to hush them. They embraced, weeping.

"Come forward, pilgrims. I am Father Matthew and I greet you as the Second to our Superior, Father Regious. You must not fear." He waved his hand to dismiss the other men with the wooden staffs. "When we saw you approach, we were concerned that you might be the thieves who attacked our neighboring abbey to the west. We feared that you held these sisters in bondage."

When we approached, Father Matthew greeted Darius the pilgrim and me warmly while the other pledge stood in silence behind us. The priest regarded Julian and his sisters sadly, then turned to us.

"We have learned much since a runner came to us last night from the Abbey of Saint Barnabas, which lies to the west," Father Matthew said. "The superior and the second were horribly murdered three nights ago. We also learned something of which we can barely speak. A terrible secret has been revealed." Now he looked sideways at the family in grief, then down while he folded his hands and sighed. Hushed so the siblings could not hear, he said to us, "Julian's sisters were not going to be allowed to stop here. They were being sold by Tulio into the care of the Superior and his Second at Saint Barnabas. It is unspeakable. I cannot bear the pain and humiliation for our order and what that would have meant for Julian and his sisters." He turned to enter the gates as though he had said all he was going to say about the matter, but then he looked at us. "Somehow, this horror must be reconciled and accounted for, though whoever the murderers were, their visit was sadly propitious." He inhaled and looked upward, not wanting to make eye contact. "The thieves must have been tipped off to the enormous sum Tulio was to be paid for these young women by the superior at Saint Barnabas Abbey. It is scandalous beyond mention."

He looked furtively at the sisters, smiled, and began to turn, then added, "But the sisters must go to the village to stay with the young novice nuns and the other women of God who are dedicated there. We will provide every resource for your needs."

"Matthew," I said, "may I ask—"

"*Father* Matthew," he corrected gently. Of course, I despised these titles. The leaders who had once been humble shepherds, deacons, and elders were now haughty priests and fathers.

I continued, "May I ask when we can meet so that I may fellowship here, and learn how we can grow together in the knowledge of Emmanuel?"

Father Matthew met my gaze and made a stern, arched smile while directing Julian with a significant glance and a tilt of the head. Then he left. I looked at Julian and his sisters, confused. He touched his sisters' hands, then waved Darius and me inside the gate toward a tiny stone hut that extended from the wall. They touched briefly one more time before he raised a finger, instructing the girls to wait in place; then he bowed. Outside the abbey gate, they stood looking at each other, incredulous and desperate. The dazed and silent pledge was leaning with his back to the wall, gazing across the desert until Darius took his elbow and led him inside with us.

Two veiled women had come from the settlement near the abbey, and nodding to Julian, led his sisters away. Resigned to the situation, they followed without protest.

Inside the abbey gate, we entered the tiny porter's hut, each wall no longer than a man. There was a short cot where Julian slept and a crude wooden bench beneath a shelf, nothing more. Under a window framed in twisting mullions lay a sheaf of papyrus. Julian's hands were shaking in grief as he slid two of the papyrus sheets toward us and asked if we could read Latin. I said I could, and Darius shrugged.

"Julian, why are you kept from your sisters? What is this?" I asked.

He held his breath a moment until he could speak, pointing to the parchments. "I am commissioned to tell you that these are the first of the rules of our order that you must memorize. These were delivered to great Pachomius by an angel of the Living God." He paused again, took a breath, and continued, "When you know these by heart and by mind, then return. I will summon two elders who will listen to your recitation. Over the weeks, when you have memorized all the rules, you will—"

"Weeks! Who...? Julian, I must...." I calmed myself and stepped back. I did not need to burden Julian with more, but I was here to learn, pray, and find fellowship, not memorize mindless drivel. Darius was scanning the page that had been handed him and nodded understanding. I stepped closer to Julian. I looked out the door into the abbey's courtyard. "Julian! When can I enter? It is for freedom that Christ has set us free! What is going on here? Your sisters! You must want to see them now?"

"Yes. Uh, no! I—cannot! I...." His voice broke and he held his hand up, unable to finish.

While we waited, a youth appeared at the door with coppery hair, freckles, and a red beard that looked like a handful of dead grass. "This is Bearic; he's the Guestmaster, and he will show you to the village," Julian stammered.

"But, Julian, I need to see Matthew—Father Matthew. I...."

He held up his hand again, looking away nervously, and walked from the hut. He stood near the gate, looking down, shaking his head and pointing toward the settlement that lay away from the abbey. There was nothing he could do, and I was not going to put him at any more risk than his sisters had already brought upon him.

Bearic was a nervous youth. Smiling, he was eager to lead us away, unaware of all we had endured or what we had discussed.

Outside the gates, the donkeys had been led away to stables and the carts stood unattended. The sisters had taken their things and the men of the abbey would retrieve the shipments in the carts. We lifted our packs out of the carts and took a path that lined the trickling stream toward the village. Desperately tired and thirsty, we shuffled under palms golden orange in the setting sun, washed by the last heat of day swirling with the sweet spice of cedar.

The gregarious Bearic led silently but looked at us frequently, as though he were about to speak; then he would smile, surrendering to the monastery's silence. It was darkening as we followed a ragged street that cleft the small huddle of stone buildings. Bearic pointed to a hut. Pushing open the door, he stepped aside.

The hut's darkened interior was larger than Julian's gatehouse and smelled of sweat and musty straw. A single window was hung with a ragged drape. Our eyes adjusted to the weak flame from an oil lamp set on a cracked jar between two broad mats. One of the large mats was already occupied by men huddled near the light. We ushered our silent pledge to the other mat, where he sat and pushed himself against the wall, staring ahead. With a reed, Bearic used the lamp flame to light another lamp that sat on a shelf near the door. The men on cots raised their eyes to look at us, their faces like Darius and the mute pledge: young, wondering, silent, and lost. They each held pages like those Julian had handed to us. Quickly, they turned back to the task of trying to learn their rote lines.

Bearic bowed and left.

"I am Lazar; this is Darius, and this is a man who is here to pledge, but we had a fateful encounter that I am afraid has left him unable to speak."

"They will like him," the older of the two whispered. "We have been instructed like Bearic not to speak unless it is urgent or if we are speaking to an elder or priest. I am called Mark, and this is Stephan." He reached under his cot and lifted a jar. "Water?"

We had forgotten our thirst and drank greedily. The silent pledge refused.

"I will not interrupt your study," I said, "but how many pages must you learn to be a believer? Yeshu said...." I stopped myself.

Mark grinned. "Only four. We are on the third, the Creed. We have learned the Psalm and will learn the dismissal next week."

"Nonsense," I whispered. Darius looked at me nervously.

I lay awake, restless on the barren mat. *What hell have I gotten myself into?* I wondered. But despite the horror I had seen, tormented by disappointment, I drifted into a death of sleep.

I jolted awake just as light grayed the shabby window. I stepped to the door to see men gathered outside other huts like ours; each hut had been given two jars of water at the door.

Darius followed me into the dim morning, nervous that he had not learned his verse because of his poor Latin. Skeptically I was reviewing the sheet when Bearic appeared as spritely and eager as the evening before. Yawning and sniffling, men from other huts were assembling into a crew. Bearic indicated that Mark and Benjamin would be going with him, but Darius, the silent pledge, and I would wait another day until we had memorized our parchments. Searching for another reason to confront Mathew, I told Bearic I wanted to say my verses now, though I had hardly looked at the parchment. Bearic had no authority to deny me. His constant smile shifted nervously as he tilted his head for me to join the others.

Just before he was ready to lead us back to the monastery, Darius called from our hut. "He's gone!"

The silent pledge had wandered off sometime in the night and vanished. We had heard nothing. We never saw him again. Bearic assured us he would report the pledge's absence immediately, but I doubted the Superior or Father Matthew would stir themselves to pursue him.

As we made our way back to the monastery that morning, I was fraught with regret, gripped by an overwhelming restlessness. I had made a grave mistake by coming here: I had been nearly murdered by the Immortals, and I had been mistaken in thinking I would find the place I was seeking: a place of communion, holiness, and the freedom to learn from others again the precepts of our faith. I had come here to seek Yeshu in the lives of others, but I had found a sham, a circus. Reverting to slavery, this enclave disdained the free gift of life. *As a dog returns to its vomit*, followers of The Way were enslaved as Pharisees. Fathers? Priests? We were lurking in shadows memorizing rote phrases instead of stepping boldly through the torn curtain into the Holy of Holies. Yeshu conquered; then we threw up our hands and surrendered to a defeated enemy. Yeshu led triumphant; we forfeited unfettered citizenship to become aliens.

I stopped in the middle of the path and allowed the others to go ahead. The tops of the palms were shining as I watched the others shuffle beside the sparkles of trickling stream toward the abbey. I sighed and turned back to the village to find the sisters.

There were separate huts for the women on the far side of the village. I found them gathering among a group of women. When I approached, I held up my hand to deflect the protests of the veiled women. I held up my pack and spoke to the two sisters, "We are finding Julian." They asked no questions, retrieved their things from their hut, and followed. The women scolded, grasping at their arms, but the determined sisters shrugged them off.

At the monastery, Julian came out to meet us while the sisters stood nearby. I confronted him. "Your parents are dead, Julian. You must return to your family, or they will be lost. You are the only one. You have obligations to God and to your sisters that supersede this carnival."

"You are wise to cut your losses and leave now, Brother Lazar. You will not find more if you stay longer," he replied. "I know this. I see what you see, and have grown sick of it, myself."

Julian was torn, but it was clear he was exasperated, and this was no longer a place he could tolerate. He had left his home in Ethiopia, and like me, come to this enclave of emptiness hoping to find much more.

The four of us left. Neither Father Matthew nor anyone came to seek us out or to plead with us to stay. We secured our things, hitched up two of the donkeys to a cart, and left for the Nile. If the Immortals wanted to kill us, I did not care. They would have already done so if they desired. But their arrivals were never predictable or reasoned.

But I could have never imagined that soon the searing terror of the Immortals would be eclipsed when earth itself was disemboweled.

XII. Alexandria

IF THERE HAD BEEN something to learn from this detour through the desert, I missed it. Shrouded in disillusionment I walked away from the monasteries. Shattered. Where was The Way? Where was dear Yeshu? It was as though faith itself had been swept from the earth.

On the middle of the third day, the terrible oasis appeared again, serene as a lion in repose. The scrabble of brush, the flaccid palms, and the dank odor appearing innocuous and unconcerned. Our heads swiveled as every rock and shrub seemed to conceal a threat. We filled our water skins near the boulder, watered the thirsty donkeys, then fled to sleep in open desert, far from that bloody hunting ground.

Outside a scrap of tent, in the glow of mounded embers, the sisters wept as they whispered quietly to Julian: first they wept for their parents, then for his dashed hopes and foundered faith. Julian and I spoke little, sharing a kinship of misery that defied and disdained speech. But while shuffling across the open desert, he told me fragments of how the monastery had been a millstone crushing the hull of his life. The chaotic, stultifying life of rules, priests, and frankincense had ground him to a moldering kernel. Long before I had arrived with his sisters, he had been considering his escape, and he had been ready to leave with Tulio if the chance had arisen.

In the stillness of the evening, I sat apart, leaning against the cart, overhearing the sisters' gentle counsel. They spoke in their native tongue, but when they spoke the comfort of grace, they spoke Greek. This was the language of their scriptures from which they had learned of Christos.

I silently asked myself the probing questions that the sisters posed to their brother.

"Are you certain of God, brother?" Senti asked.

"Yes, I am certain." Julian blinked, replying haltingly.

I was no longer as certain.

"Are you certain that one day you will be with Christos?" Iris followed intently.

"Yes, I am certain," Julian said with a mere whisper of conviction.

I did not have conviction.

"Are you certain this great struggle will not be carried with you to paradise?" Senti probed.

"Yes, I am certain." He smiled weakly.

I was no longer certain that anything existed for me beyond the veil. It seemed that door to the other side, that land where I had met my grandmother, was closing. The portal narrowed like the drawstring around a satchel of treasure.

Iris laid her hand gently on her brother's shoulder. "Christos promised that to the one who is uncertain, he will grant certainty. Promised. Is there any pain, any struggle, any burden from which he will not grant certain peace?" She squeezed his shoulder as she spoke and drew her forehead near to his. "He said that he would give up everything for you. You alone. He laid aside his universe for you, Julian, and you alone, dear brother. He laid aside his heavenly throne so that you would not perish."

I stood and shook my mat to scatter the scorpions. I could not so easily scatter the vermin that had crept into my soul. Away from the circle of light, I laid my hand on the back of a donkey. Through coarse hair I felt its rhythm of breathing. It chuffed, looking toward me in benign fellowship. Under a vast arena of blazing stars, the sliver of moon tilted like a gaff hook.

I whispered to the skies, "My beautiful friend, where have you gone? Where are you now?"

The celestial dome seemed to throb in stillness as Iris spoke aloud in final affirmation to Julian. "Our faith is at the very power center of the universe, Julian. There is no longer room for apology or fear."

I muttered to myself doubts they should not hear.

The desert robs the senses. After days of hissing sand under the cart's wheels, tasting dust, blinded by sun, an odor of river muck arrived on a lazy zephyr. Another day of trudging and the ribbon of haze hanging over the muddy Nile stretched across the horizon.

After arriving at the bustling river port, it took an afternoon to find a merchant who would exchange the cart, donkeys, and gear for the silver to help the return of the siblings to their Ethiopian homeland.

At the port on the Nile, amid stinking river docks, the sisters were already attracting too much attention. I led them to the far end of the docks where officials and wealthy merchants docked vessels carved with scrolled gunwales and painted statues. Enlisted agents and assassins guarded the wealthy and their ships. I had stowed several of my Sardinian icons, and there would be merchants who knew their value.

Then I would hire expert mercenary guards.

Julian was adept at chatting us past the few shields that milled about. After conferring with merchants and caravan leaders, I was able to hire two Ethiopian mercenaries who, I was assured, were the most trained and competent. I introduced the looming ebony-carved soldiers to Julian and the sisters. These giants bowed low, their arms and faces scattered with swirling scars pierced and cut into intricate patterns like the twisting brocade on the twin's robes. The countenance of the men was as fearsome and foreboding as their demeanor was gentle. They generously gathered the family's belongings taking everything into their care. I would have hired them to protect me from the Immortals if I were not more concerned with protecting my Ethiopian brother and sisters. And I wanted to travel alone. I was confident that whatever the Immortals wanted, I would have to confront them at a time of their choosing, and on their terms.

Standing in the shadow of their protectors, we parted. Julian and I wept. I felt broken for their loss, for his difficult path, and for the terror and doubts we had shared on this sad mission. I embraced the sisters, their bodies like sparrows wrapped in a headscarf. They urged me to return south with them to the mysterious world of the Aksum Ethiopian kingdom to learn of their faith and their community. But I was weary of the desert. And I was weary of the faith.

In the heat of summer, death itself seemed to shimmer in every mirage. I wanted out of Africa, away from desert shores and the seedy harbors of the Mediterranean. If I were ever to die, I did not want it to be in this God-forsaken land where days scrape by like the belly of a locust. If I could not leave this body, then I would leave this hull of my life and flee—far west, far east, or far north. Far from all the life I had ever known.

But my plans are never his plans.

Had my faith been merely a mirage on a scorching desert? My immortal body and the storehouse of memories in my troubled mind should attest that I had witnessed everything that my weary soul doubted. My body concealed my length of days, and it should have been surety of a contract that had been written in another dry land so many years ago. But could Yeshu have been merely a magician who had skillfully manipulated my flesh? None of it made sense. How could the horror of these debauched priests and Christian temples sprout from the life of that simple man whom I had known and loved in a distant past? I could no longer accept the evidence of my own life or memories.

I would have to wait two days until the next barge would head downriver, but an overland caravan to Alexandria had assembled and I jumped aboard as dust rolled from camel hooves and cartwheels.

The large caravan cut across land and would return us to Alexandria in less time than waiting for a barge and taking the muddy river. Half a day before the caravan was to arrive in Alexandria, swirling from the city, odors of sewage and decay met us in the wilderness. It was late as we rumbled to the edge of the city, the oppressive heat unabated under a sky glowing smoky red. On a rocky expanse, within crumbling walls that lay east of the city, was scattered waste and ruin from centuries of civilization past. We set up our camp amid other restless caravans encrusted in dust. Three of us clambered onto a pile of stone and debris that had been gathered for later use by a band of enterprising masons. We looked down across a vast city hanging in a putrid haze above the still ocean.

The ships at harbor and the normally bustling city seemed menacingly quiet under a blanket of smoke and fog that flushed pink to scarlet. The atmosphere was apprehensive, but the city seemed oblivious to the terror that was crouching under the earth, within the seas, and from God's own hand: Oblivious man below, oblivious God above. The scene was an ominous red moment of dread that remains in my nightmares.

I sat on that pile of rubble until dark, while below, children chased, their laughter echoing through streets and up the hill. Nothing in their world could cause them to comprehend the power that surged beneath their tiny feet. In an instant, the firm foundation we stand upon can turn upon us and we may become vaporized. Into nothingness. Yet at that moment, everything about the world and the universe was beyond their tiny grasp, and beyond their carefree distractions.

Slowly, veiled stars emerged to pierce the haze while lights from homes, taverns, and campfires flickered on and mirrored the heavens.

Is this what it is like to be an unbeliever? I pondered. Is this what I had become? Like the children that night, we dance and play and live our lives, utterly blind to infinite power that stirs beneath our feet. We stand too near to comprehend.

Before dawn, I thought one of the great Roman carts had trundled past. The ground rumbled, but scarcely shook enough to awaken the other snoring herdsmen and traders sleeping in tents and near embers on open ground.

Suddenly, all along the ridge, camels and donkeys brayed, dogs barked, and sheep stampeded. Tents emptied as men chased terrified animals. Before a single harness was grasped or lamb gathered, an enormous quake took several of us off our feet and sent the animals in a flurry of dust and fur.

There were plenty of hands to control nearly all the animals. The big oxen and camels were being led back to their stakes and the sheep to their stick fences when I heard the calls and saw men standing on the hillside pointing across the city, the tops of dust clouds billowing pink in early sun. We had all experienced quakes, and this one did not appear to be terribly strong or to have significantly damaged the city, though the early morning streets were already like a nest of angry ants with people pouring from their homes.

What the men were pointing at was not a city shrouded in dust or streets crawling with awakened citizens. As I looked up, my mouth went dry. I had seen this sign—I knew what it meant—yet never like this. Never.

The ocean itself was pulling away like a blanket. Where the sea had snuggled against harbors and inlets, great ships swayed and lowered onto the floor of the bay until masts jutted above the piers. The sea itself had turned its back on this putrid city and was retreating, leaving it without harbor or refuge. At the end of a pier, large fishes and dolphins flapped hopelessly on open rock and sand. As the waters rushed away, the skeletons of sunken vessels loomed, haunting from graves long sealed from light and sun.

More caravanners crowded onto the pile of stone where I stood to get a better view of panoramic horror. The seasoned sailors dreaded what they were about to witness.

Our attention was drawn far out to sea where a pod of whales wallowed, chasing the receding ocean. We wanted to shout, wave our arms, cry out, but people were already scrambling off the docks, scuttling like crabs over rocks to grab at fish and every other sea creature that lay for the picking from deep-sea gardens. Men threw baskets down to women grasping at squirming bream, mullet, and snapping pike. A herd of sheep had broken from stock pens near the docks and streamed across the mud among gleeful children, jumping and chasing in the strange early morning light.

Among the caravans, many of the less-seasoned travelers cried that the quake had opened the floor of the sea and drained away the water. The Hebrews among us, who knew the old scriptures, spread their arms like parting seas, shouting Moses was visiting Alexandria and had laid open the seas to create dry land. But the rest of us on the ridge above the city knew. We had seen this—never like this—but we had seen this and could not imagine the scope of the horror that was to follow.

We forced ourselves to overcome our shock. In desperation, we began to wave tunics and tent scraps, while some let go with a chorus of shouts. But we were too few and too far away. Desperate sailors below on the docks also shouted and waved to the scavengers, but they soon abandoned their imploring and fled for the streets.

What God giveth, God taketh away.

More than a mile from shore, a cloud bank lay: common for a cool fog to form on a hot summer morning and then slowly move on shore. The hordes of people glanced up for a moment and returned to their greedy harvest.

Like a shark, the bank moved toward shore with predatory callousness—or was it like the insensate God above? —its jaws yawning, hungry for misery and human suffering.

It was too late by the time they saw the wave. They were frozen in the mud. The sheep had stopped to look stupidly toward the liquid mountains rolling toward them.

Screams and wailing spread from the bay and along the docks as streams of humanity poured into streets and away from the harbor. All too late. I sank to my knees in awe as the great arm of God swept into the bay, gathering the souls, raising the great ships, peeling away docks and stone, and toppling buildings like children's beach castles.

Countless bodies, arms flailing, struggled among the debris amid a deafening thunder of seas as the mountain of water crashed over the city and muffled the screams of thousands. Ships careened toward us on the surf, scraping over tall rooftops. A second wave followed, and in moments, a third: Each smaller, but no less terrible, churning the horrible laundry tub of chaos. The sea continued expanding and pressing in. The walls and canals that were once the grace of this ancient city now created a terrible kettle holding a stew of shattered ships, floating debris, and broken bodies. The waters roiled as if massive serpents were seeking the last of the living.

The long, torturous act drew to a slow finale. Then silence. A long, strange quiet, as though we could close our eyes and nothing we had seen would have happened. But our eyes were open, and we saw, and soon our ears could hear again: babies. That horrible, high-pitched death scream, mothers wailing for their babies, fathers for their families, the poor and destitute wailing alone. God's butcher bucket, all sloshing in a massive tub of death and pain.

Waves of soaking refugees surged up from the city, engulfing us as the tidal wave had engulfed them, fleeing in terror, dragging stunned children, and carrying infants, faces shrouded in the gray-blue serenity of death. They were fleeing the sea of bilge, fleeing the city, and they would not stop until their bodies failed them.

By mid-day, most of the caravans thoughtlessly packed up what they could and headed inland or somewhere they could find a ship or meet up with another caravan. They brutally pushed off straggling survivors and their whimpering children.

As the days wore on, a few of us lingered, spending muggy hours traipsing through mud, while bloated faces stared down at us from bodies hung over gunwales of ships perched high on gilded palaces. There was nothing that could be done and few to rescue. The city had made a perfect killing ground. Like a battlefield the sea had encircled, and crushed its inhabitants more efficiently than a thousand brutal armies.

Ultimately, our response to irrevocable misery and inescapable stench was simply to wander off. The citizens quickly abandoned the corpse of Alexandria or huddled in destitute camps encircling the city, fighting with one another over scraps as they slowly starved.

In several days, new ships were arriving from upriver or into the harbor. I was able to sign on ahead of others because of my experience and the few names I had acquired on my passages since Kalliste.

On board, I drifted away from Alexandria in silence, and I drifted away from myself. I was an empty hull without a kernel, flesh without a soul. Did I believe there was a God? I did not care.

I barely remembered Yeshu. I asked myself again: Was he just a magician using the secret powers that Elymas the sorcerer on Cyprus had discovered? Could he have been mistaken, his power coming from a source he did not understand? Or had Yeshu simply been one man meant solely for a different time? I simply no longer cared to ponder.

I would walk on; that is what I do.

Broken. As drowned and broken as any of the victims of the tidal wave, I possessed a life I did not want and a faith I found unsupportable. I silently vowed no longer to make any effort. I would do nothing to maintain this life or my faith. I despised this flesh and disregarded my tattered faith.

There I was, broken and unsalvageable—exactly where Yeshu wanted me.

XIII. Mila

I am not proud of my life after Alexandria. Nothing was of consequence to me. I drifted back to Sardinia like a leaf, my head spinning on currents, drawn by inevitability and a complete lack of intent, resolve, or faith. Nothing remained; nothing to live for, nothing to die for. I sought that place where I would be undisturbed by the whims of earth, man, or God. Sardinia had been unshaken by quakes, and its high cliffs were impervious to tidal waves. I also longed to be among people who were equally unshaken and impervious. The solid and unpretentious Sardinian natives existed far from the world or The Way.

I had two images of Yahweh, where there had been one. As if by a quirk of double vision there had been one figure, and now I saw two again. My life was no longer tended by the gentle hand of Yeshu, but I was unfettered and adrift beneath the gaze of Yahweh: that silent monolith beyond time and eternity.

Where had Yeshu gone? Had he been taken by Yahweh never to return?

I did not witness it, but my sisters told me the story of what they had seen when Yeshu left the world after his resurrection. Overlooking Bethany on a quiet evening, they were gathered with Yeshu, the Disciples, and several followers. They watched as Yeshu ascended into a great plume of mountain fog gilded by setting sun. It was no less astounding than when they had seen him after his resurrection. The hilltop where they stood, scattered with stones and brush, seemed utterly abandoned after he left, until angelic messengers appeared and assured them he would return soon. The disciples looked around, shuffled their feet, murmured to one another, then descended again into the broad valley of darkness.

But that was long ago.

I bear in my flesh the mark of my resurrection by the hand of the Savior of my soul. However, like life itself, this became nothing more than a strange mystery to me. And this, my longevity, was less a mystery to me than a Savior who could smash a hole through our prison walls, make contact with the imprisoned, then retreat to safety before those he rescued could follow. "Where are you?" I wanted to ask, but I did not care to know. If he were knowable, I....

No. I would stop wrestling—or caring.

My eyes fixed off stern at the looming cliffs of Sardinia, I waved off the curses and prodding of the captain imploring me to heft a rope, until in the harbor I was shoved onto the pier, my bundle thrown after.

I returned to the Nuragic village having only been there a season before. Though I had known the residents for many generations, they were again unfazed by my return. But I could tell I was not the person they had expected. Instead of their usual gregarious greeting, my sullenness caused them to withdraw and stare silently at this human anomaly. Certainly, I had never been a god to them; my comings and goings were simply an aberration to be studied like the weather. The value and meaning of my appearance were appraised like a red moon, an early harvest, or an eclipse of the sun. I was expected to hunt, harvest, share my food, and defecate in the same pit as everyone else.

For years after returning, I simply wandered the island alone, scavenging and hunting, living in crude huts or caves and staying clear of the other native villages or Roman scouts. The villagers watched and tolerated me. On occasion when I circled back to the village, I would offer recognizance on the location of other tribes or on scattered Roman troops. The tribal people were forgiving and patient. There were no tribal customs for how to host an immortal.

My perimeter of journeying moved closer to the village month by month until finally I settled with them and stayed. My standing in their community improved as I drew on the skills given me by my father. I helped to build dwellings and offered my meager skills rebuilding the nuraghes into functional fortresses that would continue to keep the diminishing Roman forces from attempting to attack without sustaining severe casualties.

I learned far more from them than I taught them. For my efforts, I was given training in Sardinian metal working. I had dabbled in the rich copper resources of Cyprus, but my skills were like child's play compared to the skills of the Sardinians. I was taught how to create weapons made from alloys that far outperformed the tin swords and brittle arrowheads of the Romans. Rich ores and abundant resources of charcoal and heat provided all I needed for trial and error. I was reminded of those splendid hours working in my father's shop, serenely lost in creation and crafting.

They taught me much more than metal working. I had never possessed a warrior heart, but now I would need to learn how to fight if I were to maintain a place in their village. They had developed martial techniques and military strategy that ensured not only an offensive victory, but also defensive strategies so they would not need to often use their strong offensive strategies.

As I settled into their routines, it would have been an affront to their traditions if I were to stay in their village unmarried. On this island, there was no place for a single man unless he was widowed or had made the rare arrangement with another man. They could not abide someone living alone.

I took a wife.

My Nuragic wife was Mila, daughter of the chief. Mila was a rambunctious child, stout and muscular; her wild, black hair was plaited in shells and seeds, encircling her feline features. I believed the chief and his wife were glad to have her out of their dwelling, because I soon learned I had no ability, desire—or inclination—to control this feral young warrior. And she was a remarkable warrior. I carried the bruises and scars to prove it. In other lands, I may have been disgraced by this tiny, ferocious woman, but all the warriors of the village had scars enough from her to also live in fear. They did not berate me for the harm I endured when training with her; they pitied me.

Mila and I developed, what might be called, an alliance. Maybe she was simply fascinated because the cuts she inflicted on me healed more quickly than the wounding she wreaked on others she terrorized. She brutally and eagerly taught me how to fight her. She wanted a worthy opponent, and she was determined to make me into someone who could challenge her enormous skill.

Her father and mother were warriors held in high esteem within the tribe, and our training became more frenetic when they joined us. And, fortunately, those occasions provided someone other than me to take Mila's abuse.

Her size was always her advantage. She forced you to strike down as she parried upward until, without warning, she would leap shoulder-high on ropey legs to batter head and shoulders. Nuragic strategy was intuitively defensive. Their approach, whether on the field or hand to hand, was the same. Ingenious gamesmen, they anticipated an assailant's attack by several moves, waiting with precise countermoves. The Romans were like children with sticks against these warriors. However, Nuragic warfare did not involve much killing. Ambush or repelling a decisive attack, while critically wounding the leading edge, were usually adequate.

As I blocked and parried with Mila, I saw how defenseless and defeated my lack of martial skills left me. I had participated in few fights, and only to defend myself. With my lack of ability, it was a wonder I had been able to avoid or survive the many threats and brutalities I had witnessed in hundreds of dockside fights.

This glaring incompetence of mine revealed to me how similarly incompetent and defeated I was in the spiritual realm. Especially in the company of Paul, I had witnessed brutal spiritual encounters: exorcising screeching demons, the blinding of Elymas, turning back cursing mobs, and curing the sick. But those had faded into the mists of time.

I regret that I had not understood how real and deadly spiritual warfare is. What if I, what if The Way, had maintained such skill in spiritual warfare instead of becoming the comfortable, sad, and bloated clerics abroad in the world? In spiritual warfare, we are incompetent trainees, clumsy conscripts in the war against unseen enemies. Why do we never train ourselves in the skills or competence required to wield spiritual weapons? We demonstrate no skill, no strategy, and little experience. In his rhetorician style, Paul had written eloquently of our weapons. The Word is the one devastating offensive weapon in our arsenal. How often I had failed to employ this weapon when launching any new exploit or attacking a prevailing enemy.

I would not have found myself far from Yeshu in this savage world, living an animal existence among a primitive tribe, if I would have learned to use the defenses of my shield of faith with the same skill that Nuragic warriors used their shields to deflect, distract, and extinguish the flaming arrows of their enemies. In his familiarity and knowledge of the Romans, Paul also spoke of the standard issue defensive equipment: the breast plate of righteousness, the helmet of salvation, and the belt of truth. All his words had been lost on me. I had allowed myself to be as defenseless as a lamb amid wolves.

But Mila would have disdained encumbrances such as breastplates and belts, plunging into battle bare-breasted and often with little more than woven reeds around her waist. She would embrace Paul's admonition to throw off every encumbrance that gets in the way, and run the race set for us.

Spiritual warfare seems merely a lofty and distant notion when contrasted with Mila and the grueling blood lust that infused our warfare. Though skirmishes with other tribes could devolve into little more than childhood gang fights, they could also escalate desperate, cruel, and deadly.

That is where I found myself on that bleak day. That day I killed someone.

If I could come to this, I knew I had fled as far as it could be possible to flee from the bosom of my Savior. I had left the side of gentle Yeshu and arrived upon a brutal killing field.

I had opportunities to witness violent squabbles and strife in my time at sea. I had seen more corpses than I want to remember. But I had been fortunate to have avoided killing anyone. There had been many on the docks more capable of killing and more competent at killing than me. I had scraped up my fists and bloodied a few noses in desperate self-defense or while defending someone else, but I had never been guilty of anything more. I had never been seriously injured fighting or seriously injured anyone else. Until that day.

Most Nuragic skirmishes were minor feints, threats, or vicious family feuds. But there were occasions that required us to protect our lands, our children, and our women—though most of our women could protect themselves.

A village from the south had outgrown its borders and come looking for game and land along the river in our territory. For months, we had been able to scare them off by lobbing a couple of spears and shooting a few arrows, but as their resources continued to dwindle, they became more desperate.

Ultimately, they organized a brazen assault. They came with hides, tent poles, cooking pots, and sheep with the intent of establishing a small settlement on the edge of our lands. Across the island, clan and tribal land had been marked for generations, so no one would have attempted an assault like this unless they intended to stay. If they were allowed to build camp for one night, they could build defenses and it would be much more difficult to extract them. They would place a wedge that could topple us before the next crops were harvested. Our village would be at serious risk for starvation or conquest.

In war council, the spicy smoke rose over our heads. Our faces shone with grease from our feast and from the paint that had been applied according to strict design. Mila and her father scratched frantically in the dirt floor as they sketched and debated a plan that laid a full-on frontal assault on their camps. Arrows and spears would be followed immediately by a wave of long knives and clubs. Though blades suited for battle were never in large supply, we had the best blades of any tribe on the island. We would save them for our final attack. Our plan would be an overwhelming assault designed to insight panic and fright. We wanted to scare them into leaving, not kill them. Higher casualties simply led to more retribution that would stretch on for decades.

Plans sketched by Mila and her father always arose from a simple design that I saw everywhere in the village: a circle surrounding a square with two lines that divide both the circle and square into four sections. The pattern was on their shields, painted on their dwellings, and scratched in the dirt by children. They also played *Battle Stones*, a complicated game that used the same pattern played with white and gray stones. Another secret of their success: Everyone, from childhood on up, knew the basics of the plan.

Their planning for war explained the significance of this design. They would draw a large circle—what the Romans would have called the theatre of battle. They would cut the circle in half by drawing a line across the middle from east to west. This was the front line of battle:

the enemy on one side and our forces on the other. Then they drew a line cutting the circle in half, north to south dividing the theatre into quarters and the front line into left flank and right flank. Their core strategy was their belief that if you could control three quarters of the theater, your forces would win. Much of their time was spent on how to win just one more quarter.

From there, they also drew a large square that filled the center of the circle. A square within a circle. The large square was portioned into four smaller squares by the cross marks dividing the quarters of the circle. This square was the actual battlefield, and nearly all their planning was focused on the four squares within this larger square. Each of these four smaller squares required its own detailed plan. I never understood it all, but there was a plan and a strategy for each quarter in the circle and each of the four squares of the battlefield.

Many in the Nuragic tribe had a variety of tattoos that contained variations of this symbol. It was written in their minds and on their flesh.

Stars still twinkled low in the west and blue haze hung over hills to the east. The tremor in my knees was not from the chill of early morning but from fear and anticipation. We approached across a low rise above the enemy settlement. Mila was calm as a cat. As the plan unfolded, Mila and I were sweeping to flank. More than a flanking maneuver, our position also anchored our line to keep it tight. We did not need to contain, surround, and kill; we needed to establish a broad, unbroken front to force them away. The line would have to be held and the edges crisply maintained, or they could pierce our lines or outflank us. It was essential that we deliver a fierce and decisive assault to flush them from our territory and send them fleeing south again, too frightened to return. If we were lucky, we might wound enough of their best warriors so they would not be tempted to regroup. Mila would not have been disappointed if we killed them.

Waiting for the others to array to our left, Mila and I wedged between a boulder and a twisted cedar. Mila would give the cry to attack. Excited, her head darted like a sparrow. Nestled together in our dim hiding spot, I was enthralled so near this leonine beauty; the scent of our nearness, her rapid breaths, and dilated pupils. When she nodded, I ignored my frightened, jabbering mind, and we both stood and leapt over the rock. Before she could make her battle cry, we found ourselves face to face with three of their scouts who were either returning or had already anticipated our attack and were trying to outflank us.

To them, we were but a girl and a foreigner leaping foolishly from cover. I would be easy to overcome, but they would capture the worthy young female. With their stupid grins, their eyes were on me alone. But Mila did not wait for them to decide their next move. She applied her assured strategy: skill and swift aggression are the best defense. They never had a chance to square before she was upon them. With no choice but to thoughtlessly follow, I hoped that all our drills would take possession of my reluctant limbs.

Mila likely thought this was a romp, while I thought I was in the struggle of my life. Her small body shook with screams that both ordered our warriors to attack and momentarily paralyzed our three rivals. She was on them like a lioness, delivering a crunching upper cut with the shaft of her spear that split the jaw of the frozen scout on the left. Before he was halfway to the ground, she shifted her spear and returned with the tip of the blade, gashing a deep wound across the belly of the man in the middle, his intestines bulging at the wound. He began to lean forward, but she was already returning with the shaft of her spear delivering a crunching blow to his forehead that whipped his head backward.

The third man was coming across with his spear, and I swept with my long knife, hacking the shaft of his spear. My slashing forced the spear aside so that he lost the force of his lunge, but it did not sever the shaft. He quickly recovered his swing, slamming my forearm with the shaft. He would have broken both bones in my arm had the shaft not cracked at the point where I had struck it with my blade. His spear broke in half. He wielded the broken shaft as a club with the intent of battering Mila.

Gripping the broken shaft in both hands, he raised his arms, intending to deliver a broadside to Mila before she could get her footing. He exposed his ribs, a foolish mistake for a spearman, but he was rattled by how efficiently Mila had destroyed his partners. As Mila had always taught me, under the arm was the prized target. The flesh is thin and with the shaft wedged between ribs, if the blade does not kill, at least the arm is hobbled by the spear, knife, or arrow protruding from beneath it.

She was in immediate danger from his club. With the man's ribs exposed, all the hours of training with Mila flashed before me, and without a thought, I instinctively forced the point of my long knife into his side.

Everything slowed to the whisper of a blade. I could see his lashes flutter, the sweat from his forehead floating, colliding with droplets of blood from his wounded partner. As she spun, Mila's uncoiling hair fanned with the slow beauty of a sea creature. His eyes met mine, and with his telltale squint and eye roll I knew he realized his mistake.

I felt everything. The point of my blade hit rib, depressing his chest slightly before it slid upward, going deeper. For an instant, I thought the blade would be deflected too high to reach the heart and would be lost in empty lung. I felt my arm muscles tense, felt the thrust push deeper, sluicing back and forth to sever the nest of vessels above the beating organ.

Stuck in his side, my long knife was carried down with him as he fell, and the blade made a moist sucking sound as I withdrew it. I was mesmerized, watching the man gasping like a dying fish, his jaw opening and closing while his hands reached blindly for his chest where the wound blubbered like bloody lips. Red foam gushed from his nose and mouth. Three guttural animal sighs came from his throat; one leg shook and kicked until he pissed himself. He retched; his jaw wide; then all muscles went limp. His eyes became vacant like a dead horse. He had been a man and now he was not. *I was not. I am. I am not. I care not.*

Mila struck me in the arm where I had been hit by the spear shaft, and a world of pain and noise thundered back to me like wild seas. She was running ahead, the scout in the middle with the stomach wound was running in the other direction, holding his guts. All our fellow warriors were charging the encampment. I looked down at my victim again, then chased after Mila. While I remained in a fog, we soundly routed their forces and were back in our village before midday.

If we were not fighting together, Mila would rather scratch me than look at me, but after a victory, she was hungry. I watched her gorge herself on meat and fruit by the handful until her small stomach was taut. She belched and laughed, rubbing her belly. But often after battle, she was hungry for something more. Without hesitation, she grabbed my belt and pushed me into the hut where we were soon lost in a torrent of passion.

I had been willingly diverted from the vision of the hapless spearman. With our desire spent, I lay back, trying to sleep, while in my anguished thoughts I killed him and killed him again, over and over. As darkness enfolded us, I knew the spearman would not be coupling with his mate as I had. That night in his empty hut, his worried wife, maybe his children, would fret because he had not returned with the rest of their fleeing warriors. Someone would arrive to tell them. Then his mother and brothers would gather in his hut to mourn. Yet he would be lying out in the dark, on cold stone with foaming blood drying on his chin, his eyes waxy and vacant, animals sniffing his wounds.

Then he blinks dead eyes. His hand slides across his chest, reaching for the heart that I silenced. He fingers the wound, feeling the ragged edges, and folds his hand deep into his side, groping through lung. From lips blackened with blood, he says, "Turn away. Do not look at me. You are not worthy. Turn away. Do not look at me." I gasp, awakening to Mila's breathing beside me, gentle as a kitten.

In my nightmares he visits me, even now.

Of course, I loved Mila—and her vivaciousness and enthusiasm for life, the way she relished the struggle. I may be bold enough to believe she acquired an affection for me, too.

As time passed, she was not fearful of having children, but I did not know how she could fathom caring for an infant: a year or two of suckling a child or tolerating the stumbling attempts at training her children into warriors.

But the time came when she was with child. She became more fierce, if that were possible, more the lioness. Her widening girth and enlarging breasts did not inhibit her speed or skill. She would rub her tight, round belly, look up at my face, and scream her laughter like a sea heron: perfect wide smile and glittering eyes.

In our hut, she allowed me to put my arm around her shoulders, small and smooth in repose, not chiseled and taut. She would smile as I pulled her near and we would watch the smoke curl out of the roof of our hut until she sank into a deep sleep. It was the only time I saw her small, hard body relaxed, chest rising and falling, snoring loud as her father.

Maybe it was the clumsy hand of God that seemingly desires to give good gifts but haplessly and inadvertently swipes away lives. When no warrior could set a finger on Mila or deflect her blade, one small warrior growing inside her, arriving before its time, without tact or intent was able to disarm her, overrun her flawless defenses, and deliver the wound that would bleed her to death in minutes.

I sat there in the corner of the hut as the women tended her. I saw the last struggles of the child, no larger than a kitten, thrashing in blood. As though smeared in red, my last shreds of hope and truth were extinguished. *It is finished*. I sat huddled, as sallow, pale, and emptied as my lifeless Mila and child.

I mourned for Mila; I mourned for our unborn warrior child; I mourned for Miriam, for Yeshu, for Alexandria. All dead to me and gone.

As a widower, I was accepted into the community, and my status was enhanced by having proved myself in battle, but mostly because there was sympathy for the loss of a brave woman like Mila. Their grief for me and the legendary princess were sweet and sincere. But before Mila's pyre had cooled, I knew I would not be staying long on this island.

On previous visits to Sardinia, the winding river from the docks to the Nuragic village had been escape from the world of time and change to a savage kingdom hidden in a cleft of timelessness. In my tainted vision, I had delivered my unique turmoil to these serene people. I had refused to see that their lives were not always bravery and bliss but consisted of precarious strife.

I would follow the winding river back to the world of time.

Christian enclaves had arrived on Sardinia. I avoided those weaponless, toothless, and conquered spiritual warriors with their impotent rituals and finery. I assumed there was no longer anywhere in the world where anyone continued to follow the simple Carpenter of Nazareth. They had long ago been disarmed or had laid down their weapons, while they looked to saints and servitude, toward a new pharisaical law, decreed not by the writers of the scriptures or the letters of the Disciples, but by generations of misguided, weak, and foolish usurpers. A law not devised by true followers of The Way, but by wanton souls eager to replace freedom with ritual and grace with captivity. Pharaoh was not as effective a jailer or as cruel a master as this Church.

I longed to leave once and for all the heat and all those putrid harbors that surrounded this ravening green sea. I wanted to leave the world, leave this life if I could, but I had never been able to conceive of a way to accomplish this until an intriguing solution presented itself to me.

Just as when I left Alexandria, I felt broken and unsalvageable—again where Yeshu wanted me.

XIV. North

On the docks of Sardinia, I loved to hear the stories told by red-bearded Northmen who might interrupt their brawling long enough to tell their tall tales and blatant lies. Then with arms draped around one another they would blubber in their cups and weep songs about their homes among the green valleys, mountains, and deep snows of winter. Their long hair was intertwined with beads, silver, and leather, and they wore fur vests reeking of flesh on the hide, and leather pants often splattered with brown blood stains—animal and human.

Of course, throughout the years, I had seen a few low mountains, and occasional snows sketching fields and thatch roofs in white. As children, we would slide on scattered patches that had blown across a barren hillside. No one in this arid land believed the Northmen when they bawled their stories of snowdrifts deep enough to bury a stable, wading in hip-deep snows to find their cattle, or sniveling brats or whining women who had wandered from the safety of their hearth and had been lost to a blizzard, only to be found as stinking corpses torn by wolves the next spring.

The men from the north were usually seen in Sardinia in early autumn to stock up on grains and oils that were hard for them to acquire elsewhere. They also bartered their leather and furs for precious Sardinian metalwork.

While I stayed near the docks, deciding where I would find escape, one young Northman stood apart from his boisterous comrades. He was the one scratching on tablets or pushing his gullible mates aside before they could ruin a bargain in their drunken haste, then he would weasel a deal to include one more jar of wheat or measure of oil. He sidled up to me late one day while I was bargaining to sell a short, curved kopis sword I had crafted. I had brought several with me from the tribe, and I had sold all the others. Speaking a few broken words of Latin he interrupted my sale, which was not going well anyway. He asked to see the sword, then he clenched his jaw, furrowed his red brow, and narrowed his blue eyes as he hefted the weapon. I thought he was miming to affect a bargain. He slashed the air and ran his finger beside the slow curve of the blade. It was a design I had copied from similar blades I had seen from the East and I modified it to resemble a Nuragic blade. Quickly, he pivoted toward a scruff of weeds jutting from the base of a dilapidated shed and clipped them off neatly with a practiced swipe. Then he cut another tuft of weeds. He raised his bushy brows and smiled.

He paid full price without bargaining, then pointed at the weapon to ask if I had more. I shook my head. But I liked him, so before I lost him, I wanted to learn more about his world of ice and snow in the far north—and I was more than interested to keep a customer who would pay full price for my work. I could figure out a way to get more blades later. I do not think I needed the coins, but as with anyone, there was always the unique pleasure of selling what I crafted. Money simply symbolizes value, and there is an intrinsic joy in the exchange of value for value.

I knew a place away from the drunken taverns along the docks where two men could share the best brew on Sardinia along with a fish and lamb stew that had a balance of vinegar, ginger, and basil flavored to perfection. Sardinian fare was renowned, but the best food was hidden far from the rabble on the docks.

An old Nuragic woman kept a small room off her house where a few of the native merchants gathered. It was a place for the Nuragic to meet or stay when they came from the interior to trade. If he were in my company, she was happy to welcome the hearty Northman, but she scolded him never to bring his raucous mates there because she would always have plenty of her tattooed tribesmen and warriors in the wings to support her. He nodded in startled assent.

Edulf, as the Northman introduced himself, was creative with his limited Latin. Our understanding improved as he was able to spice his coarse Germanic with a sprinkle of Greek. With his few words and generous flourishes with his hands, he painted a fantastical picture of mountains to the sky, forests deep and dark with standing trunks larger than ten masts, green fields to the horizon, and snow—deep and cold. He had me enthralled with his majestic world—even if it were an exaggeration.

His father was a farmer and shepherd. Edulf had left his home to seek adventure, but he had spent his time developing a healthy trade between northern tribes and the broad bazaar across seas of the Mediterranean. The prodigal son became the profitable son.

I was ready to leave Sardinia, to lose myself in his great northern continent, but he was adamant that I wait until spring because no one unaccustomed to that harsh world could survive a single month if he had not established his own hearth and family. He was also shrewd to have me stay and amass weapons and tools for him to carry home in time for planting and harvest the following year. I was satisfied with this arrangement. It was a solid deal; he made a generous down payment and we parted at the dock. He waved my short sword—he called it a sickle—and he continued the painstaking task of loading a ship that was already laden dangerously close to the water line with grain and treasure. From the time of Markos, I had learned that the best captains can founder on an ocean of greed. I wondered if I would see him again, or if he would suffer the fate of many merchant captains I had known. Now they reside as skeletons at the bottom of the seas, picked clean of flesh, while their souls pilot ships laden with worthless treasure into the fields of Elysium or the halls of hell.

The winter had been severe in the north, forcing Edulf to lay over in the south while sending as much wheat and a few items along with my "sickle" upriver and overland to keep his people from starving. He was back in Sardinia earlier than I expected, but in my eagerness, I had prepared plenty of sickles along with other weapons and implements designed with the hopes of catching his eye.

I stayed in the city that winter working with a local smith to convert much of the treasure I had left hidden on Sardinia. We wrapped silver into leather belts and made buckles and hasps I could hide in my baggage. A Nuragic local joined us, helping me to create hollow iron ingots and filling them with small amounts of gold. Each piece had thin seams that could be cracked with a chisel. The rough iron was valuable, but it would not attract nearly as much attention as the gold inside if it were discovered. I traded what I could, but I left treasure on Sardinia, hidden in the secret cave if I ever found my way back again.

I was a wealthy man by any standard, but it meant little to me except for the freedom and escape from my past that it provided.

Though we were once again laden to where the cargo and seas nearly met at the deck, the journey from Sardinia to Massalia on the northern shores of the sea was slow and calm. Edulf proved to be an able sea captain. I had been on the southern reaches of that great continent, but I had never taken the great river highway that riffled cold and steady as it skirted the massive mountain wall that hedged the Roman territories.

In Massalia, Edulf and his men were joined by a fleet—nearly an army—of other Northmen who would shepherd the ships upriver as far as they could be rowed, laden with all their goods.

Within a week, I was no longer aware of river, or men, or the ships bulging with cargo. At a waypoint, we docked several vessels and transferred cargo to log rafts and barges. I was entering a world of green. Embarrassingly, I asked if all these hillsides, valleys, and fields were tended. Were these the farms of all these hardy souls? After gales of laughter, Edulf slapped me on the back and said I should have listened to him the previous autumn when he described the world of the north.

"This is scrub land: brush groves and foothills," he said.

Of course, he was right. As we veered east in days ahead, the world expanded like a vision. They hired on more carriers and added slaves to portage the massive cargo along Roman roads beneath mountain reaches that defied all the descriptions I had ever heard. These monoliths were as massive, silent, and distant as the God I believed I was leaving behind in the south.

After weeks, we came to a valley pregnant with abundance, an Eden slung between soaring forests and looming mountains. Edulf's home; a land that reminded me of the land of life after death before I was raised by Yeshu. I felt a kinship to this world, and I could not imagine again returning to deserts, heat, and squalid docks.

I stayed with Edulf's father, Azvald, that summer and on through winter. Though heavy with grief and sadness after the loss of Mila, and weighed by the doubts and tribulations I had endured prior to her death, the weight of wonder in this new world tipped the scales and my sensibilities began to thaw.

In autumn, the lush green valley of summer transformed into waves of scarlet, orange, and yellow. Mornings would sing with the taut crispness of frosted fields and sparkling treetops. Smoke, laden with the scent of porridge and salt pork, curled from the roofs of the long house and the round, thatch hovels. Rosy-cheeked toddlers smiled through huffing gusts of frigid air; their eyes lost in the brim of fur caps as they tried to look up at this dark stranger. The huddled sheep befriended the oxen as they nestled, steam rising from their backs.

Delicate autumn yielded to stern winter. The first heavy snow arrived abruptly, washing down from the mountains and through the valleys like a hungry white leopard. What started as cold spits of frost in the morning soon turned into gales that would shovel layer upon layer of deep snow over the farms and village. Man and animal were driven into their shelters.

I stepped out of Azvald's door and walked several steps into the blizzard, tilting my head to taste the cold, delicious crystals on my tongue until Azvald staggered out and grabbed my robe, yanked me back, cursing in a stream of Saxon, much of which I thankfully did not understand.

The widower Azvald was tolerant and eager for companionship. He would clutch my shoulder, his stout body shaking with laughter at mistakes I made in Saxon. He was an elf with a red beard, broad broken nose, and bald head rimmed in long, graying hair. I had never met a people whose use of humor could equally celebrate abundance or manage strife. They loved to laugh. And even the women and children were quick to disarm me with their wit.

Through the winter, the village became a maze of trampled trails with the long house at the center. Other trails led from house to barn or from home to home. By late in the season, the last of the dried meats and turnips were shared with those who had not planned as efficiently, or more likely, had been too generous in feasting and sharing earlier in the season.

Finally, springtime arrived in the broad valley on the north shield of this great continent. It filled the head to dizziness: perfume wafting from carpets of wild lilies, blue buttons, and yellow marigolds tumbling over the hills and sweeping up the valley walls all the way to snow-covered pinnacles. I inhaled the aroma as I watched cloud shadows chase across the landscape and listened to flute-like birds and the mewing lambs that speckled the slopes.

Yet I felt almost nothing.

I tried. I could see it, I knew it was beautiful, but I could not feel it. After dark years, I feared I had become peeled of emotion and my soul cored. I no longer looked up to see the graceful curve of the earth and all the wonder it held. I walked with my head down, looking only at the surface.

Though I was received into the midst of the village because of the endorsement of Edulf and Azvald, I was an enigma to them. They distanced themselves. It was not because of my dark skin and curling black hair, which was an obvious contrast to the flurry of color with which they had been painted: blond hair, red beards, blue or green eyes, and delicate pink freckles. They were familiar with dark-skinned slaves and settlers from the east. They distanced themselves because I was struggling and withdrawn. My demeanor repelled them more than anything—and my terrible grasp of their language. The Saxon language was the most difficult of any language I had tried to acquire. But the village remained unfailingly kind and patient.

Farther west, and across the world, were lands possessed by aristocracy and chieftains who extracted every drop of blood from the poor who lived there. To the east, warlords and marauders exercised the same powers using different means. But in this valley lay a peaceful thatched village, dwellings like great mushrooms hemmed with stick and bramble fences, sheltered for a time from the winds of terror that blew overhead. Encircling the central village were farms that radiated like spokes spreading across the valley.

Though it had been a narrow generation of peace, free from major incursions, the number of men had been thinned by local skirmishes or other calamities as simple as felling a tree or as harsh as being gored by cattle. A man's life was short. It was common in this situation for outlying herdsmen and farmers to take in widows or young female relatives.

Though rarely publicly acknowledged, it was known that often during lonely winters, these women became wives. This custom had a way of avoiding chaos and protecting the women. If they were not sheltered, the life of a lone maiden or widow was one of poverty and abuse and could spark family feuds or brutal contests between men.

Whatever these circumstances and arrangements were, it was not a convenient situation for a single man like me, especially one who preferred to stay single. An old widower like Azvald might stay single, but not a man who was expected to father children. I had to learn the customs and conform if I were to survive.

Though I was both a foreigner and new to the community, I was pressured to find a mate—or two. In this grueling land, with scarcity of men, and high death rates among the children, there could be no role for a man unattached to a child-bearing woman. At the same time, a man had to be cautious not to look at anyone's daughter or a woman under another man's protection unless they were prepared for a harsh challenge from her protector or clansmen. Mila had taught me skills that none of these Northmen possessed, but I was outnumbered and I had no interest in using them. Bereft of feeling, haunted by regret for Miriam and sorrow for Mila, I resisted a partner for as long as I could.

Azvald was a shrewd businessman like his son, but also a generous patron. In addition to providing shelter for me, this simple, joyous man was generous with his knowledge and insight. He was eager to take advantage of my metal-working skills after Edulf had given him the curved blade the year before. Azvald had removed the handle and tried to crudely heat, pound, and bend the blade to slightly change the curve.

On a damp spring morning, he led me behind the barn where a few penned sheep huddled, their hopeful faces turned upward as we approached. With blade in hand, he snatched a ewe and crouched with the mewling beast clutched to his chest. Using the new blade, he began shaving great swaths of billowy wool from her belly and sides. Smiling and nodding at me, he held out the blade in one hand while the other hand showed four stubby fingers. He would like four more blades like that one. I was eager to provide them.

By cobbling together a hearth, charring wood under a pile of rocks, gathering bonemeal and hair to temper blades, and scrounging metal and scraps, I was able to deliver the four blades to him in three days, just as shearing season was to begin. Preparing the blades was a familiar routine for me, but shearing sheep was not. I had watched, but I knew nothing.

I doubt that I had ever seen so large a herd shorn with such efficiency. Azvald was giddy as he hummed and did a little jig while demonstrating his new blades. Among the farmers he proudly proclaimed to have invented the shearing blade, though he was generous to give me credit for my smithing skills. With the swipe of a shearing blade, I had gained my place in the community.

Azvald took the opportunity to provide materials and a space to build a smithy onto the end of his barn. In the weeks that followed, I had plenty of eyes watching and gregarious company helping with my work. They were fascinated to see my round nuraghe-shaped smithy and conical stone char kiln taking shape behind their neighbor's barn. Though it lay everywhere, stone had been used only for low walls or to shore up a barn or fence. I had villagers of all ages eagerly slogging through their fields to find stone to haul behind Azvald's barn. Then, impressed by the smooth form and the efficiency with which these structures could be built, the villagers had taken less than a week to complete my smithy. With the heaps of extra stone they had gathered, I later built a lodging by adding two adjoining rooms to the smithy. Soon, other simple stone structures like mine were taking shape on their farms.

Careful not to reveal the solid gold core in my iron bricks, I kept most of them hidden under the raised planking that circled my dwelling. The rough boards had been bartered from a woodsman. With the small down payment I gave him for the wood, he was willing to wait a week or two until shearing was done to receive delivery of his new axe heads. As deals unfolded, he became a dependable supplier of charcoal and tool handles.

I finished a mattress shelf and the low platforms that surrounded the raised hearth in the center of my main room. With branches and the remaining boards, I built simple furniture, shelves, and framed a window and door. I was not used to the cool climate, and though spring was arriving, I relished the warmth from the charcoal in the adjoining smithy. I had lived in heat and sweat for several lifetimes, and a warm spring in the north was like winter to me.

By autumn, I had crafted enough plowshares, harrows, and implements to fill a cart. The young men wanted swords. That worried Azvald, all the wise parents, and certainly the young wives. Every young man wants war in his time to prove his prowess to peers and women. And for battles lost, and to preserve their stature in the community, old captains are too willing to lead young men to war.

By offering my minimal skills and learning from Azvald's hired hands, I was able to help care for the sheep during the busy season. I drew on my brief experiences in Judea living with the wealthy farmer, Amos, and on Cyprus with the small farm Miriam and I had managed. I would also help Azvald by delivering a bundle or two of wool to the weavers when I visited the farms and merchants to deliver the tools I made.

Small settlements intertwined with other settlements, linked by their farms and herds. In a neighboring village, Laerke and Valda had a yarn shop with their daughters Uma and Bruna. They sorted, carded, dyed, and spun wool. One of their sons was a voyaging trader with Edulf, and another had never returned from a skirmish. Every time I returned from visiting Laerke's shop, Azvald was intensely interested to ask about everything that had been said, especially by Valda and the daughter Bruna. Valda detested Azvald and staunchly avoided talking about him. There were few words exchanged. Laerke would pay for Azvald's wool, Uma and Bruna would smile, their cheeks in a row like four ripe apples, and I would leave.

On one delivery to Laerke's shop, I was surprised to find Uma and Bruna alone. Their parents were at market. The dim shop was heavy with the musky smell of wool interlaced with the forest scents from boiling dye kettles filled with cedar bark and berries. Standing behind a plank table, the girls sorted wool by color, ranging from creamy white to dusky gray. Their oily, blackened fingers flitted among the fibers, picking burrs and sticks, then tossing the wool onto downy mounds.

I had noticed the sisters on my previous deliveries, but their heads were usually covered with bonnets or hoods as they toiled. They would look up occasionally to smile, brushing tousled hair from their eyes. On this muggy day, they both worked bareheaded, flushed with heat, their hair tied back with a length of yarn. Uma was a stout girl with blond hair and blue eyes, while Bruna had brown eyes like a doe and red hair like sunset. Bruna knew I was watching her—before I did. She turned her round face with narrow chin toward me, her sly smile creasing her cheeks with dimples.

"I like the dark one," she said, broadening her smile while looking back down to her work. She blew a lock of red hair from the corner of her mouth and brushed her cheek with the back of her hand.

"Huh?" Both Uma and I said stupidly at the same time.

"Do you like the dark ones better, sister?" Bruna held up the dark gray wool to Uma while looking slyly at me.

"Oh, yes...no, I think I like the white ones." Uma held up a twisted strand of white wool. Then catching up with Bruna's wit, she added, "I would choose the red, but there be no red-haired sheep in these valleys, right now. Is that not right, sister?" Uma laughed.

"No, indeed. No red-haired rams are available in our valley." Bruna shook her head slowly, looking down, tsking while stifling a laugh. "But I hear tell of a stout black-haired ram that old piece of dung, Azvald, keeps at his farm. That black wool would be a fine sight to look at, and soft to fondle I would guess."

The girls giggled and bumped shoulders, unconcerned with my embarrassment.

"Where are you from?" Bruna asked, looking up confidently while leaning over the table, her chest pressing forward. "Dark one?" She imitated my broken Saxon. They both giggled again.

Something stirred inside me like a baby bird, just broken from its shell. It lay there, damp and thrashing, searching for anything the world could give it.

"I—I guess I am from almost everywhere," I stuttered.

"Well, Sardinia is not exactly everywhere now, is it?" Bruna bunched the wool and spread it on the table. "I'm sorry; Pa is gone so we cannot pay you today, but I'm sure old *Arse*-vald will understand." Bruna laughed. She seemed to have as much contempt for Azvald as her mother. I did not understand why they seemed to hate him. He had been kind to me, and he was always more than fair when he dealt with them or with anyone else. In fact, I often thought he had been quite overly generous with Laerke and Valda.

"So, when are you coming back, Mr. Everywhere?" Bruna asked.

I was trying to keep my composure as that little bird inside was finding its wings and beating on the walls of my chest. "Not soon enough," I said.

She smiled and nodded, knowing the arrow stuck.

And it had.

On a sweltering early autumn day, Azvald unstrapped his stinking dung-crusted leathers, dropped them outside the door, and dragged a rough stool into my cramped smithy. He sat staring at me, brows raised in anticipation. I had many orders to prepare for the harvest, but finally, pulling a red-hot blade from the charcoal and setting it on the hearth, I gave him a single quick nod.

He licked his lips, ran a hand over his bald head, and smiled broadly. "So, Lazar, more than a year you have been here now." He looked quickly around the shop. He delighted coming into my shop to look at the walls hanging with rusty tools, shiny blades, and plowshares.

"It has, indeed, been more than a year. And my gratitude to you is great, Azvald. I confess I am busy today, but it seems there is a bellows blowing inside your head and your tongue is stoked." I smiled, wiping my hands.

"Aye, Lazar. Well said!" He slapped his knee. "Our speech suits you well."

I was not sure I agreed.

"I will not keep you today." He wiped a finger across his mouth. "But I was thinking I would like to offer one more shovel of charcoal to build a fire in your mind."

I had enough grasp of the language to be aware that Azvald was much more than a simple shepherd. I was learning to listen more carefully when he spoke.

He continued to hesitate. I feared he was about to engage me in another business deal I would not have time to complete. He took a deep breath, leaned forward, and locked eyes. "I was in the east field where the sheds are. I was doing a lot of thinking."

So, he is going to ask me to help build a bigger shed? I thought.

He was uncharacteristically tactful until he spilled, "Lazar, you are not from Sardinia, but by your name and accent, I would be a fool if I did not know that you were one of the chosen ones of God from the land of the Son of Man."

I knew he could see the shock on my face, and I was left fumbling for Saxon words, but there were none.

He held up his hand. "Your people are known to us. There have been rare caravans of merchants, and there have been those despicable slavers who have been through here with an occasional, pitiful Jew in tow."

I looked away, lost for words. He stared at me in silence until the charcoal snapped and I flinched. I carelessly yanked a bolt from the fire, burning my hand.

He stood, setting his hand on my shoulder, while I shook my scorched fingers. "No, there is nothing to fear, my son. I am not talking about your heritage to alarm you," he said, and stepped away.

I looked up at him and raised an eyebrow. "The Son of Man. That is a unique phrase that I have rarely heard, at least not for a long time."

He smiled, showing his several missing teeth. "You have heard of him, then?"

I gave a single shoulder shrug.

He nodded slowly, pleased. "But we will talk of that another time. What I have to say has been heavy on my mind. I was out there slopping out the sheep pen and thinking about you."

I laughed.

He grinned. "Yes! I was thinking that for a young man to have all your skills, and to know all that you seem to know, you must have seen a great deal of the world. You seem to have seen much for a man of middle years—or younger?" He looked up hopefully, but I did not take the bait and offer my age.

He moved on. "I am certain you are a man who has been through much."

I nodded.

"I am a simple widower; I have lost much. But sometimes, I wish I could be a young man like Edulf and travel back to distant harbors. I want to know more of the world, and I want my understanding to grow." He folded his arms and glanced around the shop, hesitating. "I would like more understanding, but I would also like to grow in my crude faith, I suppose." He stepped toward the door, then turned, while his smile widened. "But why is it that every time that a man wants to grow, we just seem to get more fertilizer—more manure—dumped on us?" With a gust of laughter, he leaned toward me again, raising his finger. "Ha! Well put! Right, Lazar?"

"Well said." I nodded and smiled.

"I do not know what you are waiting for, young man. The people here have accepted you without hesitation, and now, after little more than a year, we could not be without our blacksmith. But I must say it." He quickly glanced toward the door as though someone might hear us. "The people want you to take a wife. And why not, I say?" He spread his hands and shrugged.

"I...I just..." I began.

He held up his hand. "You will never have ideal circumstances in this life, dear friend. There is no perfect labor for us to perform; there are no ideal wives—or husbands—" He winked. "No perfect homes. You are well-blessed if you should have even the taste of good fortune, though there is a better chance that you will feast on bad luck."

He sat on the stool again and pointed around the smithy. "The good, the excellent, and the ideal arise solely from our ability to grasp a moment, to steer repeatedly toward the tiny flicker of light we are given." He folded his hands around a knee. "That is the light that draws us from this difficult, dark, and cluttered valley of souls and helps us to salvage brilliance from debris and despair."

I could not answer but looked down, my brow furrowed. How had I traveled across the world this long life to find this toothless, balding shepherd who could speak with an authority I had not heard since Yeshu and Paul? The Word had found an unblemished path, all the way around the world, arriving in this northern wilderness, and those nearest to the death and resurrection of the Messiah had utterly lost his message of truth.

Azvald pressed forward, not hesitating. "Laerke's daughter has noticed you, my son. Laerke knows it, and I have to say, you know it too, and so does everyone for several villages around!" Another burst of laughter, slapping his knee.

My fate was set. I had been backed into a corner. I cannot say it was a corner I was willfully avoiding. I could no longer deny my affection for Laerke's witty, cheerful Bruna.

XV. Azvald

Amid Azvald's tireless prodding and meddling and cradled in the grace of the community, Bruna and I married before the first snow that second winter. I was troubled by the thought that the old shepherd was too enthusiastic about this arrangement, but I assured myself it was simply the bluster of a wily trader who did not want to see me miss a good deal.

With Bruna, the cold and snow drifted overhead while inside our home, our hearth was as warm and vital as a beating heart.

The previous year, I had been incredulous when told that my first winter was mild, as winters go. During my second winter, I was buried by a blizzard of emotion, swept away by my precious Bruna. I had forgotten laughter before I saw her in Laerke's steamy yarn shop. I hardly noticed the winter because Bruna brought a warmth like spring and happiness like summer: bright, spontaneous waterfalls of laughter, gusty belly laughs, and giggles like the patter of ducklings.

We made our nest in the two rooms I had constructed beside the smithy where the heat of the charcoal and nearness of our bodies kept the deep winter at bay while winds howled, and snows piled high.

But it did not keep Azvald at bay, and Bruna became uncomfortable with his meddling, his unannounced visits, and general curiosity.

Azvald had a side of which I had not learned. The villagers would not share with me the circumstances of how Azvald had lost his wife and daughters. It was custom that the one afflicted with such pain should be the one allowed to share it.

One evening before our marriage, while I was a guest in their home, Bruna's mother, Valda, inadvertently disclosed the tragic story of the fire that had taken the lives of Azvald's beloved wife and daughter. Then Laerke tried to hush Valda, but she seemed unconcerned about Azvald's feelings and decided to press forward until Laerke reluctantly filled in details that Valda had forgotten.

On these farms, larger sheds for sheep and pigs are usually separated from the homes, but often, a cow pen is attached directly to the house where grain and tools are stored. The arrangement of houses and cowsheds is continuous, often encircling a small courtyard. For warmth and convenience, a cow or a litter of sheep or pigs may be kept in the quarters with the family. At the time of the tragedy, Azvald had a simple cowshed attached to his house.

The tale was more tragic because of the commonplace circumstances. Azvald's wife had pushed him from their home because he had been drunk and contentious. Being winter, he had decided to sleep it off in the warmth of the cowshed. As he stumbled out the door that night, lantern in hand, he heard his wife secure the bar on the inside of their door, locking him out. With his sodden brain, he thought he could do her one better. He went into a shed, retrieved a pitchfork and hoe, and wedged them crosswise into the frame of the door. No one could get in—and no one could get out. Self-satisfied, he weaved back to the cowshed, propped his candle on a stone, lay down next to their old cow, and fell asleep. He had not bothered to douse the candle, and in the night, the cow stirred and kicked it over. The dazed, drunk Azvald awoke to the sharp pain of a frantic cow stepping on his ankle, snapping it like a twig. By then, the cowshed was ablaze, and the fire had already spread to the house. Amid the screams of his family, limping, he dragged himself out of the cowshed. The rest was unclear. He was likely too dazed to remember the tools he had jammed in the doorway and his ankle was too twisted for him to hobble. He could do no more than crawl near as the thatched house was consumed in a gust quickly as a dry cedar bough. Edulf, his son, had been sleeping alone in the narrow loft and was able to shimmy his way between slats and thatch to escape. The boy found his father scratching at the burning door, but too late. He pulled his wailing father from the flames.

The shepherd never remarried. He and Edulf rebuilt, and over the years, Azvald resumed his standing in the community as an honorable man. His expertise with sheep and shepherding became an asset to the entire region.

Despite having learned of his pain, I still found his interest in Bruna unsettling. Before we married, he would inquire about my visits with her. He would ask about Valda, but Valda continued to detest him all the more when she feared her daughter might live closer to him. Bruna had inherited her mother's disdain for him, but Bruna did not seem to know why they despised him. In a close community, beset with brutal weather and the threat of raiders, simple disputes and anxious disagreements were magnified beyond anyone's understanding. And women were too often brutalized. There were quiet men who had done brutal things in drunkenness or anger that they regretted or never spoke of. I tried to ignore all of it.

By the following spring, Bruna insisted we move because her mother refused to visit our home near Azvald. My wife was intent on having children, and no woman wanted to have children away from her mother. Azvald was reluctant to see us leave, but after I coaxed him with a variety of excuses, he offered a site that he had claimed for his sheep at the border of the village fields. I was concerned it was distant from the other homesteads in case of a threat, but it was adequate, and included a tidy shepherd's hut and small shed. Bruna accepted immediately. She liked the hut and saw opportunity to expand it—with my sweat—and then she would give it her gracious touch. I had to accept. We could have moved away to a nearby village or farther. I had the resources to build a house and homestead, but I would have to trundle all my heavy metal working supplies and tools. And I would have been too ignorant of the north and its winters to strike out on my own, claim land, and try to build and bargain in a strange village. We were both content with Azvald's offer. Plus, it lay in the direction of Valda and Laerke, so Valda would never have to concern herself with passing around Azvald's homestead.

Unfortunately, it did not to seem to influence Azvald's meddling. After we moved to our new home, he would constantly find an excuse to hover around Bruna. It became clear if I were to find peace for my wife, I would have to risk my relationship with my benefactor whom I had grown to respect in this wild land. My wife was bold to take care of herself with an old man if she had to, but she was concerned about challenging him and creating discord. The man was annoying her, and I could not allow that to tear our home apart.

Spring was the overwhelming busy season for a shepherd and a smith. Azvald eased into my new smithy near our home to ask if I would take a walk with him. He wanted to check on ewes that were lambing in a thicket on the southern slope beyond our small home. I was busy, but I was eager to usher Azvald away from Bruna. I knew it might be finally time for me to confront him about his visits.

We left the village behind as we walked. I was overwhelmed by the vastness and beauty of the land in springtime. There was much to learn in this new world, and I had never experienced the wonder of seasons. This was not the unvarying world of two seasons—unbearable heat interspersed with a month of sniffling cold—that had stretched on unbroken and dull, decade after decade for me. I had spent lifetimes living in unchanging rocky deserts, on sandal-searing roadways, passing carcasses of animals dead of thirst, and aboard steaming decks in stifling doldrums.

In the north country, each season was a bounty. On autumn mornings, with frosted breath, in awe I would stroll under sparkling canopies of red and yellow forests. I had naively assumed these lovely trees were being killed from the cold. How could these beautiful, delicate trees survive? Did they sprout new limbs? Azvald, Edulf, and the villagers were often as astonished as humored by my questions. In winter's deep snows, I would track through barren forests. Had those trees been killed, never to green again?

But walking with the old shepherd on a spring day, the world had been resurrected, and I felt as alive again as on that bright day when I shuffled from the tomb.

Azvald and I cut through a corner of forest that I traversed regularly throughout the seasons. I was ceaselessly astonished at the changes I would see. I knew I could confide my ignorance of this world and the changing forest with this gentle man. He was patient as I stopped in a familiar clearing and looked about. I had paused here a few months before while in the dead of winter.

"I am amazed. How can a forest endure such an assault as winter without being destroyed?" I asked. "It is dead and frozen and then rises again stronger than ever. Year after year. Can fire alone destroy something so beautiful? Can fire...?"

Azvald was silent, and I regretted what I had said before it had left my mouth. "I'm so sorry, Azvald. I did not mean...."

He waved it aside with a smile, then lifted his hand and swept it across the broad and beautiful forest. "Just like this old shepherd, a forest endures because it was prepared by its Maker," he said. "The trees do not prepare themselves to endure the deep winter; they have been prepared by water, soil, and the seasons. I have been told that to survive, we must be deeply rooted in our Creator and drink the waters from the Word of Life. And trees do not survive alone; they survive together." He set down his pack, folded his hands behind his back, and swiveled to look at the budding forest. "For a long time after I lost my beautiful wife and daughter, I was a tree alone, unsupported, and ready to rot and fall. By grace, I was rescued."

I waited. I knew he was a man with wisdom to share that defied his elfin demeanor.

"We sometimes see after a storm that a great tree has been toppled. We think this must have been the worst storm in many years to topple this grand old tree we have walked near and regarded for so long. But no. It is simply that this great tree had become so lofty and self-reliant with its spreading branches and soaring crown reaching toward the skies that it attracted the winds and was easy to topple. I had become that tree. I fell hard, limbs snapping, leaves scattering." His voice broke and he stooped to pick up his pack.

"But, Azvald, I'm sorry; I..." It was best for me to be silent.

He waved me off, not willing to say more as we crossed a gurgling silver stream and marched, knees pumping across the deep grasses and flowers of the plush meadow.

We heard the sweet, plaintive squall of the new lambs before we arrived. The ewes were huddled near a pen as their wobbly kids skipped about, taunting their tired mothers. Azvald crouched near a serene ewe and pulled away a suckling lamb, holding the warm, struggling creature in his arms. While he nuzzled it and smiled, its mother looked up placidly, grateful for a brief reprieve.

"Azvald, we need to talk about your visits to our home when Bruna is there," I began.

He said nothing for a long time while he plied the stiff wool of the tiny lamb. He furrowed his brow in thought. "We began to talk in your smithy one day," he said, "and as I told you then, I know you are not from Sardinia. But you did not want to tell me more." He glanced quickly at me, then back to the lamb. "I have said this to you before. By your name and accent, I know you are one of the chosen ones of God from the land of the Son of Man." He continued to caress the lamb.

I waited.

"Lazarus was raised from the dead long ago by the Savior."

With tense watchfulness, I wondered how Azvald would have acquired his knowledge of Yeshu and the writings of the Disciples. Most of the inhabitants of these farms and villages marked their hearths and homes with pagan rune marks. They tacked symbols and stick figures to their barns and fence lines. Devout followers of their gods, they held bonfires heralding the equinoxes and kept shrines or figures tucked into corners of their homes. This practice was no different than anywhere else I had traveled. They talked about their gods like they talked about the weather. Despite some of the things he had said, I assumed that Azvald still followed many of these same ancient rituals.

In a distant village, there was a small abbey with a few monks connected to the Imperial Church in Rome. They would rove throughout the region, but no one paid heed. They were avoided by most, including Azvald and Edulf.

Azvald looked up at me, waiting for a reply.

"I...I do not understand," I said. "Tell me what you are talking about."

"The story of Lazarus raised from the dead," he said. "I despise those monks, and the priests with their finery, their grasping hands, and hungry eyes. I have nothing to do with them." He held the lamb away from him and stared into its eyes. "But I know of the Great Shepherd."

I was astonished. He handed me the writhing lamb and I fumbled with it. Nuzzling it, I hushed its incessant bawling.

"Someone told me the story of the one and ninety-nine." He reached to stroke the lamb as I held it.

"I would very much like to talk with you about this Savior, as you say, one day, but I wanted to talk about Bruna...."

"Yes, I know," he said, looking up at me from the lamb. "I am careful when speaking of what I believe," he continued. "There are many men from many beliefs in the world today. We must be careful how we speak."

He lifted the lamb back from my arms. I thought he was trying to evade.

"I was this one." He nodded at the innocent creature. "Helpless. But the Lamb of God rescued me. I had heard of him in our meetings. We have meetings when we can—away from the Imperial Church and the monks. I have not told you because we are...cautious. But we have texts; the words of God that we share among ourselves. The robed ones in their churches do not share this Word with those who attend their *masses*. Like pagans the monks have their ceremonies or *masses*, but we do not. The monks perform their show then keep the Word for themselves."

"Bruna is concerned about..." I began.

"There is another story from the old texts," he said. "An old prophet confronted the king, David. You know King David?" he asked.

I nodded, exasperated.

"Of course, you do." He smiled. "Anyway, this prophet pressured the king because David had taken another man's wife. In fact, King David had become so selfish and wicked in his lust that he was going to kill the woman's husband so he could have her all to himself. He sent that poor man into battle so he would be killed. Can you imagine that?" He shook his head. "The prophet told the king that what he had done was like taking a precious lamb from a poor family and slaughtering it for his own feast." He held up the lamb and met its gaze again.

Clutching the lamb to his chest, Azvald turned to look across the valley. I waited, unsure what I should do until he looked at me again. He pawed a tear from his grizzled face. "I lost my wife and daughters because of stupid carelessness and because I caused myself to be separated from them when I should have been near them." He looked down, hesitating until he took a deep breath and sighed; then he plunged ahead. "Then I took Valda for myself. I robbed her maidenhood before her marriage to Laerke." He looked up to me again. "Then along came Bruna," his voice cracked, he smiled, "my little lamb. It pained me enormously to leave her with Valda after losing my own, but it was my punishment." He took the lamb and laid it by its mother. It rooted and suckled with rhythmic murmuring.

He laid his hand on my shoulder. "I lost my lambs; I took another man's lamb—Valda—and was given another. But Bruna is a lamb I can never hold, and she can never know I am her father and that I love her. It would destroy her family—and maybe yours. I accept Valda's wrath. It is more than just. I will not cause her pain just so I can receive a pardon. There is that sin that can be buried, but the stench is always there. It is up to a Shepherd greater than I to resolve it." He withdrew his hand from my shoulder and looked toward the meadow. "And I will live with Bruna's disdain in the same way. May there one day be a way for me to seek forgiveness from all of them for all I have done."

We walked back across the field silently until he stopped. "I do not know who you are or where you have been, Lazar, but I know you are a good man, who plies a good trade, and you will take good care of my little lamb." He shook his stubby finger. "But you must *never* tell her."

"Of course, Azvald."

"I will no longer visit unless invited by Bruna, except...."

"Yes?" I asked.

"When the little ones come, can I...?"

"Of course." I smiled, and hesitated, not sure if I should tell him. "And with that, you must know, friend, that it *is* lambing season. Even now, as we speak."

Azvald began to turn away but snapped back when he realized what I was saying. He grinned broken teeth and crinkled cheeks, and punched my shoulder. "Ha! Congratulations, Lazar. You will be a good father. A good father!"

"Thank you." I paused. "But I'm curious." I was afraid to press further, but I felt the moment had opened a door and he had made me enormously curious. "Are you a follower of The Way, Azvald? I never heard you speak of religion."

"Oh friend, I am not religious. How I despise religion! Religion enslaves us." He shook his head gravely. "The monks, the priests are all circus performers, jugglers, and dancing bears. I meet the Lord out here, Lazar." He swept his hand across the landscape. "The same place that you do. Right?"

I nodded slowly, not sure how to respond. I felt my life being carefully peeled away and exposed again, and I was grasping to hold onto anonymity.

"But you will be a good father, Lazar. You just wait." He smiled.

There would be no reason for me to explain to him how miserably I had failed at marriage and fatherhood in the past. There was no reason to reveal anything more. I resolved at that moment that I would do better, and I would take care of Azvald's lamb. This little lamb that brought me such joy and laughter.

XVI. Bruna

Never deflect love.

I had walled myself off and forgotten happiness. After those brutal, lost years ending on Sardinia with the loss of my feisty Nuragic princess, my heart was laid up behind walls of stone as solid as those built by my Judean father. Bruna was love and happiness unsolicited and unexpected. I shouldered into this life with all my strength and with a heart restored to receive love. It was as though I was hearing the echo of my sisters' laughter down through the ages.

We dwelt on the edge of Azvald's land, and we also remained on the edges of his small gathering of believers that met irregularly far from the monks of the Imperial Church. Bruna rarely followed me to the meetings unless we met in the home of one of her friends. There she loved to sit and listen while the women stitched cloth or fussed over a mound of roots and berries. They were also responsible for stitching together and fussing over those matters of the heart that knit together our small community.

Quietly entering and quietly leaving, I would also sit apart at the meetings. I was there to slake my soul's thirst with deep draughts of their simple faith—and with a few draughts from their foamy jars of dusky ale. Their gatherings were unpretentious, seamlessly moving from chatter about the fickleness of the weather and the cost of grain to discussions of the fickleness of faith and the cost of the Gospel in this land far removed from towering basilicas and squirming cities. A reading or prayer was often interrupted by the bleating of a ewe chasing its wayward lamb through the tiny assembly or a snorting hog offering its objections to Azvald's ramblings. Disputes were common, and often not settled until the next meeting or until a fellow believer needed help calving or winching a stray cow out of the muck.

They carried shreds of written scripture—one or two of them had the ability to read—but they held volumes of simple faith fed by years of loyal adherence to the truth. In my mind, I stitched and fussed like the women, working threads into my tattered soul to reestablish a crude truce with my faith and a renewed peace with Yeshu.

I avoided reading when we were assembled, but I listened, controlling my sweet sadness as faces of those I had left centuries before emerged through the scraps of transcribed words from the Disciples' letters and gospel accounts. However, I willingly participated with them in one of the two rituals they retained: the commemoration of the Passover Supper held by Yeshu and the Disciples. This, along with baptism, were their only rituals. "This is my body broken for you," one of the men would declare as the coarse, crusty loaf crunched and crumbled in his hands, breaking apart just as Yeshu's body had been crushed. The man would pass the loaf to all assembled, and they would break off a piece and eat it, a symbol of incorporating the body of Yeshu into the tissues of their bodies so that the sacrifice of his body would substitute for the sacrifice of their own bodies. In the ritual, we were each made one with Yeshu again.

Then the man would take a cup of ale. "This is my blood poured out for you. Take and drink." The men and women would drink, and the frothy fluid would enter their bodies and flow through their veins like his: a symbol of their blood becoming like his blood. These Believers, generation upon generation, were being knit together by his sacrificed flesh and blood into the one body of all the Believers throughout time and across the world.

Long days were rolled into years working in my beloved smithy, lost in reverie. While nestled on the northern shield of the world, vivid memories drifted back as I labored. Bruna and our children would flit in and out while farmers or woodsmen would sidle in to discuss their work or to help me design a tool to fit their task.

I would think about my father while I worked. Though he had been a mason by trade, he had been resourceful—a trait he bestowed upon his children. As a young man he figured it would be easier and more profitable if he did not have to pause for the carpenter to frame a door or wait on a smith to fashion a hook-latch or peg-hinge. He acquired the tools and taught himself carpentry and smithing skills so he could finish his stonework and move on to the next project. There had been no shortage of stone in Bethany, so he was able to build a sizable shop that contained all he needed for his masonry tools, but also had room for a small work bench and simple forge. Fresh pine and the odor of charcoal beneath the patter of rain are my ancient memories of that shop where he allowed us—my sisters included—to spend hours creating our ideas and building our simple inventions. Though our little creations were little more than sticks and tacks, skills acquired by simple experimentation were among the most precious things he gave me. They have always served me well. Of course, I allowed our children the same use of my tools and smithy—with much cautious instruction under Bruna's stern brow.

As I worked in my shop, another precious memory often returned to me: Yeshu's hands. Should not this single memory alone have sustained me through all my years of wandering and debauchery? In my childhood home, among my family and sisters, I had watched the hands that wrought the universe: dirt under his cracked fingernails, hammer in one hand, chiseling a curve into a corbel that would support a simple shelf for my mother.

Thanks to my delightful Bruna, life in the north had grown into a melody sung sweetly. On this great continent, much that remained of the Roman forces were ghosts and stony walls covered in ivy. There were seasons when armies and tribes terrorized the continent from every side. Since then, I have heard of the Huns, the Vandals and Visigoths, Goths and Ostrogoths, but that was history, not our day-to-day life. Tucked into a corner of the world, we eked out a generation or two of respite amid a roiling world. Somehow, our daily lives survived for a season.

Not that we were not threatened. And more than I care to remember. But I used all my father's resourcefulness, and the resourcefulness of Azvald, our village, and that of the surrounding communities, to survive.

And our little family thrived.

Bruna was uniquely lovely. I do not mean she was not a beautiful woman, but her loveliness eclipsed a sense of feminine beauty. A strong woman by any measure, not large, but strong.

I relish my memory of her. I would watch her bathing. Beautifully sculpted shoulders, her upper arms moving over her breasts as the muscles between her shoulder blades and beside her spine would flex under fair, damp skin. I loved that her name meant "brown," while her skin was as pink and lush as sunrise.

Her firm shoulder and arm would be delicately exposed while a small, red-haired melon rooted and whimpered at her breast until comforted into squeaks and sighing hums. I touch that infant's soft head and Bruna's firm shoulder in my dreams.

In time I had built—*we* had built—and expanded our fine farm on the land Azvald had provided. Located on the village outskirts, we could fence a small, adjoining field to allow room for larger gardens and a few pigs, sheep, and cattle.

Our village was strong. Our long house, supplies, and central homes were well fortified by berms and pole fences. But to stay safe, we each needed our own strategy for fending off raiders and thieves until our well-armed community could arrive to defend us. Azvald was one of several competent warriors. Edulf and many of the young men might be away much of the year voyaging and trading, but when they were settled into farming during the summer, we became a trained and efficient force.

I had been the dark-skinned blacksmith and mason who had taken one of their women for his wife. As they became more comfortable with me, I was able to share with them a few of the fighting skills I had learned from Mila and the Nuragic warriors.

But despite all that preparation, an occasional gang or marauder could slip between the farms to carry off livestock, metal, women, or whatever they could wrestle.

In those years, Bruna and I enlarged Azvald's shepherd hut into a fine wood and stone house with a broad thatch roof. We appointed it with simple but well-crafted features. It was not ostentatious, to avoid attracting raiders or envy, but it was adequate and well-built. My smithy was a stone building attached to the house so we could bask in the heat from the small forge in winter or use it in autumn to preserve and dry food. Two small barns with stick fences circled behind the house to form a courtyard. We had built a separate small barn nearby that kept the stench and mess of the pigs and our old she-goat away from our house.

Hanging on the wall near the door to our house and slung on the pig barn was a small collection of my quality shields and axes. I also tied a few scraps of metal or wood to the thatch. It was like hanging a signboard, but I also had hopes that these items would seem valuable to raiders and distract them from those things of real value to me: Bruna and our children.

If the raiders came, they would take what they wanted anyway, but maybe, if they were attracted to my craftsmanship, I had a chance to bargain, and we had a chance to survive. I gambled that they would not be as likely to "kill the bird that laid the golden egg" as they said in the east. Azvald said "kill the goat that shat silver," but "golden egg" sounded a bit more palatable as I explained it to my children. As a further distraction to marauders, I poorly hid small caches of silver or metal just in case they were not satisfied with the decoys of shields and metal scraps. Honed during my years with Nuragic warriors, I used strategies of bait, distraction, and defense.

It had been a normal day. Bruna worked in the house with our little Lazar and Swanhilde, their chubby hands in the dough or scuttling under her feet. It had been a cold summer, even for this land, and I was using the cool day to cut up a tree that had blown over in a storm. I needed to restore our wood supply for the following winter, and the forge was always hungry for charcoal.

Suddenly, Bruna sprinted across the yard toward the animal shed with the children crying and thrashing under her arms.

"Raiders!" she yelled.

"Where?" I cried, looking around frantically but seeing nothing.

"West! Stump Hill!" she called back, already in the shed, the children wailing.

Bruna, ever watchful, had seen them before I did. A small band of raiders was just visible at the crest of the hill. From that distance, I could not tell if they were watching us or looking away until they began moving down the hill: one horse with a rider and four men on foot. Bruna was doing her part in the plan we had devised; it was time for me to do mine.

I should have taken Bruna's warning and sounded an alarm to alert the village, but there was no way to tell who they were, and I admit, I still felt awkward in my adopted community. Foolishly, I did not want to be responsible for a false alarm.

A glance toward the house assured me that my small variety of shields and metal scraps were hanging outside. The men were already halfway down the hill and approaching the meadow. In full view of the raiders, I ran to the base of a drying post set at the side of the yard and flipped over a large, flat stone that lay slightly embedded in the earth. I looked underneath, then dropped it back in place. I pretended to run frantically into the house and back out. I did this again, returning to the stone at the base of the post, lifting the stone, and repeating my charade.

Chasing into the barn following where Bruna had scurried with the children, I hung the axe I was using for wood cutting, assuring that my other axe and long blades were hidden. The children were sniveling nearby in the goat pen, while Bruna had crawled into another pen, shimmied through a hole in the wall, and crawled into the pig run outside.

"Ugh!" she said.

As the raiders closed in, I ran back to the pole and flipped the rock one more time to be certain I had caught their attention while they picked their way around the huts, sheep pens, and fences of our neighbors. Anyone in those sheds would have been defenseless and gone to cover.

The men were not far, fewer than twenty rods, and bounding toward our farm. The man on the horse was out ahead; four men behind veered around the last berms and hedgerows. None appeared to be heavily armed, but two carried shields slung on their backs. If they had helmets they were stowed, and only one of the thugs brandished a long knife. All looked ferocious: wild hair tangled into bones and shells, and thick leather armor hung with battered medallions of tarnished bronze. Slapping on a helmet, the horseman drew a sword. My heart pattered in fear that wavered between keen alertness and god-awful terror. These men were more dreadful than I had imagined, and they could gut us all without a care. As they were bearing down, it was far too late to sound an alarm. They would kill us and flee. A last time I looked desperately from field to field, to see if any other farmer or villager might be sprinting to our defense. But I had been foolish to wait so long. All that was left was for me was to fall to my knees as they clomped into the yard.

"Get up, filth," the man on the horse said while sliding deftly off his horse and stepping forward in a single fluid movement. The shields and metal work on the house glinted in the light.

"You know how to use those?" He pointed with his chin and spoke Saxon with a lisp between rotted teeth. I glanced quickly at the crude tattoo roughly shaped like a bird, possibly a beaver, etched on his cheek. I dared not make eye contact.

"Oh, no, lord. I am but a simple tinker banished to this land," I pleaded, "to this dung heap of a farm. I make these shields to remind me of the man I used to be." I bowed, hoping my broken Saxon accent would not draw more attention.

He said nothing. That was good. He walked over, took down one of the shields, while the others looked from me to the horseman. I prayed they would keep their distance. From half way across the yard, they smelled like horse dung and rancid pork.

"Then you will not mind if I relieve you of a couple of these bad memories of the man you used to be." He sniffed, running his tongue over his gums. I was quite certain I was about to be skewered. "And do not call me a lord, pig piss."

"No, master," I said.

One of the other men lifted the last shield from the house and lashed it to the horse. Another was looking in the house; he turned to the horseman and shook his head. They were looking not for treasure alone; they were looking for flesh.

"Mem, Mem," Swanhilde cried.

I squinted shut my eyes and wilted.

At first, I thought they had not heard. But just as my hopes were growing, their faces changed.

"Mem, Mem," my little Swan whimpered again.

They froze. The horseman dropped his hands to his side and squinted at me. "So where is Mem, Mem, tinker? We did not see sign of a woman's work as we rode up, and it does not look like you have your sow in the hut."

"Mem! Mem!" both toddlers squalled.

The horseman headed toward the shed, glanced back at his men with a smile, lifted a brow, and turned on his heel in a clumsy jig. The others chuckled and started to follow.

I held back for a desperate instant. "Oh, no, master. I fear that you would be offended. I am not a fool. I know I would have no choice but to offer you my wife; it is just that...."

The others had already overtaken the horseman. He cuffed one of them to back off. They leaned into the barn while I stood, looking over the shoulder of the one most foul-smelling at the back of the pack.

Lazar and Swanhilde were huddled in the goat pen, inches from the distended and dripping udder of old Wixxie, our she-goat. I was certain these raiders had little use for screaming, coughing, soaked-pants babes. I could hope they were not so wicked they would kill my tots.

I trusted our plans were working, or he would have killed me when he took the shields.

Confused, the raiders looked at the children while one pushed by me, shaking his head as he left, heading for the pig pen at the side of the barn.

"God of thunder!" came his cry as he rounded the corner.

I stepped back and the others piled out the door, toward the side of the building where a tattered pen was built of sticks and vines. Bruna's portion of the plan was working. I checked the axes on the wall, prepared to take advantage of her diversion to overcome the raiders while they were distracted.

There in the pen lay Bruna. She was mumbling incoherently, staring into the sky like a blind woman, while covered in pig muck from head to toe. She squealed so that it frightened the two young sows tramping next to her in the pen. I had to look away, but not before she shoved a hefty lump of dung and mud into her mouth and let it dribble away. I wish I had never seen that. She squealed again and lunged at the fence. The raiders jumped and continued to back away.

The horseman elbowed one of his men, a big man, and nodded toward the pen where the two sows were cowering. The big man and another slid around to the back of the fence, keeping their distance, then suddenly hurdled forward, snatching at one of the pigs. Bruna was not slow. She nearly caught one of the men's arms in her teeth, and I thought he was going to cuff her, but the big man was able to reach past her, grasp one of the sows by the ears, and scrabble it out of the pen. Bruna squealed as loudly as the pig.

With more noise and commotion, they killed the young sow and flopped it over one of my shields strapped to the horse. While they secured the load, I could not escape the hint of pity in their eyes as they looked from the shed to the pen, then back to me.

I lost two shields, but the horseman made a deal with me to make a few shields and weapons for them, assuring me their next visit would not leave us unharmed if I did not. I meekly bowed and debased myself as much as possible. I could not help but think he made the deal as a clumsy condolence. They knew they could never attempt to raid the same farm or village twice. In addition to losing my shields, I also had a dead sow—but a living family—for now.

Raiders, who had probably spread rape, ruin, and bloodshed, and who had seen every side of human debauchery, were somehow flummoxed by a poor tinker whose children had to nurse from a she-goat while their mother wallowed in a pigsty.

As they drifted away from the farm, my legs were shaking uncontrollably. I saw Bruna reach for the top of the fence to peer over. I glanced back toward the raiders. Suddenly, the horseman turned and said something to the youngest man. The man shook his head. Quickly, the horseman cocked his fist, delivering a sharp crack to the young man's jaw. He fell to the ground, struggling. Bruna ducked back into the pen and the children were quiet.

The horseman and one of the men jogged to the pole where the flat stone lay. *Damn*, I said to myself. The man lifted the rock, and the horseman bent a knee to scoop up a small box. Undoing the latch, he opened the lid, snatched a leather sack from within, and clawed out the ragged metal scraps. He looked up at me, smiled, stood, and hefted the sack in his hand before slipping it into the horse pack. I tried to look defeated. They left. I do not know why they never ransacked the house. Apparently, they had seen enough. They would have found a hundred times more if they had bothered to dig deep under the hearth.

But that was not what Bruna and I had planned.

We were proud of our risky scheme. Of course, they never came back for the shields and weapons that the horseman had ordered. Someone probably skewered them for my shields and the sow.

Getting the pig dirt off Bruna was interesting. On most days, Lazar and Swanhilde could be restless and raucous children, but I had never seen them so still and silent, brows pinched in confusion, Swanhilde sucking her thumb, while they watched us that day. My wife just laughed her great muscular laugh that I loved. After the third scrubbing, a trip to the creek, and a lavender rub, she was almost new.

That night I held her, and by holding her, I held my family. I felt warm, full, and grateful. She was precious. A tiny waft of pig smell, but precious. She turned away from me and lay on her side. I heard her sniffle and felt her gently shaking. She would sniffle, cover her mouth, then shake again. Feeling badly for her and the serious threat she had endured for her family, I reached over to rest my hand on her lovely, sculpted shoulder, comforting the mother of my children. In a low quiet voice, so as not to wake our children sleeping nearby, she squealed like a little pig and her shoulder shook again—in laughter. I punched her lightly on the back before turning her over and rolling on top.

Beautiful salmon swam in the creek above the farms. In the days following, I wandered along the path to check my fish-weir. I had strolled along this path countless times, often with little Lazar in tow, skipping, his incessant talk causing the birds to hush and take notice. Today, I looked up toward the towering peaks and across lush valleys sketched in sparkling streams, inhaling the pine and clover scents.

There is the great and silent voice that calls us to return. I was not smitten like Paul by a flash that would knock me off a Judean donkey or by the bolt of revival I sought in a distant monastery. Instead, as gently as if my little Swanhilde were placing her tiny hand in mine to lead me to a butterfly, I was being led back to one I had abandoned. Despite the blessings I had witnessed, I had been unable to reconcile the God of despair in the ancient scriptures, or the God of destruction whom I had witnessed sweep away innocence in the horror that was Alexandria with the gentle goodness I had beheld in Yeshu and that I now beheld in men like Azvald and in my dear family. I had thought for a time that Yeshu was gone, yet in these dear people, I saw his face again.

On a morning when all the world was pink and frosty with a stillness that could have been shattered with a breath, I stopped at an overlook. I stood there with my son, able to hush him for a moment to point out the features on the mountain that we called Old Man Mountain. Though I was often inadequate as his teacher, Lazar was incessantly inquisitive. He had lived in this land nearly long as me and was learning its language better than I had.

Until mid-summer when its snow-swept pinnacles melted into silver rivulets across its bare shoulders, Old Man Mountain's snow-swept pinnacles were uninhabitable except to the mountain goat. Across its broad chest was a vest of alpine green dotted with crystal lakes reflecting rocky crags, stark cliffs, and sharp spires misted by waterfalls. Sweeping into the valleys, was a broad skirt green with forests.

One mountain, many features. I was learning of one God, many faces.

Restless in my thoughts, I scanned Old Man Mountain from valley to summit and thought of Joshua. He was a mountain goat. He witnessed and participated in gruesome atrocities at the Almighty's discretion. He saw Yahweh both vicious to defend and loyal to care for his people. Joshua's faith may have been shaken but endured. He understood not only what he saw; he also had faith in what he could not see or in what he could not understand of Yahweh. Joshua had not seen and did not need to see the entire mountain to believe.

I had pretended to know of God's character based solely on my narrow perceptions. I have seen much, but I have not seen all. What I had seen was the cold and windswept reaches of the mountain, while here with Bruna, I found myself once again dwelling in the green and fertile foothills.

Too much to ponder on a brief saunter with my dear son along a lovely alpine path. As I stood watching the mountain while Lazar picked up sticks and swung at pinecones, I realized I had become too preoccupied with the flow and span of my life, too focused on somehow deciphering a purpose and a path in a world that is infinitely mysterious and complex. I had insisted on knowing. But we are adrift in a universe of boundless complexity that we cannot know, and that we may never fathom.

I looked back up to Old Man Mountain and reminded myself of something more: We are never the mountain. Throughout much of my life, I had put myself, my needs, and my understanding at the center. We are not the center of creation. We are merely a stone, a weed, a flake of snow on the face of the mountain, a tiny chip in the corner of the mosaic of creation, never the centerpiece. We are part of an infinite panorama with Another at its center. At best, we are a mere sketch inspired by the love between Yeshu and the Father.

Arriving at the fish-weir, we waited for salmon to waggle into my rickety weir while I continued to whittle my life down to the heartwood, the essence. Just as in the mundane life of the salmon, which finds its way upstream from the ocean, I considered the utter routine and smallness in my life. For the salmon there is birth, migration, spawn, and death. We are distracted by the vastness, yet God has layered all the world, deep with ordinary life. In this, he has granted holiness to the world. The small life possesses holiness.

A kernel of truth had been planted, but unknown to me, it would take root at another time in other soil.

The fish smacked together as we hefted them over our backs with a sound that assured me that Bruna would be pleased with fresh fish for supper and plenty for the drying racks. Our damp leather footings, laced to the knee, skittered on the trail through gravel. The sun hung omnipotent above all and over Old Man Mountain.

Lazar slipped his hand into mine.

XVII. Warriors

Young men, their foolish hearts never pierced by sword or spear are soon enticed by the whore of battle; her face painted red with blood, her flaccid thighs yawning as filthy fingernails dig into their backs, pulling them nearer to her breasts, sagging from centuries of suckling hate.

First arrive the enemy raiders, who test our weaknesses, and in return are taunted by our young fools. As months or years unfold, raiders give way to enemy scouts, scouts lead the squadrons, and squadrons lead armies.

Reluctantly, I was soon conscripted to make weapons. The inevitability of war was becoming tragic and overwhelming. We would be compelled to go to the enemy, or they would soon come to us—to our farms, our women, and our children. I was enthralled by how easily corpse breath and slaughter could seduce these young men—and alter the contours of our peaceful existence.

As often happens, this festering boil came to a head by a single event. We knew the Norsemen were camped to the east and that they had raided several farms and villages like the renegades had done to our homestead several years distant. But this time, these raiders were not going to be placated by a few shields and a wife feigning slobbering insanity.

In the beginning, these raiders were merely stealing a few chickens, prying metal scraps off a barn door, or worrying the women. Soon, they would no longer be content with a few birds and scraps of metal. If they were not challenged, they would begin raids to steal cattle, invade our homes, and steal our wives and daughters. One bold provocation was so heinous that even the most peaceable or cowardly among us would soon be stirred to act.

A small settlement surrounded by a wide berm and a tall post fence had grown where six or seven families scratched out a comfortable existence. This extension of our community, in the foothills within sight of our farms, had been started by two of our young men together with a few men who had migrated from other villages and married into our families. They were within our trade circle and were a part of our simple defenses and militia.

One night, just past sunset, in the firelight of our quiet home, Bruna was preparing jars of food to bury for storage, and I was showing young Lazar how to polish blades to sparkle like quicksilver. He had grown nearly to my shoulder and was a loyal brother to graceful Swanhilde and the other two tots who had been added to our litter: Ansgar and Aletta. Bruna and I had been magnificently blessed not to have lost any children. That was uncommon. Though Swanhilde had nearly died of a fever and Lazar of a festering injury, they had survived. For the young, disease and death were sad playmates throughout the world.

Despite his early years, Lazar's serenity and intellect was as compelling as Swanhilde's beauty and intensity. I relied on him as counselor and interpreter. His mother taught him more about custom and language than my thick head and tongue had been able to master. His character reminded me of his aunt Mary, my dear sister. As much as Lazar may have been like Mary, Swanhilde was like Martha. Her lips were set and scolding while she bustled around our house, or while clutching her skirts as she stomped about the pens marshalling her small herd of sheep. And like Martha, she was devoted to her siblings and shepherded them like a mother hen.

From outside in the darkness, our quiet evening was ripped by a banshee howl. Hairs stood on the back of my neck. Bruna scattered to pull the children close as the horrible wailing crept nearer.

"What is that?" Bruna hissed, clutching the wide-eyed children.

I grasped the handle of a blade we were sharpening, hustled Bruna and the children into the corner, and tipped a table to shield them. The dreadful sound was circling toward the village. This was not a wolf, lynx, or wounded wisent wandering in the night. I slowly unbarred the door and opened it a crack, my eyes adjusting to darkness. Men with torches were streaming from their homes. Lazar slid beside me with his small blade in hand while Bruna sat the other children against the wall, shaking her finger for them to stay, their worried mouths frowning, owl eyes staring. She lit a candle, handed me the lamp, and peered over my shoulder.

In the pale evening glow that rimmed the horizon, we were able to make out a scuffle circled by torchlight. A woman, her apron and hands bloodstained, cried, "Alfurd, Alfurd!" I had heard that voice in every nightmare since Alexandria, carried on every dark breeze and in the call of every night creature: a mother's cries for her dead child.

Bruna looked back at the children, pointed another stern finger at them, and then pushed past me. "I will help; you stay," she said to me.

Bruna's sister, Uma, was first to reach the grieving woman. Uma crouched, her arm encircling the woman's shoulders while two men met them with torches. Blindly, the collapsed woman looked around and muttered. They were able to shepherd her to Uma's house, where dim light from an open door enfolded them. Under the moonless night, beneath a canopy of crisply blinking stars, gusts of cold breath huffed from the lips of the few villagers and farmers milling about, murmuring, their flickering torches falling on worried faces. Over the mountains flared the fearsome Auroras—sunrise winds—as Markos and the Greeks had described to me. I had never seen them in my sailing days in the south. While in the north, I had seen them infrequently on brilliant, clear nights. They were always an omen to the villagers, who thought they were sparks from the tail of the Fire Fox.

On a night like this, the fearful sign reminded me of the pulsing destruction I had seen wrought by the dreaded and capricious Immortals in Egypt. Foreshadows of doom, the lights in the night sky slowly danced, spreading and flowing like green and red angel gowns, hems skirting the mountains and reaching upward, beyond the stars and swirling to the horizon tracing the curve of the earth.

In the night, Bruna returned from Uma's home. I had checked the barns and smithy and sent the twittering children to bed. They peered down from the loft and from their mats near the hearth as she hustled in, clutching her shawl. She sighed, her lip quivering. I had rarely seen her this fraught. Bruna told me that before the desperate, wailing woman had collapsed into a stupor, they learned she was from the new settlement near the foothills and her beloved child had been torn apart by terrible beasts. The children gasped and scuttled back to their mats.

By the middle of the night, everyone in the village had returned to their homes. Men, armed and nervous, checked their barns and pens, then pulled shutters and barred the doors.

At first light, the woman's family arrived. They had spent the night looking for her and thought she had wandered into the mountains. They told what had happened to the child, Alfurd.

Late in the afternoon, the boy of five or six summers had wandered to the outside of the berm to play. On a fine day, children would often roll their toy carts—or their giggling bodies—from against the fort walls and down the sloping berm, or they would play with battalions of stick soldiers in the loose dirt. Because of recent vandalism by the raiders and the general unrest, the villagers had been wary, though not terribly concerned, as long as the children did not wander out of earshot. They could not have prepared for what would happen to little Alfurd.

Before a watchman could jump, three great Roman Alaunts had bounded into the clearing. These monster dogs of war had been legend, never seen, but feared by everyone. The Norsemen had taken a fancy to these beasts and adopted, bred, and trained them to hunt and kill not only wolves and bears, but also men. They were chimeras created in hell. For speed, their hind quarters were narrow and willowy as whippets, yet their chests and shoulders were built like bulls. Slavering lion's jaws were set in black and brown heads as broad as an ox. A small pack of Alaunts could stave off a detachment of warriors. How these Norse raiders had secured these dogs was unknown. It is doubtful they would have risked bringing them on their ships.

As innocent as a kitten, the child had frozen in terror as the dogs attacked. As he squealed, all the men and boys spilled from their huts and barns, falling upon the animals, stabbing and hacking. Several other men split off to chase the raiders who had been trailing the dogs. Fleeing into the hills, the marauders left, whistling to the dogs that loped behind, limping and bleeding, dragging remains of the child who had been eviscerated and ripped limb from limb. The men were left to gaze, stunned, at what lay before them on the gory berm. As darkness fell, the mother had wandered off, dazed in grief, searching for her little boy's remains.

The call to take up weapons was inevitable. This spark lit the dry tinder that had been piling up for years.

Days later, despondent, I hugged Bruna and the children.

"Where are you going, Papa?" Lazar asked, his chin up, black hair sheltering riveting black eyes. "Can I come? I have my wee blade."

"Not this time, my young man. Your mother needs a man here for a time." I placed my hand on his head. He narrowed his eyes in resolve, with a quick nod accepting his charge. He had much of his mother's resourcefulness. He would be fine.

"Will you bring me a lamb?" asked Swanhilde. She had her grandfather's red hair, Bruna's cheeks, and my dark eyes. Uncharacteristically pensive, she hugged my waist and pressed her cheek against my side.

I laughed despite myself. "If I can find a lamb, you shall have it."

Bruna carried the toddler, Ansgar. I kissed his dirty cheek while he distractedly sucked his thumb. The baby, Aletta, crawled on the floor, her chubby little fingers pinching at crumbs. She whined and wiggled when I picked her up to kiss her while inhaling her sweet and musty baby scent, tears brimming my eyes.

I reached for Bruna and hugged her near, nuzzling my wife's hair and taking in her clean aroma, laced with the odor of breakfast cakes and lard. I slid my hands across her soft shoulders and down her firm back to rest on her graceful hips. This was a moment we had dreaded but knew may arrive eventually to every hearth.

We both asked unspoken questions: When would I come back? Would I come back? What would come next for this family and for me? It was time to shut the heavy, wooden doors of my mind and drop the bar before I could ask myself the most relevant question: Could I be killed, surrender this endless life, and what horror would I endure before dying?

Mila, my bold princess, had taught me how to prepare, but her lesson was not needed. It comes to the mind and heart of each warrior. That morning, I had to force my thoughts deep inside myself, to a place of bleak indifference where I could feel nothing. I should have been good at this.

But I was not.

I knew this tortured feeling. Which face of God would he reveal? Which wilderness reach of Old Man Mountain? God was once again silent, while my life, my family, my hopes became as expendable to him as little Alfurd. This tiny hamlet had been loosened and set adrift down a cold, deadly river. It was beyond senseless: the death of this child, the theft of my life again by a ridiculous battle, and the loss to fate of my innocent family. The utter capriciousness of God: a hollow din reverberating across the universe. The eternal *why*. A season of happiness offset by a lifetime of desperation. No one can know him.

I was angry in my heart, but as Bruna and I released our embrace and I touched her fingertips, I looked at our home, expecting to see the line of gold painted by Martha around that house with Miriam long ago. No gold ribbon encircled this house. It did not need to. I felt somehow inexorably, blissfully, forever married to Bruna and this family.

Maybe it was dishonest to withhold the truth of my agelessness. Did I believe that if I did not speak it, I could forget and live a mortal's life? I rationalized I would tell her one day. No one would suspect for many more years. I had determined that this time I would devise a way to live on without walking away. I would not repeat what I had done with Miriam.

I felt seething and callous as I joined the other men where paths ran together. When I saw Azvald, he silently nodded and hefted his shield. I did not want to edge near him to hear pithy words of faith.

We learned that a large contingent of Norsemen had come upriver with two or three ships and established their main encampment about twelve miles away. We would join up with a band of nearly thirty men from a settlement we called Roman Town. Originating mostly from this region of the continent, they had been former conscripts of the Roman army who had peeled away from Rome as the empire's grip loosened. They had returned to their homeland to establish farms and families, keeping mostly to themselves because of their bond of battle and the stigma of having been Roman soldiers. I would sell an occasional sword or plowshare to them, while Azvald traded wool. A rumor had spread that the dogs of war that had killed Alfurd belonged to them. But those of us who had been in their village knew it was not true. They were good men who had shunned Rome in every way except for the small monastery they had built outside their village.

Their settlement was closer to the Norse than ours, but they had fended off the enemy with skill and training. We were grateful to be allies as we formed a deft band of warriors.

The Norse maintained their camp near their ships but had been running incursions of five to ten men into the region, scouting for plunder. They had been less a threat than a nuisance, until a few successful forays emboldened them. When their dogs killed the boy, we were stirred to action. We had become united in the grim reality that they must be pried from our land before more ships arrived.

Surrounding our fires, the night before battle, we sung none of the bawdy choruses or carnal odes that were sung around our circles at elk or bear hunts. One mirthless man gazed into the flame, offering a sweet lyric about a man who wished he had been a better husband to his young wife, while pining for his brave sons and lovely daughters.

As the fires burned to embers, some never slept. Others, their heads would bobble and drop onto a knee as they slept in tortured snatches from which they would awaken, wild-eyed and sweating.

Still other men would slip away from the fire, fall into a heap, pulling their cloaks around their shoulders, and sleep as stupid as a house puppy, legs pumping, arms twitching, and hands clutching. They might awaken for a moment, look around quickly, and fall asleep again to snore and fart, unfazed as drunken kings.

Edulf's young son, Gustof, moved among the camp in the morning, jostling the sleepers. Most of us were awake, buckling and fitting cobbled and dented armor while securing our weapons. There was little talk, only the squeak of leather or the occasional, careless dull ring of metal on metal. The men sniffed or coughed, trying to summon courage from the fact that they had breath.

Gnawing at a hank of dry meat or black bread, we moved toward assembly while others scattered into the brush where they shat or pissed. As we formed ranks, some would bump shoulders, slap another on the back, grab an arm, or parry with swords. The mindless men who had slept like dogs were the first to chatter. Or maybe they were mindful, having found the way to quiet their terror.

Our chief was Azvald's nephew, Gunther, who had proved a competent general. I had imparted to him what little I knew, and he had been wise to spend days in Roman Town learning strategy and technique from former legionnaires. Without another word, he pointed a sword west and we departed. We did not march or form ranks, nor did we cheer or sing valiant war chants. We stumbled away in the deep gray, following Gunther in a scattered line.

As they trudge toward their fate, men daydream of battle: finding an opening in the line and rushing forward to kill twelve men, or taking the head of the enemy's captain, or dodging the mighty sword of a champion, while twisting, crouching, and springing up to sever his hand. And war-mates cheer them on. They envision the kill: that moment when a sword skims off an enemy's breastplate and plunges under the arm, through to the heart. They sweep from their minds that same moment when another sword skims their ribs and drives through a lung into their own heart. But I shake my head, place a thumb under the edge of my leather breastplate, and lift it closer under my sweating arms.

The mountain valleys poured onto wide flats of rich farmlands and brushy, winding swamps, scattered with hummocks and bogs. This would be our battlefield.

Two bands of raiders had settled together in a clump of trees surrounded by wetlands. If we could destroy them, it would trim their forces by a sizable number, and protect our farms from raids until we could reach their main encampment near their ships at the river.

From the patch of island squatting at the center of the marsh, our enemy could overlook the mucky expanse of tall grasses and reed mace while hiding in branches of spiky spruce. We had to draw them out to slaughter, or we would be decimated by spears and arrows long before we reached their brushy fortress encircled by hazel and alder.

As Gunther, Azvald, and others whispered strategies to address the challenge, I slid beside to offer a suggestion for a strategy I had witnessed on Sardinia. My small warrior wife had been adamant that one of her most reliable weapons was not blades or arrows, but simply the impulses and eagerness of young men. In this land, I regretted that we did not conscript our Saxon women into our ranks. The perceptiveness and rational fear of woman warriors had been indispensable on Sardinia. In training or in battle, Mila, disadvantaged by size, used the foolishness of young men to raise her stature. The Norsemen would be introduced to the strategy of a Sardinian princess.

Early morning, more than fifty left our camp. Fifteen or twenty of the men from Roman Town had split away to engage with a band that had been harassing their village. Led by Gunther, our remaining troops had halted in the scrub and forest far from the tuft of trees that stood at the center of the marsh. The enemy had raided the day before, so we were convinced they would lay low today, hiding out, while they drank and counted their spoils, preparing to raid again in a day or two. We had heard that they had taken women, and we feared what other debaucheries could be occurring in that swampy grove.

It was early as we silently spread out in a wide half circle in the forest, overlooking the open foreground of marsh and grass. We waited. They often expected an attack at dawn, so their guard and their attention would start to diminish by later in the morning.

Our plan was to leave six of our youngest men back while the rest of us crawled and slinked through the grass, often on our bellies, through the cold marsh. Instead of a rapid rout, a Nuragic tactic could be to use grindingly slow patience. We advanced one bunch of grass, one tadpole puddle at a time. Each out of view of the other, like cats pursuing a bird, we were moving too slowly to be seen by their scouts in the trees. This time of year, mosquitoes and flies would have been our most ardent enemies, nearly flaying our flesh until midday when we reached our positions. It had taken us hours to advance unseen a hundred paces.

When we were in place, Gunther, with coarse raven caws, signaled to our young men waiting behind in the forest. In clumsy charade, they stumbled into the swamp, crouching, craning their necks over the grass, crouching again, and approaching the enemy encampment. Jesting and punching like cubs, feigning concealment, splashing in the muck, they slipped past where we lay, toward the enemy island where smoke curled lazily through upper branches of spruce.

Silently concealed, we remained arrayed in a semi-circle behind our jester troop of young men as they advanced.

The Norsemen were more reticent than we had hoped. They eventually sent out four men. The four enemy also tactically feigned concealment. When our boys saw them, they whooped and taunted, pretending they had met the entire enemy encampment and were prepared for combat.

But we were stunned to see our boys scuttle our strategy and rush forward. That was not our plan. They were to hold back, allowing the enemy to come out to them. But during the long hazy morning, as they sat slapping at flies, our boys had time to devise a plan of their own.

We hissed and frantically fanned the grass trying to get their attention.

Our boys had approached fewer than ten rods from the island of trees, dangerously within spear and arrow shot. The small band of four, poorly concealed enemy, confident of the forces behind them, leapt from their scant cover. Our boys abruptly turned on their heels, pretending panic, pumping their knees as they sloshed through mud and hummocks, back toward our hidden crescent of warriors. This caused an explosion of Norsemen from the hazel brush surrounding their encampment. Crashing and splashing, twenty or thirty Norsemen in full battle gear screamed toward our young decoys, water flying as they plunged toward us through grass and mud.

They were among us in seconds. Gunther let loose the heron's cry, and we thrashed from the mud like Nile crocodiles and fell upon the raiders. The young men turned back to fight, and their swords and spears kissed flesh first because the Norsemen had been completely distracted from them by our attack and had no time to respond to an assault from the youth.

My conscious mind fled on bats' wings.

A big, balding man, with twisted braids flying at the sides of his head, wielded an axe, his chest exposed as he lifted his broad weapon. I felt the meaty slice of sword slipping between ribs, through lungs and heart, and saw the sluice of crimson trail behind as I withdrew. The man behind him flailed, as a spear skewered his neck and exited above his collarbone. He groped the dripping spear in front with one hand while attempting to reach back with the other at the shaft held by our young man behind him. The youth kicked the impaled man onto his face, planted his foot in his back, and withdrew his spear. The man moaned and died.

Our side held the overwhelming advantage of surprise and in a few vicious moments, it was over. Several of our soldiers had dashed around to the other side of the island and cut off the few escaping raiders.

The code of the North was death. There was no thought of merely wounding an opponent or allowing them to escape to fight another day. After knifing the last of the whimpering Norsemen, we rushed their camp, where a small band of women and children sat wide-eyed and filthy. The prisoners had been fortunate because we had been able to draw the Norsemen away before we secured victory. The Norse never allowed prisoners to be recaptured alive. For me, at least, the helpless prisoners vindicated our brutal attack. At a minimum, it was something I could hold in my mind to stave bloody memories and soothe my brutal conscious. The memories are tougher to kill than the most combat-hardened enemy. And those memories are the last to fade before sleep and the last to die across eons of time. Never. Even after the mind grows dark and feeble.

We freed the captives, fed them, gave them water, and made them secure with us while we carried off what we could of the stolen possessions the raiders had stowed.

In the days that followed, the enemy's other two flanks were not quite as easy to defeat, but within a couple of days, we had at least stemmed the raids and much of their force had fled toward their main encampment near the river. When more than a week had passed since the battle in the swamp, we were certain we would prevail, and the Norsemen would either be dead or sail away. We were cleaning up the forest of stragglers and chasing them back toward their ships. We all thought we would be in our homes in plenty of time for harvest. For us, casualties had been mercifully small. Gunther and Azvald would have to deliver sad news to one young widow and one old woman who had lost her only son. Several had sustained serious wounds that might hobble them for life; those farmers' families would be dependent on our community.

One of our young men, Valdus, was like a worry-ridden child, terrified of battle, but his father had forced him to join us. He had stolen something, maybe it was no more than a maiden's virginity, but his father had condemned him to march. Edulf, Azvald, and I took a liking to him. He was kind and witty, drew runes on our shields, and reclaimed a raucous mood at our camp when he sweetly sang all twelve bawdy songs the god Ing had sung to his ancient lover Nerthus.

Valdus had joined the three of us as we executed a simple flank maneuver skirting a grove where a small band were rumored to be hiding. But we anticipated that they had fled and there would be no enemy left to fight. It was a simple sweep. Valdus, of course, was frightened, though he had proven himself well in the previous days as we were close to securing our victory. We were in a light mood, convinced triumph was in our grasp.

As we emerged from the forest, angling down the side of a narrow, rocky valley, sliding on scree, we were foolishly exposed. We had allowed ourselves to be cut off from sight of the remainder of the right flank as we slid into a thicket.

Unaware that we were being stalked, we were startled when three of the drooling black and brown Roman Alaunts suddenly leapt from cover. Drawing blades, we crouched reflexively. Valdus squealed as one beast clamped its massive jaws onto his arm and another onto his leg. With stupid smiles, two of the Norsemen's dog handlers slid down the scree into our midst, their grins betraying their confidence in their dog pack and in their lack of readiness. Edulf planted a knee on stone and put an arrow through the neck of one while I lunged, sidestepping around a ravening dog, and took the other raider in the groin. His feet stuttered on the slippery stone, until I withdrew my curved seax from my belt and sliced it across his throat.

The third dog whipped its slobbering jaw toward me and fastened like a vise onto my arm. Edulf swung with his sword and severed its spine below the neck. I shook off its grip and spun while sinking the seax into the heart of the dog on Valdus's arm. Valdus continued to scream, the third beast ripping his ankle. White bone flashed and shreds of flesh hung from his leg. Edulf wrenched his sword out of the dog that had bitten my arm while a third man emerged from the thicket. The sword sluiced out of the dog's flesh in time for Edulf to swing wide, taking out the legs of the third man who now scrabbled and screamed until he was silenced by Azvald's sword to the chest.

A dog was on Valdus's ankle, but Edulf was occupied, my seax was stuck in another of the animals, and my sword had fallen in the scramble. Azvald was distracted, delivering assurances to the bodies of the scouts. I could not find a stick, rock, or any other weapon to lay hold of and beat the animal off the lad's ankle. I slid one hand around the snout of the growling monster and slid my other hand into the corner of its mouth, grabbing the lower jaw. My palm was impaled with lower teeth as the beast shook and snarled. Its head was like a bear, thrashing, eyes wild and unfocused like a shark. I managed to spread the jaws an inch and immediately plunged my bleeding hand as far down the throat as I could. Squinting, my jaw clenched, I pushed farther until I reached the root of the tongue. When it gagged, I shoved my arm all the way to the elbow, deeply scraping my arm on teeth. I squeezed whatever I could find and held on. The beast coughed and thrashed, while dragging me away from Valdus.

Flailing at the dog, I had no idea what to do next until Valdus suddenly rolled over and pulled my seax from the dead dog, then thrust it into the animal wrapped around my arm. He missed the heart. My arm was stuck, and I was pulling away at the dog's innards with all my strength when suddenly it released, and I flew backward. My arm was wearing a dog's head and Azvald was grinning down at me, sword in hand.

"You could have taken off my hand!" I spit.

"It could have taken off your arm," he replied, laughing. "But you make a fine blade!" He looked at his weapon and thrust it in his belt.

Our attention was soon drawn to Valdus, who was whimpering in a strange, wavering inhuman moan, not because of his wounds or the horror of the attack. We followed his line of sight to the edge of the thicket, fearing another attack. By the insane intensity of Valdus's reaction, I feared it must be an army with more men and dogs. But there was neither. It was something far worse.

My mouth went dry, and I steadied myself so I would not collapse in fear. I could not speak or turn to Edulf. As though the Aurora had settled upon us, silver, red, and green light flooded the small clearing on the side of the hill. The air became infused with a metallic odor and the valley thrummed with terrifying whispers, and otherworldly music. There was no army, and there were neither warriors, nor dogs. There were two. The Two: in long robes, trimmed in gold with hands resting on massive swords planted upright before them.

After years, the Immortals had found me again. Their terrible faces roiled as their eyes narrowed, looking at us and through us.

Edulf's last move was to raise his sword while Valdus continued his eerie squeal. I did not see how they had approached, but over the scrabble of stones and brush they drifted, their robes billowing slowly in breezes from another world. My life passed in a flash: I saw Bruna and our children, our farm, our hopes, and our secure life, growing small and receding in murky dusk. *What will happen to them without me?* I pondered. I knew to struggle was futile, and I believed at last, on this northern hillside, I would know the finality of sweet death.

Then a flash, followed by darkness.

XVIII. Slaves

I imagined I had been laid again into the wreaking tomb: The smell of rotting flesh encasing me in moldy shroud. I coughed, gagged, gasping from the odor of death and the grating pain in my ribs. Searing pain wracked my arm and hand from the crushing wounds and gashes left by dog's teeth. I shivered in the bone-shaking cold.

I became aware of others surrounding me in this gray purgatory. Winds whipped the woven walls, snapping and seething like torn sails of a ghost ship. Between gusts, the wheezing moans of other ragged souls swirled in darkness. In this vestibule of hell, I lay, my head splitting, and my chest cleaved in pain. I could not be a frayed ghost if I were tortured by such pain and gagged by foul stench. Even a denizen of hell would be pardoned from torture horrific as this.

As I pondered my desperate situation, an abyss of loss yawned before me: loss more precious than life itself. I knew that wherever I was, however I had arrived there, and whomever it was that held me, it was unlikely I would ever see my Bruna or our children again. As the shroud of despair lowered over me, my loss eclipsed my suffering. In that stark moment, I pictured each of them: strong Bruna; worthy Lazar, already with a temperament more like a man than me; my precious cygnet, Swanhilde, with hair like sunrise and a smile to match; and the babies Ansgar and Aletta. I lay broken, mourning another family lost, more love squandered, and another home I would never see again. I had laid my entire life down for them, but my life had been mercilessly spared. Worse than losing my life, I had lost them.

The tent flap whipped open, and we squinted in blinding light. I cowered, fearing it was the light of the Immortals returning. But it was merely a haggard soldier with fear in his eyes. Frantic, he shouted at us in Norse. Though no one understood what he said, we knew we were prisoners, and we knew he was a captor.

With the point of his spear, he roused the ragged captives slumped near the tent flap and screamed at us in urgent fear. Another soldier stormed into the tent and began wrestling, punching, and pushing until we dragged ourselves out while the tent was clumsily brought down around us. We stood in a whirl of bright light and confusion as soldiers ran here and there and captains shouted.

The six or eight of us were quickly roped together. Many were covered in blood or festering sores. Some had soiled themselves and had been sitting in their filth. A cluster of women, more frightened and abused than us, was dragged before us and led stumbling out of camp. We were captives of the army of Norsemen we had routed, and they were breaking camp in tremendous haste. If I were never to see my family again, at least I had hope that we had secured their safety from this hoard.

Like an arrow out of darkness, I was suddenly possessed by crazy, overwhelming thirst. I did not know how long I had been unconscious. Days? I whipped my head around futilely, looking for any jar or puddle until we were pushed away to follow the flow of warriors.

The darkened sky was streaked red and gray, clouds tumbling toward the horizon. I assumed it was dawn by the motion of the clouds, but it was not obvious to me. We were soon moving at a steady trot, though several were ill or wounded, forcing those bound together to drag or prod the ailing. Movement had loosened my pain, though injured, I shuffled along.

The Norsemen were panicked and did not look back. I had confidence our warriors were not far behind, though our chance for rescue would be slim. If they were alive, I could imagine the faces of Azvald, Edulf, and the others, jaws clenched in stern resolve, weapons hoisted, feet pounding in swift pursuit. But if given the chance, the Norse never allowed prisoners to be recaptured. Our options were hopeless.

When we came to the river, I was able to see the current, look back toward the mountains, and understand where we were. It was not dawn as I thought. The sun was retreating over the horizon.

Hustling down a steep slope, clumsy in our fetters, we sloshed and slipped toward the river where a pod of ships sat near shore. I stumbled and bent as far as I could to take two muddy gulps before being jabbed with a spear shaft in my damaged ribs. I collapsed into the water, writhing in pain, bringing two prisoners with me, who also tried taking frantic gulps of soupy river water. Three Norsemen rushed upon us, and we flinched in expectation of more blows, but our enemies were too frantic. They lifted us out of the water and ran ahead. With shouts and clatter, the soldiers climbed aboard their ships, yanking us over the gunwale, ignoring the wails of the women and our screams from grating bones and gashes torn open again.

With the Norseman's skill, the entire fleet was soon afloat, at oars, and edging downriver away from the bank where my companions were already bustling out of the rushes, too late to rescue us. The Norse had secured their prisoners and were underway. On shore, my companions were left to shout, launch spears that landed short, or shoot arrows that clanked hollow on the hull. The ships had eased farther away. My men stood nearby along the shore, shoulder to shoulder, muddied, many spattered with blood, several holding cracked hickory spear shafts or broken swords. I grieved to watch these good men ebb away. They were not just my brothers in battle; these were my landsmen, the merchants I traded with—my family. I would never see them again. They stared silently at us, we stared silently at them as we lofted away on roiling waters. As though drifting on the river Styx, we gazed across the gulf between life and death, toward family, and all we had known and loved.

The Norsemen were not watching our warriors lining the river. A strange apparition stood silent and more dreadful beneath this red and darkening sky. The men aboard ship chattered nervously, while pointing in fear and awe at what stood far above my fellow warriors on the bank. Frightened, the Norse on board took cover behind the mast or crouched behind the rail. Though they had safely launched and were heading downriver, what they saw made them stutter in greater fear than they could have felt for my shabby kinsmen lining the shore.

On a hill in full view of the Norsemen, but hidden to my countrymen, stood The Immortals, appearing tall as giants, in purple robes trimmed with gold, their drawn swords raised and glinting red in the setting sun. The Norsemen, thinking we had conjured gods from hell to be our champions, feared them as much as me. I alone knew the terrible truth and the horror that might be visited upon my people.

We drifted away, the sun skittering below the horizon as though fleeing along with all the world in mortal fear. Lighting the evening sky were scathing red and green flashes, followed by deep, concussive thuds and the roaring thunder of destruction. I was certain I was seeing my landsmen slaughtered and my family decimated by the Immortals in swift and total retribution.

But why would I presume to know anything? I was nothing. The great pendulum, its pivot far above the heavens, was swinging: Soaring inexorably again from grace to destruction.

I made brutal reckonings and cold calculations. Swiftly, I had been returned to that place where there was nothing to lose. I calculated the Immortals would have slain Azvald, Valdus, and Edulf, or they would be prisoners with me. The flashes and tumult seen in the sky convinced me that either the power of these Immortals was increasing or they had now called upon other minions intent upon destroying our lands, my fellow warriors, and my family. I desperately wanted to be there to throw myself on the swords of those monsters and end these taunts and this hopeless sport. How could God allow such creatures under the sun?

Farther from the mountains, the rivers slowed to serpentine, marshy tributaries, little more than wide streams that led through marsh and muck. The waters, swollen by early season rain, would have been higher when the Norsemen had ventured upriver. The prisoners, including the women, were forced out of ships with whips and spearpoint, to work beside their captors to lift, push, and portage,

Most of us were hobbled by ropes and wounds as we slogged through mud up to our thighs. One of the stinking men of the north, stout, but smaller than the women, was standing back and using his spear point to prod us. He riddled us with nicks to our backs and shoulders. When the women would shriek at the wounding, it would result in lashes from one of the other soldiers. This stunted, ugly pup enjoyed his sadistic game while the other men laughed and hurled insults at the women.

The captain found his way to where we were lifting and prying under the ship and saw the little tramp tormenting us with his spear, impairing the fleet's progress. The captain thumped the little man, sending him sprawling in the mud, which produced howls of laughter from his shipmates. The captain found his way to another ship, while we were left alone to deal with the weasel. He ignored the scoffs of the other men.

Amid our number was a girl who reminded me of my Bruna with her stout shoulders and sturdy frame. We were all struggling despite our pain and weakness, but the little man seemed to target her among all the women. In these circumstances, I did not care much about anyone, but I was desperate to get us far from the Immortals. And the sooner we could get onboard, the less we would all be tortured by the Norse. The way to be done with this miserable work was to move the ships through the mud.

I heard the young woman shriek again; then swiftly, in guttural rage, she grabbed the little man's spear and clipped him neatly across the side of his face, sending him sprawling in the mud again. Everyone stopped, knowing we were about to witness her brutal murder—or worse. When she threw the spear down at their feet, the other sailors laughed and dragged the pointing, sputtering piglet out of the mud. Another stepped up to take the weasel's spear, kicked the fool in the arse, and pointed him toward the other ship. Grinning, the larger man just shook the spear at the girl. We quickly returned to skid-logs, levers, and muck.

Soon the ship was slithering toward open water. The girl grinned to herself as she clambered on board. Raiders were interested in selling their slaves, so she had taken a great risk. But because she had survived, she may have increased her value as a slave and given herself a small chance for a better position off the auction block. Any gamble is worthy when the stakes are hopeless.

By the third day, we had left the marshes and were gliding lazily down the broad river. The farmers on the shore would flee and women would hide amid their fields of grain. But the Northmen were hurrying, intent on leaving this land. Their excursion into our territory had been thwarted, and their plan would be to make a quick trade for slaves and treasure and arrive home ahead of the heavy curtain of winter.

We were kept below deck amid searing stench until not even the Norsemen could stand it longer. They brought us up twice a day to relieve ourselves over the edge of the ship, which was profoundly humiliating to the women who had to endure the sailors' greedy, toothless grins. We were given a chance to rinse ourselves in buckets of silty river water.

Below deck, we began to feel the roll and pitch of larger waters. One morning, though it was earlier than usual, we assumed we were being brought on deck for our usual humiliations. But as we emerged from the dark hull, we were blinded by an ocean sparkling beneath silver sun. The Great North Sea was as tossed, blue, and wild as in all the legends told by former shipmates.

Tied together in two squads, we could relieve ourselves, but as the women clumsily readjusted their ragged robes and stepped away from the gunwale, we realized the crew had more in mind today. With a bark and the help of two of his men, the captain forced us men to remove what remained of our clothing and stand naked on deck. We knew it would be fruitless to resist. The captain shouted and his men rushed forward to gleefully tear the filthy rags from the wailing women. The women were badly used. They were stripped, crudely handled, and jostled in shame until the grinning captain whipped his men away. He cared to protect the women only so far that they were not seriously damaged. Nothing more. The crew splashed freezing water over us, and we were thrown brushes and rags to clean with. We were washed like cattle for market. The captain did not want the value of his human cargo diminished. For the women, this was shame on top of mortification.

Two of the men brought a chest on deck, and another carried a pile of clothing that he dropped at our feet. It mattered not that this clothing was likely to have been torn from corpses. We were forced to find anything that fit. The women were frantic to cover themselves with any scrap. They slapped and pulled at each other in their haste, bringing more taunts and gales of laughter from the wretched sailors.

After fighting for days and then lying as prisoners in pain while our wounds healed, we were overcome by scorching thirst and raw hunger. It eclipsed the severity of the other depravations we endured. We knew a change for the worse might be near when the Norsemen began to give us larger rations of their moldy black bread and stale fish. The Norse relished a despicable pickled fish as slimy as eel that smelled worse than the bilge that sloshed below ships. Our hunger severe, we wolfed down the putrid mess.

In several days, we neared the broad mouth of the river leading to Londinium, but the captains of our small fleet would not be piloting upriver. They hovered far out in the wide river that first night. Afraid of ghosts and banshees, nearly all the sailors stayed awake that night, their worried faces turned toward shore as they whispered and gestured. Londinium had once been a great Roman city. When the legionnaires abandoned their forts and the city walls, it had become a sprawling nest of wraiths and living dead.

The following day, three small vessels appeared, rowing from shore out to the Norse fleet. Having established nefarious ties long ago, these merchant ships had been waiting for the northern ships. Two larger ships had been hidden along a shoal. Those ships began to drift toward us to take their place in this grim dance. A few of the sailors on our vessel were skittish until the Norse captain signaled safety. As prisoners, we watched in dread as this meeting unfurled between the Norse, the merchant boats, and the two larger vessels, knowing our fates were being determined in these moments.

XIX. Cletus

As the three smaller vessels approached, the women struggled until slapped into submission and crudely bound hand and foot. They knew they were fighting for their lives or at least for their sanity.

The bindings on our wrists were checked and the ropes between us cinched to assure we would all drown if we tried to escape. We watched as the six women were thrown like cargo onto one of the three smaller vessels. We knew as well as they that Londinium would be a world of pain and mortification beyond hell.

We waited to be tossed after the women, but this was not to be our sentence. As more cargo was offloaded onto the small boats, we realized there would not be room on these skiffs for us.

Listing with cargo from the Norsemen's other ships and their human tonnage, the three boats put oars to water. We watched the faces of the women: the girls bloodless and terrified, the women with wan resignation. I ached for my Bruna and Swanhilde, desperately hoping that if they had met their fate, it had been swift and painless. The stout girl who had defied the little tyrant held her chin up, but we knew her defiance might serve only to assure that her road to submission would be more brutal than that of the others.

Swaying like drunken giants, the two large ships loomed nearby. The ships dwarfed any ship in the Norsemen's fleet. Nautical design evolves generation to generation, yet in all my voyages, I had never seen such ships: broader than many seagoing vessels, but with bows more graceful and sterns narrower, squared, and tall. On the lead vessel, surreal and out of place, seven monks looked down at us indifferently as from a perch in their dark heaven. Fascinated, I could not look away. Two were older priests and five of them appeared to be wide-eyed novices, two of whom seemed at least minimally affected by the plight of slaves.

I looked along the gunwale, where another pod of four men stood with long beards and the ostentatious dress of clergy. Their apathy was palpable, seething. I expected rabble and cruel merchants on these ships, not churchmen. Soon, a captain and several sailors, looking more like the barbarians I had expected, elbowed the monks out of the way and threw down ropes to our ship.

We were clumsily and painfully hoisted upward, followed by bundles of spoil and jars of treasure. The captain above held up two bags: one of coins and a larger of chop metal and jewelry. The Norse captain waved, and the bags were thrown down onto the lower deck with a thud and clatter, spilling pieces of treasure. The Norse captain kicked and elbowed aside the sailors who had fallen like hungry jackals onto the spoils while the sailors on the bigger ships brayed with laughter.

As we rose to stand on deck, the novices and priests moved back, the clergy lifted perfumed and filigreed sleeves to cover their faces. We were hustled below, returning to the familiar odor of bilge, and rotting cargo we had endured on the Norse ships. The hull was far larger than the bunker we had shared on the smaller ships.

With the rocking of the hold, creaking beams and rolling hull, we felt the large vessel pulling away. Within hours, secured to our bench, light from the hatches above faded to night and our world was shrouded in darkness except for a small oil lamp that swayed on the other end of the cavernous hull.

One man alone was assigned to guard us, but it was apparent by late the next day that he was becoming more animated and beginning to talk rapidly, engaging us in conversation in a tongue none of us understood. His frequent weaving excursions to the other end of the hull, and his increasingly slurred speech made it obvious he had discovered how to tap one of the jars of wine wrapped in dunnage. After a long harangue of waving arms and pumping fists, he spiraled into occasional mumbles and fell asleep. Secured and going nowhere, we looked at each other.

The rolling seas were becoming violent, and more of the fetid bilge splashed around our feet. Fortunately for him, the drunken guard was awakened by the storm before his shipmates could discover him. Several sailors scrambled below to check cargo lashed to the planks and platforms beneath the swaying lantern. They rolled jars and bundled together smaller items. When the sailors lit another lantern and came toward us, our drunken guard did all he could to stand upright, cursing as his foot slid off the narrow walkway into stinking sludge as he swung out of the way of his struggling shipmates. Across from us, the sailors arranged bales and laid two smooth planks. I assumed this would provide space to strap more cargo or for the sailors to seek refuge from the swaying decks above. Before they were finished, one of the sailors brought a leather sack filled with lime powder. Coughing while covering his mouth with his elbow, he spread it along the sides of the walkway into the bilge. It cut into the fetid stench, but we coughed and gagged as the scorching dust fogged the hull.

After cargo had been reshuffled, they left with the lantern, but soon returned to the hatch. Step by step, mumbling and swaying, the monks unsteadily descended the ladder to be led out of the storm. The four clergymen in their finery had apparently bullied their way into better accommodations on deck. The monks tilted cautiously along the narrow gangway until they were motioned to sit facing us on the bales and planks that had been laid across from us on the gangway's other side. The two priests protested while the five novices stared at us like frightened children. A roll of coarse blankets was cast toward them. The priests glared around them, but there was no room in the packed hull to sit anywhere else.

Our guard was replaced by two men no more competent. The extra man was there simply to allay the monks' fears. Bound and powerless, we were not a threat, and the sailors knew the monks were harmless. But they may have been wrong. At least one of the novices was neither fearful of the slaves nor harmless.

The dim lantern swayed, the bilge sloshed, and soon the guards were again asleep.

Harsh weather and rough seas persisted for days. The sailors would bring dry bread and meat for the monks but throw us a few dried fish that smelled bad enough that the priests could not eat what they had been given.

On the second day, I asked them in Latin, "Where do monks go in this God-forsaken world?" My fellow prisoners did not understand what I had asked, and they would not have cared, lost on seas of misery.

The novices looked at one another, then at their superiors, who shook their heads sternly, trying to shame the novices into silence.

"I do not think monasteries exist in the middle of the Great North Sea," I continued.

"Hibernia," said one of the novices, drawing a sharp rebuke from his elder. "But he speaks Latin, Father; could he not be a Christian?" he pleaded.

"He is a barbarian," huffed the elder. "He may be speaking in the tongues of devils. He has done something dreadful to deserve the punishment God has wrought."

"Are you a barbarian, our Latin friend?" the novice asked. He glanced back to his superior. "Or a devil?" He grinned. "We of all people should know that not everyone sentenced is guilty."

With a deep frown, the priest made that strange configuration I had seen among other Christians, touching his forehead, chest, and shoulders ostensibly in the shape of a cross. I had seen pagans make odd flutters over their face or chest in various configurations; now Believers were again imitating pagans in mindless ritual. He also clutched the cross-shaped talisman that hung around his neck. Configurations of various Greek letters had been used as symbols among The Way since the early days, but the monks seemed to have adopted a crucifixion charm.

"I am not the devil. And Hibernia is only a legend across a fabled sea," I said. "Why would you think there are souls to save on that savage island?"

The novices chuckled. "Tell that to the spirit of dear Saint Patricius. Before he died, he opened Hibernia to the gospel of Christ," the novice said.

While keeping a wary eye on the dozing guards, the two priests were distracted by groaning timbers and the closeness of the dank hold. They soon paid no attention and drifted away as I talked with the novice into the night. The others had fallen asleep amid the dim light of the swaying lamp and the muffled drum of the seas against the hull.

The novice's name was Cletus. He was fascinated when he discerned my accent was Jewish. I did not betray my years, but I ventured to tell him about Judea and the monasteries of Egypt. He wanted to pledge at the Egyptian monasteries, but he was seeking more than solitude. He wanted adventure in addition to ministry. He had decided to follow the steps of Patricius and sail to the fabled land of Hibernia.

"You are Lazar. I know of Saint Lazarus who was raised by Jesus and became a bishop on Cyprus." I did not know if he was speaking legend or if possibly my son had become a bishop while The Way had been vibrant on Cyprus. Cletus's demeanor and brilliance vividly reminded me of my precious son Lazarus on Cyprus. Down through centuries in times spent in loneliness and privation I still held a chanting whisper of heartache for Miriam and my first son. But to embrace the thoughts of Bruna and my dear family in the north, I had dimmed the lamps of love that yet burned in me, like a warrior in battle, building walls around my heart and mind.

As the seas remained tossed and driven, the priests, unaccustomed to sailing, were stricken by severe sickness and would fight their weak stomachs and unsteadiness to find their way above deck as often as possible.

Strung together, the prisoners talked little among themselves, groaning in their private worlds of silent torture. We rarely saw light except on those infrequent occasions when one of us was led by a guard to empty the pot over the side of the ship. Seeking the prized duty, the guards changed frequently, as wine jars and a molding cargo of cheese was steadily pilfered by the crew. It was not hard for us prisoners to cajole extra rations from beaming, drunken sailors.

My injuries had quickly improved by degrees, and having Cletus to talk with was like gasps of fresh air and glimpses of sunshine. The young novice was relentless and returned to talk after the seas calmed and the priests and other novices had been led back above deck. The stench of bilge and rot had returned, but it was ignored while the two of us shouted to each other when the seas rolled rugged or edged nearer to talk when the seas were quiet. As much as the guard would permit, Cletus would return to minister to the prisoners. He often came with one or two of the other novices, including Petra, who looked too old to be a novice. The priests could not be bothered with such inconspicuous charity and never returned to the hold.

The greatest favor the novices bestowed on us was to humble themselves with the revolting task of shaving our greasy, louse-infested hair and beards. Comically wedged against cargo, Cletus would hover with his sharply honed eating blade, concentrating with arched smile as the darkened hull rolled. Waiting for the blade to slip, the guard was too entertained to intervene. Despondent or incredulous, the other prisoners willingly submitted to the grooming. Losing those festering, itching mats felt almost as comforting as loosening our tethers.

I was developing a bond with these young men, especially Cletus. The other novices watched or would offer a word, but Cletus was eager to talk, listen, and learn.

The young novice would lean forward, elbows resting on his thighs and hands hanging between his knees. His head had been shaved when he received the novitiate, but a few lice had been led in exodus from our filthy heads and found their promised land with the generous young men. While he talked, he would scratch at black stubble that was returning to his head and at the sparse, red whiskers that prickled like cactus thorns. When he listened, the corner of his mouth drew upward inquisitively, his startling lake-water blue eyes locked on mine. He was not like those other aspiring monks whose wealthy, exasperated fathers had put them under the charge of a priest who would take a father's coin, then hustle the young men away to a monastery to brutalize the fear of God into them. Cletus was here by choice. He was a Roman citizen whose father was a mid-level official, and the young man had become enamored of a small group of Christians he had encountered through a worker who had come to patch their roof. After the gregarious Cletus had engaged the man in conversation, the roofer had led him to their assembly and eventually to knowledge of Yeshu.

"I was cornered," he said, smiling. "I came from a home of idols and ritual. I doubt my mother—and certainly not my father—had any use for those icons, but you could not allow anyone to learn you had no gods. Our neighbors would have had nothing to do with us. They would have shunned us, subject to the wrath of their gods. My father would have been under investigation if it were found that he did not worship the emperor and his gods." He looked down and rubbed his face. "But I hated the burden of my wantonness. After I came to know that small group of Believers, I relished the clemency they offered, and I lived as though I had obtained it, though they did not know I was not ready to let go of my life of drunkenness and lust." He paused, shaking his head.

"I was so lost that I had actually propositioned one of the pretty young Christians." He smiled, miming. "She punched me on the shoulder—she was tough! —and said, 'You fool, you remain a prisoner of sin, and I want nothing to do with you.'" He swept his hand. "'You think you have earned forgiveness? No prisoner receives forgiveness without admitting their guilt. You cannot just apologize; you must admit your guilt.' That is what she told me."

"Did that get your attention?" I smiled, leaning back against the ship's hull.

"Ha! Yes." He nodded. "I pondered all she said and took it to heart. Besides, what did I have to lose?" He shrugged. "Since then, I have learned that when an impasse occurs, I should err on the side of holiness. Better a righteous mistake than an immoral success."

"Yes, true," I murmured, mulling the young saint's words.

We felt ourselves lifted and rolling as the ship creaked from bow to stern; the lamp swayed, and we slowly felt our stomachs tossed. The restless vessel settled. Cletus looked at the guard who snored in his stupor; then he turned to me and continued.

"I was shaken by what the girl said to me. I finally came to admit my guilt. But I was stumbling. I saw how decrepit I was, and I confessed. But then I felt hopeless. I was tilting to the other extreme, overcome by guilt. Back and forth. No matter how often I would try to convince God that he should not love me because of my sin, he would again press his insignia into the soft wax of my soul. Over and over his seal said, 'I love you.' The evidence of his love is overwhelming because it supersedes the evidence not of our sin alone, but the evidence for our own existence. Every scrap of proof for my unworthiness that I held up to his view: my self-loathing, my defeat, my excuses—my sin—he would stamp again on each one of these fragments 'I love you.' But I can say more." He pointed at the ropes that bound my wrists. "I long to sever those for you so you can experience in living what I have experienced in my soul. I know it sounds trite: with me sitting here and you there in bondage. But the farther I travel on this journey of the soul, the less I am astonished by what he has rescued us *from*, and the more astonished by what he has rescued us *for*."

"No, young Cletus, I do not think you can understand, but I accept your sympathies. I have seen many in bondage and slavery, but I did not understand until I was on this side of the ship," I said, looking along the row of my fellow prisoners. I was captivated by the insights shared by this young man. I knew I was once again beholding a face and a mind like that of Yeshu. I listened.

I was always seeking the face of Yeshu, yet I was too distracted by myself to realize that in the faces of those like Azvald and Cletus he was never far.

Cletus paused, looking over my head, his face vacant in thought for a moment. Then he leaned close, looking into my eyes again. "I had to become dead to myself. The cross of Christ cannot be empty," he said, pointing at the emblem that dangled from his neck. "Either Christ is on the cross and we are left to our own devices—lost—or he comes off the cross into our lives, and we assume our place on the cross: crucified, dead to self. It cannot be both ways. The cross is hungry; it must be satisfied. I chose to leave myself on the cross."

I nodded in silence.

"I hesitate to speak it, but you inspire me!" he said. "I am to be a slave of righteousness; my struggle is a slave's service. Though I fear that these priests, and certainly those proud clerics, have no concept of being a slave to anything but themselves: to their vanities and their perceived *goodness*, which they parade about with a pride that would embarrass the Pharisees." He shook his head, disgusted. "A corrupted goodness, blatantly paraded, has lowered them into a realm of vanity deeper than bloated accolades, and worse than their vain self-righteousness. Many Believers abound in public goodness. They feed the hungry masses their scraps, then feed others the tales of their goodness. They clothe the naked with their cast-off finery, then clothe themselves in the accolades of others. They give alms to the poor, but merely to buy God's approval, or more importantly, man's approval. Do they not know that goodness on display, this vanity of goodness, is utterly worthless and demeaning? It is deadly. It is worse than any vulgar display of public debauchery. Imagine the sordid scenes of despicable degeneracy seen in the back alleys of Rome or Athens. These scenes do not compare with the decadence seen in these preening acts of goodness."

Smothered in bondage and loss I was fascinated, yet cynical. I feared that the path of this earnest young man could lead like mine to disappointment. "I understand and agree with you. I am assured that my faith is your faith. But I want you to know..." I paused, not wanting to dishearten him, while reminded of the fates and difficult journeys of many: the Disciples, Miriam, Julian and his sisters, and even Azvald and my Bruna. They had endured lives that were worse than they could have anticipated. I continued cautiously, "God loves us intimately, yet we are quite dispensable, are we not? As though God could exchange one of us for the other with barely a thought."

"Exactly!" He plunged ahead. "I am dispensable. You are dispensable. God does not need me, and he does not need you." Then he smiled. "But more importantly, he *wants* you! We are each where we are at this moment because it is where he wants us to be, and he has built within you something special. But what a great relief that we can be replaced!" He slapped his knee and laughed. "We are never here just because of what *we* need. God is sovereign. You are placed here for a service, and if you do not do it or if you decide to leave, or if I jump off this ship, someone else will take my place. How could I ever be so proud as to think I am indispensable?"

"It sounds so brutal, so cold," I said.

"Right! It *would* be heartless and cold," he replied, leaning in, "but, like I said, there is one truth that surpasses: God does not need you—*but he wants you*!" He grasped my knee, bringing a cough and a wave from the guard.

Cletus paused, folded his hands, his head down, the bristle of his scalp giving him an appearance older than his years. I was reminded of the fervor of Paul.

The novice Petra had fallen asleep and was snoring gently in rhythm with the waves. I thought Cletus had also finally grown tired.

"Cletus, are you sleeping? I am sorry," I said. "I must ask something."

He looked up. "Praying." He grinned.

"I'm sorry. But I must know," I began. "I have known many of The Way."

"I believe that you have," he said.

"I can say this because I am not in your position. But you are a novice, a mere pledge, yet you possess more of Yesh...Christ than your priests or certainly those soulless clerics. Why do you submit to them? I have known frauds like these. They have nothing to offer that you do not already possess."

"Mmm...yes. I..." he began.

I strained forward on my ropes. "Cletus, you above all have come to realize Christ is real; he is God made flesh. You do not have to play these stupid children's games of religion and ritual that Believers are playing. You know him intimately—a friend and brother. There is never a place for ridiculous ritual or shallow pretense between brothers."

"I—I understand what you are saying. I believe you. I am here because I am following where I have been led. That is all I can say. I am nothing extraordinary. I simply try to live in his presence from moment to moment as best as I can."

I adjusted the ropes around my wrists to relieve the chafing.

"Praying," he said again. "It is our sustenance."

"But does he hear?" I held up my twisted ropes.

"My poor friend. Any comfort I give is hollow. But prayer is simply being in the presence of God. We are praying as we speak. Talking to God is one side of prayer. The struggling and the listening are another side. When it is said that the holy ones spent the night in prayer, it is not just that we are talking to God, but we struggle through the night, a grave problem plunders our thoughts. That is also a side of prayer. Then there is the sweetness of our fellowship, allowing the Father to minister to our minds, our relationships and our whole person all become the prayer."

"You are a fountain, Cletus."

"We will pray. It is critical that when we feel desperate, overwhelmed, or confronted by an unmovable force, we pray. When there is no faith, no hope of an answer—we pray. No matter how trivial, insignificant, or impossible our cause may seem—we pray. I am teaching myself that I must respond to everything in prayer."

I admit I was not convinced, but I desperately needed to hear him.

"I confess that I feel hopeless. I need hope, and I need rescue for my family—and for myself," I said.

"The time of your release will be at exactly the right moment. I can assure you of that," he said determinedly. "Let us pray."

Within days, we arrived at Dubhlinn.

XX. Atonement

"Rescue is achieved in that moment of great sacrifice," Cletus said as he lowered his cowl and untied his sash. We stood on deck, ice pellets stinging our cheeks, scrambling like fleas down our necks and into our tunics.

"You cannot do this, Cletus. I deserve this; you do not. This is madness!" I pleaded. Nearing harbor, the row of prisoners had been brought on deck to stand amid stacks of cargo shifted from the hold in anticipation of offloading. Conscripted to wrestle a heavy bale, the guard checked our ropes, secured us to a ring on the gunwale, then shoved past the line of monks facing us. We shivered, partially hidden out of the wind amid barrels of cargo and bundles of wool.

"Oh, my brother, we all deserve this, and much worse than this. But Someone took our place. It has already been decided; it is out of your hands, Lazarus of Judea," he said, smiling. "As I said, it is better if I make a righteous mistake than have an immoral success."

The prisoners stumbled while the monks leaned into one another as the ship crunched into the rotting dock.

Sailors hustled more cargo out of the hold to surround us on deck. Cletus pulled off the sash, dragged the robe over his head, and handed it to one of the novices. With his small eating blade, he urgently severed my bonds. I groaned through clenched teeth as the ties were swiftly torn from my shredded wrists and cast overboard. Looking quickly for the guard, he snatched a kerchief from his robe, ripped it in half, and neatly wrapped my wounds.

I looked helplessly at his superior, Father Comgall. Impatiently rolling his eyes, he turned away, sneering meaty lips while sucking his teeth, his greasy hair a mushroom cap and his thin, pallid face the stem. He was Gaelic and spoke Latin with a heavy accent, but he said nothing to his young novice. To him, it was another wrinkle in the long assignment of escorting novices back to the monastery on this lost island. He resented Cletus's zeal, and he thought he was a foolish child who probably needed chastisement. But I knew if this young novice were to become a slave on this brutal side of the Northern Sea, it would be more chastisement than any man deserved or would be able to bear. I had been prepared to accept the state in which I had found myself as due punishment for a hapless life and my abandonment of Yeshu and Miriam, among my myriad other sins. I had little hope of salvation, and I deserved none.

"Stop, Cletus! They will murder you if they discover what you are doing!" I cried.

In wide-eyed disbelief, the other prisoners were too hopeless, and the other priest and novices too surprised, to react. Petra chewed at a fingernail and began to step forward until Comgall thrust a hand into his chest and shoved him stumbling backward. Because of hunger and deprivation, I lacked strength to resist Cletus as he hefted the frayed end of the rope and secured himself to the prisoners.

"Cletus, you fool. Stop!" Father Comgall hissed. "You'll get us all killed! Not now."

The novice bent on one knee, wiping his untethered hand on the grimy deck, then spreading the filth over his head and onto the singlet that had been under his robe, then using his eating blade, he made cuts and tears to his covering. As a sailor was emerging from the hatch, Cletus took his robe that the other novice was holding and handed it to me, setting the blade on top. The view of the sailor was obscured by the bundle he pushed ahead of him.

"Put the robe on, Lazarus, or we will both be dead—and hide the knife. Now!" Cletus said with stern authority, no longer sounding like the bright novice I had known mere days before.

I slipped between the novices, hustling into the robe, and leaning with my back against the gunwale as the sailor pushed past to stack more cargo. Cletus had his head down when the guard returned. The guard carelessly eyed the ropes as he walked past and went on. In our days on the ship, they had never looked at any of us closely enough to know one from the other.

I hissed at Comgall. "Do something! Stop him! What are you thinking? This boy will never survive. It will never work."

A square smile of gray teeth creased his cheek. "It was his decision, and I cannot dispute the Spirit of God. This was Cletus's idea, and so we drew lots to determine if his decision was of the Holy Ghost. The choice was God's."

I never trusted the casting of lots.

"Cletus, I cannot..." Before I could finish, the guard was untying the rope that secured the prisoners and pushing them toward the plank. Shivering, Cletus looked back with a sad smile, then was gone. Forever gone.

"You fool," I said to Comgall.

"That is not the way for a novice to speak to his superior," he sneered.

Finally, when given the signal, we snaked through the mass of cargo, picked up the few bundles the monks had brought on board, and shuffled toward the gate. The prisoners were nowhere to be seen. For the first time in a long while, I prayed. I prayed for Cletus, and I prayed for the worthless man I was.

But I walked on. That is what I do.

Eventually, we were shepherded into a dank monastery at Dubhlinn where we stayed for several days until a small force could be commandeered to lead us in safe passage across this island of tribes and kingdoms.

While aboard ship, we had not seen the haughty group of four clerics. They had been sequestered on board like prize roosters, then hustled away without having to look upon or touch the lowly monks and prisoners. In Dubhlinn, the clerics had been allowed to stay in the home of a local official and would depart to a larger monastery in the south. Unashamed, Father Comgall gossiped freely about them to the priests at the monastery. Comgall's demeanor changed when he found himself in the presence of other priests. He engaged them, chatting, laughing, and drinking their hard cider.

A friend to all, yet a friend to none. These priests seemed unimpressed by Comgall. I hated him for allowing Cletus to be led away, taking the place of someone as worthless as me. I am certain Cletus's sacrifice was never mentioned because it would put Comgall in a lesser light, and make Cletus seem a better man than he.

I tried to engage the priests at the monastery in hopes they would know of a way to find Cletus. Unconcerned by the plight of slaves and overruled by Comgall, they ignored me as a foolish novice. There seemed to be no avenue to secure his release. When I returned to the docks, I was told that any slaves sold there would have been sent north or taken aboard the last ships of the season.

I schemed how I would leave this place and return home again, but I was rendered helpless by sallow emptiness, while grieving for my wife, family, and a life I knew was lost. Wandering back to the harbor again, the shabby buildings surrounding the docks were being shuttered for the season, and the last bales of cargo were shuttled away or stored in sheds. With no money and only a monk's robe to my name, I would have had no way of securing conscription on board a ship, even if it were available. I was nothing and none of it mattered; venturing home would be futile. I was convinced that the insidious power of the Immortals would have decimated our army, and certainly they would have sought my family and murdered them in twisted hate or revenge. Our lands and villages would have been laid to waste.

Maybe this island was that corner of the world where I could stay tucked away, where these monsters would not find me or wreak havoc on those surrounding me.

The monks hoped to cross the island and reach the west coast ahead of the snows and gales of early winter. Once a caravan of pack animals and swordsmen were assembled, the shuffling train started down the broad Esker Riada on a bright day with blue sky and skittering clouds. The ancient highway was as smooth and dry as any Roman street and wound along the high esker spine that traced the back of the island. By the second day, stone road gave way to rocky trail, and we clambered over low hills and heather on our westerly route. Again, I was being swept along on a current not of my own making, that I was incapable of discerning, and that I did not have the courage or wisdom to escape. I was treated like a novice, and I decided I would wrap myself in this role and in Cletus's robe. Why would I not? My life was lost, and I had been left with nothing. When all is lost, surrender is easy.

If I had any shred of a plan, as impractical as it seemed, it would be to lay over until the following spring, then return to Dubhlinn and sail east again. Of course it was folly to imagine sailing strange seas, then traveling alone across the wild northern continent again only to return to devastation. But my yearning for home and Bruna forced me to at least plan and dream.

My relationship with Father Comgall was terse. I could not fathom whether he despised me for what Cletus had done, or more likely, simply despised me because he saw me as a slave. Never interested to know more about me, he regarded me as indifferently as he had the other novices.

I caught up to him on the road. "Where are we going, Father Comgall? What sort of place can there be in this God-forsaken land?" I asked.

He did not answer for a long time, then looked sideways at me. "The monastery was established by Saint Patricius himself and has been a devout establishment for all these years. Never say God-forsaken." He sniffed.

Unless you were that God-forsaken novice of yours taken into slavery, I thought.

He teased a smile and added slyly. "But at our abbey we have a certain notoriety that may one day extend well beyond Saint Patricius."

"Cletus told me much about that venerated saint," I said, vainly trying to remind him of his novice. "Who could be greater than Patricius on this island?" I mocked, knowing this priest thought more of himself than he deserved.

We stopped. He was a tall man, his eyes cast down at me. He quickly looked around conspiratorially, moved a pace closer, and lowered his voice. "We are charged with holding captive a demon, maybe the Dark Lord himself. The Morning Star." He raised his brows, nodded once, and we walked on.

I stopped after a moment, narrowing an eye to let the idea find my brain. "What do you mean, Father? That is not possible." I scampered to catch up. I had heard of the false relics and magic these priests were capable of foisting on the innocent.

"Oh, it is possible, son," he said over his shoulder. "He came to us in the guise of a novice, but it was obvious he was a demon of hell. I alone discerned it."

"Now he lives at the monastery?" I scoffed.

"He is held prisoner there until God imparts his judgment. Two of them. He and his whore whom he tried to smuggle into our cloister. Well, anyway, they were there when I left." He laughed. "He's not going anywhere. At least for as long as our monastery stands."

Sweeping his robe across his shoulder, he walked ahead with long, ungainly strides to catch up to the caravan. He stopped to look back at me with a quizzical grin. "The demon has mentioned your namesake, Lazar. This spawn of hell claims to know Saint Lazarus himself, whom Our Lord raised from the dead. Indeed, that is how we knew this to be one of Satan's underlings." Sneering, he said, "Now we taunt the two of them by calling them The Mortal Ones."

Frozen, I watched until the caravan had trundled far ahead, disappearing over a rise. I looked back from where we came, then to where the caravan had faded. I pondered leaving, but my dilemma persisted: If I turned back, where would I go? Both curiosity and fear finally led me to scamper ahead and follow the monks. My fate lay ahead, and fate would pursue me if I did not pursue it.

The Esker Riada led straight and reliably across the island. We detoured south and had reached the great western seas in less than a fortnight.

As we arrived at the monastery, we were greeted by a sudden misty shower off the ocean that swept over us, vanishing like a specter. The constructions lay as little more than a nest of thatch and slate buildings clinging to the last coast of the world. A shamble of stone and stick walls hugged the enclave as if the embrace of these shabby walls would prevent it all from sliding away into the ocean. To the north of these walls were crude barns and sheep pens, and to the south, slightly hidden by a berm, stood a pile of stones, little more than a pen overlaid with rotting thatch. Half a world away from Egypt, these hovels were thankfully dissimilar to those ostentatious monasteries I had visited.

After the brief shower, everything sparkled in the setting sun. The sky was sketched purple and gold above infinite seas beyond the cliffs, fading to pink and blue to the east as it overspread green hills surrounding the monastery's shining roofs. Sharp, briny wind met us as we stepped over a bridge crossing a silver stream that cascaded around the walls and toward the ocean, where seas curved toward infinity.

Something stirred in me that had been lost. I had endured this long, meandering life and found few places where I felt as though I belonged. I could feel my dark and barren soul being sown into the fabric of this beautiful, lonely land. I needed to be here at this time, in this place. In a broken sense, I deserved to be here: barren and lost.

Suddenly, I was distracted from my thoughts. Like a serpent slithering along our spines, a moaning howl arose from the disheveled hut that lay south of the walls. Father Comgall turned to us, smiling. "They know. They know I have returned with fresh recruits." The other novices looked wide-eyed at one another, then hurried to catch up to Comgall. I stared at the ragged hut; no longer certain I was ready to face the next chapter of my life.

We entered the tiny main lodge while the armed contingent, which had escorted us without incident across the island, helped us wrestle our packs and supplies. They were left to bivouac outside the walls. Though they had traveled with us and protected us all the way across the island, Comgall would not invite them to stay inside the walls, or welcome them around our fires, for fear they might desecrate these shabby grounds. They made camp on the north side of the complex, beyond the pens, and far from the hut of the bloodcurdling howls.

We were shown to our meager quarters while Comgall hastily removed himself to join the priests; then he hustled off to hide in his private quarters, leaving us all to find our way.

XXI. Friend and Enemy

Before sunrise, Father Comgall shuffled into our quarters bleary-eyed, rubbing his forehead and breathing the acrid, fruity odor of spent wine. I doubted any of the novices had slept. All night, gusts from the sea had shuddered the thin slate on the roof like cloven hooves dancing. We shivered, covered with a single moth-eaten wool blanket that bristled with interwoven horsehair; some trembled from the bone-chilling cold, others from fear as the winds were punctuated by throaty, lupine baying.

"It will soon be time to meet your enemy, boys." Comgall swayed and sniffed. He lowered his chin. "I must show you the spectacle, so you know why you are to give your life to Our Lord Jesus Christ—to know your place in the battle that is quaking heaven and earth. We meet in synaxis at the chapel; we pray." He belched. "We eat a simple breakfast, and then the battle will be joined."

"Where's the latrine?" I asked.

He left without answering.

"He told us last night. Not that the piece of sh...that priest would care." Petra made a quick tilt of the head toward the door, kneading his black beard.

I nodded agreement.

A fetid bowl of water sat on a low table. I tapped the surface to see if it had frozen, then wet my face to remove the greasy layer of travel soot. All the novices, except for Petra, were roughly shaven like Comgall, but my hair was growing back at the same length as my beard and ringed my head like a curly black bramble patch. A few of the monks had beards, so I hoped I would not be forced to shave in these cold lands. This order of monks did not seem to have strict sanctions on how to grow hair, of all the things, but I was sure I would soon be informed of their other myriad rules. I guessed that ascetics like Comgall bizarrely thought, among all their meaningless tripe, that sin or holiness resided in hair follicles. Of course, they had never seen Yeshu and the disciples, and certainly not John the Baptizer.

A young priest soon appeared to tell us he would be our guide that morning. He quickly led us through the ritual of washing and latrine with whispered banter. In near darkness, we were hustled along stone paths to gather in the chapel with the monastery's other inhabitants.

While the other members of the small order assembled, a priest nervously touched Comgall's sleeve and murmured to him about the sounds emanating from the hut, which to them seemed much worse than usual. "New novices: It is the new novices it wants." Comgall nodded smugly.

Lit with few candles, the musty sweetness from old incense and damp stone was soon overcome by the odor of the scruffy hermits packed shoulder to shoulder in the small chapel. Behind the crude altar, Father Domnan, the aged superior, stood unmoving, head bowed, hands folded like statuary from an Alexandrian basilica. The only sound was the rustle of the rough parchment that he held between his tremorous hands. We waited. Above the altar, an irregular round window patterned with obsidian shards and seashells shown the first dim light of morning.

The hewn beams overhead creaked from another gale and then, as if from the underworld, a long, curdling crowing as if from a rooster the size of a bullock filtered in from the shack beyond the walls. Three long, banshee-like rooster calls to greet the dawn and clot our cold, guilty blood like the three cries of the rooster heard by Peter as he denied Yeshu. The assembly shuffled, as even Comgall looked around nervously. With sad expression, Father Domnan slowly nodded to the priests to begin the service.

The monks and priests in unison took a breath and began with a low refrain. The voices soon swelled unexpectedly in splendid notes. The uninitiated made wide-eyed sideways glances. The voices grew; a chanting melody that filled the tiny space, rising upward on the stone walls like a flood, flowing to the rafters, rebounding off the wooden vault, and silencing the ocean gales and the intrusion of devils. I closed my eyes, the face of Yeshu flooding my inward vision, recalling to me the struggle of the Disciples, the cruel deaths of my companions and others of The Way, the beauty of heaven and the despair of hell. From the dawn of creation to the closing of the age, they sang of Yeshu sitting at the throne of God amid visions of angels and celestial seas, all reverberating from the stones of the tiny chapel. My mind wandered back to the land after death, the spicy sweetness of otherworldly trees and flowers drifting among the assembly. Amid the monks' song, I could hear notes from birds I had heard only while in that infinite world. The beautiful chants of this band of men continued to swell inside us until the service passed like a dream and we stood a long while staring at the floor, the wind huffing at the roof.

The spell broken, we shuffled into the refectory to eat in silence. The novices looked toward the priests uncertainly, assuring themselves they were eating according to proscribed doctrine. Petra and I crunched the dry bread and slurped the small bowl of rancid porridge without looking up to engage the stares of the priests. After the meager breakfast, the monastery relaxed into routine as monks left to carry out their assignments. Later, they would return to their cubicles for prayer and study.

But for the new initiates, Comgall had other plans.

Led out of the refectory I fell in with the novices, following Father Comgall single file, our hands folded. In the cold dawn, Comgall stopped. "As I told you, you must know why you are to give your life to Our Lord Jesus Christ, and you must know your place in this battle because now the battle is joined." He made a rueful smile, dramatically swept his shawl around him, and made a patting signal by his side for us to follow.

Petra looked a question at me. I shrugged.

Down the narrow path leading to the stone hut, we walked in silence, the gusts teasing us to wrap our thin robes closer. Halfway there, carried on the wind, the stench met us. The novices exchanged glances and two stopped in the trail, unwilling to go farther. By the time we reached the shack the odor was worse than a tanning yard. In fear we expected to hear the chilling howl, but like a leopard crouching, there was silence. Untended grass and weeds grew along the walls of the hut, a gnarled nest of dying ivy wound over rotten thatch.

"When the door is opened, you are not to speak, not to answer the demon's questions. You are to remain silent. He will try to taunt you. You are to be silent," Father Comgall said sternly. A long, low growl rumbled inside the hut.

Several of the novices lifted the corner of their robes to cover their faces against the stench, looking back nervously toward the safety of the priory. Father Comgall nodded to the other priest, who unhitched a large iron latch and cracked the door.

I had imagined that Comgall had unknowingly procured a beast from the wilds of Africa like those I had seen sadly caged along the docks and in the cities where the animals were mercilessly taunted by sailors feigning fearlessness. But now I was wary, losing grip on my skepticism.

Father Comgall steadied the nervous old priest, placing a hand on his shoulder. He swung the heavy door outward. The inside of the blackened door was raked with long scratches where gobbets of excretions slid down the wooden planks. Though we had no intention of going forward, the old priest held up his palm, keeping us until Father Comgall could peer inside. We jumped at a piercing squeal more porcine than human, like a score of pigs to the slaughter. The squeals wailed and quavered, rising and twisting. The novices dropped the robes covering their faces and covered their ears. One young man fell to his knees, swaying and weeping; another bolted for the monastery.

Then silence. Father Comgall motioned the first novice forward. He resisted, shaking his head. Comgall gripped the man's arm and thrust his head in the door. A thrashing, wolf-like snarl sent the novice twisting from Comgall's grip. He ran, following the other along the path, then the remaining novices bolted.

"Get back here, fools! The creatures cannot escape!" Comgall shouted, then shook his head in disgust. "All must meet the enemy," he said to himself. He nodded to the priest to latch the door. The old man was eager to comply.

"Lazarus a Bethania" came from deep inside the darkness of the hut like the hiss of gas from a corpse. The priests stepped back. Comgall creased his brow in confusion, the corner of his mouth pulled up into a grin as he motioned me forward. I could no longer look away. What captive specimen or creature from hell could this insane priest have imprisoned?

Covering my nose and mouth, I trembled, my eyes adjusting to light through decayed thatch that filtered across a floor strewn with straw, bones, and excrement. The floor sloped down sharply toward a shallow cave divided into two pens, little more than sties. I saw their eyes before I could see the forms of their bodies. Pasted to the stone at the back of the cave and separated by iron bars, two creatures lurked.

One of the monsters peeled from the wall. I shuddered and moved back. It huffed, deep and slow with each breath like an ox, while crawling forward ape-like on knees and knuckles. Its movements wafted more stench toward the door, and I drew back.

"Lazarus a Bethania," it hissed again, tongue darting, licking black lips.

"Do not speak, Lazar. It is taunting you. It knows nothing," Comgall scolded.

Decrepit human features eased into the scattered light. I grimaced. Where flesh had sloughed off its cranium, white skull protruded through the scalp. One ear was a remnant of blackened skin that hung near its neck. Cheek and brow bones were stretched with leathery flesh that it scratched with boney fingers.

The other creature may have been a woman. It lay back, chest heaving with raspy breaths, scarcely moving other than to follow me with painful, piercing eyes.

The creature that had spoken drew near, and thrust back his head, howling, the throat quavering. The stones of the hut rattled, and the other creature moaned in response.

I gagged and retched, but I could not turn away from this beast. *The Beast,* I thought, *could Comgall be right? Is that possible?* The Enemy is called The Beast because it has a predator mind. And this creature seemed coiled, ready to attack impulsively, raging, without any concern for its victim. Like a shark or tiger, the Beast is not so much the scheming adversary as the impulsive monster. It does not care where it bites, who it kills, or how much pain it inflicts.

"The blind wizard, that blind priest. I followed him." The voice was coarse, but measured, almost thoughtful. "I wanted to live forever. Forever." Licking its lips again. "Elymas, you bastard!" it shouted, then scorched the interior of the cage with a blistering litany of vile curses and verbal excrement worthy of a sailor plying the rivers of hell.

"Do not speak, demon! I command it!" Comgall shouted.

"Shut up you, drunken fool." The demon coughed and growled. The priest stumbled backward. "You miserable bowl of flesh. Did you bring new prey—or are they *your* prey?" The creature's eyes seemed to clear, and his voice strengthened as it focused on Comgall. "You—you stupid fool. Bring me your sister, priest! I must have her. I lust for her more than you do," it cackled. "Does your simple mind yet dwell upon her moist nether parts as you abuse yourself in the night?"

"Shut up!" Comgall said. "Lies! The Father of Lies. I do not fear you." With hands shaking, he lifted the cross from around his neck.

Brooding unfazed in silence with narrowed eyes it regarded me. Crawling back into the recesses, it mumbled as if to itself. "I knew it was you. I knew you had found me. Oh, I was such a fool. After I thought I had flung you to the seas to be swallowed like Jonah by that whale, I followed that...that charlatan, Elymas."

It cannot know. It cannot be, I thought, my heart pounding, breathing fast and shallow.

At the back of the cave, I saw the glow of its red eyes. In a voice almost human, it hoarsely continued, "Come forth, Lazarus! Come forth from the grave!" It scratched itself with simian claws. "Oh, Lazarus, how I have always hated you. I will always *hate* you," it growled. "And here you are, still flaunting your brazen youth." It took another wheezing breath. "Here to torture me. Here to see me die." In dim light, it showed a broad toothless grin. "Will you sail away with me again someday to find your beloved Miriam?"

I gasped aloud. "Do not..."

"Stop." Comgall grasped my shoulder.

"Markos!" I cried. "How...? Why...?" I said.

"Do not speak, novice," Comgall said. "It can know things about you that you do not know about yourself."

I could not believe it. I had seen Yeshu and the Disciples confront demons. This had to be the Evil One conjuring thoughts from my tortured conscience. I tried to assure myself this was a demon from hell. More than the Father of Lies, Satan is the Father of Discouragement. This is an attack, slipping my defenses and coming at me when I am most vulnerable, to discourage and defeat me. Yes, that is what this was. A demon. Comgall had been right; he had indeed penned up demons. I tried to steady myself, reminded that such discouragement would come from the Enemy, never from God. It is the mark of the Evil One. *Do not listen*, I told myself. *Turn around.*

As though hearing my thoughts, he replied with a rumbling chuckle that rose to wheezing laughter, then howling, screaming, and lunging at the iron pen nearly bending the shafts. It spat at us and screamed, "I followed that fool, Elymas. Why did you not tell me, Lazarus? Why? Why?" His foul hands with broken flesh and splintered nails gripped the pen.

Between the bars something around its neck caught a glimmer. Something familiar. I leaned closer and gasped: Markos' phallic necklace.

"Markos!" I leaned in, shouting to him. "I tried to tell you everything. You would not listen when I..." Comgall and the other priest grabbed my shoulders and pulled me out, slammed the door, and threw the bolt. Screams from inside shook the ground and rattled the rocks of the shack.

"Gone! All gone!" Markos screamed. "Your fat, stinking Germani family and pigsty farm, wiped from the face of the Earth by the Immortal Ones." Like hyenas, the other creature joined him with wails, panting breaths, and laughter. "Immortals have delivered their reckoning to you, just as you have always deserved," he said.

I flew at the door, but others had poured from the monastery, hearing the commotion. They dragged me back to the monastery. There I was barred in a room for three days, visited by Petra and a young priest to supply me with food and water and companionship while I recovered my composure.

Comgall sent for me on the fourth day. I assured him I had simply been overcome by the horror of the creatures, though I doubt he was convinced. He acknowledged that he had seen the demons have similar effects on others. I puzzled with his delight at possessing creatures such as these.

I needed answers. However, returning to the reeking hovel in the days that followed was increasingly futile, not because of Comgall's constraints alone, but because each visit was met with nothing but wailing and thrashing.

Then we heard none of the ravaged howling for days, and I had heard a rumor that the creatures had stopped taking the scraps of meat and old pottage.

One evening before the Lord's Day, while Comgall had retreated to his quarters, I crept unseen from the priory, taking a circuitous path, going first to the sheep pen so I would not be spotted by the priests. I rounded the walls and skulked toward the hut where Markos and his companion rested.

Covering my mouth against the stench, I lay my head against the wall near a space between the stones. I heard the deep animal-like chuffs and restless scratching. I feared riling Markos and drawing the attention of the monastery's inhabitants. I breathed deeply and held it, then whispered, "Markos. Are you there?"

The restless movements and scratching stopped, but the heavy breathing continued, without response. I waited a long while, then called his name again. Finally, I leaned away from the wall and readied to leave.

"Lazarus a Bethania," said a voice like that of the Markos I had known.

I whispered, "Yes, Markos."

"Lazarus a Bethania," he said again.

I did not reply, waiting.

There was a long sigh. "I have sailed on the seas far beyond Byzantium. Disembarking on frozen shores to enter the Forests of the Infinite where men become animals." He coughed and spat. "And where animals become men. I touched the Aurora and scaled mountains from whose heights you can see stars at midday. I saw—"

"Markos, I..."

His voice began to rise. "Shut. Up," he snarled. "Silence!"

"I lived for eons near the sacred, bottomless freshwater North Sea of the Four Seas of the East. No anchor, length of rope, or sounding chain was ever long enough to reach its clear, black depths. Into the freezing deep I was lowered. I was told I had drowned and that I hung suspended there in watery darkness for three days. When shamans of the East revived me, I was told I would never die."

I began to speak, but he silenced me again with a deep growl.

He breathed deeply, fatigue measuring his words. "Lifetimes I thrived in dynasties of the East that far exceed all the opulence of Rome, Greece, and Egypt."

He was silent a long while. His partner whimpered where she rustled in pain.

"But I never found the heaven of which you spoke. You can be assured it does not exist. You may live forever, but there is nothing there. Meaningless. Everything is meaningless."

"No, I only..."

Beginning as a throaty moan, it grew into a high, wavering howl. "Silence. Damn you! Damn you to hell!" His breathing slowly settled again, and I could hear him shuffle near the crack in the wall where I leaned. "You fool," he said, brooding, "you thought there was meaning; I found only meaninglessness. Ha! I wanted immortality but I found a mortality more fetid than a slug's life." He breathed deeply. "You wanted meaning and found a meaninglessness as bleak and bland than anyone could have imagined." There was coughing I could mistake for laughter.

"Markos, I am sorry. I..." He was silent. I continued cautiously, "We were on your ship. I had left my betrothed and felt alone and abandoned by my Messiah. You came to me and you only scoffed at what I believed."

I heard a snuffling and low groan.

"You have seen great wonders," I said. "I told you when we met how we were implanted in creation because great beauty and genius cries for—demands—awe wherever it is found."

He snorted but did not interrupt.

I continued cautiously. "Remember how I told you that the created world needed to be witnessed, as you have been a witness: the curve of a shell, the curve of a growing fern, the curve of the crescent moon, and the curve of the earth." I plunged ahead. "If our adulation were involuntary, it would mean nothing, so we were granted that single sacred *flaw:* the ability to choose. In leaving Cyprus, I chose. You have made choices your whole life. It is our stubborn will that leads to our downfall. That is why we were rescued by a Messiah, ruthlessly executed in our place."

I believed he had retreated into the cave and was no longer listening, but I spoke as though reminding myself. "His death was our rescue. I had scuttled my relationship with Yahweh." I paused, thinking as much of my foundering life. "There exists purity and perfection or there does not. One speck, one infinite imperfection and purity is tainted, and any connection with purity must be severed. Infinite perfection cannot be destroyed. Never. The speck of contamination must be destroyed—death—it cannot be merely plucked out. Death, Markos, we all face death." I heard the deep gusting breath of pain or denial. With nothing to lose, I pressed on, making one last attempt to somehow rescue my old captain. "Yet in his infinite love, he took our place and became death for us. Death. When God looks at us now, he sees Yeshu. I ask for forgiveness; then God looks toward what I have done and sees Yeshu. Not me."

Silence. The wind rustled the dead vines and lifted patches of old thatch. I pushed myself away and stood to leave.

"Go," he whispered. "Go. I am finished." I heard him shuffle and scratch as he sunk into the recesses of the shallow cave. He said no more.

In the weeks following, the creatures' howls were infrequent until we heard nothing but voiceless moans, then silence. I could have hoped that Comgall would either release them or stop feeding them, ending their misery. But I knew such a deed would be merciful beyond the priest's capabilities or his ambition for gain.

I came to believe that a need had been met in Markos's desperate, rotting heart. He had waited to deliver one final message to me. Now this final time, he would be captain of his fate and allow himself to starve or merely wither, to die in utter meaninglessness. Mortality would be visited upon him. I prayed at least one word had penetrated the carapace.

Comgall had grown unconcerned about the creatures in the hut. It was apparent something about Markos's revelations about me had fascinated and disturbed him. I hoped Comgall believed poor Markos did not actually know who I was. I sensed the priest's suspicions sprung not only from curiosity, but from his rising disdain for me. However, I was not kept entirely at arm's length, and I feared Comgall had found his new relic.

I tried to convince myself that Comgall could not have believed the decaying Markos's assertion that I was Lazarus of Bethany. Not allowing him to speculate, I tried to assure Comgall that I was but one of many Lazars from the Holy Land. But, like all relic merchants, I feared that authenticity of the artifact would matter little to him, only value.

Novices were rarely allowed into the private quarters of the priests, but as long nights stretched into winter, I was summoned often to Comgall's rooms. On those nights, he would sit on his cot with a flask and extoll his opinions of every saint he could summon to mind. I was silent and merely nodded as he wove legends of celestial virtues and damning faults of persons he never knew; Paul, Barnabas, or Mary of Magdala. None of these men or women were the models of virtue the Church had come to believe, nor were some of them the debauched unfortunates this priest wanted to believe they were.

In awkward moments, he would begin a story about his sister, Athracht, then suddenly trail off. Monastic gossip was embarrassingly rampant, and the other monks liked nothing better than to chatter behind Comgall's back about his sister who was growing in prominence as a woman devoted to God and who was ministering on this very island.

Comgall possessed an unseemly fascination with Mary of Magdala. When the wine took hold, he would describe her alleged lascivious exploits in wincing detail and then ponder how a woman of such promiscuity and shame could have been allowed in the presence of other women so virtuous as Mary, the mother of Yeshu.

Lifting his cup smugly, Comgall would say, "It is testament to the overpowering virtue of celibacy that these men and women could tolerate Mary Magdalene until she was converted," apparently unaware that few at that time, other than Yeshu and his cousin John the Baptizer, had chosen to remain celibate. Custom determined that all would have married or been betrothed.

Yet there was a subtle grace I found listening to the fool drone on. For a short time my mind could drift back to those heady days with Yeshu, the disciples, and their followers. Until I would be snatched back by an outrageous claim Comgall would make, or a statement too audacious to let slip by.

Though there was little I could do to alter his lewd fascinations with Mary of Magdala, I had to interrupt one evening when his rant became egregious. Without causing more suspicions about my identity, I tried to defend this beautiful and complex woman.

I struggled to quietly explain this captivating woman. It was a mistake.

"Maybe she was never a prostitute, never lewd, but simply a person like all of us, who had a great debt that had been generously forgiven by the Messiah," I said.

Comgall looked at me incredulously, his roving cup and swaying head seeking his puckered mouth.

But I reveled in my thoughts of Mary of Magdala. Though pained, she had been lovely and lively. She had struggled with a shattered past, having been brutalized by a violent husband. Her ensuing thirst for wine and her struggle with false accusations had pursued her as she tried to establish herself among merchants. After her forgiveness and restoration by Yeshu, her skills in trade had made the second half of her life a blunt contrast to the first.

While Comgall sat on his cot leaning back on the stone wall, sodden and slurring, I remembered the woman in our home with my sisters. They were enthralled by her, as any woman would have been. She had silver jewelry twisted into long curls that lay behind her ears, and as she reclined with us, she fingered the silver in her hair, causing it to lightly jingle against her earrings. I recalled her words. "'If you will do *alpha*, then I will do *beta*'is all that Yeshu said to me. I was convinced. Because there was certainly nothing I could do on my own to restore my life. I knew my husband was a brute, but my failures were within me. I had no one else to blame." She nodded thoughtfully. "Yeshu told me, 'If you give me those things that trouble you, one by one, and give me your life, then I will take care of each thing that you bring to me. I will live in you, and my life will become your life.'" She leaned forward, shrugging, her palms upturned. "You see? It was never up to me to make any of this work out. I could not overcome my taste for wine. I gave it to him; he dealt with it in his way and in his time—as though it were *his* problem." Resting her hands in her lap, she had a lovely faraway smile. "For some, rescue takes time, yet they are granted a way to survive in the midst of their sin or until delivery is complete."

Comgall tried to mumble something, but I interrupted him. Mary had said more about the ravages of sin and the beauty of God's grace. But he was oblivious to the chastisement I spoke to him as though from Mary's lips, "Ah, yes, Father, I think it was a wise person who told me that sin is never free, not even cheap. But the price must be paid, because the Almighty is perfection. Thanks be to God that he has provided the means of reparation if we give our lives to him."

He paused, looking at me stupidly, his meaty lips smacking and his eyes heavy with stupor. "Y-yes, sin. That is what we were talking about, was it not?"

"And I believe it is a good thing to talk about," I chided him. Remembering more of the thoughts spoken by the woman he was berating, I tried to impart her wisdom. "I recall when a wise merchant rebuked me one time, reminding me that 'Sin always incurs debt or demands our resources, and those resources will be drawn from our minds, our families, and sometimes our finances. We always owe. But righteousness always pays dividends. It is always a deposit, though seldom with immediate returns. The complete sum of sin is zero, while the sum of righteousness is infinite.' I believe that is how she—I mean they—said it."

A dumb smile creased the corner of his cheek as if he had thought of it himself, and he sloshed his cup in agreement, unaware he was being chastened by the very words of dear Mary of Magdala.

He paused. "Are you wanting to confess your sins to me?"

I laughed. "No, that is not what I was saying. This wise merchant had led a tortured life and knew the torment of regret that could seem impossible to overcome. It helped me to understand the ruins of sin and the complete restoration by the Savior—for all of us."

Comgall was listening.

"As I was saying, this merchant liked to say that sin and righteousness are not deposited or withdrawn from the same account." His brow raised at the mention of accounts, but he was oblivious as I took aim at him, recalling more of her reflections. "Father, while we are talking of sin, imagine this: Sin and righteousness cannot be measured on the two trays of a merchant's scale. Good deeds do not balance out despicable acts. It is like balancing dust with a millstone." I wiped my finger on his dusty table and held it up. "They are of immeasurably different weights and value. The weight of even a crumb of our imperfection, our sin, could not be balanced by mountains of our worthless righteous acts." I evened my upturned palms. "And we can at least hope that not even a cart load of our constant, foolish mistakes will outweigh our small offerings of true righteousness." This is what Mary of Magdala, earnest and hopeful, would have said to Comgall, arrogant and lost.

The priest's response was a rumbling snore and blubbering fart. He had fallen asleep, along with the entire Church. Drunken fools everyone.

The stone hut where Markos and his partner were held had been silent for months before any of us were allowed to go near. Eventually, the door was cracked; the decrepit bones were removed under the darkness of night. Comgall would not allow the sun to bless anything so defiled. Before dawn a pyre cremated the bones, and the ashes were cast into the ocean without ceremony. The door to the hut was barred, a torch set to the thatch, and no one came near the walls again for years.

Within the monastery, under the pendulum's sway, years inexorably passed. I had long ago steeled myself: As much as I missed my home in the north, I could not return unless I was willing to endure the pain and regret that the journey home would require. On this island, I had tenuously carved out the life I had sought in Egypt among those rigid monasteries of Pachomius and Antony. Despite the restraints of monastic life that I had to bear, like my marooned life near Kalliste, I had found a refuge on another island of contemplation.

But here I was not alone. And though I considered them a minor farce, I learned to tolerate the doctrines and decrees of the priory. I consented to live their life, vowing to myself that I would be a loyal friend and brother to the monks and novices, while around the priests, we would dance to their decrees and vain religion. Moreover, living by rules is always easier, though far less exhilarating, than living by faith.

Old Father Domnan died, and Comgall for a long time had conspired to make himself successor to the Superior. In his zeal, the monastery grew to two score monks and more. Outside the walls, like the monasteries in Egypt, a huddle of thatched huts had cropped up for pilgrims and others in service to the growing community. To create a stream of income, Comgall was inventive at gathering a collection of false relics and managing visits from eminent priests

He had worked and preened his whole life for this position, like a lanky marsh hare padding a nest with fur and fluff, yet fierce as a lion prepared to defend his lair.

XXII. Comgall's Wrath

As the superior, Father Comgall was as conniving as he had been fawning while he was Second to docile Father Domnan. To many of the pilgrims, and among several of those within the monastery, Comgall was a saint, sure to be canonized or at least attain high office—maybe the highest office, God willing—in Rome or Constantinople. However, to this vain priest, earthly office would be far more appealing than saintly immortality.

The Imperial Church was expanding feverishly in all the world that lay east of our primitive island. There were competing doctrinal councils, there was interference by ambitious emperors with dubious spiritual intent who sought political gain as their true salvation, and there was interference by ambitious men within the Church with similar political intentions. As always, I ignored all of it. Comgall would accost us breathlessly with a shred of gossip from a visiting pilgrim about this potential pope or that new encyclical that he would herald as a sign of God's overarching control of world events. Many of us were merely bewildered, thinking we had come here to escape the world and men's maneuverings.

Little councils were enjoined by Comgall to debate doctrine. These silly councils could include any number of visiting clergy or renowned pilgrims. This caused strife within our community, which he would manipulate to his advantage as faction squared off against faction. Then *benevolent* Comgall would position himself as great peacemaker, mediator, and saint. Most of us knew what he was doing but did not care. We allowed storm clouds to stay in the skies above.

To remain out of the fray, I tread cautiously along that narrow fence between factions. I was Brother Lazar, and no one except Father Comgall noticed that I was not advancing through the order.

It was not difficult to stay where I was in the fellowship. I had aged enough over my lifespan to be accepted with the older novices. The revolving array of priests, pilgrims, and pledges allowed anonymity as I bustled about fulfilling my duties as mason, carpenter, and builder. I withdrew into my work and into myself. I had nothing left. By what I had witnessed when taken captive, and by the taunting words of the decaying Markos, I was convinced that my family and my village in the north had met a terrible fate. There was no place left for me.

Burying my thoughts with the steady work of my hands, I had decided to stay on this island for as long as time and fate would allow. My skills permitted me to keep my low station, where I was needed, and not worry about being forced to advance in the order.

I enjoyed the solitude and rhythm of my work and life, and I did not mind the occasional intrusions by kind and inquisitive novices or gentle priests, though I tried to avoid intrusions by Father Comgall whenever possible. He seemed to regard me as two people: one on the outside amid the other monks, and another while I sat in his dreary rooms. He would rarely speak to me outside his chambers. But he did not ignore me. His work assignments were often passed to me by one of the other priests, yet I knew he watched.

And he continued to invite me to his rooms for his drunken ruminations. He was incessantly attempting to pry stories of my past, and he was frantic about affirming my loyalties. I knew he possessed vague impressions of me as he watched, but he was careful to keep those to himself. I believe he rarely talked about me with the other priests. That would not be his approach. He was keeping me as his private artifact, trying to decipher how he could use me to his advantage. He would be legend if he were able to somehow prove his vague suspicions of who I was. But if his suspicions proved false, he would need to know enough of me so he could conjure a plausible fable. He was content to allow me, for a while, to hide as quaint Brother Lazar.

Within the community Comgall should have been considered a tyrant, but his control was by cloying manipulation not punishment. A friend of all, yet a friend to none. He was pulling the strings and changing the sets on stage: moving the pieces, playing to those who imagined themselves in his favor. Though they were being humiliated, maneuvered, and foiled without ever knowing the source. They were in his thrall, game pieces to be promoted or moved to other monasteries, never suspecting their benevolent superior of evil.

But often held captive to his drunken rants late into the night, I remained saddled with the unique privilege of being his reluctant confidant. Why would I endure the pain and fatigue of being detained in his stinking quarters, breathing his alcohol breath, and enduring his gossip? Why would I listen as he ranted against the nuns and all other women, spewed his disdain for Church leadership, and painfully jested about the foibles of his priests and novices? I endured this for a singular reason. It was not for penance but nonetheless a price I had to pay to hold on to a dwelling place and way of life I had come to cherish. I would stay close to Comgall, and hold to a certain mysteriousness if I were to maintain my grasp on this haven.

I could also serve as a foil against Comgall's machinations as I carefully gleaned scattered bits of information that occasionally served to rescue a guileless man within the monastery from the Superior's harsh resentment.

More than once, I was expelled from his chambers in a sudden outburst of anger. An opinion would arise about Yeshu that he could not fathom. Or as I had done with Mary of Magdala, I would mention a unique insight I had about the Disciples, such as the conflict between Paul and Barnabas, or the simplicity of the early Church, or the integrity of those early women of The Way.

"What do you know, fool?" he would hurl at me, which would be my cue that the evening was deteriorating, and I was about to be expelled. "Show me that in the Epistles, you...you novice!" Usually by then, he was slurring and weaving like a concussed sailor on a sinking schooner.

Why did he keep company with me? Did he not care that there would be whispers if I were seen frequenting his chambers? Though he did not trust me, he was captivated and curious. The alcohol gave him increasingly unwarranted suspicions about many things. When he asked if I were a spy from Rome, I sensed his fear of me was becoming irrational.

As the years went by, he would have noticed I had not become gray and hunched like he and the other monks. He tolerated me because of his suspicions and because of his fascination, though that was growing thin. But there was one other reason he kept me around:

Walls and buildings needed repair, and his broad ambitions bred designs for expansion and extravagant structures. He envisioned a sprawling abbey, but his ideas were impractical. When I offered my insight and contributions toward his designs it only added to his envy and resentment.

We headed for a tipping point.

The walls of the hut where Markos and his partner had died captive were hidden in tall thorns with stems as thick as serpents that grew out of the cave and covered the stones. It would take little effort for Comgall to make it a prison again—my prison. Often novices, pilgrims, or one of the priests would be assigned to apprentice with me for a season. I suspected Comgall had maneuvered them into position to steal my trade so he could do whatever he wanted with me.

But invariably the apprenticeships ended in disappointment, or worse, disaster. The novices and pilgrims were mostly the pampered offspring of aristocrats and Roman nobles who sought an ascetic's penance for their years of debauchery. Spared of callus, their smooth hands were no match for mudstone and granite. Most days spent working with these apprentices were punctuated by squeals from their pinched fingers, split toes from dropped stones, or lacerations inflicted by their clumsy use of axes and draw knives.

Their private tutors had schooled them well in philosophy, religion, and social graces, but they had not grasped the basic concepts of calculating the span of a wall, the length of timber, or the depth of footings, their blistered hands fumbling with hammers, rasps, and chisels. It was not likely they would have amounted to more than pampered breeding stock in their father's stable of corpulent offspring. The monastic life seemed the only choice that remained for them. Desperate seekers found mistaken worth in the hopeless meaninglessness of aestheticism.

If a pilgrim lasted a season, it was rare. Novices scarcely stayed long enough at the monastery to replenish the population of monks. Comgall's recruiting was always at work, and he felt he had to make the monastery ever more sprawling and laden with mysteries to attract more interest—and gold.

I cherished one precious privilege granted to me. I found my greatest contentment in a refuge that was not part of this monastery and barely known to many who lived there. Despite Comgall's grumbling, I never allowed pilgrims or novices to follow me there. I did not want to spoil this place by attaching Comgall's rules and bitterness.

In a little valley with cascading waterfalls glittering in the green, less than a half day's journey, a convent had been established. And the nuns and postulants were far more tenacious than those sniveling novices at Comgall's monastery. These women would not harbor foolishness. I had been sent there despite Comgall's reluctance; later, I learned it had been because of the intercession of his sister, Athracht. She was not living at the convent, yet, but she oversaw and fostered a growing following and a devout fellowship of women.

To Comgall's enormous chagrin, authorities and pilgrims had become more enamored of her than of her conniving brother. Holding many in her sway, she was known throughout the island, bringing with her a reputation that had spread as far as Britannia, if not beyond. Novices and pilgrims who had arrived at Comgall's abbey assured me her reputation was more than rumor. She was worthy, and her work seemed loving and true. She was never at the women's monastery when I was there. Until I met her, I was withholding judgment, knowing her brother too well.

The buildings comprising the convent and grounds required repair and expansion. Though Comgall tried to begrudge them so much as a tack, I schemed to assure that Comgall's monastery provided what the women needed. As Superior, Comgall was equally miserly in providing for the nuns' spiritual needs. The priests he favored least would be relegated to care for the sisters. He rarely set foot on their grounds unless it was to impress a visiting dignitary, or unless there was compensation he could finagle.

Outside the convent walls, I had built a slate hut where I stayed while I visited. It had a thatch roof, and I had set a small window that I had inlaid with a few pieces of lucent broken pottery and shells. Until I would be grudgingly summoned back to the monastery, I would spend weeks in the sisters' company, helping to repair and construct strong, safe structures so they could protect themselves from marauders.

Defense was important in this wilderness. I awkwardly tried to demonstrate a few Sardinian defense techniques. I am certain I was not the best teacher, but they had enthusiasm and skill, so I was willing to show them a few skills. I laugh when I remember, but I cherish, the happy, ridiculous hours training those joyous women.

The life the nuns and pledges had withstood was more difficult than that of their male counterparts. There were few aristocrats among them, but because they were women, those of high estate endured worse treatment, had worse prospects, and had fewer resources to improve their station than their male relatives. Though individual stories were rarely revealed, many had arrived in this monastic outpost with scarred souls. The tragic lives of these women could be stitched together by inference: banishment for an alleged affair, pregnancy, beatings, fleeing marriages arranged with monsters by monsters, or as prey escaping paternal predators.

If it had been permitted, I would have brought several of the nuns back to the monastery and used their calloused hands to help with construction and repair, or their sparkling smiles as encouragement to my soul.

At the monastery on the western coast of Hibernia, my years were not always content, but it was a life of rhythm and symmetry. There was joy in the designing and building, but that was balanced by the strife of living under the thumb of Father Comgall. There is a tempo to an isolated community that is hypnotic, that rocks the mind to sleep. Floating on the rhythm of these waves, I could forget the past.

But my conflict with Comgall and his Church was becoming hard to suppress. I despised the ceremony and ritual, but my soul had been content to be mollified instead of edified. To see the pure, sweet doctrine of Yeshu and his Disciples turned into empty ritual was painful, but I was forced to ponder: Was my early life in Judea merely an illusion? What I remembered as perfect and whole had been reduced to something utterly flawed and broken. It gnawed at me. But if there was an answer, it would not be found at this monastery, and I could not have continued to allow Comgall, the worm, to eat away my insides and consume my soul.

The end came swiftly. On the morning of that final day, I never could have imagined what would transpire by evening.

Our routine allowed us a period of unscheduled time on the afternoon before the Lord's Day, ostensibly to be used as preparation. Comgall would go into his chamber late in the day, telling the novices he would be fasting and preparing for Mass the next day, and they should do the same—and not bother him. Usually, no one would see him until he emerged the next morning for Mass, blurry-eyed and bad-tempered. Many of us knew he spent the day before the Lord's Day with a loaf of bread, a block of cheese, a stack of honey cakes, and a jar or two of wine. He had a private cache of the monastery's best vintage that he secured in his quarters. Then after Mass on the Lord's Day, he would repeat this routine so that often by the day after the Lord's Day, he was absent for chapel and breakfast. Then this saint would insist that he had been in a stupor of prayer and communion with the Lord and His Saints.

Those afternoons before the Lord's Day, Comgall would summon me or, rarely, one of the priests so he had someone who could listen to his pontification or his vicious derision. If one of us made an excuse that we were ill or had special assignments, irritated, he would choose another victim. A small band of us had to endure this abuse, but we were never able to talk among ourselves because Comgall's spies or someone trying to get in his good graces could be anywhere.

On this occasion, I had decided to meet with him because it was urgent he approve plans to widen the sacristy in order to create a closet for more vestments. He also wanted a way to allow the morning light to fall more directly on the priest at the altar—meaning him.

He was unexpectedly sober. As usual, he offered me a cup, and as usual, I declined. He smiled, pointing to the plans I was carrying under my arm. I quickly agreed to reviewing the sketches, though I did not need to review them; I had drawn them myself, and he would not know what he was looking at. He had learned nothing in our years of working together.

Gray wisps of hair spilled over the back of his collar and white stubble speckled his wrinkles. He had the mushroom cap tonsure, now white-flecked and poorly kept. His face sagged and his nose had grown red and bulbous. Wiping his chin, slumping into his chair, he emptied his cup, sighed, poured another cup, and finished it before he spoke. I never spoke to him before he was ready to listen: Until his blood was sufficiently saturated with wine.

He was troubled. It took three cups to loosen his tongue.

"How long have you been here?" he asked, staring into the candle flame.

I was no longer confident in his memory. "A short time, Father; the candle has not shortened since I entered. I—"

"No! How long have you been at this holy monastery?" he said evenly.

"I do not know, Father. Are we not here so that we can elude the constraints and rigors of time?"

He smiled and chuffed. "Well, you alone certainly seem to be eluding time—Lazarus."

I was Brother Lazar. No one had called me Lazarus since the decaying Markos.

"Twenty years? Thirty years? Or is it more?" he asked.

"I do not know, Father. Has it been that long?" I evaded.

"You never seem to age. I am not the only one to have noticed," he slurred. "It started with that decaying demon. You let slip a name, I believe. Was it Mark? Marco? Marcurio?"

"It has been a long time. I do not recall much about that dreadful creature."

"Brother, you have many skills, but lying has never been one of them." He glared.

I saw no reason to speak. He was determined to take this wherever he wanted.

He held out the jar to me and I shook my head again. While one of the priests might drink eagerly with him, I suspect the novices and pilgrims only pretended to sip in fear.

His cup shook as he filled it.

I recalled our conversations about Mary of Magdala. I was tempted to speak of my concern for his slowly eroding debauchery, but wisely stopped myself. I allowed my mind to drift away from the stench and tension of Comgall's quarters while he began his usual litany of jealousy and scorn.

I thought of this woman who had often been the focus of his derision. Her profound warnings about sin were spoken, in part, from her struggles with wine. She would have had much to say to this sot in his dank room, but if she were to stand before him, he would not have acknowledged her or understood her. She was all that Comgall would never be, and he was not worthy to tie her sandal.

I recalled her crouching next to a woman in a tattered robe who sat upright in the dust, legs splayed, head slumped in stupor, with a cup that lay broken between her ankles. Mary's dark face upturned toward us, lovely despite the weariness of slowly healing misery. Under her left eye was a small scar and her nose was subtly askew from past injuries. With her confident smile, she reiterated, "Sin is never free, not cheap; it always demands our resources." Mary rested her hand on the woman's shoulder, seeing a mirror of herself. "Wine is counterfeit for our longing for God. I know this. These longings find their origin in the same place, and the Creator made this space within us to draw us to him and to be filled by him, by Yeshu." She swept her palm gently across the woman's forehead, then turned to grip the hand of my sister, Martha. "God is calling us. He wants us to be his friend, but we fill this space with wine. He so desires to be our friend." She wiped her eyes and grasped the woman's shoulder. The woman awoke with a start. "Come, sister; we have much to fill you with."

Mary looked up at us. "This is the battle for the mind, friends. This is our battlefield." She made a fist on her knee, looking down as though talking to herself, reminding herself where she had been. "This ecstasy, these pleasures are meant to be our rewards, and these struggles are critical for growing and equipping us. Wine leads to brief ecstasy—without the struggle. It is a thief. It was the thief of my life."

Comgall cleared his throat and I snapped from my thoughts. His shaking cup had been filled again as he scanned my face, searching for something. Like a hungry squirrel, Comgall would dig and search, then dig and search some more, moving from topic to topic until his sharp ears perked up and he sensed he had found the nut he had been hunting for. He had found his prize. He set down his glass.

"As I was saying, lying is not one of your skills. In fact, I do not think I ever suspected you to lie about anything, Lazar." He scratched his cheek and pointed at me. "You will not lie to me, will you?"

"Of course, I would not, Father Comgall."

He could sense my apprehension.

"Tell me who you are." He sat back, relaxed, and picked up his cup. He had his prey; he could wait to finish the kill.

"You know, Father," I said, smiling. "I arrived here with you after the generous exchange made by the novice Cletus on the ship all those years ago. God be with him wherever he may be." Despite my pleas, and his false assurances, I knew Comgall had never bothered to enquire after that dear monk any further. I fingered the edge of the small stand near my chair. "I had been taken a slave while fighting to protect my lands in the Germanic territories. I had a wife and children whom I left behind and I am certain were killed by raiders more vicious than any enemy in the north."

Comgall was not in a hurry; he allowed me to ramble, patiently cracking the shell of each answer, removing the morsels inside.

"Who are you? You have evaded me long enough. You have acquired several lifetimes of skills and experience. These skills are not from Sardinia alone. We know you were born in Judea." He poured another cup. "But dear, Brother Lazar, *when* were you born? This is what I must know."

"Pardon me? We have never celebrated birthdays here," I said.

"When...were...you...born?" His teeth clenched. The wine was thick, yet he was honing.

"Father, I, uh...."

"Stop! If you will not answer, will you at least confess your faith to me?"

"Of course, Father; my Faith is in God the Father, Son, and Holy Ghost. My love for Yesh...Emmanuel is evident and open to all the world."

"I watch you. I see how you come back from that whorehouse of nuns." The wine was rearing like a serpent, ready to strike. "Where is your loyalty?"

"My loyalty is to Christ...." Then, lying poorly again, I said weakly, "and to his Church."

"Exactly!" He pointed a wavering finger. "What is the Church? Tell me what you think is your true religion?"

"Um, I think the Disciple James himself said that if you cannot live without religion, then go and take care of widows and children and the like," I said. "I suppose that is religion."

All the while I spoke, he was slowly shaking his head with a frown so deep it seemed it would exceed the bounds of his chin. I had never affirmed his religion; he perceived my hatred of religion, and now he had me cornered. In all these years, I was held in Comgall's quarters in order to listen to his ranting. He never cared what I thought about anything.

"What is the One True Religion?" he drilled in.

I felt foolish, stalling while I rubbed my face with both hands.

"What is the One True Religion?" he asked more patiently, knowing he finally had found a way to put a knife to my neck.

I tried to continue diplomatically, but I knew, before I said it, I would say the wrong thing. I took a deep breath, feeling myself sailing slowly off a cliff, though I felt freed in a way I could not have foreseen. I sat forward in my chair with confidence, hands folded. "If you are speaking of empty ritual, then I do not love any religion. I accept your question, though. What is the One True Religion? I suppose One True Religion would be like Caesar's Rome: The One True Government."

He seemed confused. I hoped he was too drunk to understand so I continued, "As I said, the One True Government of Caesar's Rome was all government enforced all the time. So, I imagine that One True Religion would have to be a creed where religion and ritual were enforced all the time: All religion enforced all the time. I suppose we could start with Judaism, that was all religion—"

But before I could continue, he stood and hurled the cup, smashing it on the wall above my head, splattering my shoulders with wine, shards striking my head. "Damn you, Lazarus! Damn you to hell!" He pointed. "Outside these walls, that stinking hut covers the cave where your old sailor friend, Markos, starved himself to death. I guess he and his bitch were not as immortal as they thought." He slurped a hand across his mouth. "To this day, pilgrims lay their gold outside that grove of brambles, thinking it will protect them from Lucifer and his dominion. We collect it...." He fell clumsily into his chair, groping for the cup he had shattered, then guzzled the last wine from the jar and pointed his trembling finger at me. "That sty would bring more gold if it were occupied again. And there, Lazarus a Bethania, you shall...." He shouted, struggling to rise from his chair again but slumped back.

I bolted while he hurled garbled rants at my back. I could not stay here to listen to his ranting or allow him to condemn me to the hell that had befallen Markos and his consort. Despite whatever twisted and bizarre path my former captain had taken, no creature deserved to die as he had. I could not wait for Comgall to sober. Whether he genuinely believed who I was or not, his intent was clear. He would soon fall into stupor for the remainder of the day, so I had to act quickly. Having endured Comgall's whims and impulses all these years, I had kept a bag with most of what I would need to leave.

At the monastery, I thought I had found the cocoon where I could dwell anonymously, allowing the plodding years to pass, outliving unconcerned monks. But I had been flushed from hiding.

XXIII. Sister Athract

Deep in the night, I fled. Starlight illumined the dome of sky, giving a gray luster to heather and dewy stone. "Where now?" I said to silent stars. Was it possible to find another path? Where else would I go? Was I prepared to begin the long journey back to Germania, Sardinia—or Judea? But it was not to be from silent stars above that I would find my bearing; it was again from those shining Yeshu-souls here among us.

I arrived as first light blushed the east, awakening those shy, feathered sentinels excited to be first to herald the dawn. Candlelight glimmered from slender chapel windows and poured from the doors of the refectory where shadows of busy women dodged and flitted. In the early light, crude tents ruffled outside the walls and several pilgrims were picking their way toward the gates of the abbey. I had not expected to find throngs of visitors in this quiet glen. But I knew of no other place to find sanctuary. Comgall would suspect I was here, but he would not dare to make the journey or trust his priests to attempt to detain me.

And he would have known something more: His sister was here and had been appointed Abbess. Knowing she was here was likely to have spurred the fury and distress he had displayed.

At the gates, I was greeted by two sentries who were unknown to me. They were attentive, but gregarious amid the bustle of visitors filing by. Aware that I had not been among the other pilgrims, they halted me as I approached. Quickly familiar when I told them who I was, they were pleased to tell me they were the brothers of one of the nuns, and like a story that mirrored the Ethiopian twins in Egypt, they had been retained as guards after they had arrived and located their dearly beloved sister. When they were unable to convince her to go home with them, the convent agreed to an unusual arrangement for one season. They happily found the accommodation a better choice than returning to their overbearing parents. They possessed a few basic skills as soldiers, no special competence, but they would at least be there to hold off marauders until the alarm was sounded and the nuns had time to seek cover or initiate the security we had developed.

The two brothers reported that pilgrims were there because Sister Athracht had arrived and was installed as permanent abbess. I had not been back in more than a season, and now I understood why. Comgall would have known for some time that she would be arriving, and he would have been laying obstacles and denying requests for my return there.

I feared Athracht's arrival was simply fate hounding me. Anyone who had a connection to Comgall troubled me. I worried the women's gentle abbey might become dominated by a self-absorbed tyrant who was simply Father Comgall in a nun's robe. It seemed like an arrangement made in hell. But I had no choice and nowhere else to go. My plan was to slip into my tiny hut outside the walls and hole up for days or weeks until a caravan traveled east to Dubhlinn.

Sister Athracht was staying in another part of the small monastic settlement. Designed with elegance and order, the nun's abbey was wonderfully efficient. Built of wood and stone with conical thatched roofs and arched doorways, the squat, round buildings huddled in clusters. The buildings were connected by winding slate pathways, all nestled inside concentric stone walls.

I was always pleased when allowed to do repairs within the compound. Although I was not allowed to be alone with anyone, except the abbess, I was permitted brief conversations with a bevy of sisters. Their conversations were always enlightening. Those from wealthy families had training in the arts, literature, and several languages. They had been diligent students who had acquired knowledge while ignoring myriad distractions pursued by their idle brothers. Now they freely shared their training with the other women.

The two sentries allowed me to wait until I was announced to the new abbess. I assumed I would be invited inside the walls to meet her. Pilgrims had taken over my slate hut so I wandered a short way from the walls where I could view the rosy and golden dawn.

One of the novices arrived outside the gates, handing bread and dried fish to pilgrims. She glanced around toward my hut, then saw where I stood nearby.

"You are Brother Lazar?" she called. She quickly pushed back in place a feathery strand of copper hair that slipped from her veil.

"Yes, sister," I said.

"Our abbess, Sister Athracht, would like to see you," she said, veiling her eyes from the rising sun with a hand. "It is quite crowded inside. Please. Wait here outside the gate," she said, motioning. "She would like to come out to meet you when she is ready and view the sunrise." She hurried off, forgetting to leave my portion of breakfast. Smiling pilgrims offered to share their food, but I waved them off. They looked as though they needed it far more than me.

Wandering a short distance from the gate again, expecting the brothers to summon me when she was ready, I stood looking away at the hills, glittering in the first breath of spring. A sliver of silver sun was spying over the hill, and an uncommonly warm breeze rustled the heather. The birds twittered, the abbey's roosters crowed, and cows lowed for milking.

"From the womb of the dawn to you belongs the dew of your youth," a woman said, startling me. I felt a stab of shame, hearing these words I had contemplated long in the past when I had made the tragic mistake of leaving my beloved Miriam. "Brother Lazar, a name so like Lazarus of Bethany," the small woman continued as she inched up to me. As if she had slipped past the sentries unseen, I had not heard them greet her at the gate or heard her steps. She stood next to me, vibrant and lean, intensity in her eyes that would embarrass a king. She was much younger than her brother. What had been sad, wilting excess in her brother's features was a serene and lovely countenance on her. The full lips, and straight brow expressed grace and not the disdain of Comgall.

Latin was spoken at the monastery, sprinkled with some of the Gaulish Gaelic native to Hibernia. Her brother had refined his speech to overcome his rural accent and tried to banish the rustic Gaelic at the monastery. But Athracht's tone was full and sparkling like a Gaelic waterfall set in a country glade. Though the language was not entirely removed from Germanic speech, the Gaelic tongue had twists and turns that made it different from its Gaulish roots. On her lips, it was melody.

Comgall had done nothing to help me learn the language's intricacies, so I had gathered what I could from the monks and sisters.

"Yes. Yes, sister," I stuttered. "Brother Lazar. Abbess Athracht?"

She nodded curtly. As quickly as her brother was able to call alarms to defense, Athracht disarmed and all defenses fell away in her presence.

We stood for moments watching the wink of sun as it continued to lift its pink eyelid over land. Green turned to glistening emeralds, diamonds, rubies, and sapphires and spilled carelessly on blades of grass, displaying the profoundly skewed economy of Earth: shameless abundance.

"I love this world simply because of what I see in it of eternity," she said.

"Excuse me, Abbess; who has said this?" I asked.

She smiled and raised a brow. "I just did!"

I nodded stupidly, looking down, then back to the horizon.

"Do you see how our souls are nestled here in creation? How is it that the Creator should weave a nest just for us?" She paused. "No. Not my words, it 'twas a dying farmer in Connacht. He had been a donkey's arse to us until he realized he was dying. This imparted to him the profound knowledge that he would finally have to separate himself from his cozy nest. He said he had seen it in a vision." She grinned and shook her head. "I doubt it. He did not want to admit that he had been wrong toward us and had missed the entire point of life in the bargain. He then turned over all his holdings to his daughter, except for the small corner of his property we had requested for our tiny convent. But the memory returns to me on mornings like this." She nodded toward the horizon. "Maybe the old farmer had a vision, maybe not. But he was right. Here we are, our souls are nestled for a time."

She handed me a narrow loaf of warm bread that steamed in the fresh morning. From a bag, she began to withdraw pieces of dried fish, then changed her mind, shook and hefted the bag, shrugged, and handed it all to me.

"Here. You will need this for your journey," she said, eyes narrowed. She tipped her head quickly. "And with that, I have something to tell you."

"You have already told me. Somehow you know I am on a journey. That may be more than I myself know," I said. I held up the bread and she nodded, allowing me to eat. "So, I imagine I best listen to what you have to tell me."

"Yes, that may be wise. Where do you go from here, do you suppose?" She smiled, looking back toward the brightening horizon.

I shrugged. I thought I would be staying at the abbey for a time, but Athracht seemed to know more than I did. Or maybe they needed to hold onto my hut for a special guest. I did not have time to wonder.

"Why do you suppose I was bothered with a dream about you, good sir?" she finally asked.

"What do you mean, Abbess?" I said.

"Call me Athracht." She smiled at me sideways for a second, sniffed, and faced the dawn. "I was visited in a dream. I have to say, despite stories about me, this is not something that happens often. Dreams. So, this troubles me; intrigues me."

She grinned at my confused stare.

"You know my brother. *Ach*, of course you do. I have not spoken to him in many years. Can you believe it? But that man hated it that I had a dream that led me into my life of devotion. All that steered him was pride." The corner of an eye watched me again; she shook her head quickly. "No. I will not disparage him more."

She swept her arm across the gold and green valleys. "Describe this to a blind person." She closed her eyes and inhaled the morning aromas. "Describe that scent to someone who cannot smell." She placed her hands on her hips, elbows flaring. "Explaining spiritual things to someone who has not been ignited by the Holy Spirit is like explaining this glorious sunrise to the blind or the morning breeze to someone who cannot smell. Explanations of the heavenly would be meaningless to a poor man like my brother. I have found that when someone is bankrupt of the Spirit, they are only interested in what they can experience. The Spirit opens our minds to a world beyond.

"Yes—your brother. I am very familiar with him. That is why I am here." I skewed a smile, cautious to proceed. "Our lives became...incompatible."

"Comgall is incompatible. Many of us carry around these little peculiarities, these little eccentricities, thinking they make us seem unique, wise, or somehow righteous. These, too, we must give over to our Lord. We must ultimately be willing to cede, subdue, submit every facet of ourselves to him for his glory alone, until he is seen *through* us by the world, not despite us." She sighed. "My brother thought his little peculiarities were special—a gift from God. His terse manner, his superiority, his vain interest in relics and ruin he thought should be fostered to make himself seem unique. But these qualities make him more...incompatible."

Looking down, she shook her head. "Finally, I gave him over to the love of Christ." As though grasping her thoughts, she made a fist with her small hand. "There is a love so powerful that it flies true as a bolt, smashes through the walls of sin, and shatters the hardened heart. And there is love so deep that no wall can stand against it or stem the rising tide of his grace. His love overwhelms the feeble barricades that we have placed in its way. It can be true even for those like my brother." She placed a hand on my arm and smiled. There is a touch sufficient as a hug.

"But you already know this, gentle traveler," she said. "Is that man still in his cups? Oh, do not answer that." She waved her hand. "'For all have sinned'—that is you and me— 'and fallen short of the glory of God.' Deep down in his heart, I fear my brother concentrates so painfully and narrowly on sin that he cannot see the Hand outstretched." She slowly shook her head. "Out of a frothy tide, we have been lifted from drowning, yet we continue to flail, trying to improve our ability to swim. This effort is meaningless. I fear my brother works hard at becoming an excellent swimmer, but he does not realize that by the sacrifice of the Lamb, we are all fishes now!" She giggled like a girl, paused, and clapped her hands. "I am sorry," she said catching her breath. "I hope I am not becoming a fountain of repetitious sayings. Oh, my! I do hate platitudes. I am working on that. Just last night, I was reading the ancient text of Ecclesiastes: 'A season for everything.' I was castigated to stop using foolish platitudes. The book teaches that meaningless sayings are just that—meaningless, because every platitude has its opposite: Is it always good to be silent or is it always good to speak? Is it good to gather or is it always good to cast away? The wise man wrote that everything has a season, a time determined. He knew that life unfolds. It is not written like a song of foolish sayings."

Her silences were long as though she were not in conversation with me alone but listened to another voice speaking from beyond her deep thoughts. The corner of her mouth creased her cheek, and she shook her head slowly, amused and a little exasperated with herself.

"Sister, I think you were about to tell me of a dream," I said.

"Oh, yes, my dream. Good heavens. Of course."

"Brother Lazar!" We turned to a joyous, familiar voice: Sister Bernice. She had been one of the stout farm girls who had been a novice and now, a bit stouter, a nun. Before I could flinch, she swept her foot to the back of my knee, grabbed my hand, and dropped me onto the soft grass, planting her knee on my chest. She looked down at me with a smile dimpling her red cheeks and curls of black hair escaping from her veil.

"Sister Bernice!" Athracht scolded.

"I thought he would defend himself," she pleaded as she stood, pulling me up while firmly gripping my hand and arm. She found my piece of bread, picked off bits of grass, and handed it to me.

"So good to see you again, Sister." I brushed myself off. "Well done," I said, wary.

She laughed and slapped my back. "Are you stayin' on a while?"

"I don't know. Am I safe here?"

"Most certainly you are not safe if you cannot defend yourself better than you taught us." She laughed again, turning to Sister Athracht. "May we start our meeting without you, Sister?"

"Oh my, yes. I will try not to be too long with our guest," Sister Athracht said.

"Later, friend." Bernice punched my shoulder.

Athracht grinned. "Thank you for preparing these women, Brother. I have known of no other monastery like this on the entire island. You have given them much."

"It was all joy," I replied, rubbing my shoulder.

"Brother Lazar, I will tell you about my dream—if there be no further interruptions." She tilted a smile at me, grasping her forearms inside the long sleeves of her robe. "So, in this dream, a woman, whose name I somehow knew to be Mary, approached me on a hill. At first, you see, I was in awe because I thought this could be the Madonna, herself. But no, it was not she." The nun began to walk away slowly, and I followed her the few steps to a low stone ledge overlooking the valley. She sat on the cool rock, patting the mossy surface for me to sit beside her.

"Behind this woman named Mary walked another woman, whom I was led to believe was her sister."

"Martha," I whispered.

"Yes, I suppose that was her name—it was—Mary and Martha from the Gospels. And you are Brother Lazar. Maybe that is why I had this dream," she said with a slow, secret smile I was unable to decipher. "But scattered behind the other sister were others making their way up the hill. They dotted the slope, stepping carefully around tufts of grass and heather. And I specifically remember a bright light at my back that was shining down the slope in their faces. It was not the rising sun, but it lit their faces beautifully as they came up the hill. It was as though this procession were headed not toward me, but toward the light at my back." Her brows drew together, briefly touching her lip with her finger, concentrating. "I felt as though I was not worthy to turn and look toward this light."

I nodded attentively.

"This woman, Mary, held a parchment in her hand. I knew it was one of the Disciple Paul's letters. Mary paused in front of me and said, 'for our brother, these words....'. Then she read to me from the parchment."

"W-what did she say? What did it say?" I interrupted. Though beneath my excitement was a vague sense of impending guilt.

Athracht looked at me, sensing my eagerness. Narrowing her eyes, her lower lip protruding, she looked across the valley from where we sat. "It was a verse I know well. Maybe that is why I dreamt it." She pressed her fingers to her forehead in thought, then recited the verse. "This is the verse Mary read to me: 'For since death came through a man, the resurrection of the dead comes also through a man. For as in Adam all die, so in Christ all will be made alive. But each in his own turn.'" As she continued, her fist beat the rhythm of the verse on her knee, "'Christ the first fruits; then at his coming, those who belong to him....'" She turned to me. "This woman, Mary, came closer to me and said more."

"What did she say?" I asked, anxiously.

"She said, 'For as in Adam all die, so in Christ all will be made alive.'"

Not knowing what to say, I did not speak.

She patted my knee. "It is a strange coincidence to me that a man named Brother Lazar should be so interested in, so quick to recognize, a woman named Mary, and another named Martha—as you said. I say this merely as an observance, though I cannot help but sense something profound—hidden—about you." She shrugged. "But I have seen many mysteries in my lifetime. The Holy Spirit is very much alive on this wilderness island. The good Saint Padrich has indeed riled up more than serpents! He has riled powers and principalities we can barely imagine. I have seen it: pagans and druids, strange spells, mysterious signs foretelling the future, ancient ruins. And years ago, that horror that my brother was rumored to have kept penned up next to the monastery."

I set the scrap of bread on the stone between us while I sat silently searching the tops of the trees dipped in gold from the rising sun.

"I am here to deliver what I saw," she said. "Nothing more. I do not pretend to be a prophet or the mouthpiece of our Lord Jesus. That would be presumptuous beyond words. My intuition told me you would be interested." A smile was in her eyes.

I did not feel the tear winding down my cheek. "As in Adam all shall die.... Does this mean I shall know death, then?" I mumbled before guarding myself. "Are you telling me this dream because my name is Lazar, or is there more that you know? Am I to be given this gift of death soon?"

Her laughter was as pure as the tinkling of tiny bells. "Oh, Brother Lazar! 'Gift of death'? Jesus, Mary, and Joseph! You are the gloomy one. I do not know any of what this could mean. I am telling you that I had a dream. That is all. We will all taste death. It is always soon, I believe. At least it always seems soon as it approaches, I suppose.

"Wait," she held up her hand. "Oh, goodness. I almost forgot. The woman, Mary, said two final words. I thought she was speaking to me, but now that I think of it, they could have been for someone else."

"What did she say?"

"Stop seeking. That was the last thing the woman told me."

"Stop seeking?" I asked myself. *Stop seeking: Death? Happiness? Home?* It deeply touched me, though I could not discern what it meant.

She held up a finger, pausing my thoughts. "I had one more impression that occurred to me as I awoke. Also from the Disciple Paul: 'We are pressed on all sides, but not crushed; perplexed, but not in despair; persecuted, but not forsaken; struck down, but not destroyed. We always carry around in our body the death of Jesus, so that the life of Jesus may also be revealed in our body...' She rubbed her chin. "This has always been a mystery to me. We carry—you carry, I carry—the death of Jesus so that his life can be revealed—in these very mortal bodies of ours." Leaning back, she laced her fingers around a knee. "Imagine that; first consider how 'in Adam all die, so in Christ all will be made alive.' Then comes 'so the life of Jesus may also be revealed in our body.' Fascinating."

Could it be, I wondered, *that his life was being revealed in me in not one lifetime, but many? Lifetime after lifetime? Each with another opportunity to reveal the life of Yeshu. Was it up to me to figure out what my immortality meant?* We gazed across the valley, watching a small dule of doves flushed from a cedar as it circled and returned to roost.

"You have given me much to think about," I said.

"I do not know who you are. I could speculate if I were one to do so, but I am not—not about things I cannot comprehend. I was simply handed a letter and I delivered it. That is how I see it." She wrapped her small arm around my shoulder.

I wiped my eyes. She handed me her small kerchief.

"Thank you. Bless you, Sister. You have given me much assurance," I said.

"I have to often remind myself that I have—we have—but one job," she said. "It is a simple one. I am like the sister Martha. I want to do so many things and get so far out ahead of what is needed that I forget we have one task: to minister the restoration that Jesus provides. He provided it; we just hand it out. We are directing pilgrims—and often each other—down that one-way road. How hard can that be? We are so busy preparing and ordering this material world for Jesus that we neglect to simply sit, gaze, and listen to him: Like the other sister, Mary."

"Sweet sisters," I whispered to myself.

"I do not know what you know. You do not know what I know." She swept her arm across the valley again. "Dreams are mysterious, yet they are not so different from life. We do not really *see* anything now. All the things we behold with our eyes are mere reflections of light striking our eyes, merely a bland representation of what is there. All objects that we see are according to our interpretation, nothing more, drawn and defined by our private vision, emotions, and experiences. We do not see with our eyes the invisible physical nature of an object or the mysterious laws that keep it in place. We see things merely as they exist in relationship to other things—and to us. When we look across this landscape, we are overlooking countless details and interactions that we lump together into a unified picture. Not that it is not real. It is real. Real to me and real to you. But both you and I may look at the same scene and see similarities—on the surface—but for each of us, our vision is at best an interpretation of what is before us. We share the simplest, the least common understanding of what is seen."

I may have been staring at her with my mouth open.

"Oh, I am sorry, my friend. My brother thought these ramblings were the fantasies of a foolish schoolgirl. My sisters here at the monastery can abide me for only so long, and now I see that I have wearied you, too."

"No, not at all, sister. I have not had opportunity to hear such things for a very long time," I said. "And I certainly never heard anything like that from your brother," I blurted, then winced.

"Oh, my. Your face!" She laughed, scarcely able to catch her breath. "Oh, yes." She dried her eyes, then held her hand to her mouth, trying to control the impulse to laughter until she regained her composure. "I am sorry, but dreams like this set me off on these journeys of the mind, I fear." She nodded thoughtfully. "It just strikes me as remarkable how in dreams we create a world of sensations, emotions, and interactions all within our minds. It is just like those things I was saying about each of us having our singular view of the world. It is wonderful to have someone to discuss these things with."

"I am afraid I have been blessed mostly to listen. I wish I had more to say. I am captivated."

"Well, thank you for being captivated, then." Her laughter was generous. "It is like I was saying, in dreams—like the dreams about your sis...those women—we create illusions while we sleep. Entire worlds spring to life in our heads." Then, cupping her hands like a shell, she said, "My dreams, anyone's dreams, are like this shell of perception and illusion that we retain without all the reality inside of it. It just confirms what I was saying about that individual portion of our view of the world. The world is perceived by and shaped by us through our five senses and our emotional responses to them; they are merely tools with which we record. Our senses are the pen, ink, or parchment. If you do not connect these tools to the mind, they are like tools used for writing;

merely a reed, some pigment, or the fibers of parchment. Nothing more. Worthless items on their own." She took a breath, then continued. "In my study of Ecclesiastes, it also states that 'the eye never has enough of seeing nor the ear its fill of hearing.' They are organs recording the world around us. Our eyes and ears will never be satisfied; will never be filled. They cannot be. They can never stop mopping up sight and sound. Just look out there! I am so inspired." She lifted her chin toward the landscape. "It is what our senses do. The world of humanity equates wisdom with how much one has seen and heard, how much our senses have acquired of this world, whereas our Lord equates wisdom with one thing: what we have seen and heard of him. That is why we must remember how important it is to have victory in the battle for the mind." She tapped her finger to her head.

I felt small, the same as I had often felt in the presence of Yeshu. Like Old Man Mountain, I was seeing another face of God: the face of his Son, cast on the countenance of this small woman.

She swept it all away with a brush of her hand. "Oh, dear man, why are you listening to my nonsense? I can just rattle on and on if you let me. I am already missing my appointed time with the sisters. I am terrible and I do this to them too often. Will you hear my confession?" she grinned and shoved my shoulder.

"No. I—"

"I am sorry. I have been studying a lot lately, so my head is crammed up. I am searing much into my brain. But I have learned that when the way is clear and we are growing, we need to use these mountaintop experiences to gain momentum for the way down, using spiritual height to its full advantage. When we are on those clear, lofty heights, we must study harder, pray often, and share—like this—whenever we have the opportunity. Then I may withstand it when I plunge back into the valley."

"I know so little, sister, but I know when I need to listen, and I know those rare times when I need to speak. I am inspired by all you say. You are lighting a pathway on this journey. Though, I do not know how much farther it will be or how much more I can endure."

"I wish, dear brother, that I could tell you that God will not give us more than we can endure. But that is simply not true. It never has been.

I know this." She looked earnestly at me and patted my knee. "And I believe you know this, too."

Together, we paused to watch the landscape. The breeze had picked up to a steady Gaelic wind; the sun was now balanced on the top of the hill wicking away the dew. "I am sorry I have caused you to tarry, Sister. You are awakening in me again something buried, something forgotten: the central language of the Universe. I can say it no other way," I said.

She nodded quickly, urging me on.

"At those rare times when I hear wisdom like yours," I said, "I am reminded that in my life there are few precious things that reappear or recur. But I see this communication between the Creator, his creation, and his people is recurrent and constant. What you are sharing is the central language, the constant voice of the universe, the life blood and respiration of the cosmos. It is the Word, and this Word that became flesh. At least I have learned that much."

"Well said. Yes, there is no better way to put it," she said. "And I am convinced that if we were to peer into the depths of this vast universe, into the mind of God himself, and hear his communication with his creation, and if we were somehow to understand this voice of the cosmos as you put it, we would hear one word. And if we could see into the furthest extent of his plans, we would see written that same word: love. How remarkable."

We were both silent a long while, missing the warnings as two ravens passed overhead calling alarm. The doves were flushed from the cedars again and did not circle back.

"I hope you can stay a while. Like I tell the sisters, there is not always joy, but there can always be comfort; there are not always answers but there is always assurance. There can...." But she was no longer looking at me. She stood, stepped away from the ledge and gaped across the valley washed in sunlight. Her face was drawn and confused. She pointed.

There on the crest of a hill, shining in a manner that gave challenge to the early sun, stood those horrors of my dreams. They were little more than brilliant points of light in the distance, their shapes barely discernible, but above them the skies churned with turbulent color that defied the sunrise.

With dry mouth, I stuttered, "Was this in your dream? Is it...is it as Mary indicated in the dream? I fear that my death approaches."

"What do you mean? What is it? What sort of infernal creatures pursue us? Angels? Demons?" she asked. Fear and confusion defiled her gentle features.

"No, Sister. I do not know what they are. I believe these are beings biding their time in jealousy—and fear. But truthfully, I do not know what they are, and their arrivals are unpredictable and unexplained. They may be here to find that old acquaintance of theirs whom your brother had imprisoned long ago. But they are too late, so now they will continue searching. I will depart soon, or I fear they will descend here to take me. They will spare no one."

Hurriedly I told her the little I knew of them. We watched. They did not turn around but appeared to recede into themselves and vanished over the hill. They would not be far. I feared for Father Comgall's monastery and now for the nuns.

XXIV. Leaving Hibernia

THOUGH IT BECAME URGENT that I flee, I was blessed when more of the women rushed out of the abbey toward us. Brief greetings became sudden farewells, and Athracht drew me aside. "There is one more thing." She motioned to one of the women who dashed inside the gate, then returned carrying a simple cedar box. The Chi-Rho symbol, which represented the first two letters of the name of Christ, was inlaid on the lid. "Do not look in it now. You will know the right time. But carry it with you; I believe it will bring blessing to you," she said.

I took the box with thanks, then wedged it in my pack among the few items I carried, including a small selection of my blades. Such things were always useful for trading. After years in the monastery, I owned nothing else of value.

My morning with Sister Athracht had been too short.

Throughout the day as I walked east, the Immortals stood far off. I saw their light or their shimmering visage on distant hills. Though I had never been able to discern their intention, I was pleased with the possibility that I might be luring them away from the monasteries. Not understanding their nature, I could not know for certain if the creatures had left me as I hiked across the great island. I could hope they had not returned to those holy enclaves to visit terror upon the monks or the sisters.

Toward evening, I was searching for a rocky outcropping or a pile of rubble where I could seek shelter as deep and protected as possible. It was a futile strategy, knowing who my enemy was, and knowing they could sunder rock as easily as bodies.

At the foot of a steep hill, I scanned upward to where the last rays of sun washed rocky heights while in the valley where I stood it was darkening. I did not want to scramble all the way up this mountain, but

I surveyed the slopes and crags. Standing like a row of sentries, a wall of stone leaned away from the face of the rock. This would be my refuge.

It was a short climb, but the sun had set when I reached the wall. As evening crept toward night, I gained solace knowing I was not seeing the ravaging displays of destruction or the glow of fires in the sky over the monasteries, which would have signaled that the Immortals were carrying out their devastation. I held out hope that they would spare these innocents.

I tucked in behind the wall and found a small cleft that seemed as dry and snug as though it had been prepared for me. I laid a mat of grass and moss over a few twigs and climbed into the crevice surrounded by utter silence amid the damp odor of rock and earth. Resting my head against my pack, I felt burdened with my foolishness and my long and meaningless life. Trying to remember the caring words of Sister Athracht was not enough to comfort me in that long night. Weighed down, I sank into sadness. At the core of this misery was the loss of my simple, satisfying life at the monastery. I had not been aware how precious that life had become. Though enduring the abuse from Comgall, I had found a corner of the world where I may have survived if I were able to outlive that conniving priest. And I had found an uncommonly bright light in Sister Athracht. But I had been cheated, immediately forced to leave her. Like tar, my despair settled into the cleft in the rock as I twisted on my bed of sticks and moss.

Melancholy is a comfortless garment. Its fibers knit into my heart and across the fabric of my spirit. Pure and stark, emotional suffering lays a pattern over the entwined threads that weave our soul. I am not inclined to give into this darkness, but I cannot deny it. In the tapestry of my life, it provides perspective and draws attention to depths I would have crossed unaware while skipping freely on the surface of life.

And what tapestry could be woven without black? God intends to make the best people, not the happiest, and because we are damaged vessels, the best of us are formed in a crucible.

Within the cool embrace of the rock, amid my emotional suffering and the tatters of my squandered life, I fell into fitful sleep.

I may have been inspired by the dreams of Sister Athracht. In the moment before awakening, in that strange sentience between soul and mind, I had a dream that unfolded more a simple story than a dream:

like the puppet shows or a Roman play from my childhood. Though I played a role in this story, there were few images. In this tale, I was a small boy, and I had been given a lamb by my father. I loved the lamb, and I wanted to train it up and care for it, but the lamb was impossible to control. It was constantly breaking out of its pen, ravaging the garden, or running away into the wilds. This little lamb was impulsive and careless. In desperation, I came to my father. Strangely, it was not my father from Judea. Someone else was playing my father in this story. Azvald? Paul or Yeshu? It seemed to be someone from my distant past. The father had spread a scroll in front of his face; I could see his hands on each side as he casually studied it, but I could not see his face. I approached to talk with him.

"What is it, Lazarus?" the man asked kindly.

"It is the lamb, Abba." I spoke as I would have addressed my father when I was a child.

"What is wrong with your lamb, son?" he asked.

"I cannot do anything with him. He will not do as I say, he is getting into trouble all the time and I cannot train him. He will not obey or do anything I tell him."

"Well, son, what did I tell you when I gave him to you?"

"I do not remember," I whined.

"I told you that if you do *alpha*, I will do *beta*." I knew the man behind the scroll was smiling, though I could not see his face.

"I do not understand," I replied.

"I told you that if you give him to me, I will train him for you. Then I will give him back to you." He said it as though it should be as easy as handing him a stone. "It is simple as that. It has always been that simple and it will always be."

I thought I was awakening as I heard myself saying, "Yes, Father, here then; take it. I cannot manage it." Once again, I was giving my little lamb—this life—into the care of those hands.

Then I heard another voice.

"Lazarus, come forth!" The tone was strident but gave assurance. I stirred. Cramped in the cleft of rock, my stiff joints resisted.

"Lazarus, come forth!"

I jolted, my heart racing, my fear melting to wonder as I began to recognize a familiar voice. The most familiar voice any soul will ever hear.

"Rabbi?" I whispered. I was too frightened to be certain.

"Do I have to come in there to get you?" the voice asked.

Confident that I was dreaming, I pried myself from the cleft and stepped out.

Red and lavender, laced with scuttling clouds, the beauty of the morning sky could have been diminished only by the beauty of the man's gentle laughter carried on the warm spring breeze, sufficient to brighten the entire mountain and the valleys that stretched below. He was dressed in a simple tunic with a golden sash around his waist. A long, purple mantle was pinned to his chest, draped around his shoulders, and fell along his right side. It took several rapid heartbeats before I recognized him with certainty.

"Rabbi? Yeshu!" I rushed to him. Overcome, I fell at his feet, tears pouring from my heart and unraveling from my soul. I felt the surge of strength in his fingertips as he took my hand and raised me to my feet. I could not look away from his face, his wonderful face; profound, yet ordinary, distant as infinity, yet as familiar as a sister.

"When may I go with you?" I blurted.

"It is not time. Soon. Not now. I know your path has seemed long. I know it has. But each of your steps has been set in eternity. This is not true for you alone, but for everyone. You will simply have a few more steps than most." He grinned.

"But, Rabbi, I...."

"No, not now. You are not the only one to have lived so long on the earth. You are not the only one who has traveled—or is traveling this long path. Why do you always think you are the only one? You are never the only one." With his hand on my shoulder, he was chiding me more than chastising me. "You will see."

"Rabbi, you said I am not the only one. Those terrible beings that pursue me and have wrought tremendous destruction wherever I go, are they...?"

"I know of whom you speak. They are not your concern. They are on a path parallel to yours and part of a plan that is likewise finite. Do not concern yourself—not about any of this."

"But Rabbi...."

"My time is very brief, but you will not be alone. You were never alone. Never. You will be shown a way, but it will not be to the north country. Not now. Do not seek this path. As a gift, you are to have a season of reprieve, of restoration. It is my promise and comfort to you."

"Where do I go? I fear for those in the monasteries. What am I to...?"

"If you do *alpha*, I will do *beta*." He held two fingers, then crossed them. "Remember?"

I stammered something.

"Now go. You left your pack in the rock. The good Sister gave you a box that will secure passage for you—and freedom for another who has also waited a long while. Retrieve your pack."

Was I to follow him? With my knees wobbly and hands shaking, I crawled into the crevice, scrabbling around for my pack—and awoke. In a moment, I was once again prying my stiff joints from the cold rock. A dream? No, it could not have been a dream. I scrambled out of the shallow cave and the sun was already painting the valley. As I searched for him in vain, the emptiness felt hollow and deep again.

I had tormented myself for so long, and I had surrendered much by leaving the monastery. But now I had been given a gift I desperately needed at the precise time I needed it: Assurance.

A wave of excitement crested in my spirit. Something new. I felt emboldened for discovery.

I was renewed and emboldened and my soul was light. I could have danced the straight journey across the remainder of the island. When I found the high road of the Esker Riada across the island, there was no longer evidence of the dreaded Immortals.

My mind was no longer on my safety or security. A disheveled monk traveling alone attracts little attention. Though, I may have been more concerned for my safety if I had looked in the wooden box that Sister Athracht handed me when I departed.

For more than a week, I lay over in dark Dubhlinn in dank quarters. Through subterfuge and a small bribe, I was able to stay at the sad monastery set at the end of a muddy path near the docks. I had opened

Athracht's little box to find the usual relics that were sacred currency only among the jaded Believers: chicken bones and rotting wood chips laid upon *sands from the Holy Lands*. Those who possessed eternity and the wealth of heaven regarded this as treasure? I had thought better of Athracht. The superior at the Dubhlinn monastery greedily accepted a couple of knuckles of bone when I told him they had been given to me by Athracht. I do not know which saint's knuckle or long-dead priest's finger I mentioned in the exchange, and I do not think it would have mattered.

When I left Athracht, I did not have a plan apart from securing passage that would skirt the great, seething island to the east, swarming with an influx of Saxons and Angles, and deliver me to the mouth of the northern continent's massive rivers. I had hoped those rivers would be my highway home. I had no idea if the homelands would be safe, or if after a generation, there would be anything left of my family and village.

But after my vision or dream of Yeshu, I had surrendered the rudder of my life. Like my sister Mary, I would watch and wait.

Each day, I kept vigil at the harbor to find a worthy vessel. On the decaying docks that lay above bobbing green jetsam, I kept moving, pacing the rotting planks, to avoid the teetering advances from reeking prostitutes and scabbed beggars.

Dawn of my final day in Dubhlinn, I arrived at the pier to find a barnacled vessel nodding on greasy waters, thudding against the horsehair buffers attached to the posts. For a moment, I thought the vessel had been abandoned until I heard a scuttle and shouting on board. Sailors wrestled and cursed, pulling emaciated slaves from the hold, and extracting a flood of painful memories from my soul. Cries caused by whips and prods preceded the human cargo onto the decks. The painful scene was reenacted, as it had been century upon century, millennia upon millennia, as old as humanity itself: The utter misery of slavery and bondage.

I had not noticed a meager crowd gathering along the docks to watch the proceedings. A band of eager men had shuffled around me, looking up toward the ship with anticipation. Dubhlinn had scarce legal commerce, but a few wealthy landsmen or their stewards would arrive at the docks to move their bundles of cargo or for the prospect of slaves.

These fat spiders did not traffic in goods or grain; their treasure was lust and avarice.

"Ho, captain! What have we today?" one of the merchants called.

The ragged sailors pushed forward a tethered band of five men, squinting in the light, wounds bleeding and oozing. Huddled behind them was a group of four women. They had been haplessly cleaned and roughly kept just like my battered shipmates of a generation before. But there was no Cletus to stand in their place.

The male slaves were lowered first onto the dock. I had not seen a more hopeless troop of humanity. The odor was appalling. The merchants waved sleeves and stepped back from their human cattle.

The captain, lean and wily, leapt down to the creaking dock, staying clear of his cowering charges. "Silver will do; gold coin if you have it. No brass and no minims," he said in broken Saxon. "One hundred Roman for the lot or ten a piece will do," he chanted as rote as a barker from a market stall.

The human souls on the dock kept their gaze downward toward the moldy timbers under their cracked and weeping feet, stealing a quick glance at their soon-to-be masters.

"These monkeys are trash, captain. You know our bargain. Get the women down here so we can examine them," said a leering, bulging, red-faced young steward dressed in leather with a wispy growth of red beard that barely countered his baby face or distracted from his feminine contours. "Now, t'will do no good if we cannot get a peek under them skirts and squeeze them little titties," he guffawed.

Two of the merchants made a show of rubbing their hands together, grinning. They laughed like jackals.

Just as brutally, the women were lowered, their skirts riding up. They were pushed forward by the captain, but they knew better than to look up at the merchants. Two young women and two girls who were probably not of childbearing age. My heart ached as vivid thoughts of Bruna and Swanhilde were revived in my head.

The bargaining began.

If I would ever have a chance to repay all that young Cletus had done for me, this was that moment. Unable to restrain myself any longer, I stepped forward in desperation. I feared I would feel the lash or be thrown into the bilgewater brine before I could speak.

"Captain," I said, my mouth dry.

The merchants smiled sideways at me, but the captain would not turn toward me.

"Captain, I will..." I began.

He grimaced. "I am sorry, Brother Hocus Pocus; I am not in the market for any of your indulgences or heavenly favors." He spit at my feet. "Me an' the Devil have a wee bargain, and I intend to honor it." He laughed, joined by a chorus of the merchants and his sailors on deck.

The fat, freckled steward harshly elbowed me aside. "I have no fear of your saints an' gibberish."

I was shoved onto the planks, my pack spilling across the dock, and my small trove of blades clattering. As I scooped the meager contents, I picked up the cedar box that Sister Athracht had given me. The *sands from the Holy Land* had been scattered, the bronze latch hung broken, and the cedar case had cracked, but even without the sands, the box had heft. The chicken bones rattled as I wrenched it open. The remaining bones, wood chips, and pinch of sand would be of value to relic merchants or fools. I fingered through the thin layer of sacred debris and found a tiny bronze hasp on the floor of the box. While the auction proceeded, I turned the hasp and raised the cover to reveal a hidden compartment. I gasped loud enough to briefly distract the slavers from their bidding.

"Captain, hear my bid," I stepped up.

He was becoming angry and about to enlist his sailors to deal with me. "I swear, monk, I will sell you away on my next voyage if you are not silent, and if you do not leave here and crawl back to your stinking band of buggerin' Brothers...."

I held out the box. "Then do not take my bid. But this may cover the price of these souls."

He whisked it from my hand, opened it, and slammed it shut. Tossing it back to me, I fumbled and nearly dropped it again.

"I told you I do not want your relics of Saint Hen's Bones or Saint Whittle Chips! Now get out of here, or I swear I will sell you to these fine men."

I opened the box and dumped the chicken bones and wood chips onto the dock, eliciting a self-righteous gasp from the small crowd, even the soulless merchants. I peeled back the hardened leather at the bottom of the box to reveal a deep layer of gold: Three rows across and five rows long and at least five coins deep. A pound or more of gold. I held it out for the captain to see. There was enough gold to buy his slaves, his cargo, his ship, and half the buildings along this fetid pier.

He immediately grabbed my sleeve, pulled me close, and reached his arm around my shoulders, turning his back on the merchants, despite their protests. I held the box away from his clutches.

"Can we make a deal, Captain?" I asked, wincing at the stench of his nearness. I carefully opened the gold to him again.

"We can, er...we might." He touched the gold with his fingertip, then rubbed his face. He grabbed for the box, but I swept it away.

"Not so quickly; you would not steal from the Church in front of all these witnesses?" I spread my arm toward the onlookers. "It may not go well for future sales," I said to him. "Do we have a deal, then? I claim them all. All these slaves." I nodded toward the enslaved men and then to the women who were now looking at me in confusion. I did not know what I was saying, and I could not fathom what I would do next. I squeezed the captain's hand to seal our deal before he could change his mind. The merchants were incensed, and rushed the captain, cursing. But the captain swept his hand behind him, signaling two of his sailors, who responded by pushing the merchants away. They continued to hurl insults at the crew.

I felt like I was plunging headlong into an abyss, but I could not stop myself. I knew it would be impossible for me to lead the slaves away from the dock without being hijacked by the merchants or their henchmen. If we made it to the monastery, I would have no assurance that the monks would show any more mercy to the slaves than Comgall had to Cletus, and they would offer little protection from this mob.

I gathered my pack. Then palming a small dinner knife from my sash, I quickly slid behind the band of slaves. While the captain and his men were distracted, arguing with the merchants, I pretended to check each of the slave's bonds, but using my small knife, I severed the bindings.

A person who has once been a slave will know that all slaves are more than equal to their masters, and infinitely more desperate. Only the power of restraints separates them. I had confidence as I selected those who seemed the least broken and weary. I carefully slipped a blade from my pack into the hands of three of the men and the two older women.

They did not turn back but stood with confused smiles, looking at the captain and up at the ship's deck where the seedy crew lined the rail.

I was wagering everything: *in for a lepton, in for a drachma.* I recalled Markos's Greek phrase when his ship was about to plunge into terrible seas. But here I was, in for far more than a drachma and trusting that the slaves were ready to do the same. I knew if I acted swiftly, I had a chance of turning the tide before the captain, his crew, or the merchants, realized they could take back the slaves and keep the gold.

At my back, hidden in my sash, I had secured a long blade that I quickly withdrew. It took but one gentle push on the backs of the freed slaves. Unreeling the bindings that had been around their wrists and waists, two of them lunged forward. Moving with more skill than I had hoped, one of the men quickly put his knife to the captain's throat while the other bound the man's wrists.

Knowing there was nothing more dangerous or desperate than a slave mutiny, the cherub-faced merchant blubbered and started to reach for his knife, but he immediately thought better of it and scattered with the other merchants.

Two sailors on the dock began to draw swords. With screams that could have cracked timbers, the two women attacked them. The women wielded their short blades with no intention of taking captives. Pouncing on the men, they brutally slashed and clawed. They were hungry, ravenous to avenge their long voyage of torment. While the sailors lay in pools of blood and gore, the women continued to slash, rip, punch, and kick the bodies.

Seeing the women's ferociousness and blades in the freed men's hands, the remaining sailors stayed aboard ship, stunned, and staring down at the scene.

I knew from generations at sea that a mutinied captain is best killed. I could not. But I did not want him to have a chance to enlist his men onboard. I motioned for the freed men to lay him face down and secure him to a post while I looked up on deck where the crew of six or more sailors looked on. With blades drawn, they were uncertain of their next move.

"You can stay here with your captain, or you can give us your service!" I shouted to them in Latin. They did not understand until one of the former slaves interrupted to tell me most of the sailors were Saxon.

Stuttering with speech I had used little in more than a score and ten years, I repeated myself. Sailors were often conscripts from different harbors, who followed coin, not captains. They looked at each other, then down at their captain sprawled on the dock. I held up my hand to stay the women holding bloody knives. The dock reeked of carnage.

Three of the sailors ran farther along the gunwale and scrambled to the dock away from the women. They huddled for a moment, but soon bolted in the same direction the merchants had fled. The women glared after them.

"Will you sail with these men?" I asked the men and women as I pointed up at the sailors who remained. They translated and murmured among themselves, made a careful calculation of the sailors, and then nodded reluctantly.

"Those men were not our problem," one of the women offered in crisp Latin. "It was those two." She pointed at the decimated corpses at her feet. "And that dog turd." She pointed at the captain.

I nodded toward the ship. "If those sailors can be trusted, we will need all the help we can get. But we must leave now. There is a garrison, and those merchants will have the soldiers here before we can put oar to water."

The sailors on board moved back as the former slaves clambered up. I recovered the small relic box of gold, climbed up and had put my foot on the deck when I heard a keening cry. One of the women, black hair flying, dropped off the netting on the side of the ship. Before I could move, she fell upon the captain, her knee buried in his back; her knife swept across his neck while she screamed again. He thrashed against her blade. With a high gurgling squeal, he flapped like a dying fish until his blood mixed with the rancid waters under the dock. The sailors above had seen the spectacle and backed into a corner behind cargo. I held my hand up to them, intending to hold them for a moment and reassure them.

The woman grabbed the netting and swung onto the ship, looking down at the carnage with a tight smile. She looked at me, her features were Greek, maybe Jewish. She nodded quickly. "Ruth," was all she said, pulling her hair back and tying it. She slipped her arm around one of the girls.

What had I gotten myself into?

I opened the box, pried out three gold pieces, and flipped one to each of the three sailors. Their eyes widened. It was probably more than they had ever made in a year of bitter sailing. "I'll give you one of these coins today and another at the end of the voyage, maybe more, depending on your service. You will take care of these men and women, and you will supply them with everything they need."

Smiling feebly, they quickly nodded agreement.

We pushed away from the dock in minutes, the sailors, freedmen, and two women all straining at the oars in haste. We were able to ease the vessel out of harbor. I had nothing to go on, no idea where we were headed, a decrepit ship of former slaves, and a handful of sailors with unknown allegiances or skills. I would need charts, navigation bearings, and a harbor where I could restock and make this corpse of a ship seaworthy. The buoyancy of these former slaves would not float this ship forever.

Then, I would find my way again.

No. I would trust that a way would be shown to me.

XXV. At Sea Again

Spray and sun awoke within me a spirit lost. I looked beyond the harbor to the broad seas where the white waves gamboled like rams and felt my soul swell. Years of confinement and solitude at the monastery dropped away as I pulled off my tattered monk's robe and stood at the bow in linen singlet. I whispered across the sea, "Here I am, Yeshu. I did *alpha.* I am not entirely sure, but now I wait for you to do *beta*—or maybe you already have!" The sailors looked at me hesitantly as they worked the patchwork sails and aging lines, and the former slaves pondered me warily, wondering if, indeed, their lot had improved as they watched a half-dressed monk talking to the seas.

I always thought I would return north if given the chance. But now at sea, the sparkle and spray, and the sway of a ship under my feet, if there were immortality, I would embrace it. This is how I would live.

Riggings, sails, and rudders had changed in the many years since I had navigated with Markos. This seafaring relic would have been a large, well-appointed vessel in Markos's sailing days. Despite its barnacled timbers and need of repairs, the hull sat high, wide and sleek, and I was pleased that the sailors understood the confusing array of sails and lines. But once again, I would be less enamored of change than constancy. Ships may change, yet the sea and its challenges would be the same. We would need to find harbor soon to restore this aging raft of timbers to prevailing ship-craft.

I made a quick survey of the ship. At the stern, I found a cramped captain's quarters that had been occupied by Eho, the ill-fated captain. The space was little more than a flea-infested cot and a few bins stuffed with worthless baubles accumulated across the world. I pawed through the debris until I found a pod of roughly drawn charts.

I took the filthy blankets and straw mattress out the door and threw them overboard in a cloud of dust and bugs. With a hank of straw, I swept the platform where the mattress had lain. As the ship began swaying in open seas, I was about to sit in the dim light of the small port window to pore over the crude charts when I spied a length of rolled leather wedged between a shelf and the cabin wall. I untied the ribbon and carefully unrolled it. I drew in a breath. Artfully burned into greasy leather was a chart of Greek design like I had once seen while peering over a wealthy captain's shoulder. This would be Eho's most valued possession. My heart skittered at seeing outlines of Britannia, Hispania, Italy, and beloved Sardinia. With a finger, I traced a dear course over the seas of the Mediterranean, across Africa, Egypt, and all the way to Judea. Then back across to tiny Cyprus, which lay like an infant in the womb of the Eastern Sea. I stroked the little island, which was barely a smudge on the smooth sheen of the chart. I imagined the soft hand of the girl Miriam.

The chart showed little of the great northern expanses where I had lived with Bruna. It did not need to. Not then. For that moment, I was with Miriam, long before many brutal and foolish mistakes. So many lost...

"Uh, monk, uh, captain, uh, we..." It was one of the sailors. His Saxon was better than his former captain's. He looked over his shoulder quickly, fearing the slaves.

"Call me Lazar. And what is your name, sailor?" I asked, smiling.

"Theod, Captain Brother Lazar," he said, scratching his arm.

I smiled. "No, just Lazar. Theod, where are you from? You look to be Roman or Greek, yet you speak Saxon well."

"I am Roman. My father was a centurion in Germania, and my mother was a local girl. I grew up in the north where my father was stationed until he left the forces," he said.

"Why did you not speak sooner? I know Germania and hope to return."

"On these seas, a sailor is cautious until he knows which way the winds are blowing. We have seen much. Eho was a rat. He had his two henchmen that he kept close, but the rest of us were not treated much better than he treated the slaves. The three of them deserved what the women did to them." He spit out the door.

"I understand that a sailor like you needs to take heed. I have been at sea, but I have never captained a ship. We will have much to discuss, and I will need your help. But you have a question."

I could see a glimpse of pride scurry across his features when I solicited his help, but he gulped, more nervous because of our predicament and my inexperience than he was in fear of my authority.

"We have cleared land, er, Lazar. What should be our heading?"

I could decipher approximately where we were and where we would need to go—at least enough to gain our bearings. "We'll keep Draconius off the port quarter tonight. I want to stay well off Britannia and that ghastly Londinium to avoid authorities—or worse. We will head far out to sea if this sopping spruce log can hold together. It is calm and the weather seems fair. I think we can risk it," I said. He nodded and I followed him out the door.

The other two sailors stood away, watching the former slaves who had already raided the stores and were devouring dried fish and whatever food they could find. The fish was followed by full hands of grain shoved into their mouths. They greedily passed around a flask of water. I did not interrupt.

I called the other two sailors over to get their names and learn their stories. They were both Saxons. The younger would have been little more than a cabin boy on a larger vessel. With his big head and stubby fingers, Aelf suited his name. The young man barely came to my shoulder, but his legs had been nimble as he swung from the mast like an ape. Aelf told me the name of the third sailor: Farval. He was a bulky, quiet man, who never answered with more than a grunt or a stifled word, but his smile was enough to tell me he was satisfied to be done with Captain Eho.

"Where are they from?" I nodded toward the slaves.

"They are Gauls, we think." Theod leaned toward me. "We had little to do with them. We were above decks tending the ship." I sensed his defensiveness, but the Gauls had ignored the sailors, so I had little reason to doubt the men. "Eho bought them from a band of Frankish beasts. He got drunk with them—at least, the Franks were drunk. He bragged about how he had practically stolen them. He thought he could earn a gold mine with these cheap slaves and this crumbling cargo." Grinning, Theod scratched his head. "And he almost did!"

I would wait to make myself familiar with the freed men and women after they had eaten.

The sailors told me what they knew of battles and military campaigns in the region. Together, we devised a plan: After avoiding Britannia, we would tuck in below the jutting peninsula of Brittany and along its southern shore until we reached the River Loire. If it were safe, it might prove to be the best place to resupply and do repairs. Somewhere along that winding river, we might help these lost souls to find their way home. If they had homes.

The ship's manifest would have existed nowhere except in Captain Eho's mind. I found scant records in his cabin. Aelf and Theod helped to take stock of the cargo. There was well-made chain, rough tin, and more bales of wool. The clothing and wool explained why a loaded ship's draft was high. But the most value on board was several large jars of fine oil. This was a good cargo, better than I had expected, and it would bring a good price wherever we docked.

Several bundles of clothing had been secured from the same thieves from whom Eho had purchased the slaves. Clothing was useful cargo if it were of quality weave, dye, and stitching. We dragged the bales on deck, Aelf cut the cords, and we urged the freed to rummage through the heaps to find what they could. Pieces that were badly bloodied or moth-eaten were tossed overboard.

We pried open two barrels. Sealed under cedar chips and wax, to deter the slugs and moths, were rolls of colored cloth and clothing carefully folded and wrapped. The clothing was new and fine. But the freed men and women were not interested, preferring the simple things they had gleaned from the bales of used clothing. I pointed to the captain's cabin for the women to change. I cringed to think who may have owned this clothing or how it had been acquired. But it seemed of no concern to these former slaves.

I heard the other woman, Vocera, mutter sadly to Ruth as she held up a dress with faded blue plaid; then she clutched it to her breast before stepping into the cabin. Ruth had given furtive glances toward me since she had boarded. She shepherded the two girls ahead. She had chosen a disheveled hooded cloak. "It is how we can remember," she said. Explaining the clothing was a comfort to them, allowing them to remember those who had worn it before them.

From that time, Ruth would rarely lower her hood unless her work or the heat demanded.

Fed and clothed, the nine former slaves settled into the ship's routine. The women, with minds badly scarred, huddled away from the sailors, and graciously, the sailors kept their distance. Ruth would come forward to take food and water and dole it out to Vocera and the two girls.

Though the women kept away from the sailors, they did not seem concerned with those men who had been former slaves. They huddled every morning and every evening. I was not concerned that they were planning another mutiny because I had shared with them our plans and they believed we were headed to the river Loire. We had tried to accommodate their every need from the stores we had. But on the third evening, I sat nearby the group of former slaves, pretending to be studying charts.

"You may join us, Brother," Ruth called to me. Lowering her hood, she bunched her braids behind her head and tied them. She regarded me with that same disarming gaze since the voyage began.

I waved and shook my head. "Please call me Lazar."

"No, I am inviting you."

"You have earned your privacy, and I am sure you have much to discuss," I said.

"Oh, no, I thought you would be eager to join our meeting—I mean being that you are...were a monk after all." She grinned. As sunrise graces the morning, the smile brightened her face. I stared until I became embarrassed, knowing that she sensed my fascination. Unaffected, she did not look away.

"I—I do not know what you mean," I finally stuttered.

"We are people of The Way. We may not resemble the people of The Church whom you are so accustomed to, but we have preserved this group at great cost." She raised her sharp chin, showing the graceful angle of her jaw. "The Way has never met anywhere for long unless it has been at great cost."

The small band nodded in agreement, and one of the men extended his hand and patted the bale of wool nearby for me to sit.

"As I was said, we have preserved this group at a dear cost. There used to be twelve of us. Two of the women and one of the men became shark's food after they endured weeks of unspeakable brutalization,"

Ruth said as she slid her arm around one of the girls. The other former slaves did not understand much of Ruth's Latin, but they knew what she spoke of as her delicate hands made circles that included them—hands that days before had been brutal in dispensing justice and death to the captain and his men.

"Eho had no patience for us, or our faith, and he would beat us mercilessly. He killed her sister, Damona, for not leaving our group to be his chamber slave." She tightened her embrace on the girl. "At last, poor Damona could barely stand up from rape and brutalization. Despite our bonds, we tried to surround her, locking hands or standing shoulder to shoulder as his two sailors beat us and tried to pull us away. All the while joined in prayer; this was how we were often forced to meet. This was our prayer meeting, the cost of being a Believer." She swiped a hand beneath her nose while tears traced her cheeks.

It was a stark contrast to the preening Church I had endured. A sick, injured soul, surrounded by the entwined circle of fellow Believers. They pray earnestly, while enduring the ravages of the world. It was the true face of The Way that I had sought, but so rarely found since those years after the death and the return of Yeshu. I had heard rumors and sporadic reports of the persecution endured by Believers. In weakness, I had fled. That is what I did best. And by fleeing, I had spent my years avoiding the persecution in the east and throughout Rome.

"The women were part of The Way when taken captive, but not the men. We found ways to share with them until we became as one," she said. "It is prayer alone that is power. Our rescue at your hands was answered prayer. But you must already know all of this, monk." She added, almost an afterthought, "wherever you have been." Her gaze made me feel as transparent as a jellyfish. I did not reply.

"We have been restored, and I will not stop speaking of his rescue. Once again, we have been assured that prayer is the bridge between what God intends and what he eventually does. We prayed; his will was manifested. How can his will be made known if we do not pray? Answered prayer glorifies God. What could it benefit if answered prayer was meant only for our satisfaction?" She pointed to herself, then around at the gathered men and women. "Yes, prayer helps to grow us, but more importantly, it glorifies him and helps us to know his mind. 'The prayer of the righteous man avails much' because that man is changed to listen for the mind of God. Prayers are harmonizing with God's song."

Since my journey away from the bitter Comgall and his stifling monastery, much of my cynicism had abated through the help of Athracht and the ministry of Yeshu. Yet, in the presence of these spiritual warriors, questions arose that had followed me all my life. I do not know why, but now seemed the time, and Ruth seemed like she might be the one to ask. I felt compelled to meet her bold assertion by reaching for one of the last cynical arrows out of my quiver of doubt. I had to know her answer. I simply blurted, possibly more to myself than to this sincere woman, "If God knows all, why do we bother to pray for someone to be rescued—or for anything else? What if you had not been rescued? What of your fellow slaves? They were brutalized and thrown to the sharks."

"I just told you," she scolded. "I thought you were a man of God. Prayer is not simply a pastime; it is our sustenance! I prayed for each of those we lost and for each of those who are still here. The praying and the saving are parallel events like two plants growing side by side, entwining, drawing on one another for strength and sustenance until one grows from the other. God blesses both the one praying and the one saved. He has used a single event to save the one and bless the other. I am never foolish enough to discern or question something as trifling as results. Tragedy or triumph is not our verdict. I have learned enough to know it is fruitless to question him because when I do, I am always wrong."

"But what of the ones who were lost?" I persisted.

"God knows. I am certain they would gladly endure again all the pain they suffered if they were to gain one minute of the bliss in which they now exist."

Though she smiled, her eyes bore into me. I was smitten, and I am ashamed to say, not with God's Spirit alone. This was another who possessed that uncommon soul that reflected the presence of Yeshu to me. As if Sister Athracht had followed me and continued our conversation. It was always the same One, the same Spirit pursuing me. Like my sister, Mary, if I were to sit and listen, I could at last stop seeking. But no. My Martha soul was always too busy preparing a home for Someone who needed nothing more than an invitation.

Bowing my head to think, I composed myself a moment to listen for the still, small voice: *Be calm, small child, tiny seed within an ocean of universe. He feeds us in small bites if we restrain ourselves and allow it. Know this first: a loving God reigns. Never be intimidated by circumstances or by scope, size, or measure, or by the incomparable love of the Savior.*

I heard the creak and swish as the pendulum descended again.

XXVI. And Prosperity

By the fifth day, Ruth would step forward to secure a stray line or to catch roving cargo on deck, and with her, the others were becoming emboldened. But while she worked, she watched me. She was puzzling or simply waiting to see when I would fail them.

One evening, the sails fell silent while we drifted on flat seas. The heat kept the crew and band of Gauls on deck seeking an errant breeze while they napped or engaged in silent tasks. I scanned charts while Aelf and Theod mended lines. The rosy-golden sky flattened above us.

Suddenly, sweet and warm, falling like soft petals, a quivering song wafted along the deck. First Ruth, then Vocera sang, joined by the girls, their voices twining and rising to the strains of a Gaulish melody that I had heard sung to Saxon words somewhere long ago.

The crew stared; the other men were silent. As I scanned from the sailors' faces to those of the freed men, all were captivated. Except Farval, the big sailor who hardly spoke. He hulked with broken nose, twisted ear, and braided beard. Because I had never heard him speak, I thought he might be mute or had his tongue cut out in a rending past. He would communicate with Aelf or Theod using little more than a nod or grunt.

He was mouthing Saxon words to the women's song.

I slid beside him. "You know this song? You can speak, and all this time, you did not tell me?" I smiled. "It is a beautiful song. Can you...?"

He did not turn aside but began singing with the women. The Gaul and Saxon were similar enough to build a lovely counterpoint. With a voice small, scarcely more than a whisper, he sang:

Oh, my Love
We are seas apart
Left on waves abandoned.

I am waiting, waiting across these waters
Waiting to worship again.
I grieve separation,
Your lovely hands pierced and ravaged
Your body laid cold in the grave.
But now you lift your arms once more
Your strong arms embrace me.

He wiped his eyes with both fists, rubbed his mangled nose with the heel of his hand, then looked away.

I was losing myself to the sea again.

After a fortnight, we eased into the mouth of the Loire and anchored off a broad beach on the south shore. From here, any attackers would be forced to run across the long stretch of sand, while we would have time to raise our defenses or shove off.

Late the next morning, a small band approached from across the beach, carrying short spears, two large jars, and a bundle. These were not warriors; they were farmers and traders. Yet we were on alert with the possibility of ambush. They would have been watching us since we anchored and also concluded that they had little to fear. We were obviously not pirates or a military vessel: We had women moving freely about, and we were not brandishing weapons. They stopped midway on the beach, waiting as Aelf and Theod plodded through the sand to meet them. Ruth caught up with the sailors, insisting that she join them across the beach with hopes of gaining news about their homelands.

The traders carried little except wine, thin oil, and more wool, but we eagerly traded with them for information. It had been peaceful along the river for nearly three years. Visigoths were settled on both sides further upriver, but they were likewise hungry for trade. We should be safe if we kept to the middle of the river, anchored offshore at night, and kept the women out of sight. The Visigoths had scrubbed the waters of pirates, and the traders were convinced we would have safe passage to the fork in the river at Condivicnum. Portus Ratiatus on the south fork had long been in ruins, but taking the north fork, we would be able to lay over at Condivicnum.

Our journey upriver was uneventful, and we found the port to be adequate, though the populace was on edge. There were rumors of invasion, but these proved to be mere speculation of a war-weary populace.

With the bit of gold from Sister Athracht and the value of the cargo, we had more than we would need to dry-dock and restore the ship. It took one week to find a slip, and another to lift and dry the hull. Before the ship was completely pulled into drydock, as the bow was being winched from the water, we pried a plank at the stern, and watched as the hull vomited the horrific contents of the bilge. Even the workmen gagged and scattered. It took a fortnight to stuff and caulk the cracks, repair and replace the few rotten slats, reseal all the planking, and complete the repairs to the deck and sails.

Farval was a fine carpenter. He worked to rebuild the captain's cabin and expand simple quarters for the sailors and former slaves. When not working with Farval, I helped to finish the suffocating task of cleaning out and scrubbing down the hold. We were pleased to discover this was a well-built vessel that had simply been poorly maintained by a careless captain and crew.

Soon after arriving in port, the former slaves received more bad news. Their homelands far to the east had been decimated by another incursion. We could not be guaranteed safe passage if we proceeded farther upriver after our repairs.

Meanwhile, Vocera and Epos, one of the freedmen, had taken a liking to one another. They decided they would be staying in Condivicnum along with one of the other slaves who had family nearby.

Ruth was careful not to allow the girls out of her sight, and with a few coins we rented accommodations for them away from the docks where the women would be safe.

Because further passage upriver might be dangerous, our plans for leaving were changing. Though the former slaves were disappointed, nearly all of them had seen their families killed or captured, so they had held little hope of returning to homes or families when we arrived. We had adequate funds to provide each with whatever comfort and assurance they needed, but most of them stayed with us. Our best hope would be to sail far south along Hispania's long western coast, turn east through the Great Strait that lay under the chalk cliffs of Mons Calpe, and back into the Mediterranean. By then, the season would be late. We would lay over in Sardinia for the winter and see if the insurgence that simmered in the eastern Gaulish regions had cooled by spring. Then, if any of the former slaves still wanted to return home, we could help them when the weather improved.

Summer was slipping into autumn, and roughening seas were swelling as we left Condivicnum and sailed back down the Loire and onto the broad ocean. It was a fine vessel, steering crisply, decked out with new rigging that whistled and white sails that wafted in the freshening winds. We had packed the hull with cargo of tin and copper that would be prized by the Sardinians, and lengths of hickory and bolts of cloth.

While finding merchants in Condivicnum to trade our old cargo from the ship, I discovered a pot of golden pigment laid away in a dusty corner of a shop. With only a humble monastery in the city, no ostentatious basilicas, and most of the old Roman houses in disrepair, it would be hard for a merchant to sell expensive pigments. I traded for the pot with the last square from a bolt of cloth.

As Martha had done on the house I had shared with Miriam on Cyprus, we painted an unbroken ribbon of gold around the entire hull. I called the ship the *Marta Marie*. I had been inspired to name her the *Miriam*, but then I could not.

With seasons changing, I resigned myself to the truth I had heard from Yeshu: I would not be venturing back to the north country soon. But the spray, the sparkle off the waves, the smell of brine in my nostrils, convinced me I would be content at sea again.

In the rebuilt captain's cabin, I had stacked the shelves with charts, manifests, and a few scrolls of the philosophers, along with all the scripture and writings of the Disciples I was able to purchase from the old monastery in Condivicnum. Three or four could wedge into the cabin to review charts and discuss plans. Ruth was indispensable.

I had framed the precious Greek chart onto a plank that I folded from the wall onto a stand. Ruth's hood lay on her shoulders, she tilted over the map, an arm braced on the table. With her other hand, she traced a finger across the smooth surface, past Sardinia, above Egypt, and up the coast of Judea where she stopped. She spread her other hand, fingers flat, and leaned in for a closer look.

"Home?" I said, cautious.

Swishing her hood up, she pushed away from the table. She maintained a thick shell and divulged little. It was foolish for me to ask, but my curiosity had grown. She was not Gaulish or Greek. Ruth would have been a common name in many lands, yet she looked much like the women of my youth.

I apologized clumsily. She closed her eyes and shook her head quickly, not denying my contention, but not willing to talk about it.

After sitting briefly collecting her thoughts—and resolve—she stood and pushed her hood back again, her demeanor restored as quickly as it had faltered. She turned to my shelves of scrolls and scripture. "Are you an educated man, Lazar, or do you intend merely to impress your shipmates?" She smiled wryly, her dark eyes sparkling.

"I have had a measure of training, for which I am merely thankful, not prideful," I said, leaning back on my cot, smiling, placing a finger on my lips as I watched her.

"All light and heat come from the sun just like all wisdom and truth come from God—not from men," she said flippantly.

"I understand. And what wise person said that?"

"I did!" Again, I had been playfully ensnared into underestimating brilliance. She tossed her thick curls. As she often would when in thought or resolve, she bunched her hair, pulled it behind her head, and tied it. "A highly developed mind is of no more use than a sailor's highly developed arm, if you do not know how to use it." She punched Theod playfully. "At least this man knows how to use what he has." Her thin smile settled. "Do you?"

She sat again and stared around the little group. "Less talk. Where are we going?"

We wintered in Sardinia. I was able to retrieve most of what remained of my treasures from the Nuragic tribe but left a portion safe in the cave. As expected, they had kept every piece untouched—tarnished—but untouched and had managed to replace or rewrap the tattered leather bags. Everything was accounted for just as I had seen it more than a generation ago. I tarried in the village briefly, cherishing memories of my former life with my brave princess. But I did not stay long in the tribal lands; I had another life and other charges to attend to.

Early in the shipping season, one of the first vessels to arrive at harbor was a large ship that had been intended to carry wealthy passengers from Rome, Athens, and other destinations. The man who was captain and owner had died on the first voyage and left no family or testament. Ruth, Theod, and I had been finding cargo to secure a voyage north when we overheard the mate talking with merchants at the docks. He had no desire to keep the vessel now that the owner was dead; the mate was old and ready for his ocean-going days to be over. He was looking for a buyer. I had ignored him and walked on, but Ruth grabbed one arm and Theod the other and pulled me toward the conversation.

"Did you not hear what he said?" Ruth asked.

I shook my head.

"He will be happy with collateral of a small vessel and passage to Massalia," Theod chimed in, his face beaming.

"I have no interest in..." I began.

"I do." As one would gather resolve, Ruth again gathered her braids and pulled them behind her head. She folded her arms. "Theod and I have been talking. We want to know what you are thinking, Lazar? We've heard your talk. You will not be escaping to the north when there is so much for you here. Maybe there are others who need you now, and we have—you have—the means to help us."

"No, I cannot..." I turned to walk away.

"You have an able crew, money, and a way with charts and rudder like I have never seen," Theod added.

I wiped my brow, feeling hemmed in by these two people who seemed so willing to be flippant with another's money and ability. And I walked away. "It is what I do," I said to myself.

I left them standing there.

When I was well down the dock, I stopped. "Wait," I said to myself. Maybe not this time. In a flash I saw the possibilities coming together. Turning around, I saw two people whom I was becoming very fond of. I allowed myself to consider for a moment: Maybe this was where I belonged.

You do alpha, I will do beta. Allow *beta.*

Though I had spent lifetimes at sea, I had never been a captain. And I had never seen a crew more willing and competent. The job came easily. In time, I fell in love with the challenge; plotting a course, managing cargo, and wrangling with merchants. Though Ruth watched me, she kept her distance. She was a competent partner and managed finances wisely.

The *Marta Marie* was adequate collateral in the deal, though I do not think the old mate cared. He just wanted passage home and a small claim on a bit of wealth. Soon we were able to pay him handsomely to release the collateral and he was satisfied with his journey home.

The much larger cargo and passenger vessel had been fitted with many more cabins than a standard cargo vessel. I transferred the name, *Marta Marie*, along with the ribbon of gold around the hull to the larger ship. I relented in my guilt and renamed the smaller vessel *The Miriam*, because she was the first. We split the crew between the vessels and signed on more, including several trusty tribal Sardinians.

I do not believe there was ever a ship quite like this large craft.

In spring we were able to confirm that there would be no home for Ruth and the girls to return to. It was not unexpected. The other former slaves stayed with us along with our three faithful sailors: Theod, Aelf and Farval. I had known ships with captains who might bring family aboard for a short voyage, and there might be captains who voyaged with their entire families, but the new *Marta Marie* was like a small village. Ruth had cared for the girls, Regina and Genna, as though they were her own, until Regina married one of our hired sailors, Samius. The women worked alongside their husbands, and, in time, several children scurried on board.

With Ruth's help, we purchased cargo wisely. We took on furniture and clothing and carried it to opulent markets seeking luxurious merchandise for lavish prices. We could name our price. The women worked while we were at sea, stitching and upgrading simple clothing into royal garb. With the help of our Nuragic sailors, we showed the other men a few metal working skills. They made delicate gold chains and trinkets that the women sewed onto the fabrics. The men performed similar work with the furniture. Simple box furniture was stacked upon itself to make chests while rickety chairs were inlaid with priceless trim or padded with deep cushions sewn by the women.

We were a ship of floating shops and cargo.

And we sailed on. I watched Ruth. She watched me. But we stayed distant friends and partners, her tortured past buried and distant. Often her watching came close to words; she would step near, as though about to say something or ask me a probing question; then she would turn or pretend she was merely walking past. We each carried our tainted cargo while we maintained this dance through the years.

Yet, I could not shake the desire to eventually return north. Back and forth the memories would badger me; the snows, mountains, and black earth. But I would not allow myself to dwell on these thoughts, remembering the message from Yeshu, afraid of what I would face, and certain that all would have been destroyed long ago. But my destiny was never in my hands, and I could never run for long.

As our ship's family grew, we also grew together with a measure of spirit and faith. Not everyone, but most. We did not make a sensation of it or a requirement; it was just how we lived our simple lives. We created a floating ecclesia away from the dreaded world of religion, the Church, and the constraints of authorities. In our own ways, we all disdained what we had seen of religion and ritual. I knew Yeshu was real and intimate; Ruth and her women certainly knew. There is no role for ceremony, meditation, fasting, and gawdy rituals between lovers and families, so why would anyone do such things with the one person who is closer than a brother and dearer than a friend? Religion and ritual attest only to a lack of faith and to our fear to indulge ourselves in the intimacy of a loving God.

Shipping was profitable. We expanded by purchasing another smaller vessel, and we used those smaller vessels to find unusual items from lesser ports and far-flung outposts, then shuttle the goods, stage the cargo for pickup, and load it onto the large *Marta Marie*. This made for fewer stops, more efficiency, and more trade. Alone, Theod, Aelf, and quiet Farval were simple men of the sea, but together, while piloting the smaller ships, they were competent seamen and owlish deal makers.

But all of it nearly ended on one warm and windy spring day.

The skies were clear, but a swift breeze was driving from the west. We had left our home port in Sardinia, heading for Massalia. We were to rendezvous with the *Miriam*, piloted by Theod and our other smaller vessel piloted by Aelf, named *Damona* after Regina's sister, whom Captain Eho had killed.

We were tacking north, out of sight of land and miles from Massalia, when we saw the *Damona* bounding our way at a feverish clip. The small vessel was built for speed, but Aelf was not driving toward us because he was anxious to see us; he was being pursued by a sleek vessel of Greek design hot on his stern. He was managing evasive maneuvers, but smoke was streaming from the *Damona*. Worried there might be no way for Aelf to escape, we unfurled all the sails as the *Marta Marie* plunged starboard in a vain attempt at rescue. Our sailor on the mast called out that the *Miriam* was tacking our way from the south. Theod was piloting it masterfully through large swells, guiding his ship to meet up with Aelf's smoldering vessel. We hoped the Greek vessel would give up pursuit if it saw us.

We were too late, and the situation became worse. Out of nowhere appeared two more Greek vessels, each smaller and faster than the one pursuing Aelf. Behind them was a large, lumbering ship, intended to onload spoils from the *Damona*.

Before we had departed Sardinia, we had heard no reports of any large, well-equipped pirate fleet sailing these waters. We felt completely off guard, doomed, and helpless.

While the Greek ships closed, the *Damona* plowed ahead, riding lower.

Suddenly and inexplicably, the Greek vessel in the lead was sprouting flames from its bow. I had not seen Aelf launch flaming arrows, and I did not think he had any weapons that would do damage to a pirate ship. But we all watched as the remainder of the dark fleet neared the *Damona*.

Swiftly it became hopeless—for the pirates. Two more of their smaller vessels were in flames. From blue skies, a bolt of lightning blasted the largest ship, brightening the clear day. Then more brilliant shafts struck the pirate vessels. Soon all the Greek ships were smoldering and foundering, crossing paths and haplessly ramming one another as they tried to flee in the heavy seas.

Next to our crew, we lined the rails and gaped in amazement. This scene was inexplicable to everyone—except me. The Immortals had found us, and I feared we would be destroyed.

More flashes, then the sky churned in hues of brilliant color.

Frantic, I sent up a flag to signal the *Damona* and *Miriam* to come alongside so we could attempt a desperate dash for Massalia.

Our ships came together, while I continued to search the skies for the Immortals. We quickly battled the flames then lashed the *Damona* to our starboard.

As memory fogs and folds, I would convince myself that the Immortals had forgotten about me or that they were errant memories long lost in my past, never to return. But then the reality and the randomness of their pursuit would come crashing back.

The mysterious agents of death left as quickly as they had arrived. Their intentions always inscrutable. They played with us like a cat with a mouse. Maybe they would wait until they could destroy us all. I was left again to ponder in confusion. But I could not hesitate, their destruction of the pirate vessels had bought valuable time.

Several of Aelf's men had been scorched; two had perished in the flames, two more lay on the deck with arrows protruding from their chests, and another man thrashed with a shaft in his gut. It was a miserable sight, and brave Aelf wept, rubbing his eyes from smoke and grief as he boarded the *Marta Marie*.

We were under full sail, the last of the pirate fleet disappearing over the curve of the earth, only a line of smoke laying on the horizon.

Again, I had somehow evaded destruction, but I had once more put those near me at risk.

Shocked and wounded, we limped into Massalia before dark. I called Ruth and our two loyal captains to my cabin. Aelf tried to explain what he had seen when the pirate ships were attacked, and though I doubt they believed much of what I told them, I explained what I could of the Immortals, hedging my long history. These sailors were accustomed to outlandish tales, but Ruth watched me with eyes narrowed and said nothing. I expected her to at least scoff or question me, but her silence was disarming. I treasured her trust and our bond, but as we talked, I feared she might be losing confidence in me.

It was time for an accounting. In a short while, we had become successful and there was plenty for all of us. We enjoyed the freedom that wealth can buy. But I was becoming restless and knew there was more. I was chasing the winds and the desire to return north needled me.

The harrowing events at sea underscored our fears. With lives and treasure at stake, we would need to evaluate the danger we were risking and the toll that our success could exact.

Docked at Massalia the heat of day lingered. A lifetime ago, I had arrived here with Azvald's son Edulf to depart upriver to the great northern shield. Much had changed at this ancient port. The dockmaster was orderly, directing our large vessel to moor on the end of the pier where we could meet the wealthy merchants waiting for our cargo of clothes and exotic furniture.

Standing on the dock at Massalia, I knew there were decisions to make. Though I kept a wary eye, I did not need the Immortals to pursue me again to force my hand. I had foolishly hoped my prayer to be released from them had been successful or that they had found what they were looking for years ago. It had been false hope.

I had been blessed for this brief time; my life was too safe.

XXVII. Ruth

I had retreated to my cabin to contemplate alone as the ship gently rolled beside the dock. In the gray light, I held the yellowed scroll closer to the small port window to re-read the passage of Ecclesiastes: *and behold all is vanity and chasing after the wind.*

My mind roiled. I should not have been so tormented. I had enjoyed a season of contentment rarely known to me. During all my extraordinarily long life, since Elymas the sorcerer on Cyprus, the Immortals seemed to root me out wherever I became settled, or they would launch me in a direction I had not anticipated and prevent me from returning. What would happen if I upset their schemes? With desperate logic, I asked myself: Could I lose them if I were to leave a life where I had become settled and propelled myself in a new direction entirely of my own accord?

But I had been adrift another decade on the Mediterranean and I could no longer quell my yearning for the rich, green north: mountains and rivers, the noise and charcoal smoke of my hot smithy, and the murmur of sheep.

I could afford an intermission in the theater of my life. Now would be the time. These had been good years, living in wealth, even a measure of extravagance. However, I was restless. Like everything else became with time, pursuing wealth had become chasing after the wind.

I would not be truly leaving my shipmates, I rationalized; we could meet again the next season, and I would have goods to trade from the north. If I left now, I might be able to prevent my seafaring family from coming any closer to that terrible duo from Hades.

I seemed incapable of being honest with myself: Was this about the Immortals again, and their ability to threaten those around me, or was I merely selfish and restless?

But something else was at work in me, something I had not mentioned to the others. In these years since leaving Comgall's monastery, three letters from dear Athracht had found me. All had showed up on the docks of Sardinia months or more after leaving her hand. While in Sardinia, before sailing for Massalia, I had recovered her most recent letter. She had surmised the wealth I had amassed, and she let me know of her concerns.

Dearest Brother Lazar,

I read your last letter with relish, and I am pleased to discover your shipping endeavors have been successful. We deeply appreciate your gifts that accompanied your letter. It is wonderful that an affluent man can create wealth that abounds not for himself alone, but also for all his associates, the merchants he patronizes, the shipbuilders and suppliers—and beneficiaries like your humble servant. Our unassuming ministries have been generously supported for years by souls like you. You have repaid us many times over for the generosity I was able to share with you when you left us.

If one could but stay at sea and avoid the tyranny of taxation and the greed of rulers, which so devastated my beloved parents. Money is not the root of all evil, only the love of money. I do not think I need caution you further.

I am intrigued by your enigmatic associate Ruth. Keep your eye on that one, and do not deflect her affection if she offers. I am praying that she finds solace from her deep wounds.

Our sisters are well, and the monks are content since my brother, Comgall, was transferred to Rome. God bless him! He is far too old to endure such a journey, so I fear for him. It has been nearly a year since he departed, and we have heard nothing. His greed and thirst for acclamation may have at last been his undoing. Please pray for him and forgive him. It is our way.

I cherish your letters and look forward to that day when either your next letter finds me, or easterly winds blow your sails toward our beloved island again. But I am an old woman, and already I feel the first cold draft of the final sleep seeping into my bones.

Sincerely by the Grace of the Lamb,
Athracht

For days I had been pondering her letter, examining my soul.

We had planned to exchange cargo and sail again away from Massalia. But repairs to the *Damona* would take a season, and springtime was an expensive time to buy a ship in this port.

I made a decision that was sure to rile the crew.

Gathering the three sailors along with Ruth and the girl, now a woman, Regina and her husband Samius in a tavern distant from the docks, we purchased a fine feast with plenty of ale and the excellent wine of Massalia. After hesitating, I finally took a deep breath, pushed aside the serving, and laid out my proposal to them: I would leave for the north, and until I returned, the *Marta Marie* and the smaller vessels would be under their care. I had planned that Ruth would become the principal in our small fleet and that Theod would be captain of the *Marta Marie*. Aelf would captain the *Miriam* until the *Damona* could be repaired or replaced.

Dreading this moment, I had delayed arranging this meeting, anticipating their disappointment. But nodding, they reacted as though they knew this was coming. Disarmed by their assent, I proceeded haltingly.

While I spoke, laying out my plan, Ruth sat quietly stroking her cheek in thought. As was her style, she wore her hooded cape. She could afford a smartly trimmed cloak over a crisp plaid dress worthy of the wealthy merchant she had become. She eased back her hood, revealing her black hair braided on each side. She caught her braids and pulled them behind her head, holding them while she waited for me to finish. Her dark features focused on me sharply, causing me to flounder in my presentation until I stopped.

There was silence. Ruth tied the braids behind her head, folded her hands on the table, and said flatly, "You are leaving, Lazar." She leveled her look.

"That is right," I said. "I must return north. I cannot shake this desire I have. The traders tell me there has been peace in the Saxon region for years. I feel compelled to return there and see what is left of the life and family I once had." I waited while no one spoke. "I hope to return next year, but I may resume that life again. I cannot say."

"You do not know what you will find or why you are going back. You do not know when or if you may return. This does not sound like the able captain we have come to know," she said.

"I understand. But I will not continue to live life unfinished and...and I *need* to see that land again. I cannot explain it. I must live a life that is more than just drifting from port to port, carrying baggage and cargo from one destination to another, and amassing more gold. It has no attraction for me anymore." I pushed aside my cup and folded my hands. "I am sorry."

She did not hesitate. "Then I have a counter proposal." She smiled, as if pulling the bow string taut and finding her target.

This did not surprise me. She was shrewd, and she was one of the reasons I could leave the ships in their care. I expected she might counter, and the others would also want to have a say.

"Let me start by telling you a dream I had last night. It speaks to where we have come," she said.

I made a single shoulder shrug. "Now you are a dreamer. That does not sound like you."

The others turned their attention to her.

"That is true; I am not a dreamer, but hear me out." She looked at her bowl, swirling the weak gruel, and picked from it a morsel of pork that she popped into her mouth. "In this dream, several of us—I do not remember who—were in a hilly wooded wilderness, not unlike the reaches of Celtae where I spent many years before we were taken as slaves. Sweeping away ahead of us, along the hillside, a strip of broad highway was being constructed, the way the Romans built. This area was rocky and impassable. The road had been cut right through the forest, and eventually, it had been chiseled right through the stone of the mountain, as the highway continued to curve upward until ending abruptly—right at the edge of a cliff. Rocks had been chipped and pried away, and the rubble had been laid to make a roadbed. It was an enormous project," she said, explaining with her hands, "rock walls on either side, but ending abruptly at the cliff." She looked around the table at us. "As we stood there in my dream, we all debated; why would anyone go to so much effort to build a road in the wilderness that goes nowhere?" She shrugged. "Abruptly ending a roadway at a precipice seemed absurd. Though we all debated, none of us could discern the answer."

We looked at each other around the table, confused.

"That is an interesting dream," I said, "but I do not—"

She held up her hand. "I'm not finished. An interpretation came to me almost before the scene faded, as I was awakening," Ruth said. She pushed aside her bowl, laid her small hands on the table, spreading her fingers flat, and smiled. "We have so many questions, and we spend so much of our time debating why God does what he does, what his motives are, and we try to figure out what this life is about: Where we are headed and why?" She sucked in breath, paused, the wheels of her mind turning, then continued. "How can we know the answers until the entire scheme has been laid out and the plan has run its course? The road is not finished. It is being constructed. All these questions, all this debate, but there are no answers until it is all finished. We are those who stand at the side of the unfinished road and debate its course. But these questions can be answered when viewing the end—after all the construction has been completed. He invites our questions. But questioning his *motive* is pointless."

"What does it mean? Why are you telling us this?" I asked.

"This alone: Stop trying to manage the rudder and go with the winds. That is all. If the winds are taking you back to the north country, then go with God." She laid her hand on my wrist. "Stop trying to figure it out. Not now. It is not time—yet."

She waited, began to speak, stopped, then said, "Are you a Mary, or are you a Martha?"

My mouth had grown dry, but not because of her words alone, but her touch.

I plunged ahead, trying to deflect. "But you said you had a proposal. Not to have a plan, to lurch forward unseeing, is that your proposal?" I did not mean to sound sharp or skeptical. I cleared my throat and wet my tongue. "I am sorry. What is your proposal, then?" I asked.

"The dream was for me, too. I have been on this unfinished highway with you." Her grip on my arm tightened. "We have traveled together, yet staying apart, for too long. I am continuing with you. That is my proposal—and my demand."

"But, Ruth, I—"

"I am not a fool," she stopped me. "I do not just walk through this life like you. I study life, each moment." She held up thumb and finger. "I hold each moment of pain, pleasure, and joy between my thumb and finger to examine and ponder it. This moment is just...it is simply right. It is the right time, for me—for us, Lazarus." She pulled her hood up again and looked down as a tear traced down her cheek. "You shun the bonds of affection; you always run, for whatever reason. And, yes, we are both the same in that regard, because of my painful past. But this must stop. You may walk away; maybe that is what you do." She looked up, her tearful eyes drilling into mine. "I do not walk away."

The sailors looked about uncomfortably while Regina and Samius mirrored knowing smiles.

Embarrassed, I fidgeted with my empty cup. The silence around the table was separating a curtain that had been carefully hung between Ruth and me to protect our pasts and our hearts. That curtain was being publicly and painfully torn away.

A girl came to the table, filled the cups, and set down another round loaf. Several patrons entered, several left. The cautious quiet held.

"I accept your proposal," I finally said. "I take you, Ruth...I mean I will take you, Ruth. I, uh, will take you with me," I said.

"Of course, you will!" She smiled and raised her cup. "You are not as smart as you think you are, Lazar a Bethania. We will leave together." I may have been the only one to hear her add, "Then I will tell you more."

Theod held up his mug. "A salute to the both of you. You are well suited to be together. The rest of us have begun to look like gray old salts, but you two have not aged a day. Good travels to you, and we will take care of the fleet."

Ruth snatched her hood forward, looking sideways at me, then down at the table. But Theod was right. This seafaring life had been good to her in the years since she had been freed on that dock. I was reluctant to take her away from it.

All this time we had engaged in a dance that kept us apart because we were both convinced we needed to stay alone, or we had to respect each other's need for separation.

We gazed at each other. With this curtain between Ruth and me torn down, I felt an empty corner of my heart filling again.

At the ship, I gathered my few belongings, the leather chart along with my scrolls and scriptures. I also held a share of treasure and the few Sardinian icons I had remaining. We would leave much of our treasure for Theod, Aelf, and the crews.

I walked to the bow, and for a long while, I watched the ships bobbing and rocking in the harbor and the bustle of people departing or arriving from around the world—the movement of trade and humanity. I pondered what it meant to once again leave this intoxicating life on the seas. I would miss the smell of brine, the waves slapping the hull, and the sparkle of open sky. But no. I had been on the waters long, more than long enough. There was more to discover.

I flinched as a small hand slipped into mine. Shaking as though she were offering a captive, tiny bird, she overcame the gulf of risk that had separated us. I had never held her hand. Ruth smiled up at me, her eyes moist, a tear ran down her lovely cheek. In all this time, I had never seen her weep, and here I saw tears again in the span of a single day. She leaned her head against my shoulder, and we said nothing.

How full of blessing my life had become. Yet how much of my life I spent in remorse, focusing on my regrets.

"I could die tomorrow and feel my life had been completed a thousand times over," I whispered to myself.

"Why do you not go ahead and die, then?" she said with a hint of irony, looking across the water.

"What?" I laughed.

"Why not go ahead and die, then." She looked up briefly, then back across the water. "I did. I believe I have finally died—to myself."

"I do not understand."

"Think about it. What if we were finally bold enough to let go of this life and die to ourselves?" She paused, shaping her words. "Before yesterday, I had heard the teaching, yet I had never understood what it could mean to loosen the grip on our lives and die to self. I was still holding on. Even my faith was something I thought I had to control."

"But you—"

"No, it's more than living a *new* life. If we were dead, we would *have* to let go of everything. When we die, we have entirely lost our grasp on all those people dear to us and all those places and things that we cherish. They are gone forever. You just said you could die tomorrow and feel your life was complete. So, let go of everything—be dead."

I loosened my grip on her hand and slipped my arm around her shoulder. "So we will be dead together, then?" I said.

The sky was a bright, seamless gray, stitched by gulls and divers that skirted the masts unconcerned with the bustle beneath them. Right off the bow, a pelican dropped out of the sky, plunged into the water, and emerged with a struggling scad. We stood together, silent, lost in our thoughts.

"I know who you are, Lazarus a Bethania," she said quietly. "Now you will come to know me."

I held her away from me and looked down, my brows gathered. She turned and I followed her as she stepped along the gunwale to where a rope was secured. She leaned on the rope and looked down into the water. After a long silence, she started to speak, stopped, then started again. "Lazarus, I have never told anyone. It is so hard for me to speak it."

"You never have to tell me anything that is too painful," I said.

"No, you will understand." She inhaled deeply. "There is a voice that we have heard; it is a voice that no one forgets."

"Yes, I know of your faith, and I..." I began.

She held a finger to her lips, silencing me, while looking to the sky. "There is one voice that no one can forget: *Talitha cumi*. My little lamb, it is time to wake up."

I closed my eyes and shook my head silently. It all made sense. How did I not suspect sooner? Ruth: Jairus's daughter, the girl raised from the dead by Yeshu.

She looked up at me again. "Now he says to you, Lazarus: My little lamb, it is again time for you to wake up."

XXVIII. Lord of Bretanie

THE FIRST BREATH OF spring followed us north. On barges, we eased over broad rivers that narrowed and became angry, forcing us to portage. Our caravan would join other caravans rambling cross country to connect to another river, then dip oars again until we drew near to those flowered valleys and white pinnacles that I recalled. Travel in this region was never completely safe, but in this season, most warriors were too busy with planting and calving to bother with thieving. For protection, we had hired a band of Saxons to travel with us. They would stay in their northern homes to work crops. Each caravan would have a small band of armed men. And all who poled a barge or led a donkey were as skilled with a sword as they were with rudder and reins.

On board the barges, Ruth and I would nestle, spending hours watching the riverbanks roll past, absorbed in quiet conversation. It was fate that two refugees from mortality would eventually find each other. She was not ready to tell me all the sordid details of her long life, but I listened to her struggles in Greece and Italy, where many years had passed living in estates as a house slave or manager. She had found seasons of refuge in the Far East, living in fantastic kingdoms that seemed to be cut from the fabric of fantasy. Like me, she had left behind centuries of family and broken hopes.

We were discussing our recollections of Judea and the ministry of Yeshu when discord arose.

With a sigh, I finally said, "You must have also experienced those times when you thought you knew and understood all Yeshu was saying. I believed that I knew who he is and what he meant to the world. I would grasp moments of understanding, but soon they crumble in my hands. Year after year, time after time, back and forth, I do not understand. What is the answer? When shall we find answers?"

Her brow knit in confusion; the corner of her mouth pulled into her cheek in exasperation as she listened.

"Ha! I did not know there were answers," she said. "I have heard you say this too many times. Have you learned nothing? You have told me of your long life, and I have told you most of mine. After all you have seen, are you one of those who thinks God doles out answers like little candies and baubles at market?"

"No, but I would think we should have some clue as to—"

"Who is Yahweh that he owes you answers? Who do you think you are that you are bequeathed answers from the Great I Am?" She scowled.

"Ask and it shall be given, seek and you shall find," I said.

"Yes! Sure, you can spend decades seeking answers if you want, if that is how you want to spend your years. Answers are cheap. But they change nothing."

"No," I said, "but if he cares for us personally, then...."

"Ask yourself this: What if Yahweh never knew you? He had no idea you existed, yet he was Yahweh, and you were Lazarus. Would it make any difference?"

"Well, of course," I said.

"Why should it make any difference?" Her eyes penetrated.

"Because...well, because..."

She plunged ahead. "Is your arrogance so great that you require the personal attention of the Lord of the universe? If Yahweh knew nothing of you, how would that change anything? Would you not worship, praise his omniscience, be in awe of his created world, love your fellow man? Is your affection for Yahweh based solely on how much attention you receive from him? Why should his personal acknowledgment of your meager life be of any consequence?"

"You do not believe Yahweh knows you? You received the attention of Yeshu in a personal and powerful demonstration," I said.

"Of course, I believe. But that is not the point. It does not matter to me, to my joy or my fidelity to him if he knows me or not. I know him! What more do I need? But you seem to believe that God needs to hand you the leather chart for your life, diagram the universe like a carpenter's sketch, and hand it back for your approval, just so your worried curiosity can be satisfied."

"I never asked to live forever," I replied. "When does it end? I want to live like other mortals. I want only…"

"Lazarus, this is our life. This is the life we have been dealt. What if you were to embrace it instead of being always at war with it?" she said levelly.

She was right. She was like my sister Mary, and I had been too much of Martha. She had watched and accepted, while I fretted for answers. We sailed in silence. She laid against me and nestled again.

We were well.

I sensed I was within less than a fortnight of the region where Bruna and I had worked and raised our family. I imagined those lands would have changed hands many times over. The Saxons in our company assured us the area had been sacked and burned long ago. I had grieved silently all these years, and now that I was near, I regretted that I willingly accepted an excuse to move on and had not returned sooner. I was just tormenting myself again, because it was not likely I could have come back. But I regretted that I had been ripped from here and had followed my instincts—whatever they were—and not returned.

My family and lands would be long gone, but nowhere else, in all my wanderings, did I feel like I belonged as much as here. The closer I drew, the more my affection for this land revived and fluttered in my chest. My heart had been planted here as deeply as the newly sown cabbage seeds or the roots in the blooming orchards.

On an early morning, we drifted up to a sagging pier, the end of the dock receding into muddy waters as though it had been too weary to hold itself up for one more upriver barge. Hidden from the river, a tired inn and a few mossy barns and dwellings emerged from the shaded forest. Away from the village stood a garrison of sagging logs sunk into a clearing on a grassy mound. By its condition, I guessed it had not seen troops in a decade and was now little more than a hopeful last defense for the nearby inhabitants.

Ruth and I exchanged worried looks. We needed to resupply and form a small caravan before heading inland from here, and this lonely outpost was not likely to carry what we would need for our overland journey.

The uncommonly warm early spring had graciously held, making our voyage calm and uneventful. Ruth and I ventured inside the inn. Enjoying the intoxication of the hot, humid day, Ruth and I sat at a rough table near a small window; the shutters were braced open, allowing the only light into the dak interior. A fresh breeze pushed through the window to chase the stale winter air from the corners of the room. Most members of the caravan had arranged themselves on the wet grass outside or were offloading from the vessels. As my eyes adjusted, I was surprised to find a neat tavern, enhanced by the scent of poultry and bread cooking in the kitchen. The walls had been painted with woodland murals and the space was decorated with a woman's touch. It was as clean and polished as any meeting house in any of the great cities of the east.

When we entered, a set of eyes had followed us from a slot in the door that led into kitchens or living quarters. When they had determined it was safe, with a thump, the door swung open and a big man with a red beard creased by a broad smile stepped forward with foaming cups of ale.

"Aye, and you are Lord...?" he said in brisk Saxon with a sparkle in his eye.

"I am Lazar, sir," I said, cheered by his tone. "And I am the furthest from a lord that will ever grace your opulent facilities."

He stopped but did not set down the cups. I was afraid I had offended him.

"Goodness! I apologize—'tis my son's name. Lazar." He said with a laugh loud and sincere. He pointed out the window at a young man who was offloading our cargo while onloading more cargo for the boatsmen that would be continuing upstream. Another boat had returned downriver and was taking on bales and jars. It was a busy, raucous ceremony with a liturgy of curse words and laughter.

"That is unusual. I have met few men with my name," I said. "None in this land, to be sure."

"Not such an uncommon name, my friend," he said. "Not around here, at least."

I did not reply, happy to maintain our anonymity. I changed the subject. "You have a fine tavern here...uh?"

"Lugins is the name. And my wife, Hilde, and our herd of young'uns run the place," he said. On cue, three screaming, laughing children chased each other through the inn, the last a toddler wearing nothing but a shirt, waddling on fat legs like a duckling to keep up with his siblings.

A woman's voice hollered in the kitchen. "Mother of Mercy! You stoats outta' here. *Now!* I swear you are to be the death of me. And mind your wee brother so he at least keeps his shirt on!"

Trying to ignore his offspring, Lugins rubbed his hands together nervously and smiled broad and thin. Innkeepers were notorious for their miserly underhandedness, but this man did not appear much of a scoundrel. We brightened. When people pleasantly defy our expectations, we understand how not only love, but mere simple kindness is a currency of heaven.

"By the garrison out there, I can imagine this is not always a safe place. How do you manage here in this small, distant settlement with all this traffic?" I asked.

"We have not had need of the garrison in a long while," he said. He was interrupted as a round woman bustled in, carrying wooden bowls of steaming bird and garden roots. She set them before us, stepped back, and beamed while wiping her hands on her stained apron, frazzled blond hair flaring around a blue cap. She bowed quickly, turned on her heel, and returned to the kitchen, peering over her shoulder to check the other tables. He continued, "We have been safe these long years. The Lord of Bretanie has been good to us. Why, this very tavern was restored with his generosity. His purser loaned me the money to build rooms and to add onto the kitchen, and he promised that his men would be here this spring to repair my pier, which was so damaged by the ice flows." He nodded out the window. "He told us he would build us proper docks. Like a rock in the river, the armies of the Lord of Bretanie have provided protection while the armies of invaders pour around us."

I was not sure I had heard him correctly, but I was all too accustomed to the grievous toll this Lord of Bretanie was likely to exact in exchange for his generosity. I hoped that Lugins was not simply duped. Ruth looked at me with her sideways glance, knowing I was withholding something. When he left, I explained my fears and all that I had known of the tyrannical aristocracy in this land. She nodded, having seen much the same.

In a couple of hours, the caravan had unloaded and arranged all the cargo that would leave with us. The men had been fed and filled with brew. Their singing carried with us as Lugins showed us around his small stable and supply sheds. He said he would send to a nearby herdsman for several more pack animals by morning. We would have everything we needed to assemble our caravan from here.

This night, Ruth and I would share a real bed. Lugins had only two rooms available, and we would not take both. We would be together if we wanted to sleep in the inn and not on a barge again. She said nothing.

As the hot day melted into hazy late afternoon, followed the warm evening, Ruth and I sat on a log near the river that had been shaved and whittled into a rough bench. We talked about our years together, the people we had each known, and our journey north. We talked about cargo, what the north country would be like, and what our life might hold. Then we were silent. We had been talking about nothing because we wanted to avoid talking about something we both had to face. Ruth was never one to talk much, but unlike me, she never hesitated to say what needed to be said. Swallows skimmed the lazy water as fish surfaced and the evening thrush warbled. The air was laden with rich smells off the muddy river. We moved only to swat at mosquitoes.

In our weeks of travel, we had been together always: we shared space, dozed in each other's arms as the barges poled up the river, and talked about our lives, our hopes, and our faith. This fellow-ancient had become comfortable with casual touch. All this while, we watched each other and learned.

"So, are we married, now?" she suddenly asked.

I was startled. "What do you mean?"

She gave me that sideways look. Her pretty mouth set in *you know what I mean.*

I nodded slowly. "Well, I suppose we are, then—if we say we are." My mind was reeling.

"Here's how I see it," she said, leaning away from me, cradling her one hand in the other as though ready to make a business proposition. "We were together the years at sea. We proclaimed our commitment to each other in front of the crew when I determined to leave with you. All our fellow travelers assume we are man and wife. What more is there? Maybe a monk can marry us then." She shouldered me and laughed.

"Yes, what more is there?" I said stupidly.

All those years at sea, Ruth and I had coexisted like a pair of porcupines. My quills consisting of my fear of establishing another relationship, considering all the damage I was capable of, her quills consisting of all the abuse she had endured while enslaved. But even porcupines find a way.

She slipped her hand in mine and we walked back to our room at the inn.

The innkeeper was generous with directions and locations of possible waypoints farther inland. Over land, we would travel many days, and during much of our journey we would be surrounded by holdings under the care of the generous and mysterious lord whom Lugins extolled. He assured me this Lord of Bretanie's men kept the area safe, though the occasional highway thieves could not be discounted. While he assured us that pirates and thieves had, for the most part, been swept away, I feared this mysterious lord might have replaced them with a brute force that might prove just as hazardous.

My plans became clearer as I traveled, and Ruth and I continued to share our pasts with each other and talk about our future. I no longer held firmly to any plan, but my desire was to purchase a simple farm and return to the life I once had. Maybe I would build a smithy. She shared her desire to continue to use her skills. If the wool trade were strong, she would make clothing or tapestries. She foresaw a big life, and I agreed with her that the skills and treasures we had secured would position us to live well beyond a bare farm life. With her help, my concerns faded.

Arrayed in tents, we slept on the land that first night after leaving the inn. By afternoon of the next day, we saw the bloom of smoke from a village. As we approached this settlement, it seemed unusual to find a sprawling village unprotected by walls or berms, surrounded by neat farms and fat cattle. Pigs huddled and grunted as our caravan passed amid outlying farms, the odor of fresh hay and animals bringing back comfortable memories.

Ruth and I stepped away from the caravan and waved them on toward the village as we strolled along the stick fences of a tidy farm. The caravan needed to find stables, stores, a commons area to set up an encampment, and other accommodations in the village.

A pleasant woman with a round face waved as she carried a bucket of slop to her pigs. I bowed slightly; I did not want to alarm her as we approached her farm. A pink toddler with blond hair looked warily at us, swinging from her mum's skirts, sucking her thumb.

"What brings you here, Lord? If you need the bishop, I am afraid you missed him by a couple of days," she said. "It was quite the week."

"No, ma'am; we hope to stay only the night. We are traveling far," I said. Despite the small size of the farm, the barns and stock were well kept, as was the house and grounds. Not opulent but thriving.

"You are in luck, then, good sir," she nodded to Ruth, "and lady. I am sure the church is open. We had us some wonderful feast days while the bishop was here, and there are tents remaining. I am sure the priest would be game to entertain guests of honor like yourselves when he returns."

"Oh, I am not a lord, and this is no lady," I said, receiving the immediate sharp elbow from Ruth.

The woman chuckled and winked at Ruth. "I am Ute and my man be Wilgard, but he is in the village. He was to help with retrieving a share of our lumber and fabrics from the merchant stalls and tents that had been built for the festival. But I am quite sure he is struttin' around as he so likes to do, and probably tipping back some of the left-over ale in the bargain, I am sure. But he will be along soon." She dumped steaming gruel to the greedy swine. The toddler poked a stick through the fence at the hungry pigs.

"We wish we could have met him, but we will need to find our place with the caravan before all the soft ground is taken," I said over the squeal and rumble of the hungry animals.

She scratched her nose as she watched the pigs fight over the slop. We looked toward the village. "One moment." She held up her finger. "I was just thinking. We kept an accommodation here for the festival. It is clean and tended. We'd be pleased to rent it one more night," she shrewdly spoke to Ruth. I knew Ruth was tired of the caravan and listening to the crude talk, snores, and farts of our fellow travelers.

"Can we see it, ma'am?" Ruth asked, stepping forward.

I consented without hesitation. Ruth was longing for female companionship. "I will go along to let the others know where we will be and bring back our packs for tonight," I said.

In the village, I found the tiny church. The townspeople remained in a state of celebration and mild inebriation. With the streamers, the bustle of our caravan, and the busy villagers taking down tents and enjoying the last of the food and drink, it seemed as if the festival were still in session.

I checked on the caravan and found the tiny rectory next to the church. It was no more than two small rooms neatly maintained by the parishioners, apparently kept for a circuit priest. The church was pleasantly simple, and the plain quarters would not have suited Father Comgall. I returned to the farm with growing curiosity about the changes the Lord of Bretanie was bringing to this region.

That evening, Ute and Wilgard shared a banquet of stew, pudding, and bread that Ruth had helped prepare. Ute had somehow conjured a berry pie that afternoon. After another week of dried fish and moldy bread, we embarrassed ourselves by devouring the feast.

"So where are you headed, then?" Wilgard asked.

I told him the caravan was going to reach the river and follow west, then north again, but Ruth and I would not stay with them. We were headed for the valleys a few days from here.

"Then you will see Bretanie for yourselves." He beamed.

"It seems to be good times in these valleys," I replied.

"Yes, and the Lord of Bretanie and his men have helped us in this village by his generous coin, all of which we have repaid. And his brave militia has kept us safe from marauders. Yes, these are good times," he said, lifting his cup. I shrugged and met his salute while looking at Ruth, curious. I was wary of what we might find when we reached the valleys.

"This must be a good man, this lord." I was afraid to pursue this subject further or offer my concerns about warlords and tyrants. "Salute to the Lord of Bretanie, then."

"Aye, we should salute him, but I fear he is no more." Wilgard sighed. "Sadly, we have heard that he may have passed." He reached for his wife's hand.

But whether he was dead or alive, it would not be the Lord of Bretanie I was to fear most.

XXIX. Home

As days passed, our caravan trundled through verdant lands of lowing cattle and bleating sheep. It did not take long for us to encounter the militia of the powerful Lord of Bretanie. We had skirted a pristine lake that reflected white birch in front of snowy mountain peaks and were ascending a craggy pass sheltered by cedars and mountain pine. They could have easily set an ambush, yet they approached us fearlessly in full view. Their horses were as fine as any Roman stock, while the men were crisply uniformed and arrayed with shining weapons. Our small contingent of capable men would have been no match. We knew it would be fruitless to flee or set up a defense.

And there would be no need for protections. The lieutenant of the Bretanie detachment dismounted, snicked his sword into a sheath on his horse, and approached us with helmet under his arm. When he waved and smiled as though greeting us at market, Ruth and I looked at one another puzzled. This was a ploy we had not expected. Our captain whispered to his men to stay alert.

The lieutenant signaled to another of his men, who also left his weapon behind and approached us. As they walked along our caravan, the lieutenant bowed to Ruth, but paused when he saw me. A fleeting wrinkle of recognition crossed his brow, but he shook it off and moved on. The other man quickly inspected our caravan, lifting the corner of a tarp and rustling the crates and jars in the cart. He signaled to his lieutenant who, in turn, nodded to us.

"Safe travels," the lieutenant said. "We have scouted the roads between here and Bretanie, and you shall have nothing to fear. You may encounter another of our squads, but you can show them this seal and tell them that Lieutenant Coenwolf has granted passage." He handed our captain a medallion. I could not see the images on the seal, but I expected it would be like those common seals and tokens that provided passage across lands and rivers or when boarding ships and ferries.

Coenwolf patted one of our donkeys, saluted, and donned his helmet, leaving us stunned and relieved. They had not demanded a bribe, had not levied a single coin of taxation or fees, had not pilfered any of our weapons or cargo, and had been gracious toward Ruth. They mounted their horses, moved aside to allow us passage, and left.

More than anything we had heard, this gracious treatment fueled our curiosity about the realm of this mysterious lord.

Throughout the land, men and women worked their fields while children gamboled like lambs. The shadow of this Lord of Bretanie was long. Despite our benevolent encounter with the militia, I reserved a little fear and great curiosity for what I might find. In this desperate age, it would take more than an iron hand to enforce peace this thoroughly.

From Lugins' river landing to the lands where Bruna and I had farmed and raised our family was a journey of less than a fortnight. At last, I saw the landmark I had been watching for: the unchanging white crown of Old Man Mountain. Countless times I had dreamt of this beloved valley where green meadows swept down to sparkling rivers under the serene gaze of that great mountain. I inhaled the familiar, spicy aroma of cedar and pine and glimpsed the patchwork of black earth and green fields dotted with farmers sowing or trailing their work animals.

Descending through the pass, I walked beside the cart, pointing out familiar features as I unwound memories to Ruth. Suddenly, I let go of the cart and stopped. Something was not right. A part of the land was wholly different and caused me to wonder if I had led us to the wrong valley. Nestled within this valley, set on the low hummocks where I had lived and worked many years before, where there had stood earthen berms and circles of thatched hovels, there now rose a sprawling wood and stone village that ascended roof by roof to a towering villa. As lovely as any Greek village along the Aegean, many of the village's stone facades had been plastered and whitewashed. The walls were built concentrically, and curving streets were meticulously laid to flow among graceful edifices.

Outside the city gate, our captain handed me the seal from Lieutenant Coenwolf that would allow us entry for our caravan. While waiting for other carts and pedestrians to approach the gate, submit to inspection, and be waved through, I curiously rolled the seal in my fingers. I was intrigued by the Greek lettering forged into the seal. On one side was the familiar Chi-Rho symbol. I had seen the symbol often used by the state churches since the Resurrection of Yeshu. However, on this seal, the symbol had been struck in simple fashion as used by the early Church, without the flourishes or added letters I had seen since Alexandria. It would mean little under normal circumstances; however, I feared for a moment that we might be entering no more than an enormous abbey controlled by money-hungry bishops.

The other side of the seal gave me pause. I rubbed it with my thumb to polish away the bit of road grime to be certain I was seeing it correctly. There were simply two Greek letters inscribed, again with little flourish. I assumed at first it was the *alpha* and *omega*—which were also used as symbols in the Church to represent the Christ as the first and the last of all things. I imagined I was reading too much into this. It was a reminder of a vital lesson I had been given. But it must certainly be coincidence, and I surmised the letters merely indicated a province, or possibly it was related to Lieutenant Coenwolf's command. But it was not. The back of the seal was clearly etched with the two letters: *alpha* and *beta.*

While I was turning the seal in my hand, we were signaled forward. I showed the seal to the guards, and they waved us inside with a nod. They asked no questions and did not bother to inspect our carts. This was the power of the seal we carried, not simply the privilege afforded any caravan of wealthy travelers.

Ruth and I approached an attendant stationed inside the gates. He seemed distracted by the routine of his service until he saw me. Like Lieutenant Coenwolf, his eyes fluttered momentarily, and his brow pinched in curiosity. But the expression immediately evaporated while he smiled and tried to graciously listen to our inquiries. We waited while he summoned a young boy, a steward. He leaned over to whisper a message to the boy, then sent him scampering away.

We began to tell the attendant we would like to offer our condolences at the passing of the Lord of Bretanie but were interrupted. "No, good sir, the lord lives," the attendant said, "but he is not well, and unfortunately, near death. I would be privileged to request an audience for you with one of his assistants."

"You are more than generous," I said, "but this was not what we were expecting. We merely wanted to make acquaintance with authorities." I looked at Ruth, who nodded, urging me on. "Then we would like to arrange accommodations for a time so we could explore the possibility of settling nearby or in a neighboring village."

The attendant gave a slight bow. "I understand. And I would be privileged to introduce you personally to someone who can help."

We were led into the interior of the complex without further questioning.

The streets and gardens of the village were maintained with vibrance and grace in every detail. A carved bridge led over a burbling stream to a broad courtyard. Beyond it lay palatial buildings with all the grace of a Roman estate.

We approached an alcove arched by delicate carvings of entwined grape leaves, blooming hawthorn, and honeysuckle. At the top of a short flight of steps, a guard turned to open the tall oak doors when suddenly a priest burst through the doors and swept down the steps toward us with a scowl. He reflected none of the kindness or subservience that had been shown to us since we had entered at the main gate. The gate attendant stuttered to introduce us, but the priest had put out his hand to stop us. "Why do you come here? You will disgrace the good name of Lord Bretanie," he hissed. His hair and beard were neatly trimmed, and he wore a black robe, crisp and elegantly appointed. A wooden cross hung from a sash at his waist.

"I do not know what you mean," I said, stepping forward. "You are confusing us with someone else. We do not know you or your lord." I nodded to the gate attendant. "We were merely led inside by your generous attendant. We have just arrived with our caravan. These fields and valleys were once my home," I said. "I was told that the lord had passed away; we were here to pay our respects to his family. Then your gate attendant graciously gave us the wonderful news that the good lord yet lives. We did not ask for an audience with anyone, but the attendant insisted."

The priest's gaze smoldered.

"We arrived here to ask permission to purchase lands if any may be available. We have means," Ruth added. The priest would not look at her.

A soldier came behind the priest. "Let them pass. The attendant sent ahead. The lord has already asked to see them." Then he looked at me, paused. I could see that same flicker of recognition. "The lord must see him."

The priest huffed at the soldier, then back at me. "Are you a far-flung relative—or some bastard child—that has come here to make a claim upon the lord as he lies upon his deathbed? I do not know what sort of charade this is."

"I have no idea what you are talking about," I replied. "We told you our intentions. If we are to be granted an audience with this Lord Bretanie, we would be humbled and honored. That is all."

"Let them pass," the soldier said sharply. "You forget that you have no authority in these matters." He nodded to me. "Our apologies, sir and madam; it was because of the appearance of your face, my lord. And because of your name. I am sorry. We must be cautious at a time like this."

The priest stepped aside, simmering.

I looked at the soldier, confused. "I am not a lord. But if I can be bold, this seems ridiculous," I said. "We are little more than merchants looking for...for a corner of land to purchase. I was in these lands many years ago, and now I have returned to see these splendid valleys again. We have just arrived, and I can assure you we have designs on nothing. We are not in need."

The soldier was satisfied and extended his hand toward the door. We were led through cloisters and down hallways hung with tapestries illumined by windows of colored glass. Up a broad flight of winding steps, two guards waited outside a tall door made of cherry planks inlaid with flourishes of cedar, long-necked cranes carved in applewood, and stags carved in maple.

As the guards opened the doors, we were led into a room where arched windows cast a dim glow onto adornments of painted wood, tile, and gray stone carvings. A nun dressed in white sat next to a large bed that at first seemed empty. I again feared we were too late and that the body had been removed. The woman stood, her smile warm and simple, and motioned us toward the bed.

While watching us, the priest reluctantly swept his hand toward the bed, announcing, "Lord Lazar of Bretanie."

In bewilderment, we approached. Barely seen amid the coverings lay an old man. Parchment eyelids fluttered as he lifted his head by degrees to watch us approach the bed. He licked dry lips that curled into a weak smile.

"Father." His voice was a hoarse gasp.

Smiling sadly, the nun looked toward the priest and soldier, shaking her head before speaking to us. "I am sorry; it is as though his senses are escaping him these days," she said.

"Father," he repeated. "I must be close to the next life if those who have long passed have ventured to visit me. Where is my mother, now? Is this her? Is she standing here with you in the vestibule of the heavens?"

"Greetings, Lord. This is Ruth... She is...she is..." I stopped. Something in his voice had given me pause. I cleared my throat and began again. "I am indebted to you for receiving us into your chamber. This was more than we..." Then madness must have overtaken me. It was not within the realm of possibility, and I felt foolish to venture more and risk our welcome. I knelt at the bedside, and with scarcely a whisper, I asked, "If I can be so bold, who was your mother, my lord? What was her name?" I was not certain I wanted to hear the answer.

"My mother? Her name?" He laid his head back. A skeletal hand slipped from under the blankets, trembling. He scratched his brow. His face brightened and he lifted a finger. "My mother's name? Why, I remember. Of course. It was Bruna. Her name was Bruna." His chest began to shake, and he huffed a gentle laugh. "Bruna. How could I forget?"

The room swirled. I knew people were talking; I may remember that the nun tucked in his blankets, the priest brought a cup to the old man's lips, the guards peered in. I scarcely noticed as my heart continued to race, remembering a boy I had cherished.

The nun tsked and came beside me to take my elbow, fearing I was upsetting him. But the old man waved them away as he seemed to grow stronger and raised himself on his elbows.

"Leave us, sister. Leave us, priest and commander. My time is near, and my father is here to take me home." He waved them away with the back of his tired hand. He whispered to me, "I tolerate these religious lapdogs; they are not so bad. But I hate all their ritual and religion. Yeshu, as I heard you call him, is real. He would have had none of this. And neither would you." He winked and coughed.

I nodded nervously toward the attendants and smiled assurance.

I sat on the bed, my finger to my lips, then reached a cautious hand and stroked his brow. "My...my son. Can you forgive me? I never knew. I was..."

"You went to battle to save us. You succeeded; now here you are," he said hoarsely. "Could you just lift my head a bit so I can see you better?"

I slid my arm under his neck and looked deep into the face of an old man whom I had last seen as barely more than a child bravely holding his small blade. I could not speak, only gaze. He lay amid a scent of aging and the stench of encroaching death, his tussled hair, gray and oily, ran to his shoulders. This was the brave child who had sought to join me in battle after no more training than smacking pinecones with willow sticks; the child who had walked with me in the meadows and forests and had apparently mustered enough courage to protect his family, maintain the farm, and restore a village.

"Thank you; that is better," he said, looking into my eyes as I held him. "There is nothing more important in life than family, and nothing sweeter than human touch. It is like fresh water to me. I fear these nuns and priests are afraid to touch such old age—for fear they themselves might catch it." He grinned.

"I am sorry," I said. "I should have returned so—so much sooner, but I was taken and..."

He waved his skeletal hand. "We knew. We were told what happened," he said, taking another raspy breath. He looked up at me with rheumy eyes. "Father, you returned at the right time. It is always the right time with our God. You did all you could with what you had. The wife you chose, our mother, was a competent woman and pulled together the damage that had been done by the attacks and made us into men and women." He coughed. "We knew you would have come back if you could." He drew a long, rattling breath. "You gave us the tools we needed, and we used them well. Your skill with metals gave us the temper of the blades that have kept our people safe and have allowed us to reap harvests that none could have imagined." He paused, gathering his thoughts and his stamina. "That was but one of your gifts to us, Father. I believe it could not have turned out any better if you had been here.

We forgave you. Your life forgives you." He breathed. "And—and I must add because I know it meant so much to you. I am sure in the same way that Miriam forgave you."

"Wh...?"

"You should not leave your scribblings lying about." He smiled. "We knew. We knew."

"I do not know what to say, son," I said. "You have seen all those things I wrote?"

He nodded slowly. "It was not much. Some skins and parchments, but it told us enough. We half-believed what we read, but you are here. That is surety."

"You have done much with what your mother gave you. I cannot fathom...."

He held up his hand. "Please, I have but few breaths remaining, a few more heartbeats and my time quickly fades. I must finish—well." He inhaled deeply, holding for a moment. "Father, you and old Azvald showed us the Savior. That provided for us everything we would ever need. Because I would exchange all this life that was full, large, and wealthy to live a life that had been boring, small, and meaningless if I could but have the Savior. I would have lived a meaningless life to possess the One who is meaning."

"Rest, son," I said, kneeling beside the bed.

"Meaningless. Do you not see?" He strained, looking to Ruth then back at me. "I stopped seeking meaning. Life is all meaningless to us. It shall always be. We should want to have it no other way. It is not up to us to find meaning or to know what is signified by meaning. The world is awash with meaninglessness—to us that is. The smallness and meaninglessness of it: *that* is the blessing. Embrace it. Praise our God!"

"But look at all that you have done! You have found meaning," I said.

He struggled, trying to sit up. I laid my hand on his shoulder. "I have done nothing!" He held out his empty, trembling palm. "Nothing! I merely held out my hand and the Savior either filled my hand or he took my hand and led me on. I have done nothing."

He laid back again, sighed. "The land I go to is the land of forgiveness. It has arrived and it fills my vision as we speak." He looked through me with his clear, dark eyes, speaking as to himself. "It has nothing to do with what we have done. A life is measured by how that small circle—no larger than a hug—regards you, how you have treated *them*. The world's measure amounts to exactly...zero," he said through escaping breath, then added, "You never have to seek. Your mission is always there, right in front of you. Like Mary, not like Martha." His breath was growing fast and shallow. "So now I leave." He paused. "I see the door open. Those agents of eternity that you brought with you, are they here to accompany me?" he asked, looking intently toward the window behind me.

"I'm sorry. I do not see..." I said.

"Right there, Father." He motioned his gray, limp hand toward the window.

I placated him by turning.

And froze.

I felt as drained and lifeless as my dying son.

Like a crack of lightning striking nearby, splitting the air, the Immortals stood in blinding light.

I waved frantically at Ruth to flee. As I fell over my son to cover his chest with my arm, a long gurgling sigh was escaping from his nest of bones. From the horror in our midst my feeble attempt would not save him and would not save Ruth or me. The pursuit ends here.

"What do you want, spawn of Elymas of Cyprus?" I demanded. "Slay me now. Spare this old man and this woman. Leave him to his journey beyond. Spare my son. You have no use for him. He is obviously nothing if not mortal. Killing him will not assuage your envy of my immortality or finish whatever mission given you by hell."

There is daylight; there is the first sliver of sun on a warm morning; there is moonlight that sparkles on still water. When the Immortals smiled, it was all of those. It was none of those. The room was filled with a new light. A light that has been seen on earth few times, and briefly.

"Fear not. Fear not, Lazarus of Bethany." Their voices were not the squeal, terrible shriek and gong I had heard on the desert, not a deadly siren's song, but a song sung in tinkling bells and simmering cymbals. "We have protected you; we have been there to steer you along a chosen path while you are on this tiny orb. Our faces stand eternally fixed toward the throne of the Great I Am. And your son has been lifted from time to join us. He is, was, and will be well."

Like the Disciple John, I felt my tongue had been seared. I could not speak.

"You do not see, vain mortal. You are not to know the day or hour of your passing. No one does; no one will. So much you do not know. It is so small. In our realms, we do not have a measure for the minuscule amount that has been made known to mortals. You play at immortality; you desire immortality, yet you have not learned how to possess mortality. Mortality and immortality: two sides of the same coin. Flip the coin today and you see an infant; flip the coin tomorrow, it is as your son. Tomorrow it will be you. Today is a lifetime. Tomorrow is a lifetime. Each morning, rebirth, and each night, a death. Lifetime in a day. It is that way until you will see as we do. Until you see the eternal day."

I sat up away from my son. Ruth stepped behind me and gripped my shoulders, her face dazzling joy. Where I had seen demons, she saw seraphim.

I shielded my eyes and stuttered, "You have been nothing but destruction and desolation wherever you have followed me. This woman Ruth has lived an eternity of horror and pain. Where were you then? If you are messengers of God, why have you not brought a message of peace and healing? You have brought with you only horror."

"Not so, son of Eve, in this plane of existence, in this realm of time, we dispense justice—wherever we are seen. When you witnessed light and fury churning the skies, we battled the unseen forces of the Enemy," they said as one. "If the Great I Am had never allowed evil and pain into your lives and into the world, your race would never have learned of the Great Infinity."

Ruth and I said nothing. They continued.

"In the finite universe of time, into your small race, pain and suffering are stern counselors. Without them you would not have understood the great and eternal virtues." Each word harmonized one with the other like chimes. "Justice, Courage, Devotion, Faithfulness, Selflessness, or Truth. The Great Weaver could not have weaved without black. You could not have understood except for pain."

When they spoke, each phrase completed the thought. There was nothing I could respond.

Fraught with fear and anger, I challenged them. "Tell me all that you must, Messengers, I only—"

"Stand and hear. Since we walked with your beloved grandmother in eternity, we have had one message, and it has not changed...."

Without willing it, an image was brought forth in my mind. I saw my grandmother in the land-after-death. Two children in gold-hemmed robes carrying small swords had accompanied her. "That was...? I do not...."

"On the other side of the veil, we are like children next to you, the Rescued. Here we are more. Now listen, Lazarus; this is our message—to you and to the woman, Ruth." Their voices lowered like a burbling stream.

"Tell us, if I may ask—" I began.

"Will we see mortality?" Ruth stepped forward.

"Mortality, immortality, short life, or long. Why do you seek one or the other? One is the same as the other to the Rescued. As we said, two sides to the same coin. All live their lifespans on this orb, then pass through the veil. There is nothing of mortality or immortality on the other side. Time and mortality have been merely carved out and created: tools may help you to know and seek eternity. These principles should all have been evident and simple for you, but your race makes everything far more complex than it is.

"In the Final Reckoning, mortality is granted to those who prefer to remain mortal until they are cast into oblivion. When the forest burns, the tree and the twig are both consumed by the same fire. It is of no consequence to you. Greatness or trifling; there are no such values given to human life when the final trumpet sounds, and the scroll of this age has been rolled up."

"But what does it mean? Why are we here to live without meaning? Then we merely...?"

The room trembled, as though they were stirred to the edge of anger. But it was joy that thrummed under foot. "You know nothing of what you speak. Meaning? Meaninglessness? You seek answers on this plane? Meaninglessness? Your question answers itself by affirming that if there is meaninglessness, then there must exist meaning by comparison. By what do you measure meaning? If all were meaningless—which it is not—would that not be meaningful? All that is past, present, and forever is meaning. Meaning is cradled within, what you call, meaninglessness."

We waited, unable to reply.

"Stop," they said.

"I am sorry. We said nothing. I—" I said.

"Stop," they said again.

"We do not..." I said.

There was silence. Their visages swirled and eddied like faces lowering in water, then sharp again.

"Stop seeking," they said. "Stop seeking and begin observing."

"I seek only to—"

"Stop seeking," they repeated, louder. "Stop seeking and begin seeing."

"But—"

Their brief silence silenced me.

"Mortal man, stop seeking," they said. "Stop seeking—and begin receiving."

I looked at my son. His body limp, his face ashen and vacant. I sat on the bed, carefully closed his eyes, slid near, and kissed the wrinkled forehead that had been soft and smooth many decades ago when my lips had last touched it.

The light in the room was growing dim, like a wick receding into a lamp. I turned to speak, not sure what I would say to the Messengers, but they had vanished. Their light shimmered a short time. I slumped over the body of my son.

Ruth stood motionless. I reached for her. She took my hand, then bent to take my other hand, helped me to my feet, and we embraced.

Epilogue

I talked with angels.

I walked with the Son of God, befriended his Disciples, was raised from the dead and blessed with several lifetimes of love and family. I saw the face of Christ in multitudes.

And I talked with angels and saw their ministrations on earth.

The vanity that I, of all men, should ponder meaning and meaningless or mortality and immortality. All irrelevant.

I had viewed life from the pinnacle of a pebble, while ignoring mountains at my back. Ever searching I splashed through streams ignoring spring-fed waters while ever thirsting for a drop of dew that merely fades with the morning sun.

I can claim nothing more than my life has been a testament to the stubbornness of the human heart and the impenetrable, rocky hardness of the soul.

But we stay here in Bretanie where my grandchildren, though wary, have nonetheless allowed us a generous stake near the city. It is not home. There is but one Home at the heart of all our striving; all others are mere reflections.

And we do not count our days, Ruth and I—however many days we may have. Eat, drink, be merry, enjoy life with your beloved wife all the days of this fleeting life.

All the days of this meaningless life that God has given you under the sun—all your meaningless days.

I end here and secure these pages for Sister Athracht along with a portion of my wealth. I was able to hire a small band of scribes so I can retain copies and not lose my journal to fire or thieves. I do not know if they understand what they are copying, if it is truth or a tale. But I am hopeful that the good sister will understand and keep it in a manner that she would see fit.

My days have been long, and I know not where they lead from here.

The End

ACKNOWLEDGEMENTS

Writers come and go but great readers are precious. Sally is a great reader. On the page and in our life together her eyes, ears and intuition are precious to me. I am nothing without her.

My family: The circle I embrace no larger than a hug. Thanks Jonah, Sarah, Amie, Naomi, Makaiya, Dave, Vaughn, Trent, and Sam. What they put up with!

For *Curve of the Earth* I have had a very diverse group of early readers, from all walks of faith. Life-long friend Den Nordstrum also suggested a reference or two on the early church and showed me the C.S. Lewis poem *Stephen to Lazarus.* He and Nan by reading and comments have always challenged us. Jonah helped so much with reading and in discussions. Sonja Downey, librarian and the most widely read individual I have ever known, gave me that early spark of assurance I needed to press on. Next door neighbor and friend John McConnell told me things I needed to hear. Brother and blacksmith Dan Brockman is ever encouraging. You give a whole new meaning to metalhead. Dr. Ross Michaels was succinct and went for the heart, just like a good doctor should.

Tyler Tichelaar did an early edit and challenged me with important insight. Angela R. Watts provided new perspective with a developmental edit and Michaela Bush brought it in for a landing with great poofreeding.

I am so sorry if I forgot anyone. I'm sure I will remember you soon—right after it goes to print.

How can I thank the myriad individuals and couples whose discipleship, sermons and writing contributed to our spiritual journey: all those faces of Yeshu. *I do not recall the countless meals my mother lovingly prepared, but they all contributed to my growth.* That idea and one or two others were inspired by friend and pastor Norm Thomasma. He and his wife Ellen are but one example of those countless persons who inspire me and had an impact on our lives.

There are so many more. I cannot begin to mention the cloud of witnesses, some living and some who eternally have stopped seeking and are now receiving.

About the Author

CRAIG A. BROCKMAN LIVES with wife, Sally, in Tecumseh, Michigan. Prior work includes a middle grade novel *Marty and the Far Woodchuck* and the ghost story *Dead of November: A Novel of Lake Superior.*